Sop...

and the...

"As always, Littlefield... dystopian California
with unnerving conviction, and Cass's encounters with
Beaters retain their horrifying power."
—*Publishers Weekly* on *Horizon*

"A book about what it means to love and be human
disguised as a story about a zombie-riddled dystopia."
—*RT Book Reviews* on *Rebirth*

"Littlefield has a gift for pacing, her adroit and detailed
world-building going down easy amid page-turning
action and evocative, sensual, harrowing descriptions
that bring every paragraph of this thriller to life."
—*Publishers Weekly,* starred review, on *Aftertime*

"A fantastic new dystopian series...Littlefield's
compelling writing will keep readers turning pages
late into the night to find out what happens next.
Outstanding!" **Top Pick, 4 1/2 stars**
—*RT Book Reviews* on *Aftertime*

"A fascinating protagonist and some of the scariest
zombies I have ever encountered
—a double-barreled salute."
—Jess d'Arbonne, the *Denver Examiner,* on *Aftertime*

"Wildly original, guaranteed to give you nightmares...
examines the strength of one woman, the joy of
acceptance and the power of love. A must read."
—J.T. Ellison, author of *The Immortals,* on *Aftertime*

"The End Times have always belonged to the boys.
Sophie Littlefield's *Aftertime* gives an explosive voice to
the other half of the planet's population. *Aftertime* is a
whole new kind of fierce."
—Laura Benedict, author of *Isabella Moon*

Also available from Sophie Littlefield and

Harlequin LUNA

Rebirth

Aftertime

Sophie Littlefield
HORIZON

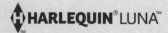

Recycling programs
for this product may
not exist in your area.

HORIZON

ISBN-13: 978-0-373-80354-5

Printed in U.S.A.

In honor of all beginnings

failed and fresh

hopeless and hopeful

And for M:

safe in His arms

HORIZON

All those shades of red—candy-apple and cinnamon and carnelian and rust and vermilion and dozens more—people arriving for the party stopped and stared at the paper hearts twirling lazily overhead on their strings. No one had seen anything like it since Before. No one expected to see anything like it again Aftertime.

Except, maybe, for Cass, who dreamed lush banks of scarlet gaillardia, Mister Lincoln roses heavy on glossy-leafed branches, delicate swaying spires of firecracker penstemon. Cass Dollar hoarded hope with character-istic parsimony when she was awake, but since com-ing to New Eden her dreams were audacious, greedy, lusting for color and scent and life.

Even here, in this stretch of what had once been Central California valley farmland—rarely touched by frost, the sun warming one's face in March and burning in April—even here it was possible to long for spring in

February. In her winter garden, homely rows of black-twig seedlings and lumpy rhizomes protruded from the dirt. There was little that was lovely save the pale green throats of kaysev sprouts dotting the fields beyond, skimming the entire southern end of the island with verdant life beyond the few dormant acres in which Cass toiled. At the end of each day she had dirt under her nails, pebbles in her shoes, the sweet-rot smell of compost clinging to her skin and nothing to show for it yet in the fields.

Cass was not the only one who was tired of winter. In fact, the social committee's first idea had been a cabin-fever dance, until someone suggested the more upbeat Valentine's Day theme. There was romance to be found in New Eden, for some—different than Before, of course. Some kinds of human attraction thrived in an atmosphere of strife and danger. Others waned. Cass couldn't be bothered to care.

It wasn't the first time she'd ignored the social committee's call for volunteers, though it wasn't like she was swamped with work. The pruning was done. She'd sprayed the citrus with dormant oil she'd hand-pressed from kaysev beans, and she covered the thorny branches whenever nighttime temperatures dipped. A second round of lettuces and cabbages and parsnips were planted. Beyond weeding and the eternal blueleaf patrol, there would be little else to do until warmer weather launched the growing season into full swing. So Cass would have had plenty of time to join the other women in turning the public building into a party room, fashioning decorations from bits gathered from all around the islands. She'd declined to help as they set aside ingredients for special dishes and tested out cocktails made with kaysev alcohol, its gingery taste overpowering anything else they tried to mix it with. The committee had even talked the raiding parties into bringing home scrap wood for the past two weeks, enough for a bonfire to burn until the wee hours.

Cass watched them as she walked home across the narrow bamboo bridge from Garden Island, stretching her tired limbs and working the kinks out of her neck, sore from the backbreaking work of checking the kaysev for blueleaf every afternoon. The sun was still high enough to offer some warmth, so they'd thrown open the skylights and French doors to let it in on their party. Once, the building had been the weekend getaway of some tech baron with lowbrow taste, a man who preferred booze cruises and wakeboarding to wine tasting in Napa. Most of the residents of the banks along the farm channels opted for trailers and prefab buildings and listing shacks, so the house stood out for both its size and the quality of its construction. Well before Cass had arrived in New Eden, all the non-load-bearing walls had been removed, opening it up; there were foosball and pool tables, bar stools, leather furniture, a community center of sorts. A clubhouse surrounded by the little town that had sprung up on three contiguous islands wedged in the center of a waterway that had been nameless and unremarkable Before.

It was supposed to be called Pison River now, after one of the four lost rivers that carried water away from Eden in the Bible. But the Methodist minister who had named the river had died in a cirrhotic coma after coughing up black clotted blood. He had the disease long before coming to New Eden, but everyone had taken to calling it the Poison River instead.

Cass slipped just inside, curious about the party preparations despite herself. There was Collette Portescue, with her signature apron and a colorful scarf in her hair. Collette was inexhaustibly cheery, a born organizer, a Sacramento socialite who'd found her true calling only after she lost everything.

"Cass! Cass, there you are." The woman's cultivated voice called to her now, unmistakable in the high registers over the murmurs of the other volunteers and a handful of early guests. Even though she'd agreed to this, Cass's gut tightened as Collette put a drink cup down and rushed toward her on—Cass's eyes widened with astonishment—teetering red satin high heels. Beneath the wrinkled linen of her embroidered apron, Collette wore a tight red jersey dress. Cass glanced around at the others; some of them had made an effort, with hair washed and tied back, even an occasional slash of lipstick or jingling silver bracelet—but February was still February and most people wore layers to stay warm, none of it new and none of it truly clean. It was a testament to Collette's fierce commitment to New Eden's social life that she stood before Cass with her arms bare and her hair in home-job pin curls.

Her smile was as splendid as ever—that kind of dental work probably came with an apocalypse-proof guarantee—and her kindness was genuine, only kindness felt like a blade to Cass's heart and forced her to turn away, pretending to cough.

"Oh, precious, you haven't got that bug that's going around, have you?" There was a faint note of the South in Collette's voice, a hint of the Miss Georgia crown she'd worn four decades ago. The early eighties would have been the perfect era for her—big hair, big parties, big spending. Austerity never seemed like a greater affront than it did where Collette was concerned.

"No, ma'am, just—dust, maybe."

Collette nodded. "Tildy and Karen have been up on ladders all afternoon, probably knocked some loose. I should have had them take rags up there with them! But, honey, come with me now, let me show you what I need...."

Collette dragged her through the milling little crowd of Edenites who held drinks in plastic cups and chatted over the sounds of Luddy Barkava and his friends warming up in the corner. On long tables at the back wall of the public building, where the wealthy entrepreneur had once installed a pair of four-thousand-dollar dishwashers, were the makings of the centerpieces, such as they were: four mismatched vases and bowls and piles of plants that Cass had cut from the winter-blooming garden near the island's shore. There were coral fronds of grevillea, creamy pink-tinged helleborus already dropping petals, tight clusters of tiny skimmia berries. Cass sighed. These were the only flowering plants she'd been able to grow this winter. The helleborus seed had been raided from a garden shed; the others plants were returners, species that had disappeared during the biological attacks and the Siege, and only now were starting to show up again.

These plants were never meant for floral arrangements; they were merely the hardiest, the sturdiest, the first to come back Aftertime, fodder for birds and insects, early drafts in the earth's bid for return. They were not especially lovely, and it would take skill to make them appear so.

And Cass was no florist.

She touched a cluster of glossy oval skimmia leaves. "I don't know—"

"Trust me, anything you do will be an improvement. June found you some stuff. Ribbon and...I don't know, it's all right there. Gotta run. You'll do a marvelous job!"

Collette was off to organize the volunteer bartenders, to untangle paper hearts whose strings had gotten twisted, to admonish Luddy and his little band to play only cheerful songs. Luddy had been in a thrashcore band of local renown on the San Francisco scene; now he spent his days building elaborate skateboard ramps along the island's only paved stretch of road. It was a testament to Collette's charisma that in her wake the band started in on a jittery minor-key version of "Wonderful Tonight."

And Cass got to her task, as well, starting with the berry stalks in the center of the vases and bowls and filling in with the more delicate flowers and leaves. She was winding lengths of wired organza ribbon through the stems—where June found such a luxury, Cass had no idea, but you never knew what the raiders would bring back from the mainland—when she sensed him behind her and she closed her eyes and let it come, the fading of the other sounds in the room, the heating of the air between them.

"Collette put you to work, too, huh?" His voice, low and gravelly, traced its familiar liquid path along her nerves. He was standing too close. But Dor was always too close. Cass pushed a hand through her hair, grown in the past few months well past her shoulders and released, for the occasion, from her usual ponytail, before turning to face him.

His expression was faintly mocking. In the sunset glow diffusing through the tall windows of the public building, his face was tawny and sun-browned from his work outside, just like her own. The scar that bisected one eyebrow had faded considerably since she first met Dor six months earlier, but a new one puckered a crease along his skull that disappeared into his silver-flecked black hair. Cass had been there when the bullet barely missed killing him. Here in New Eden, under the ministrations of Zihna and Sun-hi, it had taken him only a few days to recover enough to insist on leaving his sickbed.

Of course, he had other reasons to want to leave the little hospital, reasons neither of them forgot for even a day.

Watching her watching him, Dor leaned even closer, inclining his head so that his too-long hair fell across the top scar, obscuring it. Cass doubted he was even aware of this habit, which had nothing to do with vanity. Like so many men Aftertime, Dor didn't like to talk about himself, about who he had been and where he came from. Though insisting its way to the surface, the scar was in the past.

She was in the past, as well, for that matter.

Except neither of them could quite seem to remember that.

"Where's Valerie?" Cass asked, ignoring his question. She would have expected the woman to be here already, with her embroidery scissors and pins in her mouth, doing last-minute repairs for all the women who'd managed to pull together something special for the party. Most days, she did mending and alterations in her small apartment—just two rooms, the back half of a flat-bottom pleasure boat grounded and rebuilt by the two gay men who shared the front—but for the parties given by the social committee, she came early and sewed on loose buttons and took in seams and tacked up hems. Valerie loved to help, to feel needed. She had a pretty spilled-glass voice and a ready smile.

She was a very *nice* woman.

Dor grimaced. "She's not feeling well."

Again. Cass nodded carefully. Valerie's stomach pains came and went, the sort of thing one managed Before with medication and special diets, but that one just endured nowadays.

Truly, it would have been so much easier, so much less complicated if she were here right now, in one of her old-fashioned A-line skirts and Pendleton jacket, a velvet headband smoothing back her glossy dark hair. Sammi said Valerie looked like a geek, and Cass supposed it was true, but she was pretty in a fragile way and if she were here she would be with Dor and there would be no danger from the thing that loomed between them.

"I'm sorry," Cass muttered, meaning it. "What have you been doing all day?"

Dor shrugged in the general direction of the back of the building. "There's some rotted siding along the back—Earl and Steve brought back some lumber and we've been replacing it. Trying to get finished before it rains."

"Lumber?"

"Figure of speech—they took down an old house along Vaux Road. We've been cannibalizing it for parts."

"You smell like you've worked two days straight."

"I was going to take a shower…before this thing starts."

"I think it's already starting." Luddy's band, rehearsing their party sets, had segued into "Lola" and the conversation swelled as people finished their first round and went back for refills. Cass wouldn't be joining them.

"You gonna be here later?"

Cass shrugged, staring into Dor's eyes. They were a shade of navy blue that could easily be mistaken for brown. When he was angry they turned nearly black. Very occasionally, they were luminous colors of the sea. "I don't know…I'm tired. Ingrid's had Ruthie all day. I need to go check on her. I might just turn in early."

Dor nodded. "Probably best."

"Yeah. Probably."

A group of laughing citizens rolled a table covered with pies into the center of the room and a good-natured shout went up from the crowd. Everyone knew they'd been hunting all day yesterday for jackrabbits and voles for meat pies. So the three hawthorn-berry pies were a surprise. Cass knew all about them, though, for she had been the one tending the shrubs hidden on the far end of Garden Island down a path that only she and her blueleaf scouts ever used, or sometimes the kids when they wanted to watch the Beaters.

After an autumn harvest the shrubs had surprised her by reblooming. She could not say why or how that had happened, other than the fact that kaysev did odd things to the earth. When it first appeared, people worried that kaysev would strip the soil of its nutrients in a single growing cycle. The opposite seemed true. There were other cover crops—rye, for one, planted to give overworked soil a break and renew minerals—but Cass had never seen one behave like kaysev.

The hawthorn bushes' second bloom was scant, and after Cass picked enough for the pies, the small berries were nearly all gone. The few that remained weren't enough even for pancakes. Cass would give them to Ruthie and Twyla when they were ripe, and they would get the sweet juice all over their faces. A treat, something to enjoy as they waited out the winter.

Winter was tough on children, the cold days and early nightfalls. They had no television. No electronic games. No radios. Not even lamps, except for special occasions. Children got bored and then they got restless.

Cass could sympathize. She got restless, too.

02

An hour after sundown Cass was back in the room she shared with Ruthie, one of three cobbled-together boxes that formed a sloping second-floor addition to an old board-sided house. These were not coveted rooms, but Cass was among the most recent to arrive at New Eden and so she took what was offered without complaint.

Besides, even with that she didn't mind. What the builders of the ramshackle house lacked in skill, they made up for in imagination. The rooms lined a narrow hall that overlooked a spacious living room, the body of the original house, whose roof had been sheared off to accommodate the second floor. There were two tiny rooms at either end of the hall, and Ruthie and Twyla loved to use them for imaginary boats or stores or churches or zoos or schools, and since no one really owned anything, they were free to borrow props from all over the house. Buckets became steering wheels, folded clothes became racks of fancy dresses, dolls became dolphins bobbing on imaginary seas.

Twyla, who was older than Ruthie—nearly five—remembered some of these things from Before. But to Ruthie they were entirely make-believe.

Ruthie was telling Cass about a book that Ingrid had read them that evening. Fridays were Ingrid's turn to watch the four youngest children—the girls plus her two sons, age one and three—and she stuck to the most educational books from New Eden's lending library, biographies and how-things-work and math books. She also made flash cards with pictures of things long gone, like birthday cakes and puppies and helium balloons and ice skates. Cass and Suzanne secretly called Ingrid "Sarge"—at least, they had before Suzanne mostly quit speaking to her—but Cass felt a hollow pang whenever she saw Ingrid bent earnestly over the little ones, pouring herself into lessons they were too young to understand.

Cass had once felt that passion. When Ruthie had been missing, Cass's hunger for her daughter was stronger than her own pulse, a primal longing. Now she'd had Ruthie back for half a year, but sometimes Cass felt like she was losing the thread that bound the two of them together.

So she listened and she listened harder.

"The fork goes on this side," Ruthie said in a voice that was little more than a whisper, patting the mattress on the floor. She was a quiet child; she never yelled, never shouted with joy or rage. "The knife and spoon go here. You can put the plate in the middle. That's where it goes."

Cass murmured encouragingly, folding back the

sheets and blankets as she listened. These lessons were pointless, but what else could she do? For some, the old rituals brought a kind of solace. Ingrid was such a person.

The room was illuminated by a stub of candle melted to a plate, and when Ruthie was tucked in she blew the candle out, as was customary. Candlelight was to be conserved, to be used only when necessary.

"Can I help set the table tomorrow?" Ruthie asked, yawning. Tomorrow Suzanne would watch the kids so the other two could work, the three of them rotating every three days. Despite their troubles, Suzanne and Cass had an unspoken agreement never to let their discord affect the children.

Cass calculated what needed doing tomorrow—Earl had promised to come to Garden Island in the afternoon and look at some erosion that was threatening the area Cass had tilled for lettuce along the southern bank—but she could knock off after that, come by and get Ruthie. They could help with dinner, eat early and still have time to visit the hospital.

It had been a long time—too long—three weeks, a month? She hadn't meant to let it happen, but it had gotten harder and harder to go there.

But yes, she had promised herself she would be better.

They could get there in time to help Sun-hi with the last few chores of the day. And Ruthie actually enjoyed the visits—she was too little to be afraid.

"Yes, Babygirl," Cass said, trying to keep her tone light. "And then you can wash all the dishes. And dry them and put them away. How does that sound?"

"Will you help me?" Ruthie asked doubtfully, sleep

overtaking her voice. So serious, Ruthie never seemed to know when Cass was teasing her.

"Of course I'll help you," Cass whispered, laying her head down on the mattress next to Ruthie's, her knees on the carpet. She felt Ruthie's breath on her cheek. Before long it became regular with sleep.

Cass kissed her softly and crawled over to the corner of the room where she kept their few special things in a cabinet that had once held electronics, part of a "media center" in a time when media still roamed the earth and electric byways. She ran her hand over the books, the toys and jars of lotion, the wooden flute and the little glass bowl of earrings, and only then did she take down the antique wooden box that had held a board game a hundred years ago. She'd traded a potted lime-tree seedling for the box, which a woman had carried with her all the way from Petaluma in her backpack. On its surface, in flaking paint, was the image of a dancing bear balancing an umbrella on its snout. No one knew what the box meant to the woman, or why she'd carried it all those miles, because not long after arriving in New Eden, she cut her foot on a piece of broken bottle in the muddy shores, and died three weeks later when the infection reached her heart.

The woman had one good friend, a mute who had walked beside her all this way, who inherited her few paltry things when she died. Who now owned a lime tree.

Cass ran her fingertips lightly over the painted bear. Then she opened the box, took the plastic bottle from inside and put it to her lips.

The first swallow burned like heated steel, like justice done.

The second swallow and all the ones after that went down like nothing.

3

The singing was back, somewhere behind his eyes, a strange high-pitched, tuneless song that had been weaving in and out of his diluted dreams for days, or months, or years, for all he knew. It seemed like he had been here forever. "Here" was a place of watery uncertainty, its outline flickering and disappearing, brief flashes that inevitably faded into the nothing, over and over and over again.

His senses were gone. He was content—well, perhaps *content* was not right, but *aware* of his lack of sensation and glad for it. At one time, in that vast unknowable that was Before, there had been pain, indescribable pain. But now there was just nothing, and he drifted around in the nothing and was aware of it and that was all.

Until the singing started, a whiffling, meandering

tune as though someone was letting the air out of a bicycle tire.

The thing that was Smoke, this creation of mind and nothing, stumbled over this thought: *Bicycle. Tire.* Details came into focus: *bicycle tire* was black, matte to the touch and about the size of the round mirror that had hung above the mantel in his parents' home in Valencia.

Mantel

Parents

Valencia

No, no, no—this was no good. New thoughts intruded, and Smoke's consciousness shivered and contracted, like an amoeba under a slide. He did not want to think. He did not want to wake.

Mantel, parents, Valencia. In the trilevel house in Valencia where Smoke lived with his father, who sold… *Acuras*…and his mother, who dabbled in portrait photography—

Dad

Acura

Mom

portraits

—there were fires in the fireplace and trays of sandwiches and the game on Monday nights.

Also, he was not called Smoke.

Edward Allen Schaffer, that was his name, and he had grown up in Valencia and his parents were dead and now people called him Smoke and he'd loved a woman and he'd tried to make up for the terrible thing he had done but they'd found him first and that was all.

Wait—it wasn't really singing, was it?

What Smoke had mistaken for singing wasn't sound at all—it was light. It waited outside his eyelids but it was growing impatient with waiting, and when it became impatient it pressed harder against him and became like a sound, entering his brain and ricocheting from one corner to the other. It wanted him to come back. It insisted that he come back. Smoke did not want to, but now he understood that it was not his choice.

Painfully, inevitably, Smoke began to gather himself.

First step…somewhere, he'd had a body. Where he'd left it, he wasn't really sure, but he would not be able to do much of anything without it, and so he cast his weary and reluctant mind out until it stumbled upon the form of the thing and he traced its shape with his memory. It made him laugh, or at least remember laughing, remember the feel of laughter if not the reason.

Toes! Toes were ridiculous, weren't they? Something to laugh about? There were so many of them, and it took Smoke a long time to count each of them, two sets at the end of his two feet. These were attached to legs, which had apparently been there all along but damn if he hadn't forgotten about them. Wonderingly, Smoke recalled his legs and that was enough for a while and he let go, exhausted, and floated back out into the nothing and rested some more.

Days passed. Nights passed.

The next time he came back, the toes, feet and legs were still there and now so were arms. Fingers—these he found interesting enough to dwell on for a while, especially since they felt…incomplete. Memories of touching things, grabbing them, holding them, breaking them. His stomach. His neck. So, it was mostly all there, then. He was all there, and apparently had been for some time. Again, that struck him as funny and he smiled or thought he smiled, though maybe he only imagined either event.

Wait…there was something. Something important. The woman. The woman and the girl. Cass and Ruthie. Those were their names. Hair like corn silk, eyes like green agate.

The memories and sensations coming back too sharp and too fast now, bringing with them pain. Smoke groaned, remembering a kiss—that would be Cass. She tasted like sun and iron and oranges, her skin was silk and velvet and he wanted it.

Wanted her.

He had been at a crossroads, had been choosing the forgetting place, except now he'd remembered Cass and there was no longer a choice, only Cass, only the Cass-shaped hole she'd left in him.

Once, he thought she came to him. He struggled to come up from the wavery not here. He was willing to accept the pain of returning, willing to let go of the lovely forgetting, if only he could see her, touch her, and he tried, God how he tried. He called her name, but he had no voice because it, too, was still caught in the gone place.

The grief of this loss was as real as what he'd left behind. Whether she was a prisoner, too, or a spirit, he didn't know—only that she'd been here. That was enough, that and the memories. They strengthened him and girded him for the pain.

The nothing was gone. The pain was waiting. He breathed in deep and pushed off from the edges and broke the surface, and with a mighty effort, he opened his eyes.

When Dor came around, the sounds of partying in the distance had mostly died down. Earlier, there had been the occasional shout, laughter carrying on the breeze, a couple of firecrackers—where they had come from, Cass had no idea, since nearly everything that could be ignited or exploded had been set off a year earlier when the Siege splintered weeks into riots and looting and people fighting in the streets.

Back then, Cass had trouble sleeping through the sounds of car crashes, screaming, gunshots, things being thrown and driven over and crashed into. By the time she finally left her trailer for the last time, joining those who were sheltering at the Silva library, the street in front of her house smelled of damp ash and rot, and smoke trailed lazily from half a dozen burned structures throughout the town while corpses rotted in cars and parlors and survivors learned that the Beaters weren't so easy to kill.

Sleep had been hard then, because sobriety meant you had to let it all in, every sound, every thought, every memory. Doing A.A. the right way meant handing over your denial card; those who held on too tight never lasted long, and Cass had been in the program long enough to see people come and go. So when she lay awake in her hot, lonely trailer, tears leaking slowly down her face, she accepted the sounds as her due, just one more surcharge of sobriety.

Of course, none of that was a problem now.

Cass sat on the rough poured-concrete stoop behind the house, sipping and watching the bonfire burning down to embers in the middle of the big dirt yard in front of the community center a ways off. On warm days people played football and volleyball there. In the spring there would be picnics; if Cass managed to patch things up with Suzanne by then, they could take the girls there to make wreaths of dandelions and wild loosestrife.

The building's doors had been thrown wide and people spilled out of the party room holding their cups and plastic bottles. Drinking wasn't forbidden in New Eden, and it wasn't even exactly frowned upon, but you didn't see much of it except on nights like these. It had been hard to get used to, after the indulgent ethos of the Box—sometimes the mood of New Eden seemed like a hoedown or a revival, wholesome to the point of cloying.

Sometimes Cass missed the edge-walkers. The despair-dwellers. The ones who routinely lost their battles with themselves.

Her people.

And sometimes she wondered if people like that were just another species doomed to extinction. Aftertime was not hospitable to weakness. It offered too many outs, too many reasons to quit.

Cass couldn't quit, though, because she had Ruthie. So when she fell off the wagon, she fell with excruciating care. She did not actually enjoy a single drop of her cheap kaysev wine as she slowly sipped it down. She wanted to gulp, to drown in it; instead she parceled out not quite enough, every night—and never before Ruthie went to sleep—enough to get just a little bit out of herself. Cass thirsted for complete oblivion; instead she medicated herself to a painful place in the shadows cast by what she couldn't escape.

A footstep on gravel, a figure cutting moonlight— Cass nearly missed him, focused as she was on the orange glow of the remains of the bonfire. But it could only be one person, the one man who knew her habit of sitting out here late into the night while the community slept, the sentries at the bridge the only other souls awake in the small hours.

"Thought you were going to turn in early," Dor said, lowering his tall, sinewy body next to hers.

Cass shrugged. "You knew I wouldn't."

"Yeah, I guess I did."

For a while they sat in silence. Dor drank the dregs of homegrown wine. When he got to the bottom, he held up his plastic cup—the flimsy kind that college kids used to serve at keggers—and stared at it from several angles in the light of the bonfire a hundred yards away.

Then he crushed it in his hand as though it was nothing. Cass raised her eyebrows in the dark.

"Better not let Dana see you do that."

Dana was the compliance leader, tasked with making sure everyone reused and recycled and composted—and the most vocal member of the New Eden council. The council operated on principles of concordance and had sworn off hierarchy, which only seemed to make Dana that much more dogged about getting his way whenever an issue was brought before it. He also seemed to delight in taking rule-breakers to task, though there was no formal punishment structure, only admonishments to do better. You got the feeling Dana would have welcomed more authority as long as he was the one wielding it.

Dor flashed a bitter grin that quickly disappeared. "Dana can go fuck himself. I've just spent eight hours up to my ass in rotting siding and I have the splinters to prove it. If I want to stomp one cup under my boot for old times' sake, I'd guess I've earned the right."

But rather than tossing the cup on the ground, he took the twisted, torn mess and tucked it into the pocket of his shirt. No one littered in New Eden, not even Dor—the three islands were all they had.

"Ruthie sleeping?" he asked after a while, and when his words were followed by his warm, rough fingertips on the strip of skin at the small of her back between sweater and jeans, Cass swallowed hard, because he could take her to the other place that fast.

"Yes," she whispered hoarsely as his fingers traced circles, drifting slowly lower. This went on for a while, moments, hours, who knew…it was always like this, him barely touching her, both of them going white-hot in seconds. They never talked about it. Sometimes he would keep talking—about the things he was fixing, about nails and shingles and broken asphalt; about a bird he'd seen lighting on a fence post, or a book the raiders had found somewhere; about his daughter's latest project, a mural she was painting on the wall of their building or a jean jacket she was embellishing with Valerie's help. He would talk, and Cass would murmur in the appropriate places, the lulls and silences in their conversation, and if someone had been listening to the two of them, unable to see where his hands were going, they would never know there was anything going on except conversation. Dull conversation.

"I might take a ride out with Nathan tomorrow," Dor went on, without inflection. "Go out toward Oakton, see what we can find."

Cass nodded. Nathan siphoned gas from wrecked vehicles, using a system he'd rigged from a pump, a length of hose and some custom couplings—along with a sledgehammer and crowbar for dealing with tank locking devices. He drove out in his tiny hybrid in the mornings and came back with his cans and jugs full. Cass suspected Nathan did it more for sport than anything else—and that Dor went with him for the same reason.

"Be careful," she said unnecessarily. Beaters had been showing up more often lately along the shore, five or six times a week, where they could easily be picked off while they screamed in frustration, unable to swim. There was a certain fascination in watching Glynnis and John, the best shots on the island, taking the skiff out and shooting them at almost point-blank range, dropping them with a single shot to the head or spine, the only sure way to kill them quickly. Cass never let Ruthie watch, but she'd joined the other spectators half a dozen times, borrowing Jasmine's binoculars so the burst of blood filled her vision through the lenses.

But meeting them on land was another story entirely. Especially since Nathan and Dor had to get out of the car to siphon.

"I will," Dor growled as he pulled Cass toward him, his big hand wrapped around her arm, his warmth seeping into her skin even through her jacket.

She went wordlessly, straddling him in the dark, and her mouth met his with a hoarse cry deep in her throat. Her knees ground against the hard, cold concrete as she levered herself more forcefully against him. She could feel his hardness between her legs, and his hands slid down her back, against her ass, pulling her against him. Her teeth knocked against his, and his mouth was hot and hungry on hers. She plunged her hands into his hair—long enough to snarl in her fingers—and felt the bristle of his beard against her thumbs.

It was like this with Dor, this hunger, this need to consume him and be consumed. There was nothing tender about it. Every time, she had bruises. Sometimes one of them would break skin with their teeth, their nails. But every time, this feeling.

"Where is she?" Cass gasped, wrenching herself away from the kiss. She could feel Dor scowl, his jaw tightening under her hands.

"Can't be sure," he said, kissing the soft skin under her chin, scraping against it. He knew she meant Sammi, not the woman. Twice—only when both Valerie and Sammi were safely on the sparsely populated northern island for the day—Dor and Cass had fucked in his room, the luxury of a bed intoxicatingly heady but almost distracting, because they were so accustomed to sheds, abandoned boathouses and, most often, the cold ground at night. They'd rutted in between the rows of plants in Cass's garden on moonlit nights and on the rocky, muddy shore on moonless ones, and Dor had taken her standing up in a narrow space between trucks in the auto shed. Many times, working in the thin winter sun by herself, Cass thought about what they did and wondered if it was the shame of it, the degradation of hiding, that made it that much more intense.

She tasted the liquor on his mouth and licked it greedily. She could not get enough of the taste of him. So it would be another time in the open, another morning when she would wake in filthy clothes, dirt ground into her knees, her elbows, twigs and pebbles in her hair.

Well, so be it.

Dor stood, half carrying her until she wriggled from his grip and found her footing. Dor, who had been an investor Before, who had spent his days under fluorescent lights working at a computer, had been hardened Aftertime. Until they came to New Eden, he'd run the Box, a fenced-in pleasure mart, and he'd trained with former cops and gang members, learned martial arts and shooting and put his body through a demanding regimen until it was as imposing and strong as it could be.

And Smoke had done the same, right along with him. What else was there to fill their days?

Everyone was lean and basically fit now. Life demanded it. Physical labor filled everyone's hours. But Dor ran the length of the islands at dawn, and he lifted weights in the lean-to where sports equipment was haphazardly stored, on both fine days and rainy ones. He was even more hard-muscled now than when they arrived, and Cass suspected it was because he was no longer in charge of anything, no longer a leader, and too much energy accumulated inside him with nowhere to go. His skin against hers was hot; his muscles had been hardened by his own punishment.

He led her ungently down the rocky path to the water's edge. Here, on the southeast end of the middle island, a wooden dock extended twenty feet into the water, its pilings loose, water lapping over the far end. Soon someone would need to either fix or salvage it. But that was not for tonight. Dor led her to the center, which was dry, if splintered and rough, and pulled her against him. His breath was hot on her neck; his teeth grazed against her skin. She seized handfuls of his shirt, threw back her head and let go of conscious thought. For a moment he crushed her against him, and Cass's eyelids flickered at the sensation of her body joined all the length of his, the bonfire a golden, shimmering, wavering illusion in the distance, before she let them drift shut.

If she'd kept them open, she might have seen her coming.

By the time her footsteps clattered on the wooden boards and her shocked gasp reached their ears, by the time Dor and Cass disentangled from each other, it was too late to do anything but try to keep their balance as the dock swayed and rocked.

A flashlight's beam arced wildly across the dock, skittering over the water, until it leveled at them, shining it directly into each of their faces in turn. Cass blinked hard, but when Sammi lowered the light, she saw that the girl's eyes were filled with tears.

"Dad?" she gasped. "Oh my God—Cass—what are you *doing*?"

Cass backed away from Dor, as though to erase what the girl had seen, but really, even a fifteen-year-old couldn't mistake what they were doing for anything but what it was.

"Wuh…we were just—" Cass stammered. Dor's hand shot out and he grabbed Sammi's hand, but she jerked it back.

"Oh my *God!*" she repeated. "I can't believe— Her? *Her?*"

And then she was running, but at the edge of the shore her shoe caught on the lip of the dock and she went sprawling. Dor raced to help her up. Cass stood, with her hand to her throat, unable to breathe, knowing what they had broken, the enormity of it buzzing in her head.

Sammi refused her father's hand, crawled away from him, got to her feet and paused for only a second, her arms hugging her slender frame.

"I hate you!" she cried. "I hate you *both!*"

And then she was sprinting away, the light's beam ricocheting wildly across the landscape, back toward the bonfire, and disappearing completely around a wide building.

Dor watched Sammi go. Cass watched him watching. She ached for him, even as her skin still tingled with the memory of his touch.

Sammi wasn't supposed to see them, not ever. No one was. How they thought they could keep doing this without anyone ever finding out, in a place as small as these islands, she had no idea.

But neither of them had been able to stop. Not once.

Sammi's feet hurt like hell but you had to take your shoes off to climb up the tree without making noise. She'd taken her socks off, too, because once before she hadn't, and snagged one on the bark. It ended up stuck there because she wasn't about to go back for it once she got into Kyra and Sage's room, and at, like, three in the morning she had to sneak back to her room with just one sock. And her boots were nasty, rank and worn-out, and sticking her foot in them without a sock made her want to hurl.

So tonight, even though she'd run all the way here, even though her lungs ached from the effort and she felt like the entire island could hear her breathing, she took the time to stuff her socks into her pockets before she shimmied up the trunk. The party had ended but there were still a few stragglers making their way back to their houses, the paths crisscrossed with flashlight beams and candle glow, laughter spilling over into the darkness. The adults were drunk, some of them, which shouldn't be any surprise because they were all so fucking hypocritical, Sammi could hardly stand it.

Dad and Cass

No. *No.* She wouldn't think about it, wouldn't let herself remember the way they were groping each other, hands all over each other like they'd just die if they couldn't—but no.

The adults were drunk.

Earlier tonight she'd been having fun, the kind of fun that came along unexpectedly sometimes when you had no expectations at all. When you had resigned yourself to the idea that everything was going to suck, and then some small thing would shift or change and suddenly it was like you were in grade school again and it was chocolate cake for lunch, or your best friend gave you an invitation to a party, or your mom painted your nails with a brand-new bottle of nail polish. Sammi remembered feeling that way, that pure clean happy feeling that used to be part of her life, just like Sunday pancakes and riding in the BMW convertible her mom bought herself for her fortieth birthday—but she had forgotten what the feeling *felt* like, if that made sense, which was somehow sadder than all the rest of it put together, and then there would be a moment like tonight when it all came back for just a second or a minute, enough to trick her into feeling like maybe things would be okay.

Tonight it was when Luddy and Cheddar and their stupid friends with their lame-ass retro-emo band were messing around, and Sage and Phillip were making out in the corner, and Sammi and Kyra were helping set out the pies, and then all of a sudden the Lazlow kids were in the middle of the room where the ladies were trying to set up tables, and they started dancing. Only not really dancing. They were taking running starts—or Dane was, anyway, since Dirk was too little, and then flopping down on his knees and sliding across the polished wooden floor like some sort of old-timey break-dancer. Dane got on his back and kicked his legs in the air, and Sammi was reminded of a time when she was six or seven, when she used to take classes at Tiny Troup but she couldn't keep up with the other girls, she couldn't do a plié for anything, so her mom told her it was okay if they quit and they went home and cranked the speakers and got on the floor and made up their *own* dance, right there in the living room of the house in the mountains, under the fake log beams and the elk-antler chandelier, they jumped and danced and rolled until they were piled in a heap, the two of them, laughing so hard her sides hurt. And her mom had said, *Who needs any stupid Tiny Troup?* and Sammi said, *Yeah, who needs those guys?*

Of course, her mom had been dead two months and twenty-four days, and so had Jed, and Sammi kept a count in silver Sharpie on the inside of the plastic box she stored her last few tampons in, the days since she stopped being her old self and started being…well, her half self. Because that was how she thought of herself now, as half of what she used to be.

Not that you could tell from the outside. That was all fine, and from the way the boys looked at her, more than fine, and Sammi knew she looked good—she had sun on her face even though it was so damn cold all the time, and her hair had gotten really long and kind of wavy since she stopped using the flatiron. So the outside, yeah. But inside she was only half there at any given time. Sometimes it was her thinking half that was there, like when she was working on her chords, Red tapping out time on the back of a folding chair in the music room. And sometimes it was her bad half, her remembering half, the one that kept hold of all the things she wished she could let go. And other times it was her numb half—yeah, that was three but who was counting—the numb self she'd learned to call up from deep inside with the help of the herb cigarettes that Sage made for them. She swore they got you high and Sammi wasn't so sure but what did it matter, eleven herbs and spices or whatever was good enough for her, so she and Sage smoked like they'd been smoking forever and that was what mattered, putting that paper to your lips and sparking it up and sucking it down, with your friend beside you. And getting to the numb.

Thinking. Remembering. Going numb. But never all at once.

Right now, pulling herself up the low branches, swinging up to the ledge, the different parts were coming and going. That thing with Cass and her dad—

What the hell? Her dad would fuck anything that moved, but he wouldn't even let Sammi walk down to the water with Colton after dinner. But she couldn't think about it tonight. That had to wait. So she was pushing back on the thinking half and calling up the numb half. She was just killing time, it was nothing.

"Sage," she said kind of soft, tapping on the window glass. She had one arm wrapped around the branch, the wood digging into her inner elbow painfully, leaning down against the cold window. Sage and Kyra were no doubt sleeping, they'd left the party at least an hour ago,

Kyra looking like she was going to puke again, which was nothing new. Kyra had been puking since they got to New Eden, so much that Corryn had started making her special crackers out of kaysev flour, she even poked holes in them to make them look like saltines.

"Sage!"

But Sage was already there, pushing the window open, yawning.

"You scared the shit out of me. What are you doing?"

"I couldn't sleep," Sammi lied. "Dad's snoring again."

It was a pretty good lie. Her dad did snore, sometimes, if he'd been out all day on the road with Earl, or if he'd been doing something hard-core like cutting wood with the axe or hauling stumps with chains. Sammi figured snoring was just one of the ways old people dealt with physical exhaustion. Which was okay—would have been okay, anyway, back when they lived in a six-bedroom house and her mom and dad were, like, in a whole other wing—except that now they shared a trailer barely big enough for one person to live in, much less two, and it was nice of her dad to let her have the bedroom except he slept in the living room, which was the only other full room in the trailer, and she couldn't even go to the bathroom without having to walk right past him, which was just wrong since her dad was longer than the twin mattress he'd put on the floor and he always had a leg or arm falling off the side. She didn't want to see her dad like that and she figured he for damn sure wasn't proud of it either.

Of course, that was all before she knew about him and Cass. Cass! When he was supposedly with Valerie, who was totally boring except at least she was old and normal, someone her dad *should* date—not Cass, who had been cool until they got here when she had some sort of breakdown and barely even cared about Smoke anymore and besides she had a *kid* for God's sake, but evidently Aftertime meant that parents could just fuck around and do whatever they felt like and to hell with the kids even while they were still ordering them around.

"I thought I'd hang out," Sammi said quickly, not wanting to go down that path. "You know, I thought we could be quiet if Kyra's, like, needing her sleep or whatever."

"Oh, dude, get this," Sage said, forgetting that she was exhausted and pulling the window open wide so Sammi could scramble inside. Sage and Kyra were roommates in the House for Wayward Girls, which wasn't actually what the place was called, just their nickname for it. Red and Zihna, who were *really* old, were like the housemom and housedad and had the big bedroom downstairs. Kyra would probably have to move over to the Mothers' House when her baby came, but that was months and months away. Sage had been impregnated at the Rebuilders' baby farm too, but she had miscarried right after they got to New Eden so it was kind of like she hadn't even been pregnant. "Kyra's getting this, like, *line* on her stomach."

"What do you mean?"

"I guess it's a pregnancy thing. That's what Zihna says, anyway. Zihna says it's probably going to be a boy because the line's from testosterone and you get more testosterone in your system if you're having a boy."

"Like with the bacne?"

"I *know,* right? That's so disgusting." Sage made a face. "Here, look, she won't wake up."

As Sage tugged the blanket carefully off their sleeping friend and shone a flashlight on her, Sammi thought about how Sage always acted like pregnancy was the worst thing that could happen to anyone. Not around Kyra of course, because that would be mean, but when she and Sammi were alone. And that made Sammi wonder…maybe Sage wasn't as relieved about having had the miscarriage as she pretended to be.

Which Sammi kind of got. At least if you had a baby, there would be something to *do* all day long. And someone to love you back. For *you,* not for who people wanted you to be. Everyone was so messed up, from everything they'd seen, everything that had happened. A baby wouldn't be like that—a baby would never have seen cities getting blown up and burned down, whole fields and farms leveled, all the plants dead. And now, with the kaysev and all, a baby would never go hungry.

Of course, there was still the Beaters.

Sage lifted the oversize T-shirt Kyra wore as pajamas, and sure enough, there on her still-mostly-flat stomach was a faint gray line running from her belly button down. And a few black hairs lying flat against her skin.

"Shit," Sammi said, impressed.

Kyra sighed and shifted in her sleep and Sage pulled the covers back up over her, then snapped off the flashlight. They sat on the floor with their backs to Sage's bed. Sammi, who saw well in the dark, could make out the shapes of Kyra's bottle collection on top of the dresser, a few wilted weeds stuck in some of them.

"I saw Dad with Cass tonight," Sammi said, surprising herself. She hadn't planned to tell. Sudden tears welled up in her eyes and she pushed them angrily away.

"What do you mean, *with?*"

"Like, with his tongue down her throat and his hands in her pants. And she wasn't exactly saying no. They were down on the dock doing it like, like dogs."

They weren't exactly doing it, of course, and not like dogs either, but Sammi was pretty sure they'd been headed that way. And she'd bet this wasn't the first time.

"Oh wow," Sage said, seeming genuinely shocked. "I never would have thought that."

"Yeah, no shit."

"I thought she was, like, with—"

"Smoke? Yeah."

There was a silence, and Sammi figured they were both thinking about Smoke, how messed up he'd been when they first got here, bone showing through his skin, scabs oozing pus, missing a couple of fingers, scars crisscrossing his face and body. For a while Sammi visited him a few times a week, and then she just sort of stopped. She felt guilty about that—guilty as hell, since Smoke had always been there for her and her mom back when they all sheltered at the school. But she couldn't stand looking at him half-dead, because it reminded her too much of when her mom and Jed and all the others were killed. And none of them even killed by Beaters, but by supposedly good humans.

Smoke didn't even know she was there, anyway. Sunhi said he might never come out of his coma. Zihna said his "energy was growing stronger," but that was just the hippie way she talked all the time.

"So…what about Valerie?" Sage asked.

"What about her?" Sammi snapped, and then regretted it. She had wondered the same thing. Valerie was always trying to get close to her, asking her about her friends, Sage and Kyra and Phillip and Colton and Kalyan and Shane, offering to make snacks for them all, offering to loan her clothes that Sammi wouldn't be caught dead in. Valerie was nice, in her boring way— but there was no *way* Sammi needed another mom.

"Well, Cass is kind of…way hotter than her. I mean, you know?"

"Yeah, but—" But it was still her *dad*. "I mean, it would be one thing if Dad wasn't on my shit all the time about every little thing I do. His new thing? Now he doesn't want me going off the island without telling him first. I'm like, I always tell Red or Zihna, and he says that's not good enough. If he's off working or whatever I have to wait until he gets back."

"Sammi…he's worried about you. I mean, you're his *kid*."

There was a hollowness to Sage's voice and too late Sammi remembered the thing that made her an asshole with her friends sometimes—that she still *had* a parent, which was one more than most of the others here.

Sammi said she was sorry like she always did, and Sage said it didn't matter like she always did, and they smoked for a while and then they lay down, Sage in her bed and Sammi on the floor under borrowed blankets, and after a while Sage fell asleep in the middle of talking about which actor from Before Phillip looked most like, and Sammi lay awake and tried not to think of her dad and Cass and what they were doing and the sounds they were making, and instead imagined sliding across the wooden floor on her knees like the little kids, being seven again with her mom on the sidelines clapping and saying, *Go, go, Sammi-bear.*

"I already knew that," Luddy said, taking back his guitar after Red had showed him exactly how the chord progression went. They had been among the last people in the community center, the party having wound down to the dregs, all the good food gone and most folks having wandered home with a full belly and a pleasant buzz.

The chord progression was a tricky one, and Red remembered with wistful clarity the day he'd learned it himself. He'd been crashing in a guy's apartment in San Francisco, not too far from the Haight. Red had a little of Luddy in him back then: insecure and ambitious. He didn't dare let on how much of a rush he got just being that close to where it all started. Hendrix, Joplin, Garcia—back in those days everyone still remembered the greats.

Red used to get up before the rest of the guys and

walk over to the park with his guitar and find a bench. He'd stay a couple of hours, dicking around just for the sheer joy of it, going through the set list first for whatever dive Carmy had managed to book them into—and then he'd play his own stuff. Some of the songs were polished, as perfect as he could make them; others were just a few bars here and there, inspirations that came to him in the early hours of the morning while he lay in bed thinking and smoking after a gig.

Back then, people used to try to give him money all the time, and what the hell, Red didn't discourage it. A "hey, man" for the guys, a wink for the ladies. He got other offers, too, and now and then he'd take one of the girls home, or if he and Carmy were sharing a room, to her place. It never meant anything. It was just part of the journey, and Red back then was always on a journey. It was in his blood, in his bones. The original ramblin' man, that was him.

Not anymore, though. Red counted every day that he woke up in the same place, Zihna at his side, as a good day. And the kids—the girls who lived with them, the teenage boys who hung around the house—they were a kick. He taught them all guitar, just for fun. On a good day, it was pure magic. On a bad day, well, then it was still pretty good.

His favorite nights were when the girls got bored and came downstairs looking for something to do. Zihna made tea and snacks, and Red got out board games or cards, and they laughed and played until the girls got sleepy. On nights like that, it sometimes seemed like he had all the time in the world. That was an illusion, of course. Red was fifty-nine this year and well aware that he looked a decade older than that. All that hard living was catching up to him.

There was one more thing he needed to do before he was dead. He'd tried and failed more times than he could count on one hand. Still, he was biding his time. Making a move too soon would be even worse than waiting too long. And he had a feeling he'd have only one more chance.

In the morning Cass woke before Ruthie. For a while she lay with her daughter tucked in the curve of her body, wrapped in her arms, watching Ruthie's hair ruffle in the gentle current of her breath, feeling her good sure slow heartbeat and marveling for the hundredth, the thousandth time at the perfection of her eyelids. They were porcelain fair, with a single faint crease and long curved dark lashes, a tiny miracle, evidence of grace she didn't deserve.

Her head was thickly cottoned, sharp thorns of ache punctuating the fuzz. Her stomach rolled and burned, and she had a powerful dry-lipped thirst and a faint dizziness. She eased herself out of the covers and crawled onto the carpet, then carefully stood, holding on to the small end table that served as a nightstand for support. A tremor, a shake. A sheen of sweat on her forehead, the backs of her hands.

Self-contempt as real as salt and poison on her tongue.

This morning Cass would not go to the shower house, where a primitive plumbing system had been cobbled together by Earl and his men. The women gathered there, breathing misty clouds in the morning chill, while they scrubbed their faces and brushed their teeth with split kaysev twigs. Cass couldn't face anyone until she got her daytime mask in place.

She retraced last night's path down to the water, keeping an eye on the ground in front of her. Not many people came here; besides the problem of the disintegrating dock, the shore sloped too gently to be good for fishing, especially when a steeper drop-off on the other side of the island meant you could practically hang a line into the water and catch bass or sturgeon. Still, there had been enough foot traffic to wear a path from which roots and jagged rocks protruded, ready to trip the inattentive.

Cass reached the water's edge, and shuffled slowly out onto the dock. The river was wide here, the water calm and lazy; it seemed to flow more rapidly on the other side of the island where the bridge to the mainland was. She knelt at the point where it sagged, and a thin skim of water slid over the slimy wood, inches from her knees. Cass watched the water's behavior for a moment as she lined up her things—a toothbrush, a cloth, the plastic box of baking soda that she used under her arms—and thought about how pretty it was, the way it followed a design as endless in its variety as it was inevitable. Lapping, dripping, sluicing into every crevice in the wood, every pock and hollow in the shore.

It would be so easy to slip soundlessly into the water,

let it find its way into her nostrils, her eyes, her mouth, the breath bubbling out of her as she drifted slowly down into the reeds and muck.

The February-cold water would scour away the stale film left by last night's wine, the guilt-pall from Dor's bruising kiss.

A sound interrupted her treacherous train of thought: a crowing burbled cry carried across the water, sharp on the misty morning, sharp and close. Cass jerked her head up, and there, across the twenty yards of sluggish river that separated the island from the shore, were Beaters.

Cass fell back on her ass, the impact jarring her body, and scuttled backward several feet until she got herself under control. Twelve, fifteen...*eighteen* of them. They saw her and started screaming at her like desperate lovers, reaching and testing the water with their knobbed and scabbed and mostly shoeless feet before retreating back to the shore.

So many of them. Their rage was nothing new, but ever since the first wave appeared, nearly a year back, they had steadily evolved, like the old Time-Life picture books Cass's mother brought home from garage sales—evolution presented in glorious saturated colors, ancient dogs and apes turned slyly toward the reader with expressions of self-confident conspiracy. In no time the Beaters started searching each other out and building nests. In mere months they had learned to work together to take down a citizen, in groups of four so there would be one to pin each of the victim's flailing limbs. Not too much later, they discovered that larger groups could divide responsibilities so that some kept would-be rescuers at bay while others spirited the prey away for a group feast.

Gathering clothes and rags for their nests. Dragging their victims' remains away and stacking them into bone-piles. But some things remained beyond them—putting on warm clothes when the weather turned cold, or scaling walls, or driving machinery or building fires.

And most significantly—*swimming.*

It was the only thing that kept New Eden safe. No one had ever seen a Beater even approach waterways with intent, though surely in the crowd of lurching, bumbling creatures on the other shore there must have been some accomplished swimmers. Perhaps one of them had swum for Cal, another had been a pretty young mother who floated her laughing toddler in water wings in a backyard pool, yet another maybe wakeboarded on New Melones Lake only a few short years ago, splendid and muscular and sun-sparkling in his joyful youth.

No more. Even at this distance Cass could make out the hallmarks of the advanced stages of the disease. Some of them were missing huge chunks of flesh, and their bones flashed white and vulnerable-looking. Others had chewed off their own flesh, the thin skin covering their fingers, their nails, their own lips, tearing scabbed craters in their shoulders. When they could not find fresh uninfected flesh, the Beaters would nibble dispiritedly at each other, drawing blood and painting themselves with it, tearing off strips of flesh, but their hearts were not in it. They could tell the difference and the difference was evidently considerable. They would even eat kaysev when they grew truly hungry, and as far as anyone knew, no Beater had perished from starvation.

Eventually, they died—even the freakishly super-charged immune system that was left behind by the blueleaf fever was not enough to save them from the endless insults to their systems, the breaking of bones and rending of flesh and unstaunched bleeding. Occasionally the raiding parties came across Beater carcasses bent and splayed in the streets, left by their companions where they fell. The huge black carrion birds that had appeared last fall were not interested in dead Beaters. Only maggots would eat Beater flesh, and Cass had heard the stories of raiders rolling over a corpse to reveal its underside split and leaking a tide of fat white pupae onto the pavement.

Cass's stomach rolled and heaved and she retched and retched into the water, the remains of a meal so long ago she had forgotten it, bare lean tendrils of bile. Retching until there was nothing left, until it felt like her soul itself was expelled.

At last she wiped her mouth on her sleeve and returned to the path without looking again at the opposite shore.

It was her duty, as a member of New Eden's community, to take this bad news straight to the council, where it could be absorbed and disseminated and acted upon.

But as Cass remembered what she'd done on the dock only hours ago, she knew she would shirk this mean duty as she had so many others. Someone else would have seen what she saw, surely. Someone else would act. Someone else would have to save them.

The day was a scorched and stretched expanse of time. Cass was grateful—her gratitude lousy with guilt—that it was not her day with the kids. Tomorrow was her day in the babysitting rotation and she would not drink tonight. Or at least she would only drink a little, almost nothing. And she would not see Dor tonight. And, definitely, she would visit Smoke. All of that. She just had to get through the day first.

Earl showed up as promised and they walked the bank together, boots squelching down into the sodden soil near the bank, clumps of reed stems going pale where they met the earth, crushed flat under their feet.

"I don't know," he said, finally, when they reached the southern tip of Garden Island. Looking north from here toward the other islands, you could see only the rooftop of the community center and a few of the other buildings. A lazy plume of smoke swirled up into the clouds, the remains of the breakfast fire. Lunch was always a cold meal, a lean repast of kaysev in its humblest forms—greens for salad, hardtack made from the everyday flour.

Cass had been skipping lunch too often, she knew that. She was much too thin, her muscles taut and sinewy across her shoulders, her back, her arms. She would go join the others, just as soon as they were finished here. She would eat extra, she would nibble sustenance like a squirrel.

"Maybe hold back on this one area," Earl said, indicating a section of Cass's planned lettuce patch. "I don't think it's gonna go, but this winter's been bad for rain."

Cass nodded. She'd expected as much. She had the rows sketched in twine tied to sticks sunk into the spongy soil, waiting for a dry day to plant.

Earl hitched up his pants, their business concluded. He was a kind man, Cass knew that, the leathery kind of sixtysomething man who would have been a putterer, a retired gent who refereed Little League games and built sunrooms and gazebos for his wife. He never complained about the arthritis in his joints though it was clear that mornings brought him almost debilitating stiffness. As they walked slowly back along the path, he favored one leg; if a trove of Advil or Tylenol popped up, there would be some relief for him—but that was as good as wishing for helicopters or snow cones, since everything good had been raided from the easy scores long ago.

"So you got your crew coming down after lunch," Earl said amiably.

Cass was surprised he kept track. Benny, Carol, a few others who pitched in occasionally—they came to

Garden Island on the afternoons when Suzanne watched the kids, everything revolving around the child-care schedule. The kaysev field was separated by footpaths into six long and narrow sections, and on picking days the crew worked alongside Cass, bent-backed like the migrant workers who used to dot the strawberry fields along Highway 101 from Salinas down to San Luis Obispo fifty miles to the west. It was hard work, painstaking and slow, making sure they didn't miss a single blue-tinged leaf. The markings could be subtle—on the youngest leaves in particular, there was nothing but a light tint at the base of the veining, only the slightest crenellation along the edges of the leaves. In a mature plant the signs were unmistakable—the leaves were ruffled prettily and the underside had the blue shade of the veins on a fair-skinned woman's breast. For that reason Cass discouraged her team from picking any of the young plants at all.

Benny and Carol had become as efficient as she was and so she no longer double-checked their baskets. They were a good team, close-knit. The dynamics had shifted, Cass knew that—at first she and Benny and Carol stood together at the end of the rows, hands pressing at their aching backs, resting and talking for a few moments before heading back down the field. Now she mostly worked at her own rhythm and it was the others who took their breaks together, their laughter occasionally ringing out over the hush of the island. At the end of the day, when everyone carried their baskets back to the kitchen, the others were subdued, overly polite, asking after Ruthie and Smoke, asking if she needed anything else, help with some chore. Cass always said she was fine, she had everything under control, and it seemed to her they were happy to have her answers and be able to leave her company.

Earl wasn't like that—or maybe it was only that he moved so slowly he could not outrun the pall she cast. For a moment Cass was so grateful for his kindness that she had an urge to hug him, to put her hand in his big work-rough one. He could be like…a father to her, maybe. Her own father left her for good early on, and her stepfather was rotting in the hell he richly deserved by now, and it would be nice—so nice—to have someone who cared about her. Cass blinked at the shock of painful longing, made a small sound, an exhalation of breath.

Earl stopped, put a hand on her shoulder to steady her. "Cass, are you all right?"

She tried to evade his kind eyes. They were sharp and shining in their nest of wrinkles in his weathered face, but he had seen.

"I'm fine."

His hand stayed heavy on her shoulder for a moment. "You need to take care, girl," he said gruffly, and Cass knew it was reproach as well as concern, that he recognized the signs of her hangover. Well, she deserved it, didn't she, and as they walked the rest of the way she redoubled her fierce silent promise that tonight would be different, that tonight she would abstain from everything that was wrong.

The hardtack, spread with a bit of jam to sweeten it, did not go down easily and did not do well in her stomach afterward. Still, Cass got through the afternoon, keeping to her own row and painfully thinking up responses to the others' cheerful greetings. The sky cleared by late afternoon, turning a brilliant sapphire suffused with unseasonable warmth, and Cass's skin sheened with perspiration as they walked back together.

They turned their baskets over to the kitchen staff, who would wash the leaves and pods and roots and turn them into a dozen different dishes. Today's harvest was mostly tender leaves, succulent and pale from all the rains, so it would be salads, stir-fries and maybe even an exotic soufflé made with the precious eggs from the three chickens found in a creek wash a quarter mile from a farmhouse near Oakton. People joked that the chickens were New Eden's VIPs and everyone was anxious for the day a rooster would be found and ensure future generations of poultry.

The few pods they'd found were still young and tender enough to be eaten as is; though mature pods were edible they were tough and fibrous and usually reserved for the work studio, where they were dried and turned into a coirlike material that could be used for mats and scrubbers. But the shelled beans could be tasty if they weren't allowed to get too large—at that point, the beans would be dried, oil pressed from them and the rest ground for flour.

The meals would be prepared with care and presented with ceremony by the women and a few men who tended the kitchen. People needed to take pride in their work—Cass understood that. She even wished she could feel the same, and she envied the beaming servers who set out dishes garnished with lemon slices, the juice squeezed so that everyone could have a little in their boiled water.

Cass lingered in the yard, pretending that she was caught up in a boccie game, in reality putting off the moment when she would have to face Suzanne. That was how she came to be among the first to hear the cry go up.

"Blueleaf!"

For a beat after the syllables hung in the clear warm air, there was silence. Cass whipped around and stared at the long table where the rinsed kaysev was laid out to dry, two of the kitchen staff—Rachael and Chevelle—frozen over a sorted pile, looks of horror on their faces.

Cass leaped to her feet and ran to the table. Chevelle mutely handed over a bunch of leaves. Cass examined it with shaking fingers and yes—*oh, yes, there it is*—the cloudy blue tint at the base of the leaf, trailing up into the veining, which was almost azure before it shaded to green. The leaves were too young yet to have clearly ruffled edges and they lay cool and smooth in Cass's hand.

"Oh fuck," Chevelle murmured, as Corryn hastened over, wiping her hands on her apron.

"Is it?" she demanded in the booming voice that more than anything had sealed her position as head cook. She held out her hand for the leaves but Cass made no move to share them, only nodding.

The worst of the discovery—the first in a month—was not that a rogue plant had grown on Garden Island, but that one of them had failed to identify it when they picked it. If it had been passed over by the kitchen staff—whose job was to cook, not inspect, the harvest—it likely would have been eaten.

And one or more of the people of New Eden would have begun to turn.

"Which basket?" Cass demanded, scanning the row

on the wooden counter behind them. Rachael pointed, her face drained of color. "Whose basket?"

Cass seized the basket and spun it in her hands, looking for the metal scrap that Earl had wired to each basket, initials inscribed with a nail, to identify its owner. CD.

CD, she read, and her throat closed.

Cass Dollar

It could have happened to anyone. The kind words, spoken in an unexpectedly kind and tender voice by Corryn, were a branch offered to one drowning in a current, and Cass tried to hold on.

It worked, in the moment. Corryn had ushered Cass into the storage pantry while the others checked and rechecked the harvest. Harris and Shannon joined them in the pantry for a quick consultation; it would be discussed at the nightly council meeting, and Cass knew that Harris could be counted on to quell any hysteria. Corryn, if she were called upon to recount what happened, would be fair. She was a woman who would always continue to be kind.

These are good people, Cass reminded herself, holding her arms tight across her chest, back in the room an hour later with Ruthie. It was almost dinnertime and Cass would not let her daughter go hungry, but she did want to wait until most of the people had eaten, until darkness was settling over the dining area and they could sit alone.

But these were good people. How could she have taken them so resolutely for granted? Why had she rebuffed all their efforts at friendship, at inclusion? But Cass knew the reason why—the reason was sitting in the wooden box. In the dimming light of evening, the bear's gilded collar seemed to shine. The umbrella balanced on his nose as it always did; his placid canine expression remained unperturbed.

"Can we go see Smoke?" Ruthie asked. She was playing with Cass's bowl of earrings, taking them out and sorting them, dozens of sparkly and polished studs and dangles, some with mates, some without. Cass mostly kept the collection for her girl, since she rarely wore such things anymore, but tonight she had to tamp down her irritation and resist snapping at her daughter for the baubles spilled and snagged on the dirty carpeting.

"I don't know, honey." Cass smoothed Ruthie's hair down gently as her little girl snuggled into her lap, her skin soft and warm despite the chill of the room.

"'Cause he misses us. He told me."

Cass's fingers stilled in Ruthie's downy hair. It needed a cut. "Did you have a dream about Smoke, honey?"

After Cass had recovered her daughter, it had taken a while for Ruthie to begin dreaming again. At first her dreams took the form of daytime trances; they were often frightening and sometimes providential. Dreams of birds preceded the appearance of the giant black buzzards; dreams of other disasters followed.

But recently Ruthie had only mentioned nice things. Cakes, mostly—she loved cookbooks and pored over them at night with Cass—and adventures with Twyla and sometimes Dane.

She frowned, a tiny line appearing on her brow. "I don't think so, Mama," she said, her voice going even softer, almost a whisper. "He said he misses us."

"But—" *When,* it was on the tip of Cass's tongue to

ask. In which of their visits had Smoke done more than thrash or mumble in a coma-sleep? It had been weeks since they'd been to the hospital, and Cass had not discussed Smoke with anyone, least of all Ruthie.

"It was…" More frowning. "Before. Before today. Yesterday?"

Cass sighed. There would be no making sense of this rogue impulse, and she didn't want to disconcert Ruthie by pressing her further. "It's all right. We'll go see him soon, and we'll see what he says, okay?"

Ruthie brightened. "And can I ask Corryn for a cookie to take to him?"

"You may ask—but it might not be a cookie day." Also, Smoke was still being fed his meals ground and moistened, in a spoon, his dormant body responding only enough to swallow the mush   but Cass didn't mention that either.

On nights when she stayed over, it was Sammi's habit to slip out before the rest of the Wayward Girls were awake. It wasn't that she wasn't welcome there. She came to the House almost every day, since Red and Zihna let all the older kids hang out whenever they wanted. Sammi imagined that she could stay over whenever she wanted, that she could show up anytime, no matter the hour. The front door wasn't locked. Doors in New Eden weren't locked. Well, except for the storage sheds and the pharmacy cabinet, a fact confirmed by Colton when he had gone to the hospital—nothing more than a two-room guesthouse behind the community center—to get a cut on his ankle cleaned.

The reason Sammi sneaked in on her late-night visits, and left early in the mornings, had nothing to do with whether she was welcome in this place, but with her dad. She worried about him. She used to, anyway.

The way he always held on to her a little too long with his goodbye morning hugs, the way he was always checking in with her—at meals, after dinner at the community center, when she went to North Island with her friends, hell, even when she was with Valerie. It wasn't *exactly* loneliness, and Sammi got that it was his *job* to worry about her, and the fact that they'd been separated for so long, all the terrible things that had happened, her mom's death and everyone else's—so yeah, it was natural that he'd want to keep an eye out for her. But with her dad it was something more. It was like his fear for her made him weak and she had to be the one to constantly remind him that he was strong, and she couldn't let him worry too much or the weakness would grow.

And that was why she always made sure to be home, in their crappy little trailer, by the time he got up. It wasn't hard to do, she knew her dad had trouble sleeping and often spent the middle of the night tossing and turning, but even on those nights—*especially* on those nights—the sleep that finally found him at dawn was deep.

But all of that was different now, Sammi reminded herself angrily.

She was sitting on the floor of Sage and Kyra's bedroom for the second morning in a row. The borrowed blankets were neatly folded with the pillow centered on top, tucked under Kyra's bed, because there was too much shit under Sage's. If—when—Sammi asked Red and Zihna if she could move in for good, she would have to ask for her own room. She loved her friends, and the mess didn't bother her when she was just visiting, but she needed a place where she could have her things the way she liked them, everything in its place, arranged exactly the same every single day.

She had that now, she remembered with an unwelcome hollowness. Her dad let her do anything she wanted to the trailer's only bedroom, and didn't so much as raise an eyebrow when she took to dusting every single day. Her things—a stone and a necklace that had been gifts from Jed, a plastic barrette that had belonged to her mother and was missing a couple of teeth, her journal, a striped coffee cup holding sharpened pencils, the small pocketknife Colton had given her just last month—each had a specific place and Sammi checked them all the time, making sure they were centered on the shelves. She had begged to use the jerry-rigged hand vac, and Dana had finally relented and agreed to let her borrow it once a week, and she went over the matted beige carpet one small row at a time, walking all the way down to the shore to empty the debris into the swirling water of the river.

All of that was hers, hers alone, and all of it was good. She would give that up by moving here. Even if they let her have her own room, she would be too embarrassed to do the same things here. Besides, she would have to share everything, and even though she had no problem sharing her clothes and her food and her books, even her treasured shampoo and conditioner and lotion and cleanser—she could not bear the thought of her special things disappearing.

The stone, the necklace, the barrette were all she had left of Jed and her mom.

Too bad she wasn't more like her dad, Sammi thought bitterly. He'd started dating within a month of leaving her mom, as if their twenty years together hadn't even happened. One woman after another—Pilates in- structors and pharmaceutical reps and even, for a few strange weeks, Sammi's old Spanish teacher.

Her father wasn't the type to let things get to him. She ought to ask him how he did it. Right after she asked him if it was hotter to mess around with some- one who'd been a Beater and recovered. Fucking Cass. They said people like that had higher body tempera- tures and faster heartbeats than ordinary people, that they could heal from whatever injuries—scratches, bite marks, hickeys?—they got. Fucking Cass.

Sammi kicked at exposed roots as she took the long way back home. The path wound along the edge of the river, disappearing in hummocks of reeds and reemerg- ing only to dip down to the water and back up the banks. Hardly anyone came this way, and Sammi was in no mood to run into other people before she'd had a chance to change clothes and wash her face. She just wanted to spend a few minutes in the welcome order of her room. Touch the stone and the necklace and the barrette, in order, twice. Once to make sure and once for luck.

An exhalation followed by a curse: Sammi looked up the banks and saw an uncertain figure struggling through thick overgrowth, grabbing handfuls of grass and weeds to keep from slipping down the slope on her ass. Sammi resigned herself to having to share this moment that she would have so much preferred to keep to herself.

And then she saw who it was, the thick dark hair grazing the woman's shoulders, the grosgrain headband. Valerie, with her bag slung over her shoulder, the can- vas printed with some art-museum logo—Valerie the do-gooder, supporting the arts even after all the art museums had been ransacked and abandoned.

"Sammi—oh, Sammi, thank God," she called down, pushing at a stalk that crossed her path. "I've been looking everywhere."

Sammi looked past Valerie toward the community center, through wisps of mist and stumpy dead trees, to the yard. She had been so deep in thought that she hadn't noticed the crowd forming there, people gathering in little groups, huddling in the cold.

"How come?" Sammi asked irritably. Whatever the new crisis was, she wasn't in the mood to be a part of it.

Valerie slid the last few feet, stumbling and almost falling. "There was a crowd of Beaters this morning, on the west shore. Your dad saw them when he headed out this morning with Nathan and he's been looking everywhere for you."

"Not everywhere," Sammi mumbled, even as Valerie's words—*a crowd of them*—sank in.

"What's that, honey?" Valerie's hand—Sammi couldn't help focusing on her nails, perfectly oval and clean—settled on her shoulder, and Sammi resisted shrugging it off.

"I just said, I'm surprised Dad didn't find me, I would think Kyra and Sage's room wouldn't be all that hard to find."

"But we did look there, first thing!"

"Well—I was there." Sammi made a halfhearted effort to keep the defiance out of her voice, but hadn't she and her dad talked about it—she'd asked him point-blank, *So Valerie's, like, my new stepmom now?* This was weeks ago, when Valerie had returned a stack of

Sammi's clothes, mended and pressed and smelling, somehow, faintly of lavender.

No one can replace your mom, he had replied, as if he knew that Sammi was remembering her mom doing laundry back in their house in the mountains, singing while she folded clothes in the sunny laundry room.

Valerie was better at laundry—her mom tended to mix red things in with the whites, turning everything pink—and somehow that just made it all the worse.

"But Zihna said she hadn't seen you," Valerie said, twisting her hands together.

"So what's the big deal anyway? There's Beaters on the shore every day."

"Oh, Sammi...you don't understand. It was more than there've ever been before. Steve said he counted more than thirty before Glynnis and John started shooting."

"Thirty?" Sammi was taken aback. *A crowd*...by that she thought they meant eight or ten. The most that anyone had ever seen before was, like, nine, and that was two separate groups, one that came from the direction of Oakton and the other from straight across the field, dragging what turned out to be a split and rotting garden hose behind them. But thirty...Sammi had never heard of that many being in one place at one time, though she probably could have *imagined* it in the denser cities' ruins. "Where did they come from?"

"No one knows. It was so early...no one saw them coming. Glynnis and John managed to kill eight of them, and the rest ran. Nathan took off after them in the car, and he and Steve killed another seven. They'd wanted to see which direction they came from, but the Beaters just—they just panicked, I guess like they would, and ran in every direction."

"Dad didn't go with Nathan, did he?"

"Of course not," Valerie said, eyes widening. "He hasn't done anything but look for you since they were spotted. He's down on Garden Island now, going row by row."

Guilt made Sammi blush. She should have known—but her dad loved going out with Nathan, and she could picture it—Nathan white-knuckle driving, her dad half out the window with that big Glock of his, like it was some kind of jackass safari.

Her dad was such an idiot. Acting like it was all some sort of game, the way he went out driving around, looking for gas, blowing up cars. And he had the nerve to accuse *her* of being irresponsible.

Her irritation was back in a flash. "Well, I guess you can tell him I'm fine," she said, pushing past Valerie, taking the incline nimbly. *Sucks to be old,* she resisted saying, knowing Valerie would struggle even more getting back up the bank than coming down—and knowing she was a real bitch for not staying and helping, especially since Valerie had devoted her morning to searching for her. "I'm gonna head back to the trailer and take a nap."

"But, Sammi—"

"Look, I'll talk to you later, okay? We were up late, I'm wrecked." Sammi yawned and didn't bother to cover her mouth.

"No, what I wanted to say…look, they found blueleaf. They don't think anyone ate it, the plants were young, but there's an alert." Her worried face sagged. "There's a buddy-up, right after breakfast."

As if on cue, the breakfast bell chimed, two soulful tones carried on the mist. Sammi loved that bell possibly more than anything else about New Eden, the way it sounded like it had once hung in a beautiful old cathedral, the way it made the air still and silent and echo-y for a few seconds after it stopped ringing.

"Fuck…"

"I know they're a pain," Valerie said, not even commenting on Sammi's language, which made Sammi want to say it again, or worse. Sometimes she wondered what it would take to get a reaction out of Valerie. Of course the woman was only nice to her because she was dating her dad—if she wasn't, she would have snapped a long time ago, given Sammi the lecture she probably deserved. Sammi took advantage of her, but honestly, how could she not? How could anyone stand Valerie's fakey niceness? "We could go together, though…if you want. I mean, once we get there, I'd—"

"You're with Mrs. Kristobal," Sammi interrupted. "Right?"

Valerie nodded. "But it won't take long. You and Cindy can finish up quick and we can eat together. Your dad'll come back, I'm sure of it—we agreed he'd come back every half hour to check in. Oh, Sammi, he'll be so glad to see you. He'll be so incredibly relieved. Maybe, just to make him feel better, you and I could try to stay away from the banks until we get this all sorted out. Keep to the middle of the island, with everyone else. What do you think—shall we make a pact?"

Valerie was trying so hard to give her a brave smile that Sammi gave up and held out her hand to help her scramble up the muddy bank. Valerie took it gratefully, blinking against the sun, which had risen high enough in the sky to warm their faces.

"Good idea," Sammi muttered, wondering what Valerie would have to say if she knew that not even twelve hours ago her dad had been out on the dock, practically in the water as he buried his face in Cass Dollar's tits.

Cass knew it was no accident that breakfast consisted solely of day-old pone, a thick bread made in skillets over the fire from a kaysev-flour batter sizzled in rabbit fat. No fresh kaysev would be served until it had all been checked—in the daylight—a couple more times. This was mere paranoia—the odds of finding more blueleaf were incredibly low. Only the passage of time would get everyone comfortable again, would lull them back into a state of calm.

After most had eaten and before anyone could leave, Dana got up on the porch of the community center and clapped his hands for quiet. Buddy-ups always began this way, with Dana listing the early signs of the disease in his droning voice: the fever, often accompanied by a darkening of the skin and a sheen of perspiration; the dizziness that was traced with euphoria; the sensitivity to light; and the disorientation. He would go on to remind everyone that the old and young were especially vulnerable, things everyone already knew, and then he would lead them in the buddying.

Today, Cass felt people stealing glances at her—with apprehension, judgment, doubt?—and quickly looking away as they found their partners and lined up. Cass stayed rooted to the spot. She knew that Karen would come to her. She was efficient that way, one of Collette's best volunteers, a spry sixty-plus woman who liked to say she was a "doer."

There was good-natured grumbling that the vigilance committee, headed by Dana and Neal, had made a special effort to create as many odd couples as they could, putting people together who didn't ordinarily seek each other out, who didn't especially like each other. No one said it, but Cass guessed that everyone believed the same thing—that the vigilance committee figured you'd be more likely to turn in a suspicious case if you didn't like them that much in the first place. Much lip service was given to the promise that "potentials," as they called the symptomatic, would be treated very well, escorted to the comfortable house that had been set aside for just that purpose. The house was outfitted with magazines and books and canned food and even soda. The windows had been altered to raise only a few inches—enough to slide in a plate of food or a cup of water, but not enough for anyone to crawl out of.

The house, of course, was locked from the outside. Only Dana and two other council members had keys.

The quarantine house had apparently been used twice before, both false alarms. It wasn't that New Eden hadn't lost citizens to the Beaters—it had, more than a dozen—but in every case it had been from attacks on the mainland, and those unfortunates had either been dragged away to their fates or mercifully shot by the citizens.

One of the false positives was Gordon Franche, who now kept to himself. People said that the experience of being locked in the house, waiting to see if he was infected, had caused him to lose his mind. His illness had just been a virus, evidently, because after six days he was let out and welcomed back, but he withdrew from all social events and mostly spent his days reading quietly now.

The other one, a woman, had died soon after, drowning in the shallow waters off the mud beach up at the north end of the island. Supposedly, she had been an excellent swimmer. No one talked about her anymore.

"*There* you are," Karen said behind her, and Cass fixed a smile in place before she turned around to greet her. They lined up with the others, in two rows before the porch, and stood facing each other, shivering a little in the shadow cast by the building.

"Temperature," Dana called, and everyone put the back of their hand to their partner's forehead, like thirty-five concerned mothers checking on sneezing toddlers.

"Eyes," he said after a while, though by then most people had already checked. It was disconcerting; Cass realized the first time she did this exercise that in reality she rarely actually looked directly into people's eyes, focusing instead somewhere around their mouths, watching their lips move as they spoke. Dor, of course, was the exception, like Smoke and Ruthie, all of whose eyes she knew like the familiar rooms of a house in which she'd lived forever. Perhaps, she thought, the feeling was a self-protective fear that eye contact might alert people to the bright green of her own irises. It was something she preferred not to think about.

Karen's eyes were an unremarkable brown, and they were nested in wrinkles, the upper lids drooping and reddened, the lashes thin and pale. But her pupils were a healthy normal size.

Cass was about to make some pleasant, harmless comment, beating Karen to the punch for once—the importance of covering her ass socially was not lost on her—and other pairs of partners were breaking up and returning to the tables or walking off to start their workdays, when Milt Secco surprised everyone by walking up onto the porch and joining Dana. His face was pinched, and he leaned in close to speak. But Cass was close enough to hear him say, "A word, if I might, Dana—"

And she was far from the only one who turned to look at Dana's partner, who stood frightened and lost-looking, alone at the edge of the yard.

It was Phillip.

11

Sammi and Sage ran, taking the shortcut behind a little row of prefab houses. There was a small crowd clustered around the quarantine house, Dana and Zihna conferring on the porch, Earl visible through the front door that Sammi had never seen open before. Phillip stood with his back against the house, under the overhang a few feet from Dana, looking as though a strong gust of wind would blow him away. Phillip looked smaller, standing there. How many times had Sage gone on and on about how buff he was? Even Sammi had to admit he was the best-looking boy on the island, his blond, blue-eyed good looks saved from being too perfect by that nose of his, which had been broken in a ski accident. Now, though, he was wearing a paper mask on the lower half of his face, the sort that the dental hygienist would wear back when Sammi went in every six months with her mom.

"Phillip!" Sage burst ahead of Sammi and broke through the crowd. People stepped out of her way, but before she could get to the porch, Old Mike grabbed her arm and she flailed in his grasp, grunting and pushing off of him.

Sammi caught up to her and took her other arm. "Sage, *stop*."

"They think he's got the fever, Sammi, they're gonna lock him up—"

"Calm down, you have to, just listen to me, come here a minute…." Sammi talked fast but softly. The way Zihna talked to the girls when they were upset. The way Valerie sometimes talked to her, which she hated, but Sammi didn't have a lot of experience with trying to calm people down, though she did know one thing, and that was that Sage could not win this one.

Sage's eyes welled with tears and she was leaning out of Old Mike's grip, trying to use her body's weight as leverage. But Old Mike—who wasn't really all that old but still rather older than Fat Mike—was stronger than he looked. He used to be a mechanic at the airport, and his stance said he was determined to hold his ground.

Earl stepped out onto the porch and looked out at the crowd. Saying nothing, he put a hand on Phillip's shoulder and pushed him back into the doorway. The boy went mutely, shuffling, and now Sammi could see that he was trembling. He didn't *look* sick, though with that mask on she couldn't see much. He just looked scared, scared as shit, and since his mom had died in the first round of fever and his older brother and his girlfriend had set out for Sacramento in December and not been heard from since, he didn't have anyone to come to his aid.

Except for Sage. They'd been together since before Sammi got to New Eden, and it was as serious as any couple she knew about, even if they were young. They sat together during Red's crazy homeschool sessions, and both worked part-time in the laundry so they could spend their work hours together, too. Phillip was always trying to make her laugh, and he gave her the best parts of his meals and took her plate to the washtub. They had been close enough that occasionally Sammi felt left out, and on those occasions she just hung out with Kyra and told herself it didn't matter, not everyone had to be her best friend all the time, except some days were so lonely that she would have traded everything to have a best friend and on those days she would have picked Sage, if Sage wasn't obsessed with Phillip and didn't already have someone more important in her life than Sammi, just like everyone had something more important to them than her.

Like a certain parent who couldn't even be bothered to be here now. If he was, he would know what to do, Sammi thought and then immediately felt angry. Well, her dad used to be in charge of a whole town or whatever, to hear the way Cass talked, and Cass said he was fair and brave and took care of things and even set up a whole system of commerce and laws and shit. Which, if she really admitted it to herself, Sammi had felt secretly proud of. But where was he now? When there was a *real* crisis, when Phillip needed him—when Sammi needed him—when someone had to step up and take care of things, and it was so stupid with New Eden having this whole collaborative-governing shit. No one was ever really in charge and whenever the least little thing went wrong it was like this with all the adults standing around staring at each other and no one doing anything that would actually make things better.

"Let him go!" Sage screamed, her voice wild and unfamiliar. "He's not sick, just look at him, he didn't do anything, you just want to throw someone in there to make it look like you're doing something—"

But Sammi caught her breath, because Phillip was looking back at them, his hand on the doorjamb to steady himself, most of his face obscured by the white mask except for his eyes, which were frightened and beseeching—

—and his pupils had almost disappeared.

Tiny black specks in the sky-blue of his eyes. And his skin... Phillip was fair, so fair he wore a big straw hat to avoid getting sunburned during the day, and it looked like a woman's gardening hat so that Shane and Kalyan sometimes called him Ladyhat.... His skin was not so pale today. It had a burnished-gold tone, and there was a sheen to the skin above his eyes, that faint perspiration that made a person seem to glow.

A person with the fever glowed that way.

Sammi dug her fingers more tightly into Sage's arm and yanked her back.

"Ow, Sammi, stop, you're hurting me," Sage wailed, as Earl spoke quietly to Phillip, and Phillip stepped back, disappearing into the house. Earl closed the door and Old Mike let go of Sage so abruptly that she fell against Sammi and they almost stumbled to the ground together.

And Dana took the key out of his pocket and locked the door.

Zihna did her best with Sage but in the end it was Red who finally got her to sleep, on the sofa in front of the fire. They almost never lit fires in the fireplace. The rule was that fires were only for the public space, both for conservation and safety. There was no way to put large fires out besides an old-fashioned bucket brigade, and everyone had seen city blocks consumed by fire during the worst times and remembered just how quickly it could reduce a building to nothing.

But one of them must have gone around quietly spreading the word to the neighbors, because an hour after dark Red laid the twigs and some crumpled comic books under the dry kindling and soon he had a roaring fire going, one that reminded Sammi of long ago nights before her dad left, when they'd end a day of skiing by picking up ribs from Mountain Smokehouse, and her mom would open a good bottle of wine and they'd all curl up in front of the fire. That fireplace had been beautiful. The stone was faux, but Sammi's mom had had it installed all the way up the two-story wall, with the oil painting that she'd paid a fortune for hung above it and iron candleholders arranged on the mantel. Sammi always grumbled about having to stay home with them instead of going out with her friends, but she secretly loved these evenings, cuddled under a quilt watching the fire while her parents drank wine and laughed about ridiculous stuff on the couch.

This fireplace was junk, a metal box with a brick hearth and a strip of molding for a mantel, on which Zihna had lined up pretty rocks she found while out walking. It didn't draw well at all and the house quickly filled up with smoke, but Sage stared into the flames and drank the weak tea that Zihna gave her, the rest of them on the carpet, except for Red, who sat with his arm around Sage and she let him, soundless tears leaking slowly down her face while he mumbled words that only she could hear, *dad words,* and Sammi thought angrily that he was more of a father to Sage than her own father was to her.

She wasn't moving back in with him. He and Nathan came straight to the quarantine house as soon as they heard that Phillip had been locked up. Valerie must have told him, and Sammi was pissed at her, too. All she wanted was to be here where Sage needed her, though if she was honest about it Sage hadn't given her and Kyra a second look since they all came back.

Phillip was all alone in that dark little place. Sage *knew* he wasn't sick but Sammi had seen his eyes. Sage said she would stay right outside the house so he could talk to her but maybe she forgot that, or maybe they made her leave, because not long after Sammi came back here, Old Mike and Earl brought her home. Later, when Red and Zihna went to bed, Sammi would ask Sage if she wanted to go back near Phillip, they could take sleeping bags, a tarp. It would be cold, though, unless they took the blankets from the beds.

After the fire had burned down to glowing embers, and Sage had fallen asleep in the corner of the couch, Red got up and tucked the blankets carefully around her. To Sammi he whispered, "Let's let her sleep here for now. If she gets up, she can come upstairs, but this way she'll be nice and warm."

"I can sleep down here with her," Sammi whispered back. "I don't mind."

Zihna got her a stack of blankets and a pillow and then the two old people went to their room, leaning into each other, Red moving slowly because of his bum hip that always seemed to be worse late at night and in the morning. Sammi made herself a pallet, but she didn't get in. She sat with her arms around her knees and watched the fire for a while as the last of the logs burned low and the embers snapped and popped. The heat felt wonderful, reaching into her bones in a way like nothing had warmed her lately. She was both sleepy and oddly awake, stealing glances at Sage, who had bunched the blankets under her chin like a child.

"Sage," she whispered, feeling guilty that they were comfortable here when Phillip was alone, and no doubt frightened. But Sage didn't stir, didn't so much as twitch in her sleep, and Sammi lay down—just for a moment— and closed her eyes and felt the warmth on her face and let the thoughts and worries dribble out of her mind like pebbles through a grate until all there was was empty.

When she opened her eyes again the sky outside the sliding glass doors was starting to lighten to a midnight-blue edged with pale pearl-gray. The air smelled of smoke, but not in a nice way like last night.

On the couch, Sage had pulled the blankets up around her face, leaving her ankles and feet exposed. It was cold, cold like it always was, the kind of cold that made you wish you could stay in bed until the sun was high in the sky. Sammi crawled over to the couch and tugged the covers down, but Sage murmured in her sleep and her eyes blinked open before Sammi could finish.

"Hey," Sammi said, giving Sage what she hoped was a reassuring smile.

Sage pushed herself up on her elbows and frowned. "Is it tomorrow?"

"Yeah."

"Like, morning?"

"Barely. We're the only ones up."

Sage struggled the rest of the way up and yawned, pushing back her hair. In the middle of the yawn she jerked her mouth closed and her eyes widened in horror.

"Phillip—"

"I know," Sammi said quickly. "Look, I would have gotten you up earlier but I thought you needed your sleep. We can go over there now. No one will see us, and they wouldn't care anyway. I mean, all we're going to do is talk, right? Talk through the door?"

"They can't lock him up like that, Sammi, it's not right! He's not fevered, I saw him, he was just like he always is—"

"Don't worry," Sammi cut in, gathering up the blankets and folding them quickly, sloppily. *Don't worry*—it was a stupid thing to say, it was what everyone always said even when the shit was about to hit the fan. But what else was there?

It nagged at the back of her mind, this unfamiliar and unwelcome feeling of being the responsible one, the one who had to lie to her friend to keep her going.

She raced upstairs and grabbed her own coat that she'd thrown on the floor, plus Sage's blue puffy one. She had to help Sage put it on, urging her to hurry while she fumbled with the zipper. She practically dragged Sage out into the cold of the morning. A fine drizzle was falling, more mist than rain, but Sage didn't even seem to notice it.

There were a few women at the green latrine, one of two that served the island. This one had gotten its name from the fact that it had once been a green-painted detached garage. Sammi and Sage and Kyra always used this one because it had a big mirror that they could all three look into while they did their hair and, occasionally, their makeup, when the raiders brought some back. At this hour it was too dim to see much at all in the mirror, and the women looked sleepy and bleary, no doubt on their way back to bed. Some people used jugs and buckets at night so they wouldn't have to venture out in the cold, but most still made the trip, dressed in flannel pants and winter coats.

They didn't talk on the way to the quarantine house. Only now, approaching from across the island, did Sammi notice how it was situated as far as possible from the nearest structure. In between were the buildings that were used for the sports-equipment shed, the library and the storehouse. The thought gave her an unpleasant shiver—they were trying to isolate people like Phillip as much as possible. The only way to set them farther apart would be to build a house on North Island, which was mostly wild with a couple of decaying shacks and acres of bramble.

Only when they reached the house and were making their way around to the front, where the windows were open a crack, did they see the figure crouched there. He or she was doing something at the window, either pulling out or pushing in a dark, lumpy something. As they got closer, Sammi saw that it was some sort of fabric, a bedspread or clothing of some sort, and that the person was definitely trying to push it through the slot. Her feet crunched on the gravel and the figure turned toward her, her jacket hood falling back a little to reveal Valerie's tired, anxious face.

"Oh!" Valerie said, her hands going to her throat as she scrambled to her feet. The object hung from the slot.

What looked like sleeves hung limply to the ground. "Sammi? Sage? Is that you?"

"What are you *doing?*" It was Sage who answered, her voice shrill. She stalked forward and grabbed the thing from the slot and yanked it savagely out. It caught on a splinter or a nail and ripped, curling lengths of knit fabric tumbling down the wall, and Sage yanked even harder and the sound of the tearing echoed in the still morning as the thing came away in her hands and all three of them stared at each other.

Then Valerie sighed, her hands falling useless to her sides. "It's his favorite shirt, Sage," she said unhappily. "I was fixing a torn seam for him…please, give it back. I'll mend it again."

"He shouldn't *be* here," Sage said, in that same thin, high voice that didn't sound like her. "He's not sick."

But she allowed Valerie to take the shirt. Sammi and Sage watched her shake it out and squint at the damage, a long rip in the underarm, before folding it with care and stuffing it in the bag she carried over her shoulder.

"I brought a few other things for him," she said quietly. "Some socks. A…book. I'm going to put them through now."

Sage didn't stop her this time, and Valerie crouched down again to slide her gifts through the slot. Sammi saw that the book was a Bible, a small one with a flexible blue plastic cover. It made a muffled slapping sound when it hit the floor inside.

Sage knelt down next to her and tried to look through the slot, but all she saw was darkness.

"I was here earlier," Valerie said softly. "Around midnight. I stayed with him until he fell asleep, Sage."

Sammi knew that Valerie was trying to comfort

them, but she felt guilty. They'd been in their house, drinking tea and warming themselves at the fire, while only Valerie had come here for him. Was that going to be his future, to be forgotten and left alone each night as people found excuses to be elsewhere?

"Did he ask about me?"

Sage kept her face pressed against the house, so she didn't see the way Valerie pursed her lips, the sadness that came over her expression. But she didn't answer the question.

"You must not blame Cass," she said instead. "This could be anyone's fault. No, I mean, it's no one's fault. The blueleaf could have been so young it was hard to detect the signs, or it could have been from the roots they've been drying—they're throwing out the whole batch now—or it could have been from dried flour, even, or beans from last summer."

But Sammi had stopped listening. "What do you mean, blame Cass? Why would we blame her?"

Valerie's eyebrows pinched together, making a line between them.

"No, you *know* something." Sammi stared at her face, trying to find the answer in her silence. "What happened? Come on, I'm going to find out anyway— you know I will. What did she do?"

"She didn't do anything, Sammi, other than her job. You know how hard Cass works, she's out there every day that she isn't watching the kids, and that's hard work, bending down between the rows. I mean, I tried it and I couldn't keep up. It's hard on your back, and it's just way too hard to keep staring at the plants and looking for something out of place. It could have happened to any of them—"

"Cass picked the blueleaf? Is that what you're saying?" A horrible thrill of understanding made Sammi go cold. "But nobody ate it, did they? That couldn't have made Phillip sick—"

"He isn't sick," Sage wailed, crumpled against the house as though she was trying to embrace it.

But Sammi was remembering all the times they'd hung out on North Island, the long lazy afternoons when, if they got hungry, they just ate handfuls of kaysev. They were careful...mostly.

Valerie held up her hands, palms out, as though defending against Sammi's anger, against Sage's anguish. Sammi noticed that she had on a blouse with a scalloped collar, like something a nun would wear, something that should have been thrown out twenty years ago. How did she do it, how did Valerie keep finding things to make her look so virginal, so pure, long after everyone else had resigned themselves to dregs and spoils, the Aftertime battle fatigues? She'd smoothed her shiny hair under yet another headband, this one covered with plaid fabric, and somehow that made Sammi all the angrier.

"Why do you always defend her?"

"Who?"

"Cass. Why do you defend Cass? She's not your friend."

"Of course she's my friend," Valerie said, but the line appeared between her eyebrows again, and Sammi knew that Valerie suspected, deep down, maybe buried so far that she didn't even know that she knew something was wrong. "I think the world of Cass, she's overcome so much, and she's such a great mother to Ruthie and—"

"She's *not* your friend. She *fucks* my *dad!*"

Sammi hadn't meant to yell, but the words rang out sharp and clear on the chilly morning. Sammi watched the puff of her breath on the frosty air; it dissipated and was replaced by another and another. Breathe in, breathe out. Everyone kept breathing, kept living, and what was the point? Everyone betrayed everyone else—was that the cost of survival?

Something interesting was happening to Valerie's face—it was crumpling in on itself, like a pretty tissue-paper flower splashed with water, wilting and fading before her eyes.

"Sammi..."

"She *is*. They've probably been doing it ever since they got here. Hell, probably before that. I saw them. Down on the dock, they were like—like—he had his hands inside her *clothes,* Valerie. I don't know how he can even look you in the *face* every day, but that's my dad."

Valerie had a hand to her throat, her narrow fingers twitching against her perfect pale skin, like she was going to faint or something.

And still Sammi couldn't shut up.

"He left my mom, did you know that? Even before everything got fucked up. He went off to find himself or whatever and just showed up when he felt like it. I hardly ever saw him—" the lie rolled easily from her lips, to Sammi's surprise; lying shouldn't be so easy "—and he never even tried to find us after. He had his business, I'm sure he told you about it, right, and that's all he cared about."

"No," Valerie said in a choked voice. "He *loves* you. He always did. He told me he sent people to check on you, your safety meant everything to him—"

"You *know* what he sold in the Box, right?" Sammi felt the thrill of forbidden knowledge; she only knew this because she'd heard it from Colton, who overheard it from a couple of the raiders who used to go up to the Box for medicine trades. They'd stay there for a few days and party, and then return to the shelter they were in before coming to New Eden. "Drugs. Booze. Sex. Like, as in prostitutes?"

She spat out the last word, making it as ugly as she could, curling her lips around the syllables—and still there was a little thrill to the revelation. She realized that until now she had been trying not to believe it, trying to explain it away. She'd told Colton to shut the fuck up, that her dad traded food and medicine, that he protected people, helped the ones who needed it. But of course that was a lie. Just another one of her father's lies.

"Kind of funny," she said, making her voice as bored as she could. "My dad's a pimp, and Cass, well, since she'll fuck anyone, I guess that makes her his whore."

Valerie's arm shot out so fast that Sammi didn't have time to duck. The slap was more shocking than painful, hard and stinging and making her head whip around. She bit her lip, and tears stung her eyes. She put her fingertips to her mouth and touched blood.

"Oh my God, Sammi," Valerie said, horrified. "Oh my god I'm so sorry, I'm so sorry, I didn't mean to, I didn't mean, oh, please—"

But what Sammi felt was victory, a mean and hungry victory, and she bared her teeth in a snarling grin. The hot, stinging impression on her cheek where she'd been struck meant that she had won. "No worries. I'd be pissed too. I mean, you've been so nice to my dad.

Look at you, in your little skirts and all, and with your sewing, you probably thought you could make a *home* for you guys, with curtains in the window and a hope chest or whatever, right?"

Valerie made a horrified sound in her throat, a convulsion of shock and grief. Sammi knew she was hurting her, but *she'd* been hurt so many times and it wasn't like anyone was very concerned about *that,* was it? Valerie—with her mended dresses and inspirational quotes and wind chimes—was just pathetic. Sammi was doing her a favor. She'd either deal with this or not; she'd get over her dad or she'd sink like a stone, and then she'd be the one who wasn't careful when she ate her salad, or who went on the mainland without a weapon, or who walked into the water until it filled her lungs. Whatever. It wasn't Sammi's fault.

"I mean, I guess you could still do that," she muttered. "Get Dad to build you a little picket fence. You'll just have to move Cass in with you, so you guys can share him."

Valerie had been backing away from her, little stumbling steps, her sneakers too white, as though she'd found bleach and soaked them. But now she turned and ran, weaving and unsteady, heading for the path that led to her place, the sound of her wailing eerie and heartbroken.

"Sammi," Sage cried. Sammi had almost forgotten she was there, on her knees in the dirt, up against the house. "Sammi, look."

Jammed through the slot in the side of the house were fingers, the nails torn and bloody, deep gouges in the skin.

Phillip's fingers.

12

Cass woke feeling like teeth were working her head from the inside. Her eyes were gritty and her mouth tasted like the fetid rot in the bottom of a trash can. She staggered out of the bed after checking on Ruthie—a trembling hand pressed to her cheek, feeling the warmth and her daughter's steady pulse, calmed by the sight of her hair tangled and cascading over the pillow—and down the stairs, skipping the third one from the top, the one that squeaked. It was already getting late, the sun rising in the sky, and people would be up in the house. Cass heard voices from the kitchen and slipped out the back way, the damp cold hitting her like a washcloth dipped in ice water.

She went down to the shore and did her morning routine there. She brushed her teeth twice with the kaysev stub, spitting over and over again into the river. This time, she checked the other shore first, and there were a few of them there already, though they looked sleepy, too, bumping and stumbling into each other as they got as close to the water as they could. They kept up a steady stream of muttering, but it wasn't the desperate hungry keening that signaled a hunt. Cass tested the air with a damp finger—sure enough, she was downwind. And sheltered by the overhanging willow that was coming back into leaf, they couldn't see her.

On another morning Cass might watch them for a while, taking in the details of the clothes they'd been wearing since before they turned, of what was left of their hair. It could be a fascinating exercise, looking for clues to who they'd been—a gold watch that still hung on a bony wrist, the remains of a tattoo in the ruin of a bicep, a hank of dreadlocks stringing across a filthy scarred scalp; a T-shirt with a now passé slogan or a skirt with last season's flared hem.

But today she didn't care. She just didn't care anymore. After last night…dear God, the boy had looked so terrified, his skin already getting the sheen. He had to be what…two days in? What had they served two days ago?

It was a useless exercise, since everyone was allowed to visit the pantry freely and help themselves to the snacks the cooking staff left out each day, bowls of greens and pans lined with kaysev "cookies," the hard little nuggets studded with dried berries and sweetened with the syrup made from cooking the juice crushed from kaysev stalks.

It was just impossible to know, especially since the kids liked to spend their free days on North Island, frequently plucking raw kaysev to avoid coming back and eating at the community table. Cass understood that, remembered how much she'd wanted an identity of her own at that age, how she'd cherished the fleeting moments of freedom when she and her friends could pretend that they never had the homes and parents and lives they were all so desperate to outgrow. She knew the kids stole kaysev wine from the pantry, that they'd learned how to roll their own cigarettes. She even knew where they kept their little weed patch, although she hadn't been sure it was the kids' and didn't feel right turning it under or trying to catch the gardeners in the act. It wasn't her place to judge—that was for damn sure, especially now.

She thought of the little band of New Eden kids, Phillip and Colton and Kalyan and Shane, all the girls—Kyra and Sage and especially Sammi, oh, Sammi, and the thought of her hit Cass with a fresh assault of dread and fear and guilt. She had to talk to Sammi, had to explain again how they must never, ever eat anything that hadn't been grown on Garden Island, that hadn't been checked and rechecked and prepared by the kitchen staff. But how could she get Sammi to listen? What if Cass had had a chance to reach them, warn them, and had squandered it?

What if Phillip was her fault

No, no, she couldn't do that, wouldn't do that. It didn't help. And God, it hurt, it hurt so much to wonder about all the ways she'd failed and people she'd hurt, if she indulged that kind of thinking for even a minute she'd never get up off her knees in the mud at the edge of the river, she'd just sink into it until it covered her over and buried her. And that wasn't happening, not as long as Ruthie lived.

Cass splashed her face with water and dried it with

the cloth she kept in her kit. She squatted to relieve herself, the urine splashing into the brackish edge of the river, and as she watched the Beaters it almost looked like they were trying to copy her, crouching and crab walking at the water's edge.

Only…they weren't at the *edge* of the water. They were *in* it. Water lapped around their ankles, their shins, soaking the bottom of their pants. Stupid beasts, their shoes would be ruined, waterlogged; the skin of their feet would swell and peel and, if they weren't Beaters, succumb to rot and gangrene. But because of their wretched immunity they'd keep walking even after the skin had sloughed away and they walked on bone-ends and raw pulped flesh, never knowing and never caring.

Something almost sounded like laughter. They were playing like children, patting at the water with their hands and crowing. There was a commotion as they jostled for position, going farther and farther into the water until it was up to their chests, their underarms. They had to be freezing. A citizen could last ten, maybe fifteen minutes in that water before hypothermia sucked the life from them, but a Beater…they were too stupid to stay out of the cold water. It would serve them right if they fell facedown, dead, in the river.

The water was the only barrier between them and the island, and seeing them breaching it spurred a deep, almost insensible terror. Of course they couldn't swim, and the wide brown river surged and churned with whirling currents and floating debris and hidden hazards. Cass was perfectly safe on this side, but the dread that accompanied this odd sight was undeniable and complete.

Cass gathered her things. She would tell the oth-

ers, would find Dana or Shannon or Neal and let them
know, as they were supposed to report any Beater sighting and especially any behaviors that were out of the
ordinary. They'd know what to do. And Cass was more
than happy to let the others handle it.

She was stuffing the cloth back into the little zipped
ditty bag that held her collection of toiletries when a
startled squawk reached her ears. She looked back over
the water and saw that two Beaters had given a third a
shove, pushing it into deeper water, and were watching it flail. Water flew and frothed as it gasped for air
and flung its arms out wildly, cheered by its babbling,
grinning comrades.

The current began to carry it, slowly spinning, on
a lazy ride downstream, and for a terrifying moment
it almost seemed as though it was floating toward the
island, but of course the river carried its bounty in the
center, and only when a log or branch jutted into the
water would it get snagged and dragged and deposited
on a silty bank. By then it would be drowned, as dead
as dead could be, sodden and already starting to de-
compose, just another bit of Aftertime detritus to be
broken down and absorbed back into the earth, no longer a danger to anything.

Cass watched it struggle, beginning to tire, swallowing great gulps of river water. But right before she
turned to go, she saw something that made her pause.

The Beater stopped flailing and paddled. For a moment she doubted what she was seeing, but the longer
she watched, the more she became sure of it. Its hands
stroked the water in front of itself, a sloppy dog paddle,
fingers splayed and weak against the current. A moment
later it sank beneath the surface, the water quivering

and swirling above where it disappeared for a moment before the current smoothed it over.

The Beater was as good as dead.

But before it died, it had started to teach itself to swim.

The kids were all fussy, as though they had sensed Cass's mood despite her efforts to cover it up. Twyla whimpered and sucked her thumb, a habit Suzanne had been trying to break her of for some time, and which she had given Cass strict instructions to monitor. But today wasn't the day for it, and Cass let the little girl comfort herself, wiping her tear-streaked face gently.

Dane and Dirk squabbled, and as the morning wore on, it got worse, Dane making a game of snatching away any plaything that caught Dirk's attention. The little boy was enraged, screaming and bunching his hands into fists, so Cass picked him up and walked him around the living room, making loops through the kitchen. On one of her rotations she came back to find Dane holding his hands squeezed tightly together, yelling at Ruthie.

"She bit me! Cass, Ruthie *bit* me!"

Cass sighed and set Dirk down next to Twyla, who was giving play shots to a stuffed dog with a fake plastic syringe. Then she bent to examine Dane's hand. Sure enough, there was a perfect angry red imprint of Ruthie's teeth on the soft flesh of his palm.

"Oh, Ruthie," Cass said, and Ruthie shyly picked up the skirt of her play dress and pulled it up over her head, a new habit that Cass usually found charming. "Were you two fighting?"

Dane shrugged, and Cass saw that he was trying to hide the pile of play money behind him. Dane was a hoarder, and she frequently had to intervene when he took things from the others, only to find little stashes here and there around the house, piles of doll shoes and board books and spoons. She was always at a loss as to how to discipline for this habit; the parenting books of Before never gave advice about what effect seeing your dad beaten to death trying to defend a water supply, or watching your happy-go-lucky neighbor get dragged away by a horde of screaming monsters, might have on children and what you could do to help.

She'd tried to talk to Ingrid about Dane, but she didn't believe Cass. Ingrid's answer to every parenting problem involved more of her relentless structured activities; she suggested Cass read a book called *Red Monsters Share* and discuss it with the children.

"Dane. There's enough play money for everyone to share," she said now, digging deep to come up with enough patience to see her through at least until lunch. By the time she served the children their tea and jam sandwiches—jam made from the nectarines she'd grown herself—she would probably be able to force down a few crackers. She always felt better after she got something in her stomach to absorb the churning bile left behind by one of her infrequent all-out benders.

Which she never would have had, if it hadn't been for—

No, don't

Dane was looking at her doubtfully, groping around behind him, trying to push the coins out of her sight.

"There's enough for everyone," Cass repeated. "You don't have to keep them all yourself."

"She bit me," Dane repeated stubbornly. "Biting is *not* okay."

And it wasn't, of course; biting was one of the things that could get a kid thrown out of child care, Before. That and not being current on vaccinations. Or a failure to potty train. All offenses that seemed ridiculously irrelevant now.

"Biting is not okay, but neither is not sharing," Cass said through gritted teeth. What she really wanted to do was seize all the plastic coins and put them in a box and put the box up on the counter where none of the kids could reach it, and keep taking things away from them every time they fussed, until they had nothing, nothing, and maybe that would keep them quiet, just long enough for her to get her strength back, just long enough to *think*.

"Maybe Ruthie's got the fever," Dane said, watching her closely, a mean little smile at the corner of his mouth.

Cass froze. She ground her fingernails into the palms of her hands, forcing herself not to react. "Don't you ever say that," she finally whispered, her own voice sounding strange to herself, stripped bare and dragged over coals.

There must have been something in her tone or expression that finally got through to Dane, because the smirk left his face and his lower lip wobbled and he looked down at the carpet.

"Don't you *ever* say anything like that, Dane," she repeated. Because if an adult could accuse, who was to say that a child couldn't, as well? She was nearly positive that Phillip had the fever, but if more cases popped up, there was sure to be hysteria, finger-pointing, blame. There were people in New Eden—the weak ones, the easily swayed and those with a tenuous grip on reality—

who might latch on to an accusation, even a groundless one, even one that came from a child. "None of us have the fever. We are *careful*. We are healthy."

Before long she managed to distract the boy with a stub of crayon and pages torn from a microwave manual. The densely printed instructions were in English, Spanish, Japanese, but there was plenty of white space, which Dane and the other kids set to filling in with colorful scribbles at the kitchen table while Cass made preparations for lunch.

Long ago, Cass had practiced affirmations, little phrases from a book someone had given her at A.A. *Live life on life's terms. Faith chases away fear.* Some days they seemed utterly worthless, sentimental drivel, mindless pleasantries. And some days they worked, a little.

I can do this I can do this I can do this, Cass repeated soundlessly to herself, turning away from the children and forming the words on trembling lips. It wasn't much of a mantra. It lacked imagination and substance.

Worst of all, Cass seriously doubted whether it was true.

But she did. She got through lunch, settling only one disagreement over who got the last of the cookies. She managed to eat a few herbed kaysev crackers and the crusts of Ruthie's sandwich, and after cleaning up the kitchen she got all the children to lie down for a nap, even Dane, who was not much of a sleeper these days. When she was sure they were all out, she lay down between Ruthie and Dirk, thinking she would just close her eyes for a moment, perhaps catch fifteen minutes' rest before one of the children woke her up.

But images of the morning's discovery kept her awake. Bubbles had risen to the surface of the water after the Beater went under. Was it possible that she had imagined the other—the sudden paddling of its hands?

The sound of the front door opening yanked Cass out of her thoughts. She scrambled to her feet and smoothed her clothes. There was already enough trouble between her and the other moms without them thinking she wasn't doing her part with the children. She picked up the closest book—one of the historical romances Suzanne liked—and put her finger between the pages so it would look like she'd been reading, and sat in the recliner.

Ingrid came into the room, followed by Jay Swarmer, who headed up the security rotation, guarding the bridge and dragging away dead Beaters from the shore. His presence here, in the middle of the day, caused an uneasy cramp in Cass's stomach. As for Ingrid, her onetime friend's lips were set in a thin line and twin red spots stood out on her cheeks, and she refused to meet Cass's gaze.

"What's going on?" Cass said quietly. Getting no answer other than grim looks, she set the book down on the coffee table. "Let's talk in the kitchen so we don't wake the kids."

"I'll stay with them," Ingrid said primly. She settled herself cross-legged on the floor, the long wool skirt she wore draped over her muddy boots.

Cass followed Jay wordlessly into the kitchen, wondering if she should offer him some of the cold tea left over from the morning. They'd all grown accustomed to drinking it cold; though the cooks kept a fire going through most of the day, the hearth was usually in service for one task or another, everything from slow-cooking rabbits on a spit, to baking flat breads, to boiling river water to purify it. There was no time for heating tea or leftovers, barely even for warming one's hands over the flames.

But Jay spoke before she had a chance. "This is a hell of a thing, Cass."

She was surprised at the approbation in his voice. He leaned back against the counter, his jeans slung low under a gut that had been slowly disappearing ever since Cass had known him. No matter how much kaysev a person ate, it wasn't enough to make or keep them fat. Even Fat Mike was lean these days, though the nickname stuck.

"What do you mean?"

Jay winced, closing his eyes for a moment as if the conversation pained him. "Sammi's been to see me."

Cass set a hand on the back of a kitchen chair to support herself as she absorbed this fresh bad news. Sammi had told. Despite Cass's deep anguish over hurting Dor's daughter, she had never considered that Sammi would want revenge against *her.* But of course, Cass would be much easier to hurt than her father. Their affair didn't go against any of New Eden's covenants, and there were those who might even admire him for keeping a couple of women in play…but Cass had trouble fitting into New Eden from the start and this would only make people that much more reluctant to befriend her—

"She told us all about it. How she'd had her suspicions, about how people were talking."

Somehow the knowledge that Sammi suspected the affair troubled Cass even more. Would that have been enough—would knowing that they were hurting her have been enough to make them stop? Cass hoped the answer was yes, but there would be no way to know now.

"Look, I know we messed up. But I never meant to, to hurt anyone. We just, it was private, it—"

"'We'?" Jay's gray eyebrows, thick and untrimmed, knitted together in consternation. "Who's *we?*"

They stared at each other for several seconds, Cass spinning possible scenarios wildly through her mind.

"I am talking about your *drinking,* Cass. If there's other folks I mean, the issue's judgment, if there's partying going on, people who need to keep their wits about them to do their job, when it affects all of us— look, we're not trying to go on a witch hunt here." Jay wiped a callused hand across his forehead. "The only reason it was agreed we needed to do something was, first of all, the mistake that's got a boy down in the quarantine house. If your little problem made you care- less, then hell yeah, I think it's community business, and at the very least we need to think about taking you off the harvest detail. But as Ingrid pointed out, and I've got to say I agree with her, leaving you in charge of the kids when you're high as a kite ain't much bet- ter. I mean, I know I won't have an argument from you when I say they're our most precious resource, right? These little ones?"

Throughout his speech, Cass was trying to keep up, trying to assimilate what Jay was saying. Why hadn't Sammi said anything about what she'd seen on the dock? But the answer hit her with blinding clarity: be- cause it wasn't enough to hurt her, not in a big enough way. By revealing her drinking, the girl could hit her on every level that mattered—calling into question her commitment, her competence, even the wisdom of letting her have a role in the children's lives.

Of course, there was one secret Sammi still hadn't shared. If she ever told the others that Cass had been attacked and infected, that would be a sure way to stir up so much trouble that Cass could get thrown out of New Eden. Cass wasn't the only Beater victim ever to recover, but no one in New Eden had seen such a survivor before. And with tensions running high, there was no guarantee they'd listen when Cass offered up frantic, self-serving explanations that she was no threat to anyone.... Nor was Ruthie....

"But I love the children," she mumbled, on the verge of tears. "You can't think that I don't."

"Aw, hell," Jay said, his shoulders slumping forward, and she realized that he had been hoping he was wrong. He was a good man, a family man with no family anymore, an associate dean at Sacramento State with no one to ride herd on. And he had the broken capillaries and red nose that signaled that he too had once known his way around a bottle. "I hate this, Cass. Lord knows I don't have any beef with you. But there's too much at stake. I'm here to ask you to resign. From child care and picking both. You can stay on gardening—I don't think you'll get any argument for that, everyone knows you're the best with the growing. And that's enough for anyone—Hell, there's lots of folks that don't get a fraction of that done. We got Ingrid, we got Suzanne, we got Jasmine ready to pop, maybe we can get another of the gals to pitch in with the little ones. Valerie, maybe, she'd be good."

His words cut deep. She understood why he said it—

Valerie would have been a great mother; her patience, her soothing voice, they were perfect.

"Maybe," she said bleakly, but it was a lie because the day that Valerie was responsible for Ruthie's care would be the day Cass had failed utterly. Her daughter had been taken from her twice before, when other people decided Cass wasn't a fit mother. She couldn't let it happen again. "Or I don't know…maybe I could take Ruthie in the field with me when I work. Let me think, okay? Just give me a day to think about it."

Jay sighed and folded his hands over his gut. You could see in the gesture the shadow of what he had once been, a paunchy, proud, cheerful man. "That's fine. I don't want to take this up with the council in any official way, you know what I mean? That wouldn't serve anybody. Just, hey, Ingrid's a little sore with you right now." He hooked a thumb in the direction of the living room. "Let's let her finish out the day with the kids, maybe you go for a walk, talk to a friend, whatever you feel like. An afternoon off. Looks like the weather's breaking, maybe we'll get a little more sun, everything'll look different by tonight."

"Yeah, okay," Cass said.

She saw him to the door, and they said an oddly formal goodbye, Jay giving her a little half bow before he walked off toward the guard headquarters. He'd been right about the weather; a thick cloud scudded across the sun and was quickly gone, leaving the air warm and inviting.

She should do as he suggested, take that walk, maybe go to the far southern end of Garden Island where you could sit and stare off at the mountains in the distance, skip stones into the river. But she didn't think she could bear to look across all those rows and rows of kaysev, the chubby deep green leaves hiding a secret killer somewhere in their midst.

And she couldn't leave Ruthie here, not with Ingrid. She wouldn't risk losing her daughter, ever again.

She made her decision. She went into the living room. Ingrid stood with her arms folded, glaring, but Cass did not look away. There was so much she wanted to say, but instead she tamped down her anger as she picked up Ruthie from her pallet of blankets, and carried her into the remains of a day in which, yet again, everything had changed.

13

Smoke opened his eyes when it was quiet in the room, closed them when the people came in. He worked his hands under the blanket, flexed his limbs, tensed his muscles, always going slack and still at the slightest sound.

He was careful, because he knew the people were waiting for him to wake up. What would happen then, he did not know. There were people who wanted him dead, who wanted him to suffer.

The great irony was that Smoke did deserve to be punished, but only one other man left on this earth knew the true reason, and who knew if he was even still alive. It was Smoke's burden, to know what he had done and to be alone in that knowing. They could punish him for the lives he had taken, for the Rebuilder leaders he had killed, and Smoke would laugh—fighting the fascist warlords was only a tiny penance for his true crime, for that secret crime. They could send in one Rebuilder after another and he would keep killing them until he was exhausted from the effort, until he could no longer lift his blade or his gun, and he would never regret all the blood that got spilled. In that battle he had right on his side, because the battle against the Rebuilders was a battle for freedom and for hope.

But for his other crime, his first crime, he had no justification and no defense....

This was a strange prison, where people came and went freely and he was not shackled, and security was lax. A terrible miscalculation on their part. If they knew anything at all about him, surely they would know he'd bide his time and he would wait for the right moment.

Each day, Smoke let the thin gruel dribble down his face, swallowing just enough to survive. So too with the water held to his lips. And he felt his strength returning. Soon he was able to leave his bed at night to stand at the window, looking out on a moonlit yard; not long after that he was marching in place, doing simple calisthenics, returning to bed only when he was exhausted.

His body was not the same. He was missing two fingers, the flesh raggedly healed at the first knuckle, where the little and ring fingers of his left hand used to be. The skin of his face was crossed with scars he could not see; his arms, his torso, his legs, with scars that he could. There was a persistent ache in one arm and in his hip; his abbreviated walks around the room were hampered by a painful limp.

Each night he pushed himself. Each dawn his body screamed in pain at the effort. And each day he grew stronger. Emboldened by his success, he took to working his hands during the day, squeezing them into fists, getting used to the odd absence of the severed fingers. He flexed his limbs, bent and extended them. Worked as though his life depended on it.

One day soon, they would come for him. They would not expect a fight—but a fight was what he meant to give them.

Ruthie barely stirred, so Cass settled her into the stroller
they kept under the eaves of the house. It was a nice
one, an Italian model that navigated even the stony paths
along the water without getting its wheels jammed, but
it didn't get much use now that the younger kids preferred to walk nearly everywhere.

She tucked a sweatshirt around Ruthie, draping it
over her head to keep her warm, and set out along the
path to her herb garden when she heard gunshots, two
in rapid succession, then another a few seconds later.
Shouting followed, not just one or two voices, but half
a dozen or more. Cass hesitated, wondering what the
latest calamity could be. Glynnis and John routinely
picked off Beaters on the shore when they patrolled the
river, but they lined up their shots carefully, deliberately,
taking their time so as not to waste ammo.

In the end her curiosity won out, and she turned the

stroller toward the community center, where people would know what was happening. As she drew close, she saw a knot of people on the edge of the lawn looking toward the water, shielding their eyes against the sun.

On the opposite shore were Beaters, dozens of them. How they'd managed to assemble so quickly since Cass was last outside—only a couple of hours ago when she took the little ones for a walk over to the drying house to watch Corryn and Chevelle lay out the metal pans of hardtack—she had no idea. Now they lined the bank for a hundred yards in either direction, and from the distance, if you squinted, they could be spectators at a game, shoppers at a department store, except for their jerking, awkward movements.

Cass nervously ran her fingers over the sun-browned skin of her forearms, a habit left over from when her arms were covered with ragged scars. But her torn skin had scabbed over and fully healed from her time as... one of them. Early on after recovering, the fear of what she might have done—whether she'd joined a pack of the things, whether she'd hunted or even, God help her, *feasted*—continually worked on her mind, and her touch on the wounds brought the pain that she needed to distract herself. These days—mostly—she kept those fears at bay. But looking at the things, separated only by the river, the old terror nagged at her.

And now she had a new concern, a fresh terror: that Sammi, her fury stoked by what she'd seen, would tell the others that Cass and Ruthie had survived infection. It was dangerous information, sure to stir up distrust and anger in the community. But how far would the girl go to punish Cass?

Beyond the ragtag crowd, in the fields studded with

drifts of kaysev, more approached in groups of three and four and in some cases more. Cass could only guess where they had come from—there were more than could be accounted for from the usual nesting spots the raiders had mapped in the area. Were the wretched creatures somehow responding to a signal that citizens could not pick up on, an instinctual awakening that drew them inexorably here in this moment?

Since the early days of the fever, when the first Beaters cast off their humanity to follow their terrible hungers, they had been drawn to population centers. They preferred towns to farmland, cities to towns. Of course, at first many people believed that safety could be found in the most densely populated areas, so they set out for urban settings. In the heightened security of the new century, every high-rise featured antiterrorism barricades and could function as their own ecosystems for a short period. Most had backup power sources and filtration systems that could sustain citizens at least a few weeks while they modified the buildings to serve as shelters for the new, grim reality.

The terrible fallacy of this assumption emerged slowly. Last summer, citizens flocked to the cities by whatever means available—by the carload when gas could be found and the streets were clear, on foot when not. Through an unseasonably warm and sun-dappled autumn, those who stayed outside the city limits wondered if they'd made the wrong choice. But as time went on, the other citizens never returned, and the cities remained dark.

And so one conclusion was generally drawn by those outside: the fever thrived in the population centers, infection spreading geometrically among those who lived close together, until the skyline became a treacherous maw teeming with hungry Beaters.

Dor, crafty and careful inside the Box, probably sent his patrols to get a visual confirmation of this, Cass suspected. He'd never said as much, but that would be like him—he would want to know himself, but not wish to inflict debilitating proof of the world's end on others, if he could avoid it.

Though Dor kept his own counsel, others did not January had brought a few refugees from what Sacramento had become. Their stories confirmed that the cities were lost, taken over by swarms of maddened Beaters nesting in office buildings, in shops, in public housing and luxury town houses. Restaurants and museums and parking garages were full of them.

The Beaters were not above feeding on each other, though they didn't seem to like it. Of late, refugees passing by New Eden reported that the creatures had begun to starve inside the cities, imparting to listeners the most horrifying tableau of gaunt, bony Beaters in the later stages of the disease, kneeling over recently fallen others, feeding on their slack and waxy skin, before seeming to lose interest, and lying down next to them to die. There was not enough to feed even these voracious, implacable monsters.

Had the Beaters finally sucked all the sustenance out of the cities, and returned to the countryside to hunt? If so, New Eden would be a ready target with its seventy-some citizens living out in the open, where they could easily be observed and smelled and heard.

All that separated them was the perfect barrier of the river.

No one had ever expected the Beaters to learn to

cross it. As a shocked murmur went up from the crowd, Cass knew that she wasn't the only one thinking that if they somehow took to the water, New Eden would be lost.

There was another gunshot, and another. Cass pressed forward, pushing the stroller through the crowd, muttering apologies. When she got near the front of the throng she wheeled the stroller around so that it was behind her, and elbowed her way through.

Two canoes floated in the current halfway between island and shore. It was too far across the wide, rapidly flowing expanse of water on this side of the island to reliably hit a Beater from the shore, even with a deer rifle, which was why they patrolled from the middle of the river. John steadied one canoe expertly, paddle skimming the surface, while Glynnis sighted down her shotgun. She alone of the security staff preferred to use a shotgun; she'd learned to hunt with her father and, until last year, had gone up to Canada every year when the season opened. Now she hunted Beaters.

In the other canoe Neal struggled to keep the prow pointed at the opposite shore. Parker, one of the younger security guys, knelt clumsily in the front trying to reload, but the craft's rocking made it difficult.

"Goddamn it," a low voice said next to Cass.

Dor. She turned to him instinctively, resisting throwing herself into his arms, suddenly flooded with the fear and tension that had reemerged with these things. She couldn't give in to the urge, not here, not after what had happened with Sammi and Jay.

"What's happening?"

"What's happening is, this is what we get for not training more people on the watercraft," Dor snapped.

"Look at that. *Look* at that. They're likely to drown themselves before they get a shot off. Maybe even lose a rifle or two. I told them—" He bit off his words and fell silent, anger radiating off his tense, rigid body.

"Do *you* know how to handle a canoe?"

"Yeah. Me and Nathan—we've taken them out half a dozen times. I mean, I'm nowhere near what John can do, but I could for damn sure keep the fucking boat pointed in the right direction. *Fuck.*"

"Where's Nathan now?"

"Went out this morning, after I decided to stay back and look for Sammi. I doubt he even knows what's happening, because he was going to try going down toward Clifton. I told him not to go alone, but…"

But Nathan was another renegade, just like Dor.

He'd mentioned Sammi. Cass looked back at Ruthie for a second. "Did she find you? Or Valerie?"

"Yeah, yeah, I talked to Val. Sammi's over in the community center with the other kids. Earl's told them to stay put there until we get this under control."

So Sammi was safe for the moment, at least. By Dor's grim expression, Cass had to assume the reunion hadn't gone well. Which wasn't surprising.

"But why are Neal and Parker even out there? I mean, the Beaters are bound to wander off eventually. They always do." Even as she said it, Cass realized that what she meant was that they always *had*—there was a difference.

"Cass. They're only shooting the ones that get in the water. Trying to conserve ammo."

Dor pointed down the river, and only then did Cass notice the gray lumps being carried downstream, drifting lazily in gentle spins in the current. They looked like logs, or bags of trash, but they were dead Beaters.

The ones that get in the water...

"You mean they're trying to swim." Not a question—Cass suddenly knew it beyond a doubt. She'd seen one try for the first time only this morning, but that didn't mean that they hadn't been working up to it for a while. They were gifted mimics, for beasts that seemed insensate much of the time; they often echoed each other's movements and sounds. At times it seemed like they made a game of it, a primitive Simon Says, but when one considered that this was how they learned, it was both awesome and terrifying.

"Yeah. And some of them are coming too damn close. And they're *watching* each other. See? They're trying to figure out how to stay afloat. The ones Glynnis and Parker took out, they were paddling like dogs—nothing pretty and with a lot of wasted motion, lots of splashing, but you can bet the rest of them noticed that they managed to stay above water for a few seconds before they went down."

Just then a barking wail went up. At the far right edge of the crowd of Beaters, past Neal's canoe, a knot of them pushed forward, the momentum of their bodies propelling a stocky one into the water. It was recently turned, with a nearly full head of dark hair and most of its face intact. A woman's face, Cass could guess, through the leering and the pus and excited babbling.

A final shove sent it stumbling into the water, where it wobbled and abruptly sat down. It screamed high and shrill when the water rose up to its armpits, and splashed with its hands, making wide arcs. In the canoe, Parker was trying to aim over Neal's shoulder as he dug deep into the current, forcing the canoe around. He fired, and one of the Beaters on the shore squawked and pitched forward, facedown into the muddy bank, the others tripping over it and stepping on its limbs.

For a moment, Cass had a vision of the torn bodies clogging the river, a peninsula of broken flesh permitting them to cross to her and Ruthie.

The one in the water had rolled onto its front and began splashing its way toward the canoe. The water went farther up its body until it went under, only the top of its head visible, black curls floating, and after a moment it came up sputtering and coughing. It flailed and slapped at the water and went under a few times, but then it seemed to establish a rhythm—an inefficient and clumsy one for sure, but enough to keep it from drowning.

Yelling, from the people in the boats and the people onshore, competed with the Beaters' cries. Parker fired again, but the shot went wide, cutting the water harmlessly, and the Beater bobbed and splashed closer. Neal twisted his body in the canoe, trying to get out of the way. Parker shouted something that Cass couldn't make out over the din of the crowd, but as he turned back around and aimed at the paddling Beater—it was a can't-miss-shot, only ten feet—Neal plunged the paddle deep into the water and spun the canoe.

He'd exerted too much force, and the canoe dipped far to the left. Parker's shot missed, unbelievably, landing somewhere in the inky water, and as Neal tried to correct, the canoe lurched the other way and the two men scrambled for balance and Cass sucked in her breath and swore she could feel it too when the canoe went over and both of them were dumped into the icy water.

Screaming rent the air as John turned his own canoe toward the upended one. Glynnis took a knee and fired without seeming to aim at all and there was a burst of blood from the swimming Beater, the side of its head shredded and running with crimson. The crowd called to the men in the water to hurry, hurry, hurry—

—and then there was a splashing commotion in the water that took Cass away to long ago with her dad, when he took her fishing on Lake Don Pedro. He'd borrowed a friend's gear, and they didn't catch a thing all day, but as the sun climbed in the sky and Cass got sleepy and leaned against her dad, her tummy full of peanut-butter sandwiches, her dad's flannel shirt smelling pleasantly of coffee and tobacco, a bird had swooped down to the water and hooked its talons into a sizable fish. But the prey was too large to be carried off so easily. The bird screamed and fought the mute, desperate fish. They flailed for their lives, the water frothed by the fish's body slapping the surface of the lake and the bird's wings beating at it, and they spun and fought until their bodies blurred together, and Cass hid her face in her father's shirt and cried until it was all over, until the bird finally gave up and flew limp-winged away and the fish sank to the depths, torn up but free to die—

It seized Parker and sank its teeth into his neck. Parker screamed and fought, but the bleeding creature held tight.

Glynnis shot Parker first. A neat hole appeared in his forehead and he went still. When she fired again, the Beater stopped flailing, but it never let go, and the pair sank below the water locked in their deadly embrace.

There was a shocked silence. Only Glynnis's voice never stopped as she yelled at John to turn around.

"This is a goddamn train wreck," Dor muttered. "Cass, we've got to take out the boat. I'll row, you shoot."

"I can't," Cass said, horrified. "I have Ruthie."

"Leave her with the others. It won't be for long. It's already getting dark."

"Dor…" Panic sparked pain behind her eyes. How could she tell him, how they all hated her, how no one trusted her? Who would be willing to help her now?

But as he looked deeply into her eyes, whatever he was about to say died on his lips. Somehow, he understood—not the specifics, but the shape of her fear.

"Okay," he said. "Okay. Then leave her with Sammi. Tell her I said she should watch Ruthie until we get back. She's just inside the hall. I'll go grab my gun and meet you right back here in a few minutes."

"But—someone else, can't you get someone else?"

"Cass!" His voice exploded, so loud and desperate that people turned to stare at him. "There *isn't* anyone else. I don't know who can handle a boat and I'm not willing to take chances right now. If we don't act fast, those things might get bold and try to swarm… And… who else is going to shoot with me?"

Dor was a rogue, a renegade, and he knew it, knew how he had squandered the others' trust to pursue his own hell-bent pastimes. In that moment Cass finally understood how ill suited he was to New Eden, how much he must hate the collaborative government, the council with its endless deliberations, the constant hedging and search for concordance—it must have been torture for Dor to try to find his place here. No wonder he left the islands when he could, no wonder he took the brute-force jobs that left his mind free to stew and boil.

Dana, Harris, Neal—none of them liked Dor, none of them had ever asked him to serve on a committee or take part in a planning session. They were content for him to do the menial labor that kept him occupied and uninvolved.

It was true. None of them would shoot with Dor—because none of them would take direction from him.

"Go," Dor said, and then he bent in close and brushed his lips against hers—once, and then a second time. He lingered, and it was not so much a kiss as a demand, a promise, an acknowledging of the need they never spoke of, and his mouth on hers was hot and hard and bruising.

Cass broke away and rushed toward the hall, pushing the stroller in front of her. It jounced over a root and Ruthie woke and began to wail, and Cass pulled her from the stroller, abandoning the thing in the middle of the yard, and ran the rest of the way.

She was putting her daughter in danger once again, trusting her to someone else's care once again. What kind of mother set her child aside to go on a suicide mission? Cass—Cass was that kind of mother. She'd risked Ruthie for the bottle, she'd risked her for a moment's pleasure in the sun, for stolen moments of desperate passion, and now she was risking her to plunge headlong into a mission that was bound to get her and Dor killed, a mission no one was asking her to undertake, on behalf of a community of people who hated her. If by some miracle she saved anyone, they would never thank her.

But she had no choice. Because if she did nothing,

again, then she didn't deserve to be anyone's mother, anyone's guardian. Not in these times. Not in what the world had become.

Inside the hall she blinked and paused, her eyes adjusting to the dim interior. There—near the window, all of them, clustered on the long couches. The boys in the front, the girls huddled behind them.

"Sammi!"

Cass called her name, already running toward her. When the girl turned Cass saw not the hatred she expected, not the bitterness and rejection—but pure terror. It was written on all of their young faces, and Cass knew that they had seen: the swimming, and the upending of the canoe, Parker going down and the Beater and Glynnis's two killing shots.

"Please, I need you to take care of Ruthie," she said, out of breath. "Just for a little while. Your dad and me, we have to help." She kissed Ruthie—both cheeks, her forehead, her eyelids.

"Mama," Ruthie whimpered.

"Mama needs to go help Dor. You stay with Sammi and be a good girl, hear? And I'll be right back, I promise. I promise."

"Should we come?" one of the boys said—Kalyan, the reckless one. "Do they need us?"

"Right now they need you to stay here," she said, as calmly as she could. "Someone will come. Soon. To tell you what's going on."

Sammi held her hands out for Ruthie, who snuggled into her arms as Cass turned away and ran.

She passed the stroller in the yard, pitched sideways with one wheel lodged in a divot in the earth. She's fine, *she's fine she's fine she's fine,* she told herself. Sammi would keep her safe. Sammi might hate Cass, but no one could hate Ruthie, no one could hate her beautiful baby girl. Ruthie was innocent, Ruthie had never hurt anyone, it was just her terrible bad luck to be born into this world, this time. And no matter if Sammi told everyone in the world that Cass had suffered the fever and somehow gotten better, she knew now that the girl would never reveal that Ruthie had, too.

The crowd near the shore had grown—it looked like every Edenite was there. Cass scanned the crowd and found Dor near the front. He held the Glock against his leg, and in his other hand was a gun Cass didn't recognize, a small steel semiauto.

She hadn't fired a gun since coming to the Delta. The last time had been during their escape from the Rebuilders, and her last kill had been a citizen, not a Beater, something only Dor and Sammi and the girls they'd rescued from Colima knew, something she had hoped to put behind her and never, ever let Ruthie find out.

But already her fingertips thrummed and twitched to

touch the cold steel, her palm was ready to wrap around the grip. *I am a killer,* Cass thought, and the thought made her neither happy nor sad. Only ready.

Dor was standing near the edge, talking to Neal, who had made it back to the shore. Someone had given him a blanket and he was standing wrapped in it and shivering, his lips blue. The overturned canoe hadn't traveled far downstream, and Cass saw the reason for this small stroke of luck—it had snagged on a tree that had fallen on the opposite bank, but the current tugged at it and there was no telling how long it would hold.

There were other boats—half a dozen skiffs and aluminum rowboats, all stored on the other side of the island. In typical New Eden fashion, they were secured and cleaned and well maintained and hardly ever used. Everyone used the one-lane bridge—well tended and even better guarded—if they wanted to get to the mainland. Besides, there was little sport to be had from floating downstream or fighting the current on the way back.

Glynnis and John preferred the canoes to the other craft for their maneuverability, and the two of them had been able to handle the mostly unnecessary duty of shore patrol by themselves. When they weren't working, the canoes were simply stored on the grassy banks. Having two had seemed like a great backup plan, but the second had never been needed until now.

A woman took Neal's arm and led him away, talking to him softly.

"I need someone to swim out and get the canoe," Dor said, his deep voice carrying over the crowd. "We'll need both of them."

Everyone stared at him, making way for Cass to pass,

and she joined him at his side. She began strapping on the hip holster he'd brought.

There was murmuring, and then voices—angry voices—began to be heard.

"Why don't *you* swim out?"

"Someone's gone for the rowboats."

"How'd you get those weapons?"

"I said, *I need someone to swim out*. Whoever goes will be too cold and exhausted to also paddle effectively after," Dor yelled, silencing them. "Before we lose more people—look out there. Do you see? They're *still coming.*"

Cass turned, along with the crowd—it was true. The Beaters had to number close to a hundred now, their milling and jostling making it hard to count. The sun had sunk nearly to the horizon, illuminating them from behind, outlining their ghastly silhouettes. Glynnis and John were upstream, picking off a clump that had ventured ankle-deep into the water. All along the shoreline now, dead Beaters bobbed, gently bumping up against the bank. In several places the mud was red with blood.

Directly across from them, a Beater had gone down, but was not yet dead. Glynnis must have missed the spinal shot, and it twitched and spasmed. Two of its closest companions grabbed its hands and legs and dragged it up onto the bank, up the incline, depositing it on dry land, while others looked on. For a moment Cass thought she was seeing some sort of new ritual, honoring the fallen, but then several of them bent over the dying thing and began to bite it, tearing off shreds of skin and crowing the way they always did when they ate. Blood poured from the downed body and it twitched harder.

They were usually unenthusiastic about feeding on each other once finally dead, but something about the death throes apparently made the prospect more appealing, and it was not uncommon to see them devouring their wounded.

"Oh, God," someone said nearby.

"I'm gonna throw up."

"This is ridiculous. They can't keep this up forever."

Cass didn't know if the speaker meant the Edenites or the Beaters, but she knew that Dor was losing them. They wouldn't listen to him. They held him in contempt. And things were only getting worse here.

"Please!" she yelled. "Please, someone, get the canoe. I'd do it, but Dor needs me to shoot."

"Getting in that water'll kill you," a woman said. "It's got to be forty degrees. Do you know how long—"

"I know!" Cass turned on her, furious. "I know it. It's a risk. But do you just want to stand here and wait for them to come get us? Look, Neal made it. He didn't have to go as far, it's true, and we need a strong swimmer."

"*You* go," an angry female voice said. "I'll shoot. I'll go with Dor."

Everyone turned to see who spoke.

It was Valerie. Incredibly, since the voice sounded nothing like hers. She stood off to the side of the crowd, her face knotted in fury, her hair released from its band, tumbling around her shoulders. She'd forsaken her Pendleton jacket and skirt for a pair of tight black pants and a man's coat, and her hands were bare, clenched into fists.

"Do you even know how to shoot?" someone demanded.

"How hard can it be?" she screamed. Her eyes drilled

into Cass, glinting with fury, and Cass noticed for the first time that Valerie was actually quite beautiful, with her dark features and pale skin, her arched brows and long neck. "If *she* can do it, I can."

"This is not the time," Dor said, his voice hard. He had lowered his tone but in the hush of the shocked assembly, it carried just fine.

"Roger. You go." Dor turned his back on Valerie, and Cass, who'd been watching the other woman, saw her deflate, saw the fight leave her when she realized her desperate gamble had failed. Valerie had been willing to sacrifice everything—her life, his, the lives of everyone in New Eden—just to force him to acknowledge her, to claim her and love her.

But there was no more time for that.

Roger Taugher was staring at the canoe, trying to gauge whether he could make it. He was in his twenties, strong, a former soccer player who often led pickup games in the yard and entertained the little kids with tricks with the ball. Ruthie adored him.

He started to tug off his jacket and kicked off his boots.

"You'll freeze!" the young woman next to him protested.

"Clothes'll just slow him down," Dor said. "Everyone else, give him room. The minute he gets back with the canoe, you all take him to get warm—Cass and I will head out."

"I'm almost out of ammo!" Glynnis called, as they paddled toward a group that was splashing farther downriver.

"Dana. Go to the storehouse, bring back the box of 12-gauge shells. Glynnis uses the Browning, but she's good with a handgun too so bring one. Don't forget extra ammo for that. Take someone with you—Hank, you go."

Hank nodded, but Dana hesitated, staring at Dor with a mixture of contempt and anger. "Look, Dor, we need to consider—you can't just—"

"What the *fuck* do you think I'm doing, Dana? If I let you all take charge you'll still be deliberating while the rest of us are being dragged off. Now, are you going to go or do I need to take the keys off you myself?"

For a moment it seemed like Dana was going to refuse. But he looked around the assembled crowd, and seemed to sense what Cass did, what the rest of them did—a turning of the tide of sympathies. She knew that few people liked either of them, herself or Dor, especially after Sammi's revelation and Valerie's outburst.

But they also knew that Dor could lead them.

Roger was down to his long underwear, and he threw himself into the river and came up already stroking powerfully toward the canoe. This was the easy part, since the current was in his favor. A gasp went up from the crowd, which turned to watch him.

"Get the shit, Dana," Earl said. "I'd go myself but I'm too slow."

Hank clapped a hand on Dana's shoulder, and they took off at a brisk jog toward the sheds.

"Earl, can you coordinate getting the other boats?" Dor ticked off on his hand. "Get the Bronco from the shed, hook it up to the trailer. Sharon, Elsa, can you give him a hand?"

The two women who ran the auto shop nodded.

"Drive right across the yard, don't bother to take the road. Don't forget oars. When Dana and Hank get back—" Dor searched the crowd, his gaze falling on Harris, the quietest member of the council. "Harris. You need to take charge of arming people. Okay? You can do that? Good candidates would be Terrence, Shel, Fat Mike. Do *not* give a weapon to anyone without experience. Do you hear me? That's important. It's worse to have them in the wrong hands than to leave them unarmed."

Harris nodded. "I got it."

"Good. I doubt you'll be able to get all that coordinated by dusk, and with any luck they'll be gone by then. But this isn't wasted, because we're going to be ready in the morning. And I have a feeling we'll need to be."

Roger reached the canoe, and was struggling with the branch. Sharon and Elsa ran in the direction of the auto garage. Harris moved among the crowd, assembling his shooters.

Everyone else focused on Roger. He got the canoe unhooked with little trouble, but as soon as he started dragging it back toward shore, it was clear that he was in trouble. He sidestroked with only one hand free, kicking hard against the current. But the canoe dragged in the water and slowed him down.

"Go, Roger," a man said near Cass. Another man repeated it, and then they were all saying it, quietly.

Though the struggling man could not possibly hear them, Cass felt their energy, their frantic hope. The sun slipped a little lower in the sky and orange brilliance shone along the horizon, the last gasp of the day. In an hour the sky would be velvety dark blue, and the Beaters would not be able to see. Their tiny pupils, altered by the fever so that they were no longer able to expand, would not let in enough light for them to make out rough shapes, much less details. If they could hold off this wave until then…

Roger paused, his hand on the lip of the canoe, and treaded water for a moment. Cass saw him gasping for breath. For a moment he went still, and was it her imagination or was he sinking down, down, under the water—

"Damn it," his girlfriend exclaimed. "Do something, don't you see he can't make it, someone do something, save him!"

Cass wasn't the only one to turn to Dor. He was deliberating, his jaw pulsing the way it always did when he focused on a problem.

"You could send someone else in for him."

"And lose two men?" Dor answered quietly; their conversation was not meant for anyone else to hear. Valerie was as good as forgotten in the moment, and Cass saw that she knew it, her face blanched the shade of parchment. Defeat contorted her fine, frail beauty, and she turned away.

"Roger's our best swimmer," Dor continued, reaching for Cass's hand. She didn't think he was even aware of touching her, and in that moment she understood she was his mooring, the source of his steady courage. "No one else could have gotten as far as he has."

No one else could bring him back in—that's what he was saying. Around him the voices had turned imploring—*Roger, go, you can do it*—but when his girlfriend screamed his name again, he finally shook the water from his eyes and resumed his weak strokes.

The canoe came closer. Only a matter of inches, but closer.

"This is taking too long," Dor muttered. Cass looked where he was looking, saw Glynnis pat her jacket frantically for more ammo, knew she wasn't finding it. Saw John using his paddle less accurately now, his arms shivering—they had to be in excruciating pain, his muscles in revolt.

Roger cried out, a guttural, almost inhuman sound of desperation. He flung out his arm on the water and stroked. Again and again, he drew himself painfully against the drag of the water, and he came closer.

"You can do it," the crowd screamed.

"Roger! Roger!"

"Come on, just a little farther!"

When he was ten yards out, people threw themselves into the water, half a dozen of them, women and men, some of them linking arms. They splashed and yelped at the cold and hands grasped the canoe and others cradled Roger, who seemed to slip into unconsciousness, his eyes rolling back in his head, and Cass knew she could not spend one more moment worrying about him—she had to give all her attention to the canoe, which was being handed along the row of people in the water. It was dragged up on the shore, tugged onto the hard-packed mud.

"Get in, get in, Cass—I'll push us off."

She didn't hesitate, but stepped nimbly over the prow, feeling the canoe bottom grind against the silty bank, then steadying herself as it listed sharply. Dor's strong hands gripped the edges to steady it, and then others did too.

There was shouting from the path. Hank and Dana ran toward them, Dana looking as though he was about to have a stroke, his face beet-red and his fine hair waving in the breeze.

They were carrying the boxes of ammunition, half a dozen guns. Dor released the canoe and ran to meet them, taking armfuls of weapons. He was back in seconds, but the panicked swell of cries from the crowd told Cass they were running out of time.

Across the river, emboldened now that Glynnis had stopped shooting, more of the Beaters were taking to the river. Fifteen of them, maybe, in twos and threes, they waded and shuffled and stumbled into the water, plunged forward, went under, came up gasping and shrieking. John and Glynnis had retreated ten feet or so, but the crush of Beaters in the water made their craft look impossibly vulnerable.

Dor swung his body into the canoe and jammed his oar into the shallow water, pushing them away from the shore. A dozen hands seized the canoe walls and when they were free of the land it felt for a second as if they were weightless, suspended in air, in nothing—and then the current found them and tugged and Dor dipped his oar into the water and they were off.

Their speed belied the fact that Dor was far more powerful than John. His navigation skills were not as precise, but he was heading them straight for the other shore and Cass knew that accuracy was not his goal.

"Get the .22—that one," he yelled. "That ditty bag, it's got the shells. When I pull up close, get them in their canoe but, Cass—make sure you don't miss. We only get one shot."

She carefully reached for the weapons, aware of how easy it would be to tip over; if they did, all was lost. But the canoe glided on. Closer, she could make out individual Beaters' cries, and then John, talking steadily, intently, slurring; she caught the words "hold on" and "brave" and saw that Glynnis's head was bowed and her eyes closed, as though she was praying.

So focused was John that when Dor shouted his name he startled, glancing wildly around, his eyes going wide when he saw them. Utter, loose-limbed exhaustion radiated from his body, and steam rose off his back. He stared dumbly at Dor.

"We're coming in," Dor yelled. "We've got the shells. A hundred, hundred-fifty rounds. And the .22, I don't know what there is in the way of ammo. Enough to make this a fair fight, anyway."

Cass held the ditty bag, felt its weight in her hands. Past John and Glynnis, she saw a Beater sink into the water up to its chin and ears, like a beaver or an otter. It churned the water in front of it and then she realized that its feet were not touching the bottom, it was keeping itself afloat—swimming—and it was coming closer.

"Oh, God," she said softly.

"I see it," Dor muttered through gritted teeth. "Don't say anything until you get this shit safely in their boat. I mean it, Cass. Knowing can't help them."

If Cass alerted John and Glynnis of the approaching Beater, they might panic—rock the canoe too far, miss when Cass tossed the weapons—and then they wouldn't stand a chance against it, that's what Dor was saying. Cass nodded grimly.

"Be ready, be ready," she whispered, and her eyes locked on Glynnis's. Five yards, three—it was like softball, twenty years ago when she played on the U-12 team, waiting in the dugout for her team to bat.

And then the canoes pulled even. Cass held the bag

aloft with trembling hands, and Glynnis reached; her hands closed on the bag, tugged, and then she had it, and Cass seized the .22 and held it out by the barrel, and Glynnis took that too, and then it was only a matter of the extra magazines, and Cass lifted them from the bottom of the boat and—

"What the hell!" John roared, turning, as the Beater caught up with the canoe and slapped at it with desperate hands. It was close enough that Cass could see that it was recently turned. Only the hair along its hairline had been pulled out of its scalp, and its face was still recognizable, barely bruised or lacerated, the face of a young man. The fresh wounds on its forearms were very much like those she'd found on herself when she woke in the field.

She shivered with the realization that she could be among this throng, or one like it, if she hadn't recovered from the fever. She could be one of these single-minded things, throwing itself into the water, driven by flesh hunger. Who knew what things she had done—

Her attention jerked back with the thudding sound of John bringing an oar blade down on the Beater's head, but by the second blow the thing had already slipped below the surface, and the oar slapped harmlessly on the water, splashing him and Glynnis instead.

The canoe was slammed from the bottom, the Beater trying to claw its way back to the surface. It popped up a second later, its wet, greasy head dripping cold water, its hands paddling air.

Then its scrabbling fingers found the lip of the canoe and gave a yank.

Glynnis screamed, and an answering roar came from the far shore, all the people of New Eden helpless to do anything but watch. Cass cried out, too, but no sound came from her; her throat was sealed with terror, her body frozen.

The gun fell from her shaking hands. It hit the water with a little splash and was gone, heavy metal sinking indifferently into the depths.

Oh my God
oh my God
oh my God

"Oh my God," Cass gasped, watching the gun disappear.

She had failed. She had allowed the old fears to drift up from the place where she had banished them, and the fears had made her clumsy. She had failed John and Glynnis and she had failed Dor and the pain of her failure burst through her body—

"It doesn't matter!" Dor shouted at her, his hand reaching for hers. His touch was warm, even in the frigid air he was warm, all determination and life, and she responded, snapped back to attention and forced herself to forget about the lost gun.

John slammed the butt of the oar's handle directly onto the thing's disfigured hand, over and over, so hard that the canoe shuddered and the air was filled with the sickening sound of bones splintering. And still it hung on. Miraculously, the canoe had not dipped below the water's surface, though it rocked dangerously back and forth as the Beater hauled and tugged.

The water behind it churned and boiled, rounded shapes rising above the water. Heads. More of them— three or four more had swum nearly to the boat.

An explosion split the air only inches away and Cass

snapped her head around. Glynnis was crouched in the boat; she must have pressed the muzzle of her gun directly to the Beater's head because its blood covered the side of the canoe, her pants, the seat, everything—and its skull as it slipped below the surface for the last time was cratered and broken. Another shot. Another, and another, and Glynnis barely paused, even when brain matter slapped wetly against the hull, even when another of the infected hooked a bony hand over the side like the first one and when John smashed it with the heavy oar, a skinned and crusted finger splitting off into the boat. More and more, and then the shots ceased and there was silence—sudden, shocking silence and the smell of the shooting acrid in Cass's nostrils. She coughed, almost delicately, touching her mouth as though assuring herself that she had survived the shootout, that she still lived.

"You go down, we'll go upriver," Dor yelled, already dipping his oar in the water to pull them against the current. John only nodded, exhausted, and laid his oar across his knees and bowed his head, a few seconds' respite while they drifted downstream. Glynnis didn't stop; she dug in the ditty bag and lined up her extra shells on the metal bench.

There was no more time to worry about them. "Get me in closer," Cass urged Dor. "I'm not that good." She might be able to hit a target from where they were, but she might not, and there were too many of them.

"You're no good to anyone if they get to us," Dor said, but he arced the craft around and headed to the shore.

"So don't get me *that* close. Get me, you know, medium close."

Cass was sure she saw his lips curve, only for a second. Dear God, he'd smiled. In the midst of this madness, wearing the blood of Beaters, she'd made a joke, unconsciously, and he'd found a reason to be amused.

Dor was strong when no one else was. Dor burned bright with life, with vitality, even when people and hopes—when the world itself—disintegrated around him.

Cass reached for him, touched her fingers to his wrist. He looked at her questioningly

"God be with us," she said.

For a moment he just looked back at her, his eyes shining the blue of Ceylon sapphires. "I don't believe in God," he said, barely more than a whisper.

"Then believe in me."

They weren't the words she meant to say. Weren't words she was aware of thinking. But suddenly they were the plea that powered what she could do next, that gave her the strength and the courage to brace herself with a knee jammed against the cold metal canoe wall, to hold the gun in two hands the way her daddy taught her, to line up the Beater's throat in the sights and to pull the trigger—

A starburst of blood and the beast shuddered for a second and then crumpled to the muddy bank, but Cass was already lining up her next shot and her next. Some she missed. Most she hit. Her arm went numb from the recoil and she had to stop and reload, and Dor said things to her and she held on to the sound of his voice even though somehow she'd lost the ability to comprehend what words came out and her teeth rattled and clacked against each other and still she kept shooting.

Dor kept them to the shore, going down the line of

Beaters assembled there, and when they reached the huddled end it seemed that the crowd had thinned. Cass rested her gun against her knee, feeling her muscles stretched taut and painfully cramped, and twisted in her seat.

Beyond the scattered bodies, she could see the rest retreating, limping away in twos and threes, a whole line of them at the downstream end, where John and Glynnis's canoe turned lazily in the water.

This, too, was terrifying, however. A retreat was evidence of forethought amid their insatiable drive, of consensual thinking, of responding to events. No doubt the Beaters had learned things tonight that would change their strategy tomorrow when they returned—a fact Cass was certain of. They'd be back as soon as daylight allowed.

"We're heading to shore."

John's voice, weakened and hollow, reached them as though over a divide far greater than the water. Cass watched him dip his oar into the water, painfully, slowly; and then their own canoe turned and headed for home, Dor's strokes sure and strong, undiminished by the effort he had made.

The effort *they* had made, together. A team.

Cass had only worked like this with one other man in her life, and that was Smoke. Only once before had she been completely united in purpose as she had been with Dor tonight, each protecting the other, each reading the other's thoughts, the sum of them stronger than they could ever be on their own. With Dor, there was a hyperawareness of each other's bodies, almost an anticipation of their movements, creating a total economy of motion. Nothing wasted, working to each other's strengths.

The shore loomed solid and welcoming, lined with the people of New Eden, all of them shouting and crying and hugging each other. And then the crowd thinned slightly and Cass saw a figure limping slowly across the yard, all alone, hobbled over a stick, pain evident in every step.

She was vaguely aware of the people calling her name as the canoe was dragged up onto the bank, the warmth of Dor's hand on hers as he helped her up, the solid ground beneath her numb feet.

She was aware of all these things, but they were not real and they were not true, not the way the man walking toward her as though he might die on the journey— the way he was real and true.

Smoke saw her, and his eyes found hers and held on and all the other sounds disappeared and all the other people disappeared and all there was was her and him and he lifted his hand, he held it out to her and then he fell, crashing down on the hard-packed earth of the island that he had never walked in all the time since he arrived in New Eden, all the time between sleeping and waking and every lost moment that lay between.

Smoke fell.

Cass ran.

How could she have given up on him?

The minute she looked into Smoke's eyes, saw him trying to say her name as Steve's strong hands helped him sit up, she knew what a terrible mistake she'd made, leaving him alone in that place, untended, all because of fear.

She hadn't been strong enough for him.

"Are you…" He was struggling to speak, his vocal cords rusty from a lack of use. He cleared his throat and tried again. "Are you all right, Cass?"

"Me? I'm fine, oh, sweetheart, I'm perfectly fine. But you—I'm so sorry I haven't been coming—"

"Have they…hurt you?" He pushed weakly against Steve, trying to break free of his grasp.

"No, no, no, no," she said, realization dawning on her. No one had told him where he was, no one had explained. "Smoke, these are good people. Free people.

This isn't Colima. These aren't the Rebuilders. This place is called New Eden, and you've been recovering here, healing here."

Smoke's eyelids fluttered and he started to say something else, but the words were garbled and almost unintelligible as he slumped against Steve.

"Smoke, no—" Cass pressed her hands to his face, his neck, feeling for his pulse.

A sharp exclamation above her—Sun-hi, out of breath, clutching her jacket front closed. She cursed in Korean before crouching down and switching to English.

"Smoke is awake?"

He mumbled something, his chin slumped to his chest. Sun-hi reached for his wrist, Cass getting out of the way for her. She used her thumb to pull up one of his eyelids and shone her flashlight at his face. That got her a groan of protest.

"This is amazing," Sun-hi said. "He walked here by himself?"

"I think so."

"I don't know how he could—well, it does not matter now. He picked a bad moment for waking up. I have to get all patients ready for evacuation. Steve, you bring him now."

Steve and a raider named Brandt crouched down to pick the prone form up in a fireman's hold, linking arms to support him. Smoke's head lolled the other way.

"Is he going to be okay?" Cass asked. "Is he going to wake up again?"

"I don't know how this is happening," Sun-hi said. "I am very amazed. But right now I must figure out cars, pack supplies. You come with me, Steve. We will get ready together."

"Yes, ma'am," Steve said.

"We will take him back to the hospital, Cass," Sun-hi promised. "Take very good care of him. Now you go get ready too."

Cass put her hand gently on Smoke's face, his beard soft under her hand. Someone had kept it neatly trimmed. It should have been her.

Smoke was silent as they carried him away, Sun-hi striding purposefully ahead of them toward the hospital. Smoke owed Sun-hi his life, Cass had no doubt. And Cass owed Sun-hi too. And Zihna. And all the volunteers who'd fed and bathed him, held his hand and read to him, talked to him despite the fact that he'd been trapped in his mind as his body mended.

This should be her happiest day, the one she'd longed for, dreamed of and finally despaired of. And instead of holding him, whispering the thousand things she'd saved up to tell him, she and everyone else had to try to survive a horror that lay waiting to overrun them come the morning.

Aftertime had taken so much from her, and now it threatened to take this miracle, as well.

As Sun-hi's little group disappeared around the back of the building, Cass headed for the doors of the community center, now thrown wide open with dozens of people milling about inside. She would get Ruthie, pack their things, get back to the hospital, make sure Smoke had a place in one of the cars, and then—once everything was in order—she would finally return to keeping the vigil she had forsaken.

She wouldn't let the world take this one from her.

* * *

Sammi had organized the little kids to play a version of Duck, Duck, Goose. Twyla and Ruthie and Dane ran in a circle around Sammi and Dirk, who sat scowling at the floor, old enough to know that something was terribly wrong, but not old enough to understand what.

When Sammi looked up and saw Cass, there was a moment when her resentment and anger didn't have time to catch up, a second where she looked like a little girl again herself, frightened and vulnerable. Then the mask came down; she narrowed her eyes and got to her feet.

"Sammi!" Ruthie giggled and smacked her. "Goose! Goose!"

Ruthie hadn't noticed Cass yet. Her skin was rosy from the exertion of the game, and she threw herself at Sammi and grabbed her hands, wanting to play some more. She looked so happy. In recent weeks she had come out of her shell—laughed louder, chattered more excitedly, played more creatively. She was doing so well here—and now she would be uprooted again.

It couldn't be helped; it was the only way to save them all. Of course, not all of them would make it on the road to…wherever better. How many would die tomorrow? How many the day after that? How many of them would be alive in a week, a month…a year?

Cass forced herself to stay focused. It never helped to think about the future like that—she knew better; everyone knew better.

"Babygirl," she said, and Ruthie spun around and ran to her, laughing, arms lifted to be picked up. Cass swept her up in her arms and spun with the momentum, her little girl's legs sailing through the air.

"So, can I go now?" Sammi's voice dripped with sarcasm, her face curled into a sneer.

"Sammi…"

"*What?* Don't you have to, like, figure out which guy you're gonna hook up with later?"

"Sammi, this is serious. All I want for you—all *anyone* wants for you—is to keep you safe. Your dad—"

"Dad's already been here. I told him to fuck off."

Only the faintest quiver of Sammi's lower lip gave her away. It broke Cass's heart to see how hard she was working to preserve her anger.

"At least let's figure out what you should bring—"

"I've got that covered. I'm with Kyra and Sage, we're gonna share."

Cass sighed. If she pressed any further, she risked alienating Sammi entirely, or drawing her focus away from the important tasks at hand. "Okay. I know you girls are smart. You've got packs? How about that jogger stroller, can you pack some things in that?"

Sammi rolled her eyes and picked up Dane, who'd fallen at her feet in a fit of giggles. "Tell you what, Cass, why don't you let me focus on my life and you can go back to screwing up your own, okay?"

17

It had all started so well and gone so wrong.

The other women in the Mothers' House were welcoming at first. They gave Cass jars of wildflowers, cakes decorated with thin kaysev-syrup icing, books and toys and blankets and stuffed animals and good cheer. They made her tea and sat with her, clucking over the scrapes and bruises she'd sustained in the Rebuilder battle just before she got there. All of them had jobs. Ingrid and Suzanne both worked in the laundry, Jasmine—at that time already six months pregnant—was in the storehouse, assisting Dana with disbursement. They were happy to have another person to work into the child care rotation. In the evenings, coming back from meals, there was laughter and sometimes singing and when the little ones were asleep they gathered in the living room and talked by the light of a single candle.

And then, one day, one bad day that Cass wished she

could do over, she rose in the morning and began down the stairs only to overhear a conversation between Ingrid and Jasmine.

"All I'm saying is, a child doesn't get that way by herself," Jasmine said, in her faint East Coast accent.

"Wait until your own child starts sassing you and then see what you think," Suzanne—unflappable Suzanne, always willing to give everyone the benefit of the doubt—said mildly.

"But I mean, it's like Ruthie's *afraid* half the time. Twyla talks, like, *four times* as much as she does."

"Some kids are just quieter than others, Jazzy," Suzanne said patiently. "And Cass and she have been through a lot. Even kids need time to process things."

"But look at Dirk and Dane. I mean, they lost their dad, like, one day he was there and the next day he was facedown in the front yard, shot by the neighbor, for heaven's sake. That's traumatic, right? Right?"

There was a pause, a small silence in which the coil of anxiety inside Cass pulled taut. The silence meant that Suzanne—sweet Suzanne, humming-without-knowing-she-was-doing-it Suzanne—had doubts.

"I don't mean she's a *bad* mother," Jasmine said. "Only, you know, she's so protective. Overprotective. She never lets that child out of her sight. She even drags her along to go see that poor man in the hospital. I mean, tell me that's not traumatizing, right? I heard his eyes were gouged out."

"Oh, Christ, Jazzy, that's not true," Suzanne protested. "Go see him yourself, if you want. I was over there getting some cream for Twyla's rash, I saw him, he's not that bad."

Cass backed up the stairs at that point, her face burning.

Was she overprotective?

Yes, probably; but how could she help it, after everything they had experienced and seen?

And yes, Ruthie was quiet…but a few months ago she didn't talk at all. Cass had been happy that she was simply talking again. But these few words from Jasmine threw a pall over her progress.

The doubts magnified and escalated all that day. It wasn't the first time her parenting had been called into question; it was far from the worst time. So why did it hurt so much now? As Cass sat with Smoke late that afternoon, holding his hand, smoothing the hair out of his face, adjusting his covers, her mind reviewed every interaction she'd had with the others. The way they instinctively knew how to fill the gaps in the conversation that always left her tongue-tied…had they been thinking she was awkward all along? The way Ingrid always brought a new book for Ruthie from the library—was it because she didn't think Cass would do it on her own? The games Dane invited Ruthie to play—had Ingrid put him up to it, out of pity for her awkward daughter and her inadequate mothering?

By dinnertime, she had a stomachache and her face felt tight. As she carried their tray of food and walked with Ruthie across the lawn, headed for the table she usually shared with the other women, she saw Dor sitting alone at another. His meal was finished, his cutlery laid across his plate and half a cup of water in his hand. He was watching Sammi, who was talking to a group of teens over at the volleyball net.

In a split-second decision she went and sat with Dor instead.

Sliding her tray on the table across from him, she gave him the best smile she could muster.

"Okay if I sit here?" she said.

Dor looked surprised. "Hell yeah. I thought you were avoiding me." Then, as if sensing he'd made a mistake, his face softened. "If you hadn't come to me, I would have hunted you down, Cass."

"I don't belong here." The words, stark and frightened, were out of her mouth before she could stop herself. Worse yet, her eyes stung with unshed tears. Cass covered her mouth and looked down at the table. Someone had covered it with a flowered cloth—someone, no doubt, who had no trouble making and keeping friends, someone who was comfortable in the social milieu here in New Eden.

Dor smiled ruefully and held up his hands for Cass to see the cuts and scrapes that covered his forearms. He'd spent the day helping to remove barbed-wire fencing from a section of the lower island; they'd been using it to cultivate kaysev, but as Cass had already seen for herself on a walk with Ruthie, they had barely cleared the land since New Eden had been settled.

Pulling the barbed wire, like hauling trash or tilling the earth, was a job for the brawny, but not one that was prized. Such jobs were never given to council members. Despite New Eden's insistence on a cooperative society, it was clear that some job assignments were more coveted than others and distributed according to the council's whims. And Dor had started at the bottom. He didn't have the same reputation in New Eden as he had in the Box.

"Ahhh…hell." Dor's hands sought hers and drew them together, holding them tightly. "Come on, girl, don't go soft on me now."

Blinking, Cass took a chance and peeked at him. His dark, scarred face was shadowed with concern. His brows were lowered. He'd cut his silver-tinged black hair since coming to this settlement, and it now cleared the collar of his work shirt, though the front still fell in his eyes. The thin wire loops in his ears and the tattoos that wound up both arms—things that had never looked out of place in the Box—seemed a little too edgy here, a little provocative. Maybe that was why he sat alone, a fact Cass hadn't bothered to consider until just this minute.

Neither one of them fit in here.

"Sammi's making friends," Cass said lamely, after Dor finally relaxed his grip on her hands.

"Ruthie too."

Just like that, they acknowledged what neither had said aloud: New Eden was a good place for children. And that had to be enough.

"I just…I don't know. Maybe it's just that the others all knew each other already. I mean, Ingrid and Suzanne and Jasmine and all. They're nice to me, but sometimes…"

"Don't let them get to you," Dor said. "They're jealous. I mean, *look* at you."

Cass looked up in surprise, found Dor's eyes intent on her. They were the near-ebony that always signaled intensity, the shade of Dor's strong emotion, and he stared without blinking into her eyes, and then let his gaze travel down to her mouth, and it was almost a physical sensation, as though he were touching her instead of just watching her, and Cass felt the stirring that she thought had not followed her to this place, the hunger for touch that had been driven from her by the terror of almost losing Smoke.

And thinking of Dor touching her lips led to memories of him kissing her. They'd made love twice on the journey that took them from the Box to Colima. No. That wasn't right—they'd *fucked* twice. They'd seized on each other out of desperation, terror, need, hopelessness, anger, slammed their bodies into each other as death threatened and the world yawed crazily on its axis. They'd kept each other going, no more and no less, and wasn't that over when it was over? Wasn't that the nature of the deal they'd never discussed out loud—to get each other through, and then leave it, then never speak of it again?

"You're beautiful, Cass," Dor said, and only then did Cass realize that he'd only loosened his grip on her hands, not released them, and he laced his fingers through hers and caressed her palms with his thumbs. The sensation went straight to her core, searing, ignited from a spark to a roaring flame with no slow build. "Every woman, every man, that's the first thing they think when they see you."

His words were a buzz in her ear, confirmation of things she didn't want to hear. These were things she didn't want to know. They were a crushing rejection of the fragile hope she'd nurtured, that she could be just another mom in just another town, raising a nice girl and having nice friends.

Dor must have seen her expression slip, because his hands went still, he stopped touching her, pulled away. "What did I say?" he asked urgently, not unkindly.

Nothing, only don't stop touching me. Nothing, only—please—make me forget again.

"Tonight—" Cass swallowed, nearly lost her nerve. "Tonight, after Ruthie goes down…"

"What? What do you need?"

"Take me somewhere," Cass said miserably. "Alone."

And he did.

18

There existed on the survivors' islands one pickup and one panel van, a motorcycle, a small ATV with a trailer for hauling fuel, Nathan's little hybrid and a dented Accord, all of which were maintained by Sharon and Elsa, two women who'd met at WyoTech and worked at a Toyota dealership in Sonora until riots and crashes decimated most of the vehicles on the road. A hasty midnight session of the New Eden council divided the vehicles' cargo and passenger space among the eligible citizens, following a very specific set of improvised guidelines. Communal supplies would receive top priority: medicine, water, prepared food. Mothers and children would ride at least some of the time, as would the elderly, the sick, the disabled.

Seventy of them and four passenger vehicles. Everyone knew that meant they would be able to take very little. Cass looked around the room, knowing that the few sentimental things she clung to would only weigh them down. Elsewhere in the house, she could hear Ingrid and Suzanne and Jasmine, throwing what they could into backpacks.

"Ruthie, Babygirl, we're going exploring," she said, as she sorted through their clothes, choosing lightweight things that could be layered. Some of Ruthie's clothes were getting tight; she had hit a growth spurt and had outgrown most of her pants. Her turtlenecks no longer pulled easily over her head. Even her nightgown's sleeves didn't cover her wrists.

Her little girl sat cross-legged on the mattress and pouted. "I don't want to go."

"Oh, honey, it'll be an *adventure*." Cass didn't have the heart to put any energy into the lie. She'd be found out soon enough; horrors awaited around every corner.

"Is Twyla going?"

"Yes, of course. We can walk together."

Except that Suzanne had told her not to speak to her until she'd cooled down. *Don't call me, I'll call you,* she'd said over a week ago, a faint attempt at humor on a day when humor had no place. By now Ingrid would have told her the latest, and Suzanne was bound to be angrier still.

Cass packed the large-framed pack that she used to haul a day's worth of water and her tools every day. It was good she'd become accustomed to carrying forty pounds on her back. She could not count on much help on the road and she already needed to ask a very big favor that would exhaust any goodwill she had left.

Into the pack went her meager supplies of soap, aspirin, lanolin and dried rabbit jerky. Then hers and Ruthie's clothes, with extra coats and scarves wrapped around her bottle of wine. It was about half-full, a fact she did not allow herself to dwell on. The box decorated with the circus bear she left on the shelf, along with the bowl of earrings.

Into Ruthie's Tinker Bell backpack, a gift from Twyla on her birthday, Cass packed a soft baby blanket that she liked to sleep with, a few stuffed animals and the veterinarian play set. She added a stack of books and then, reconsidering, took out all but two.

"Okay, sugar?" she asked Ruthie, helping her try it on for weight.

"Okay," Ruthie answered through a yawn.

"Oh, honey, I'm so sorry, it's bedtime, isn't it? And we'll go to bed soon."

A lie. Cass would not sleep this night. The entire settlement was leaving at dawn, and she had to make sure that Smoke was with them. *How,* she did not yet know, and her anxiety over that fact curdled in her stomach.

She descended the stairs with Ruthie, using the flashlight she kept for emergencies. Its beam was still strong, but she had no spare batteries, and she was aware of every second that ticked by.

The house was empty. The women had left without her, just as she feared. She swept the flashlight's beam over the kitchen table, the counter, the living room—everything as it had been before, about to become part of a ghost town.

She stepped out on the porch and stopped for a moment, caught up short by the scene in front of her. Flashlight beams and candles bobbed along the paths as people hurried about. Someone had built a bonfire in the yard and piled on firewood with abandon. They couldn't take it with them, so Cass supposed it made sense to burn it. The air was filled with people calling to each other, and along the shore she could make out a growing pile of bags and boxes.

The island's vehicles were parked in a neat row in front of the bridge, and men were milling around close by. From this distance Cass could not tell who was in the crowd, but she suspected it was the council members and their trusted friends. People connected to them would decide what went and what stayed. Already the mound of belongings at the shore was more than would fit into cargo.

"Саза."

The deep voice in the darkness startled her. She spun around and pointed her flashlight straight at the speaker, who'd been standing under the overhang next to the house.

It was Red. He winced in the sudden light and held his hands up to his face; they were empty. "Hey, easy there."

"I was just. Ah, going," Cass said, backing away from him. In the flickering light she saw how he braced himself against the wall, his muscles stiff from waiting.

"No, wait. Wait, Cassie."

Cass looked up sharply. No one called her that, not for a very long time. She didn't like it—it brought back memories of times and places that she couldn't reclaim even if she wanted to.

"What do you want?"

"To help. Just to help."

"Help me?" The absurdity of the request made Cass laugh. "And how are you going to do that? You got a key to some underground bunker no one knows about? A ten-year supply of Rice-A-Roni?"

"No, no, nothing like that." In the light of Cass's flashlight, which she directed at the ground, Red's face looked ghostly, his beard obscuring all his features except those soft eyes nested in sun-weathered wrinkles. He lifted a hand and then cut the gesture short. His shoulder drooped. "I wish I—we—could offer more. But, well, I just thought Zihna and I, we could watch the little one. So you—I mean, Smoke's gonna need you to advocate for him. They're over there right now… and it looks bad. No way they're taking all the patients along, and Dana and a couple of the others want to leave them all."

"What are you talking about?" Cass's voice went shrill with fear. *"Leave who?"*

Only, before Red even answered, she knew what he was going to say, and was surprised she hadn't already thought of it.

Four cars. All that gear. The water. Decisions were going to have to be made, and a full-grown man was a lot of cargo. She knew they wouldn't necessarily help *her,* but to leave Smoke, who'd been a hero to so many when the Rebuilders threatened all… But of course: Dor, Smoke, herself—none of them were recognized for what they had been prior to their arrival, for better or worse.

"Oh my God…" she breathed, and the enormity of the truth finally sank all the way in. "Oh no."

What had she been thinking, that she could save them all? It would be a miracle if she could even make it through the journey with Ruthie. An injured man— barely walking, barely returned from the edge he'd walked with Death. She felt the porch floor tilt underneath her.

Strong hands steadied her as she struggled to hold on to Ruthie. "Let me," Red said, and he eased Ruthie out of her arms with surprising tenderness, and hitched her up over one shoulder. Her little head lolled in the crook of his neck, her eyelashes fluttering and her sweet mouth in a sleepy pout.

Red put a hand at her elbow to steady her. "Are you okay? Do you need to sit down?"

Cass took a deep breath. "No, I'm all right. I need— I just need—oh God." She needed to get to Smoke— but she needed to stay here with Ruthie. She needed to get their things down to the pile and hope there was a chance they might be loaded. Otherwise, it was only a matter of time before the packs became too heavy and they had to start leaving things behind, leaving them at the edge of the road like people did in the impossible early days of the Siege, back when families tried to take everything with them. You'd come across abandoned pillowcases stuffed with silver, paintings, photographs; suitcases bulging with clothes; bicycles and chain saws and radios and clocks and dolls and things that defied logic; vases and puzzles and garden hoses.

Would their things end up like that? And then—a half mile down the road, a mile, two—would they themselves lie down, too?

"Cassie." Red spoke urgently. "You can't give up now, girl. Me and Zihna, we talked it over. We have the trailer. We think we can rig it so Smoke can ride. I've got Steve helping me out right now. He owes me one. We'll have to take turns with Ruthie, but I don't expect that'll be a problem, not with so many of us. We've got the girls—well, Sage, anyway. Can't be putting too much strain on Kyra, not with her goin' on her sixth month. And Sammi…well, she'll come around. You'll see. She just needs to cool off a little, is all."

Cass's mind swam with what he was proposing. All those people—all the favors he was willing to trade on her behalf. She wanted to know why. What she asked instead was, "What trailer?"

"It's a little old flatbed three-wheeler. It was the one Zihna and me came in here with. Came from her place, to be fair, but I expect she won't mind sharing with her old man," he said, smiling.

What other choice did she have? Smoke wouldn't make it four steps down the road, despite his amazing journey across the island. Still, maybe there was another way; maybe she could convince them to give him passage in one of the vehicles. She had to find out who was in charge and could make decisions.

"I don't know what you've been planning," Red began, "but there are some things you should know. Milt and Jack already took Charles down to the end of the island, about forty-five minutes ago. Charles *didn't* make the trip back with them."

Charles—Cass's heart lurched at the memory of the frail, scabbed man who was in the late stages of AIDS, which he had controlled Before but which ravaged his body now that the steady stream of medicine was gone.

"Do you understand what I'm telling you, Cass?"

She stared out at the scene unfolding in front of her. The bonfire was growing, wood stacked high and sparks flying. Collette and her friends, waving their hands at the pile of burning belongings. Luddy had his longboard under his arm; for once it didn't seem like a ridiculous thing for a grown man to own. Two of the guys worked on upended bicycles. What did they think they were going to do with those—outrun the rest of them? Then they would be traveling alone come daylight, with no defense against the Beaters' speed.

Not odds that Cass would take. But still, at least they had plans of some sort.

"But." She swallowed, raking her hair with her hands. "Why? Why do you want to help us?"

Red hesitated, and then searched her face with his intense gaze, the one she'd noticed so many times before. It seemed like he was about to confide or confess something; then the moment passed, and he shrugged. "Zihna and I...we like kids. We like helping people. And Ruthie...well, we've always thought she was special."

His voice broke oddly on the last word, and Cass saw that he rocked Ruthie in his arms. It was true that he and Zihna had always been kind to Ruthie—in the days following the chill that formed between Cass and the other women, hadn't they been extra solicitous, always talking to her at mealtimes, taking the time to chat when Cass and she walked around the island?

Still, Cass was uncomfortable with Red's suggestion. Hell, she wouldn't be the first to raise an eyebrow at the two older people taking such an interest in the kids, especially the teens, even though no one had ever picked up on anything inappropriate going on with the couple.

Cass had taken risks with Ruthie's safety that she never should have. She'd left her daughter with strangers so she could work, or drink, or date. She wanted to trust her instincts. Sometimes it seemed like they were all she had left to navigate with. But right now, as the island descended into chaos all around her, was not the time.

"Thank you," she said formally. "But as generous as

your offer of help is, I'll take my chances—mine and Ruthie's—alone."

Red's face sagged, the sadness in his eyes reflected in the eerie glow of the flashlight, and he went still.

"I can't let you do that, Cassie," he said softly.

A strange premonition snaked up Cass's spine, something so familiar and yet just out of reach. "Why?"

"Because this is too important. Because she's my granddaughter. Cass...listen to me. It's *me*...your dad."

19

This time when Cass felt the breath leave her, the ground rushing up to meet her and cave her in, she did not yield to it.

No no no he's not

The man—her dad—because of *course* it was him. It was wily old Silver Dollar Haverford, shape-shifted anew, more worn but no less crafty and elusive. How could she not have recognized that voice—the one that had once sung her lullabies? The one that called from the road with ever-diminishing frequency, always a new number, a borrowed phone when times were tough, as they nearly always were. Sometimes she heard a woman in the background; other times the din of Greyhound stations or taverns.

And always, always, she asked him the same question: "When are you coming home, Daddy?"

How long did it take until she figured out that he

never would? Oh, but that was the genius of old Silver Dollar—he could make you believe. He waited until you'd just about given up hope and then he'd show up, all smiles and hugs and trinkets in his pockets, embroidered blouses and clay whistles from Tijuana, bags of apples from Washington. A dress for her mother. Promises to stay, this time and the next. The two of them would go out for dinner, come home laughing and loud, then whispering in the living room, him singing and her dancing, and Cass in her bed would be happy because surely this time it would last, surely this time he'd see that they all belonged together?

The last time he ever came home was her eighth birthday. Well, a week later, anyway—the delay broke his heart but was unavoidable, of course, and stupid, stupid Cass, she believed him. He took her to a baseball game, called her his little lady, said maybe they could go skiing that winter once it got cold enough.

And then he was gone forever.

She'd tried to find him, just once. It was after her mother took up with Byrn, after her stepfather started coming into the hall late at night when Cass was in her nightgown, pretending to be on the way to the bathroom at the same time, "accidentally" touching her down there when they passed.

Cass had searched every town she could think of that her dad had ever mentioned. She stole her mother's credit card out of her purse and used it for an internet service that promised to track down missing loved ones; the fifty-dollar report included six known addresses, but the most she ever found were a few irate landlords who remembered her father well.

By the time she finally gave up, her mother had gotten the bill and was furious. And her anger only grew when Cass tried to tell her what had been going on late at night, that Byrn lurked in the halls, touched her through the thin nightgown, followed her back to her room and whispered warnings while he fumbled with his zipper. She told Cass to consider long and hard if telling lies was worth getting thrown out of the house over and Cass—who was fourteen and had no idea how to even get a work permit—gave up and sealed her heart forever against the man who'd abandoned her to this fate.

And now this man, this old craggy man her father had somehow become, was actually crying, his cheeks shiny in the flashlight glow. Suddenly that enraged Cass more than anything else.

"You don't, you *don't*," she gasped. "You don't get to *cry*."

She seized Ruthie and wrested her from his arms, her body floppy and hot and damp in sleep. Ruthie began to wail and went stiff in her arms, but Cass fought her, holding her tightly, and backed down the steps, away from Red, away from her father.

"Stay away from us." Her voice rose to a wail, rusty and choked with sobs. "Just—just stay *away*."

She picked up Ruthie's Tinker Bell pack, the glittery wings shimmering in the dark.

Then she turned and ran.

20

Sammi was doing her best to keep her shit together, but it felt like she was becoming unglued from the inside. Sage was over talking to Phillip through the slits in the windows and refused to come back to the house. Colton was nowhere to be found. And there was something wrong with Kyra. She wouldn't get off the bed, wouldn't help pack, wouldn't even tell Sammi what was wrong. She just sat on the bed with her knees pulled up as far as she could, her arms wrapped around her legs, rocking and sniffling.

Sammi had a duffel on wheels, the sort of thing she would never have been caught dead with Before. It looked like something her dad took back when he traveled for business, back before he went through the mother of all midlife crises. Back then, her dad had the start of a beer gut, a stupid haircut that he put gel on, and he wore golf shirts with logos from all these different country clubs even though he never had time to play golf.

Hell, Valerie wouldn't even recognize him. Which was weird. Sammi would have figured someone like Valerie would have liked the old version of her dad a lot more than what he was like now. Sure, he was a lot more buff these days, but then again everyone was at least kind of cut, everyone who survived, anyway.

Valerie and her dad…Sammi could just see them the way they would have been a year or two ago. Valerie probably would look about the same, with her stupid skirts that hit her at the least flattering possible place on her leg, her sensible shoes and her headbands. She had good hair, it was true, and a great figure, but she did her best to hide it all. Her dad never would have asked her out. Although…the truth was that Sammi had never seen any of the women her dad dated, other than her Spanish teacher. All she had to go on was her mom's commentary on the subject, and her mom was pretty bitter.

And Cass—Cass would *never* have looked at her dad before. Cass was so…what was the word, anyway? Sammi used to think she could be really nice, when you were alone with her. She could make you think she was listening, really listening, and not condescending. But maybe all that was was her lame attempt to make Sammi like her because she had a thing for her dad all along.

Except…back when they first met, Cass was with Smoke. She was *still* with Smoke, wasn't she? Supposed to be, anyway.

Sammi clenched the stack of underwear in her hand. She had given up trying to talk to Kyra, and was packing for her. Her own bag was ready, and she'd jammed lightweight stuff as far down as she could, leaving room for whatever she could scavenge from the storehouse. Those idiots had better have it open—Sammi wasn't about to count on the whole commie sharing system to make sure she got what she needed. You could see how fast that was breaking down—she'd heard them all arguing earlier. But what could you expect?

Back in honors English, they'd read this book by a guy whose motto was "Don't trust anyone over thirty." Sammi figured you might as well make it twenty. Luddy and Cheddar and those guys, they were what, twenty-five, twenty-seven, and they were all fuckups. Before, they would probably have been homeless or living in communes or something. Hell, they'd probably be the first ones to get picked off by Beaters when the shit hit the fan. They'd be throwing their stupid Frisbee around at the back of the pack and *bam!* that would be it.

Well, Sammi wasn't going to let anything like that happen to her. She'd already survived one full-on attack—right before Cass and her dad showed up in Colima, she'd escaped on her own, and she'd nearly made it, too, only a nest of the things had woken up and sniffed her out. But she'd nailed a few of them with this piece of wood she'd yanked off a porch—it had nails sticking out of the end. It was the perfect weapon—she still remembered how it felt making contact with their stupid zombie heads. Somehow both hard and soft, like a melon split open. She was sure she had killed at least one, and maybe more.

Sammi realized she was holding Kyra's clothes so tightly that her hands had gone white. And she was starting to shake, too. Right now, thinking about the zombies, remembering the sounds they made and Cass screaming her name as she came running—yeah, so she'd come to help her, driven that truck of hers straight into a Beater nightmare when she could have just hit the road and never come back, okay, Cass had done at least that for her—right now she was about ten times more afraid than she'd been that night. Which didn't make any sense at all.

And she wanted her dad.

And…she really, really wanted her mom. But her mom was dead.

"Kyra!" Sammi snapped, a lot meaner than she meant to.

Kyra turned her slightly unfocused dark eyes her way. "What…" she mumbled, but at least she stopped rocking.

"I've got your underwear, your leggings, your thermal shirt. What else do you want?" She held up a couple of T-shirts, emblazoned with band logos.

Kyra bit her lip, twisting it around, and Sammi felt a little reassured because it was an expression that went back as far as she had known Kyra. "Hothouse Shears," she said.

"Okay," Sammi said, hiding her relief. "I could have guessed. That and Stacy Faith, that's all you ever wear."

"That's all that *fits*," Kyra said, and lumbered off the bed. "I'm getting fucking *huge*."

She peered into her pack, a black one with silver-and-gray trim.

"I can trade if you want," Sammi said. "Mine's probably easier, with the wheels and all."

Kyra shrugged. "I think they're gonna let me ride.

At least part of the time, me and the other knocked-up girls."

Other than Jasmine, that club included Leslie and Roan, both of whom had been impregnated at the Rebuilders' baby farm and escaped with Sammi when her dad and Cass came for her. They were cool and all, but since they were almost ten years older than Sammi and Kyra and Sage, it wasn't like they all hung out or whatever. Leslie and Roan shared a place at the north end of the island and they'd told Kyra she could live with them after her baby came, which pissed Sammi off because there were extra rooms at the House for Wayward Girls and if they all helped out, how hard would it be to raise the kid right here themselves?

But now that they were leaving New Eden, who knew what was going to happen. Poor Kyra—being pregnant for this trip was going to seriously suck. For one thing, Kyra still threw up sometimes, not near as bad as a while ago, but bad enough that she had days where she'd just lie around and moan. And she got these weird cramps that were supposedly kind of like labor, but not really real labor, which was a good thing because Sammi was *not* interested in being any kind of emergency midwife.

Although, if push came to shove, she'd do it. She'd do anything for her best friends. They were her family now.

"Girls!"

Zihna hurried into the room, her face flushed and her T-shirt damp with sweat under the arms. Sammi felt a twinge of guilt—she'd been so busy trying to get Kyra moving that she hadn't even offered to help Zihna and Red. Speaking of which, where had they been? After the Beaters finally went home, everyone kind of split up and went off to prepare for the evacuation. Dana made some sort of pronouncement, but no one was really listening—it was pretty clear what had to happen. How hard was it to understand what the priorities were? Anyone who stuck around the island tomorrow was going to be treated to the world's most terrifying swimming lesson, and then end up served for dinner.

Zihna stood with her hands on her hips and scanned the room quickly. "Okay, I'm going to go get Sage and then I want you two to come wait with me. You can sleep down there, by the water, but I want us all to be ready to move when the time comes."

"Where's Red?" Kyra asked.

"He had a little personal errand," Zihna said.

Suddenly the room lit up with a flash of searing white light.

"What the hell!" Kyra knocked over the glass of water on her bedside table, and the wet stain spread out into an amorphous shape on the carpet.

"Flares," said Zihna. "Sorry. I was just about to tell you about that. They're trying to alert any nearby shelters."

"Why the hell are they using *flares?*" Sammi demanded. "Isn't that like a giant neon sign that says, 'Hey, zombies, over here, come eat us'?"

Zihna shook her head. "Not according to Booth and them. He says they only respond to sustained light. It's the pupil thing—a flash like that supposedly just makes them dilate more."

"I think he's a fake," Kyra muttered. Booth—Phil Booth, formerly a high-school teacher from Sonora—had supposedly made a study of the Beaters before finding his way to New Eden. He told stories of experiments he'd conducted with a couple of other academics, one of them on the epidemiology staff at a hospital there. The only problem was that depending on the night and who was listening, his stories tended to shift. Often, he was featured as the guy who heroically stepped in when things went horribly wrong.

Which was a little hard to swallow given the fact that Booth was a hundred-ten soaking wet, pale and practically hairless, more of a geek than a hero. Also, there was the problem of Booth's missing colleagues; depending on the story they'd either died in a huge battle—from which Booth alone emerged unscathed—or gone to the west and north, the three of them having made a pact to spread their findings to whatever civilization they stumbled across.

"But why are they trying to get the other shelters involved?"

Zihna spoke carefully, which was her habit when any of them was upset. She wasn't the huggy sort. Though old enough to be a grandmother, she was hardly a grandmotherly kind of woman. She showed her concern mostly in the way she took the time to think first and avoided saying anything that could be misconstrued. "I believe there was some hope that other communities…where they might have avoided the attention of Beaters in these large numbers…might see the signal and come help."

"Help with what? Help us fold our underwear?" Fear was making Sammi sarcastic, and she wished she could stop yelling, but there was only one person who could calm her down fast anymore, now that Jed was gone, and that was her dad. She was still furious with him, but he'd always had a way of talking to her that made things seem like they would work out.

Zihna paled. The girls had lit half a dozen candles from their stockpile, enough to illuminate the entire room, and in the light of the candles you could see every wrinkle, every valley on the woman's face. At other times, Sammi thought Zihna pretty for an older lady; she wore her hair long and loose and smiled a lot, not in a fakey way like Collette Portescue and the rest of those uptight bitches.

But tonight Zihna just looked old.

"Help us with the, uh, departure. We can't leave until there's enough light for us to see where we're going, but hopefully still before the Beaters are up and out. But we're bound to run into them soon after that. All it's going to take is stumbling on a nest of them, and they'll start up their hollering and get the others all riled up. I think that—the thought of some of the council was that if some folks came from Hollis or Oakton, they could give us a sort of escort until we got out to the truly uninhabited land. Once we get there, we can handle the occasional pack ourselves. It's only the first few miles that have everyone worried."

"Wow, was there, like, a whole meeting or something we missed?" Sammi asked, gathering a handful of cosmetics and jamming them into an old plastic zip-around tote that had once been a Clinique gift with purchase.

A third flare went off and Sammi dropped the tote, spilling tiny tubes and bottles onto the floor. A round eyeshadow rolled across the carpet and bumped into Kyra's leg. "Shit," she whispered. "Fucking shitballs with lint."

But she looked like she was about to cry. Sammi

crab walked over to her and pulled her into a hug on the carpet, realizing too late she was sitting on the water spot. Oh, well. That probably wasn't the worst thing that was going to happen today. Or tonight or tomorrow or whatever it was.

"What time is it, anyway?" she asked Zihna.

Zihna, who wore a watch all the time, an old-fashioned one with tiny delicate hands that pointed to the numerals, squinted at her wrist. "Nearly three. Three hours until dawn. Think you girls can catch a little sleep once you get down to the shore? I promise, we won't leave without you."

"Are you sure? I mean, don't you want one of us to keep you company or take turns or something?"

"Aw, no, honey," Zihna said. "Red and me, we've got it covered. We're a team, right? I mean…Sammi, you know we want you if you want to join us."

Sammi realized what she was half asking: if she planned to walk with her dad—or stay with Zihna and Red and her friends.

"A team," she repeated quickly, before she could change her mind.

21

Cass had the foresight to go back for the stroller, hoping she'd get to it before Suzanne or Ingrid and then feeling guilty about the thought. The stroller was exactly where she'd left it earlier in the evening, abandoned in the middle of the yard, and Cass realized how lucky she was that no one had taken it. It would make a great little cart, for someone who wanted to transport food, belongings, anything at all—up to seventy pounds, according to the government label engraved on the side, something she'd never given much thought to before because Ruthie didn't weigh a fraction of that.

Ruthie had settled down after the encounter with Red, a lot more than Cass anyway, whose nerves were still jangling.

I'm your dad, Cassie

She was in a state of shock and denial, but there

would be plenty of time to sort it all out on the journey. More than enough time.

Out of nowhere, Cass thought of a picture book a babysitter had once given Ruthie—a children's Bible, illustrated with watercolors in pale, weak colors. Moses crossing the Red Sea looked more like Moses wading through a forest of camellia blooms, his placid smile making him and the Israelites all appear stoned. Still, Ruthie had loved the story and liked to point to the people in the pictures and try to repeat the names Cass read to her.

Moses, Pharaoh, Jethro, Zipporah

And now her dad, Red whoever-the-fuck he was calling himself these days, wanted to come and lead them to a promised land. Hell, he wanted to be her dad again all of a sudden. But it was too late for that, too late by a long shot. And if Cass had to make some harsh decisions to protect Ruthie the way Mim ought to have protected her, well, so be it—she had fought harder for less. Twenty years was a long time, and her father was a stranger to her, and she would not trust her daughter with him. All she had to do now was keep saying no, and she figured she could more than handle that.

She settled Ruthie into the stroller after wiping the chilly dew from its interior with her bare hands, then wiping her hands on her pants. Her pants were not clean, her laundry day was Tuesday; if the Beaters had waited a few more days to come fuck with them at least Cass would have started the odyssey with clean pants. Oh well.

Cass pushed the stroller toward the hospital, trying to narrow and focus her thoughts. If Smoke had made it out of the hospital building, all the way up the path to the yard, halfway down to the water—then surely she could convince the council that he was healing quickly enough to justify bringing him along. She would be responsible for him. All they needed was one seat in one of the cars, Cass would walk alongside, she would push Ruthie and carry their belongings and it would all work out fine.

But when she got to the hospital it was dark. She parked the stroller, behind a rain barrel, and picked Ruthie up before she went inside, but she knew the minute she set foot in the place that it was deserted. And sure enough—there, in the light coming through the windows, the light of the hundreds of candles and flashlights being squandered tonight—there was Smoke's empty bed, the covers clumsily folded, the pillow on top.

Cass went into the other room. There in that narrow bed with the crayon drawings that Ruthie and Twyla and Dane had made, pinned up on the walls behind the headboard—there was where Charles had suffered through his waning and finally unconscious days.

Cass would be hard-pressed to denounce the men who dragged him to the southern end of Garden Island and did what needed to be done. In fact, maybe it was a heroic act, stopping his suffering a little prematurely so he did not have to endure one more horror.

But not for a body on the mend, like Smoke. Sun-hi must have found passage for him, must have gotten him down to the vehicles somehow. She and Ruthie would ask around, find out where they were, maybe even get a little sleep before dawn; perhaps they could pass the night in the car with him, or barring that, at least they could bed down close by and be there at his side when the group rolled out at sunrise.

Cass came out of the hospital and deposited Ruthie back in the stroller—she whimpered, no doubt tired of all the repeated resettling—and when she stood back up, she was startled to see Suzanne standing several paces away, her arms folded across her chest.

"Oh, Suzanne…" Cass's heart fell. Not now, she was not prepared to deal with this now. "I took a few things from the house, for Ruthie. Just things she had in her room. I would have checked with you guys first, but—"

"Do you honestly think I care about a few toys now? When we're about to…" Suzanne's face crumpled in on itself but with a tremendous effort she righted it, her jaw working and worry lines appearing between her eyebrows. "I just… I have been very angry at you, Cass, and I resent everything you've—all the risk you've brought us and the children."

"I know, I know, I wish I could. I wish—I've just been so—"

"Shut up, shut up just for a minute. I'm here because—well, I don't know why I'm here, only I thought you should know." Suzanne took a deep breath and hugged herself tighter against the chill. "They took Smoke. After they took Charles down there and, you know, and drowned him, they came back for Smoke. About ten minutes ago. I saw you over on the porch talking to Red. I should have come then. I just—I just want you to understand, I—"

"Where?" Adrenaline surged through Cass's veins, clutching at her heart. "Which way?"

"Down the east way." Suzanne pointed, her tone still

defiant. "I would have told you right away, but after everything you've put the rest of us through—"

But Cass was already gone, careening down the path, pushing the stroller with its big rubber wheels absorbing the bumps. Ruthie sputtered as she bounced along, but Cass had secured the straps and she was held tight in place.

How could they justify this? Charles had been as good as dead anyway; they'd only hastened the end, saved the poor man from a final battle that he'd be the first casualty of anyway. But Smoke—he was getting better. He'd made it across the lawn, hadn't he? He'd spoken her name, touched her, talked to her.

Cass swung the arc of the flashlight back and forth wildly. So they'd know she was coming—so what? She might surprise them before they began their task, and then they'd have to deal with her before they finished him off.

There—up in the gray sedge growing along the bank. Cass had transplanted it herself in an effort to stem erosion and the plants had thrived, and they were thigh-high now, so it took her a minute to make out the figure of a man struggling with another on the ground. When the flashlight beam hit him, he wheeled around and held up a hand to shield his eyes. Cass stumbled over a clump of reeds and nearly went down, but the stroller's weight steadied her and she found her footing and stared in shock at the scene in front of her.

Smoke clutched the shirtfront of a man who was kneeling in the dirt. The man's chin bobbed against his chest and blood saturated his tan shirt and fleece vest. More blood coursed over Smoke's hand and fell to the earth.

Milt. Oh God, it was Milt Secco and if he wasn't dead already he would be soon. All that blood…Cass put a hand to her mouth.

"What happened?"

"Cass," he said, and dropped the limp body. It fell gracelessly, facedown, legs splayed.

Smoke stood painfully and hobbled toward her. He looked at his hands and seemed surprised to see all the blood there, and stood awkwardly holding them at his sides.

That's when Cass noticed the other body, half-submerged in the river, also facedown, its head at an angle that suggested a neck broken. But Cass knew that red parka. It belonged to Jack.

"Oh my God," she whispered. "You killed them both?"

"They were going to kill me. Drown me. They told me—I had to." Smoke's leg buckled as though it would go out under him and Cass rushed to help him, draping his arm over her shoulder. He was warm, even through his bloody clothes, so warm. "They said I ought to thank them. What the hell is going on in this place?"

"Oh, Smoke," Cass said softly. "What are we going to do…"

Behind them—across the fields she'd so carefully tended, the kaysev that both nourished them all and hid a traitorous poison within its cells—there was frantic activity, fear, the shadow of death waiting for them and gnashing hungry teeth. But here in this moment it was just the two of them.

"I can't believe it's you," Smoke said, his words slurred against her neck.

Cass could not find her voice to respond. There was so much to tell him, and no time at all to do it.

"What day is it?" he asked.

"February sixteenth."

"I've been gone for…"

"Almost three months. We came a few days after you left the Box. After…what happened to you. Do you remember?"

He was silent for a moment, and then he pulled back and stared down into her eyes. He touched her cheek with the hand that was missing part of his fingers, but his touch was as gentle as ever.

"I remember most of it. I remember…the ones who burned the school, I think I got at least one of them, maybe two."

"Two. And one died later." His mission of vengeance, completed before he fell. "You killed them all, Smoke."

The bitterness she'd felt at the trade he had made—risking his life for the momentary sweetness of revenge—was lifting. She'd hated Smoke the day he left the Box with nothing on his mind but finding and killing those who had murdered his old lover and the rest of his old community. At the time, Cass thought his wrath was proof that he loved them all more than he loved her and Ruthie. Now, in his arms, she understood that the truth was far more complicated than that—that his hatred had not been more powerful after all.

"I don't remember after, though," he said. "I've tried. A million times, in that place. That jail. Where are we, Cass?"

There was no way to explain it all to him now. And far off in the east, a thin line of azure tinged with pink signaled the coming of dawn. There was blood on their clothes, and two men lay dead at their feet.

"We're at a place we have to leave. I'll tell you everything," she promised. "But for now, we've got to get back and get ready."

"Ready for what?"

Cass looked across the inky waters, to the shore where the beach was choked with matted dead weeds. Not so long ago, people had anchored their boats there, set up their pop tents and their portable grills, their coolers and their lawn chairs, and whiled away long afternoons scented with sunscreen and charcoal. Children waded and splashed, teens swam across to the island, old folks watched the scene from under the shade of their sun hats.

"Ready to travel," Cass said sadly. "Again."

Happiness had once dwelled in that humble little strip of land. In the morning, the Beaters would be back, and perhaps they would trudge across that sand in their fetid rotting shoes, into the water they'd only yesterday learned to navigate, and follow the yearning that was the only emotion they had left. If any of them had been to this place before they turned, if they'd water-skied these waters or drunk pitchers of icy lemonade or read the latest romance novel or stolen a kiss under an umbrella, that memory was as lost to them as the ability to speak or love.

22

Red saw them coming, the man limping along with his
arm around his daughter, who was somehow manag-
ing to push one of those funny-looking three-wheeled
strollers at the same time. The man walked like he was
about to collapse, leaning on Cass for support.

So this is how they were to meet. Red had imagined
this day a hundred different ways, but never like this.
Red would call for Zihna. She was good at this sort of
thing. He knew the only reason Cassie had come to him
was that she had no other choice, and he accepted that.
But this was a start.

The trailer, a little single-axle flatbed utility model
with a handle he'd rigged from an old ski rope, was as
comfortable as he could make it. Earlier, Craig Switzer and a few of his friends had come by and tried to
talk him out of it, and when he didn't budge, the talk
had turned ugly.

"What are you fixin' to do, haul your guitars and shit along when there's people to be fed? We could get a hell of a lot of water and supplies on that thing," Craig said, eyeing the trailer with a calculating expression. What brave Craig didn't know was that Zihna was in the next room, cleaning their guns. He didn't know what a good shot Zihna was. Well, there was a reason Red had taught her in private. A man would have to be a fool not to see that a day like this was coming—and he'd have to be a coward not to take precautions to protect the ones he loved.

Red had been exactly such a coward for most of his life. But no more.

No more.

"And who's going to decide that, brother?" he asked softly, hand on his belt, where a holster he'd carefully modified over several long winter afternoons hid not one but two blades, each of them specialized, each of them very, very comfortable in his hand. "You? Because last I heard, no one had nominated any of you clowns for council."

An ugly grin spread across Craig's face. Behind him, his friends giggled and shuffled. Red knew that Mario had been caught trying to break into the storehouse at least once. No formal punishment had been meted out, since there was no proof to contradict his story that he'd been simply seeking a Band-Aid for a woman who had cut herself on a paring knife. But a lingering pall of suspicion had followed him ever since.

"Council's in for some changes, I bet," Craig said. "Give it a week or two, there'll be all manner of staff changes, resignations…attrition…what have you."

"I imagine you're right," Red said, his mild tone hiding a growing anger. "Why don't we wait until then and reconvene this discussion again. Meantime, my wife and I have our own plans for our property, and I'll thank you to respect that, and be on your way."

The men stayed only for a moment more, looking around the garage, no doubt trying to see if there was anything worth taking. There was not—Zihna had helped the girls pack and sent them on ahead to the docks, where everyone was assembling.

"Wife, huh," the dullest of the three, Tanner Mobley, said over his shoulder as they sauntered away. "You all have you a proper wedding I didn't get invited to?"

"Indeed," Red said, folding his arms over his chest and watching them go.

No, he and Zihna had never had a ceremony. They'd met after Red had nearly given up on life, seven months ago. Red had in mind to hang himself in a neatly tended trilevel house on the outskirts of Bakersfield. Who knew why he chose that house from the dozen on that block—but when he went inside looking for a rope or a belt or even a sheet he could rip into strips, instead he found Zihna sitting calmly at the kitchen table, shelling kaysev beans.

He couldn't believe his eyes. He had been wandering for days, and he hadn't bothered to eat or drink much since survival had ceased to be a goal. He wondered if she was an angel, sent to welcome him to the next world, the one where he could start forgetting all the things that he'd done wrong in this one.

But she wasn't an angel. And she had no plans to allow him to forget or escape anything at all. Instead, she guided him back. He owed her everything, and had pledged her everything. Where before there had been a broken man and a proud woman, now there was a union that meant more to Red than anything on this earth, aside from his daughter.

If that didn't make Zihna his wife, no vow or ceremony or holy man on this earth would either.

Now, as dawn waited just over the horizon, he waited with an old wool blanket over his lap and watched his daughter slowly approach. When they were within a few yards of his front door, Red cleared his throat.

"Cassie, I'm glad to see you. And your friend."

Cass saw him then, and the door opened behind him and Zihna came out, carrying a lantern. The porch was lit up and they could see the wounded man clearly. Zihna saw him every day, of course, but it was not Red's habit to come inside the hospital where she worked. Red couldn't abide hospitals, not even now. So the face of the man his daughter loved was new to him.

He knew the stories, of course. Well, maybe the man was a hero. Maybe not. Time would tell. For now, though, Red owed him courtesy. He'd watch him like a hawk, and if Smoke made his daughter happy, then he could stay.

He stood up with his hand extended. Smoke regarded him with unfocused eyes and it took him three tries to lift his hand high enough to shake. He looked like he was about to pass out on the spot.

"Welcome," Red said gravely.

In his mind, he added, *Watch yourself.*

23

Sammi followed the sound of her father's voice without getting up from the spot they'd claimed, their backs against the bridge supports where they took root fifty feet inland. The road rose above the ground there and was in pretty good shape for Aftertime. Someone must have kept it in good repair, Before.

Sage was sitting next to her, finally asleep, dozing with her head on Sammi's shoulder, and Kyra was sleeping at their feet wrapped up in a blanket. A little while ago Roan and Leslie and Jasmine had stopped by to see if Kyra wanted to go with them, but she and Sammi had barely managed to get Sage to come with them, practically dragging her away from the quarantine house, and Kyra had absently told them, thanks maybe later.

It was too weird to think of her with Jasmine, who had to be the oldest pregnant woman Sammi'd ever met—she was well over forty, anyway. What would she and Kyra even talk about? She could be Kyra's mom, easy.

Before Kyra fell asleep she told Sammi to make sure they stuck together, and Sammi was going to do that, though she was secretly worried about whether Kyra ought to be walking so much. But then again, who knew how far they were even going to go? Maybe they'd find the perfect shelter in a day or something. It was unlikely: rumor was that Nathan and some others had driven out to all the known shelters within thirty miles that were still reachable—many of the major roads were impassable, clogged with wrecks—and none had room, or the desire, to add on a group of their size. But it wasn't impossible, right? They could split up, if they had to, find somewhere like the first shelter Sammi'd lived in, back when her mom and Jed were still alive. The school had been fine. It wasn't like New Eden, where there were no high walls, nothing to separate them from the rest of the world but the river, but it had been all right. In fact, she missed it in some ways. Missed how small it was, how she knew everything about everyone, how everyone always asked her how she was doing.

She'd been a child there, still. It had been a long while since she felt like that.

Her father was going around talking to people about what they wanted to bring along. He was acting like some kind of expert, like someone had put him in charge. Like he was king of the council all of a sudden, when last week he was digging a new trench for the latrines. Sammi knew—she'd seen the way people talked to her dad, like they thought they were better than him. It was a long way from when her dad was a big financial trader, that was for sure. Somehow, here in New Eden where there were rules for everything, her dad never really fit in. Even when he took up with Valerie—and everyone liked Valerie, she was so perky and perfect—people still didn't warm up to him. And if Sammi was really, really honest with herself, that had hurt. *He's not perfect,* she wanted to tell people, *but you have to know him like I know him.*

Only, then she'd seen another side of him and decided she didn't really know him at all. It started with him getting all overprotective, after not giving a shit what she did or where she went for all those years. It was like he wanted to keep her locked up all the time. Her mom had been protective, but at least she had reasons, at least she'd been like that as long as Sammi could remember. With her dad it was just stupid. And then, seeing him and Cass together—as though nothing else mattered, not her, not Valerie, not the job he was supposed to be doing.

But now he was like some kind of hero, going around and talking to people, and everyone wanting to know his opinion. All because of what he'd done today, him and Cass, going out in the boat and shooting all those Beaters. Sammi didn't know exactly how she felt about that. She'd been watching out the window of the community center with Kalyan when they first set out in the canoe, and she'd been so scared she didn't have actual thoughts but just a crazy buzzing spin of fear that didn't go away until they were back onshore.

For a while there, when her dad and Cass were helping Glynnis and John, giving them the ammo or whatever, it looked like they were all screwed for sure. There were just so many of them. It got to the point where Sammi couldn't bear to look. She turned away from the window and Kalyan put a hand on her shoulder and she went very still until he got the message and went away and then Sage came up and wrapped her arms around Sammi and told her everything that was happening in a soft voice: "They're paddling upriver…Cass has this one gun where you have to hold it with two hands… damn, she nailed that one…oh shit, there's—no, she got that one too.…"

Sage kept that up until the Beaters retreated and her dad turned the canoe around and only then did Sammi stop shaking and find the courage to look again.

Now she listened to her dad talking and tried to find in his voice the man she most missed. But this was more like the dad he used to be before he moved out. He used to order her mom around, not in an asshole way but in a way like he was just used to being in charge. It wasn't like her mom put up with it anyway; she always did whatever she wanted. Maybe that was what finally broke them up, they both had "boss" personalities. He used to tell Sammi what to do all the time too, but, back then, she mostly didn't mind because he liked to spend time with her and they had their own things they did, just the two of them, like watching reality shows together and yelling at the TV, or going out for Gizmos Garlic Fries whenever they got a craving.

"Sure, sure," he was telling the Patels, one of those rare intact fairy-tale couples from Before who clung all the more firmly to each other in the face of all the dangers around them. "I know you want to take all your family stuff. But you're really going to have to pare it down. See if you can get it into just this one suitcase here, the one with the wheels, and I'll be back in a while to see how you're doing."

And then he was on to the next group.

Sammi hadn't seen Cass at all tonight, since she came to get Ruthie. She hadn't come down to the shore with piles of bags, like almost everyone else on the island. For a second Sammi wondered: the decision she'd made, to tell Mr. Swarmer about her drinking

All she'd wanted…what *had* she wanted, anyway? At the time it had seemed pretty clear. Cass was drinking, everyone knew it—well, maybe not everybody, but the other women in the Mothers' House for sure knew about it because Jasmine had told Roan, and Roan told Kyra, and Kyra told them. In the Mothers' House they weren't happy about it, not by a long stretch, and supposedly they'd had a come-to-Jesus meeting where they told Cass if she ever drank while she was watching the kids she was not only out of the babysitting rotation but out of the house too. Somehow they all seemed to believe Cass only drank late at night. But that wasn't very likely, was it? Addicts were…well, the only ones Sammi knew, maybe they weren't addicts, technically, meaning by whatever rules or whatever these things were determined, but the girls at school who were stoners and pill poppers and the ones who brought vodka to school in water bottles?—they were for sure doing it during the day, despite Grosbeck Academy's zero-tolerance policy, and despite those letters they sent home assuring all the parents they had the best record on drug use of any private girls' school in Central California, which was a blatant lie, but then again that was part of what her parents used to pay Grosbeck twenty-five thousand bucks a year for, was to be lied to and feel good about it. They all wanted to believe it so they wouldn't have to acknowledge that they were too busy or didn't care enough to pay attention to their kids themselves.

And that's what was going on here too, right? The other mothers didn't want to lose Cass because they needed her to babysit. Jasmine would join in eventually, she was going to have the kid any day now, but she'd been on bed rest for weeks because she was so old and Sun-hi thought she shouldn't move around much. And after the baby came she'd be too busy to watch all the other kids for a while.

So they didn't want to lose Cass, so that meant some-one else had to be responsible and step up and say some-thing because it was just plain dangerous for her to be left with the kids. Which was why Sammi had gone to Mr. Swarmer.

Only.

If she'd really wanted to punish her, Sammi would have told Dana, not Mr. Swarmer. Underneath his whole "nobody's in charge here" thing, Dana totally thought he was in charge. He was always ordering peo-ple around and pretending he had the council behind him. Or maybe he did, but Sammi would bet he did a lot of behind-the-scenes ass-kissing and favor-trading and threatening to get his way.

And Dana was such a Goody Two-shoes. If he knew about Cass, he'd probably make an example of her, pub-licly humiliate her, like he did when they found Mitchell Keller stealing the box of cocoa mix off the raider cart. Dana had suggested public stocks. And while the coun-cil had voted that down, they had given the thumbs-up to the reparations chair. Mitchell had to sit there for two days, with a sign he'd written saying what he'd done and how he was sorry, and he wasn't allowed to say anything until the two days were done and then Dana made a big deal about forgiving him in a big speech up on the steps of the community center.

All over a box of cocoa mix. What would they do for something as serious as what Sammi told Mr. Swarmer?

Because she hadn't exactly said that Cass never drank on the job. She said she didn't know. Which was true, sort of, but really, Sammi knew Cass would never do anything to endanger a child. Especially Ruthie. No one could say that Cass didn't love her daughter, and even though Sammi was angrier than ever, if that was possible, about Cass and her dad, she was starting to feel a little guilty—okay, a lot guilty—about telling Mr. Swarmer that she "didn't know" what time of day Cass drank or who she got it from.

At least she hadn't told them the other thing. About how Cass and Ruthie had been infected. Sammi couldn't bring herself to spread that, knowing what she knew the immunity was super-rare but if you were immune, you weren't a danger to anyone. There were people in New Eden who'd completely freak if they knew, idiots who'd probably want Cass gone, just because she'd been sick in the past. And even angry, Sammi knew that going that far would be wrong.

Besides, if her dad found out she'd talked to Mr. Swarmer, he'd probably be furious. He could be such a bastard but he was kind of rigid about right and wrong, at least his version of right and wrong. He'd be all over her about lying, even though he'd been lying to Valerie all along—one look at her tearstained, puffy face when she came by earlier with her friends made it clear she'd had no idea about Cass. But what went on between adults, *that* way, was a private matter. The council would probably all disapprove—and given what a bunch of tight-ass losers they were, she guessed they'd disapprove a *lot*—but there was nothing they could actually do about it.

Besides…if Sammi told people about that, then her dad would be implicated too. And Sammi wasn't ready to take that step. She hated him, true, but he was all the family she had left, and he'd do anything for her, to keep her safe. She couldn't let go of that right now. Maybe if Jed was still around…but no. Jed was dead.

So she couldn't bring herself to hurt her dad, and she had a ready-made way to hurt Cass, and that was what she had done, and at first it had felt really good, to imagine Cass getting her wrists slapped, having everyone spying on her all the time to make sure she wasn't drinking, and if they were watching Cass like a hawk then she'd sure have a hard time sneaking out to meet her dad, right, which was a win for everyone….

Except Sammi was starting to think she'd made a mistake. A big one.

Half an hour ago Ingrid and Suzanne had come by with Jasmine between them and Twyla holding Dane's and Dirk's hands, and Elsa had been with them and they were talking about a car. A car for the moms with little kids, and Jasmine, who was ready to pop. So that was what, three adults and three kids, which was a full car right there.

And no one said anything about Cass and Ruthie. Which meant they weren't getting a ride, even though they had every bit as much of a right as the others— or they would have, anyway, if Sammi hadn't started a rumor that might not even be all the way true.

And that still wasn't any big deal because Sammi

knew, deep down inside, that come morning it was going to be basically everyone for themselves. Sure, there'd be a lot of talk about sticking together, and the smartest people *would* figure out ways to stay in groups, while it suited them, but in the end they'd all have to fend for themselves. Everyone would be so focused on saving their own asses there wouldn't be much left over for taking care of anyone else. People would get left, abandoned. Discarded. But at least in that regard, Cass was in better shape than most. Despite her drinking thing she was strong and fit and brave and healthy.

But then there was Ruthie…

Ruthie wasn't like other little kids. She spooked kind of easy, and then she went quiet, really quiet, like she thought if she played invisible the problem would go away. In the community center earlier tonight, when Cass left to help her dad, Ruthie wrapped her arms so tight around Sammi's neck that she was almost strangling her. She put her little face against Sammi's and made a tiny little whimpering sound. Ruthie was not strong, not the way you had to be to get through what lay ahead. And she was only three. *Three.*

What if the thing that Sammi had done had condemned both of them? What if it was her fault that they wouldn't get to ride tomorrow, safe inside a car, protected by all that steel and—as long as the gas held out—able to outrun the Beaters?

Down by her feet, Kyra turned over and sighed unconsciously. Sammi couldn't believe anyone could sleep through this, and Sage was leaning all her weight against Sammi, and if she didn't move soon both of Sammi's legs were going to go to sleep. Carefully, slowly, she eased Sage off her and scooted down next to Kyra. Still neither of them woke up.

Sammi wanted to walk, to shake out her legs and work off some of this excess energy. The boys were down helping pile things up and load the vehicles; she wished she was with them. Helping out, keeping her mind off things. Or maybe going for a walk with Colton, one last trip around the island, just to say goodbye—although Colton had been acting weird for a few weeks, hanging around with Shane and that creeper Owen Mason, the guy who grew weed and taught them how to roll. Owen liked to get high, but he liked fires even more—the only useful thing he ever did was to tend the bonfires whenever there was a celebration. There were rumors that he liked fires too much. That he'd set the brush fires up on North Island.

Owen was the kind of guy who—and Sammi knew it was wrong even to think it—you wouldn't mind if he'd died in the Siege. The kind of guy who made everyone nervous, even if he held a certain kind of fascination, at least for Colton and the other boys, with his personal stash of drug paraphernalia and weird martial-arts weapons and who knew what else.

Sammi hadn't seen the boys at all since Phillip got locked up, come to think of it. And it made her uneasy, wondering if they were with Owen.

But she didn't want to leave Sage and Kyra alone. She felt responsible. This was new, and Sammi wasn't sure she liked it—feeling accountable for people. Her friends…and Ruthie, and Cass. It had been so much easier back when nobody expected much from her at all, when she was just an ordinary kid who was bratty to her parents and maybe a little spoiled, who loved soccer and listening to music and painting her nails and shopping, who wasn't responsible for anything but keeping curfew and getting her homework done, and half the time she didn't even manage that, but it never mattered back then.

Now it mattered, the things she did mattered. Or maybe they didn't. In a couple of hours the sun would rise and they would all set out. It would be their last day on earth or it wouldn't, and Sammi had watched enough people die to know that none of it was in her control anyway.

Sammi looked around one last time at everyone rushing around in the dark. She sighed and let her eyelids flutter closed, and thought about Jed, about the way they used to stay up talking until they were so tired they fell asleep in the middle of their sentences. After a few minutes she stretched out her legs to get more comfortable, and snuggled a little closer to Sage.

Just resting. Just for a few minutes.

It had been Zihna's idea to wait until they heard the sound of engines turning over, of the procession starting out. This way, they'd avoid any more of the others' logistical arguments on the way off the island. By then, presumably, everything would have been worked out—who was riding with whom, who was going to be left behind.

There was the matter of the two dead. Cass had told Red only that they had been trying to drown Smoke. Red was mystified about how an injured, unarmed man could kill two healthy ones, but Cass was not in a mood to talk. In fact, that was the last thing she'd said to him after they'd agreed that Smoke would ride with Ruthie on the trailer and the other three would take turns pulling it.

Red was a little concerned about that. He was in a lot better shape than he looked. He might not be able to erase the effects on his face from all those years on the road, but his body had certainly benefited from several years of his abstemious new life. No drinking or smoking even before the Siege, and the construction work he'd picked up to supplement his income had hardened him. On the island he kept busy. He and Zihna did yoga together, and she could make him break a sweat practicing the most innocuous-looking poses.

The thought made him smile. He and his lovely woman—they had a few surprises in them yet. But still, they were both in their late fifties. Roaming like a bunch of nomads with no camel probably wasn't AMA-sanctioned exercise in their case.

But it would be what it would be. He had Zihna, he had Cass, he had his granddaughter—a *granddaughter!* How the word could still bring him fresh, amazed, pure joy—and, though perhaps more problematic, he had a fallen hero of the Resistance. A resistance to a Rebuilder movement that no longer existed, but still.

Red had taken a little nap earlier, but at the first sign of dawn, Zihna woke him. Smoke and Cass were napping on the trailer with the little girl between them. They'd moved the trailer to the space between the house and the detached garage, which was hidden from the path by a lattice covered with dead vines. If Craig and the rest came back—or anyone else, for that matter—their hiding place was far from perfect, but it beat waiting in the garage like lame ducks.

Zihna'd handed him a glass of water and reminded

him to drink it all, and then she settled into the lawn chair he'd dragged in for her and immediately went to sleep with her hands folded over her stomach. It was one of her gifts, this ability to control her breathing and her worries; she'd been working on it since she started teaching yoga all the way back in the nineties.

Red was not nearly as good at serenity. He could feel his heart accelerating with anxiety as the sky started to lighten.

It wasn't long before he heard the rumble of the first car. The rest followed, until the earth thrummed with the rhythm of the engines. Half a dozen vehicles, when you'd heard so few for so long, suddenly sounded like a busy interstate. Red was on his feet in seconds, remembering a motel he once crashed in for a few weeks in San Diego that backed up to the highway; night and day the earth reverberated with the traffic going by. It used to help him sleep, as a matter of fact, and when he moved on he missed it—but now the sound filled him with dread.

"Time to wake the women," a low voice said behind him. Red turned quickly and realized that he'd momentarily forgotten about their cargo, his daughter's injured lover. In the faint light of dawn, he found the man making his way to his feet painfully, slowly. But with his jaw-clenching determination, he did not look much like a victim today. He did not intend to be counted out.

Well. That was interesting.

"Yes, indeed, friend," Red answered, offering a hand to help Smoke. He was not surprised when it was ignored. So he was not to be the only dog in this race, after all.

Red allowed himself the smallest of smiles. He'd had

hundreds of friends through the years, though besides Carmy he couldn't name a single one who stuck or who he missed when the road beckoned and he moved on. Aftertime had brought all kinds of interesting times Red's way, forcing him to acknowledge things he'd fully expected to go to his grave without knowing.

He'd fully expected to protect these women all by himself. They'd hate the notion—Zihna would, at any rate, and he suspected that his daughter would too—and insist up and down that they could protect themselves just fine. But Red took his late-life transformation seriously and he was damn well going to be a man and take care of his own or go down trying.

He'd never anticipated that he'd have company. Surprisingly, the notion didn't leave him completely cold.

He hid his smile and clapped Smoke on the shoulder—carefully, since the guy was still looking a little tender.

"Let's get this show on the road."

Cass knew that Red—that her *father*—was right to wait, but it was damn hard to watch the procession go over the bridge, the vehicles in front followed by the walkers, dozens of people dragging suitcases and pushing shopping carts and baggage carts and in one case a wheelbarrow, carrying packs and gym bags and tote bags, and not feel the terrifying loneliness of being left behind. Ever since she arrived in New Eden, that bridge had been the symbol of safety, with the sturdy metal gate at the water's edge, its round-the-clock double staffing of armed guards. Seeing the gate open wide, the guard chairs empty, it chilled her. When the last of the pedestrians—Steve, that wasn't surprising, as well as a few other people who'd volunteered to form the rear guard behind the slowest walkers—had gone a hundred yards down the road toward Hollis, Red said softly, "Okay, now."

But before they could go more than a few feet Red stopped her.

"Wait," he whispered urgently, looking back toward the community center.

Cass saw it too, two lean figures racing from the wide-open French doors, across the yard, toward the bridge. One was Owen Mason, a hawk-faced man around thirty who raided occasionally and worked at a few other jobs on the island, none of them with much skill or attention; and wasn't that—it looked like one of the boys Sammi ran around with. As she watched, they caught up with the stragglers and melted into the back of the crowd. No one seemed to notice.

What had they been up to? If it had only been the boys, Cass might have thought they were saying good-bye to Phillip. Throughout the night people had been leaving things outside the quarantine house, magazines and mugs and T-shirts and dried flowers, a heartbreaking if macabre shrine to the feverish boy inside, who was probably incoherent by now, dementia taking over his brain as he picked at his skin and scalp. Sammi's friends were good kids, and all of them had been friends with Phillip. But Owen…she'd gotten a bad feeling about him from the start, and avoided him as much as she could. He was just…creepy.

A shout from the front of the crowd interrupted her thoughts. It was repeated, voices joining in, and in seconds it had gone from alarm to panic.

Beaters. It had to be.

They'd waited too long. The council had been wasting time, figuring that it was too dark to travel safely, and undoubtedly that was true—even if they'd used precious battery power they could not have safely covered any ground in such a large group in the darkness. But apparently, on this day, the dimmest glow of dawn was enough for the Beaters.

"What do we do?" Cass asked, hollow with fear. To the rear of the crowd, they were safe, perhaps, for a little longer. But they had Smoke. There was no way that he was ready to stand and fight—even if he could defend himself as well as anyone as long as he had a gun.

"We can't stay here." Red spoke quickly, firmly. "Anyone on this island is as good as dead, because there's no way to keep them from swimming across now."

"All right. Let's go." Zihna didn't hesitate. She pushed Ruthie's stroller with surprising speed, and Cass followed. The trailer moved easily and it was not at all difficult to pull across flat ground.

"Let me help," Smoke protested. In the early morning, after several hours' rest, he seemed more recovered than last night. He was sitting up in the trailer, surrounded by the cans and water bottles they'd packed, in a pile of mussed blankets.

Cass put her hands on his shoulders. "Hush now. Close your eyes. Rest. Please, Smoke, please just trust me this time. We can talk about it later."

"Go, go," Red urged.

They caught up with the group by the time they reached the bridge. But there was a problem: the people running back across in the other direction, back onto the island—June, Karen and then Collette, the ringleader of their little group, her hands raised to cover her ears as though she could protect herself by shutting out the screaming. They raced past, heading for the community center, and others followed.

The crowd had stalled on the other side of the bridge, people shifting around inside it strangely so that it was like a living organism, ebbing and flowing across the road, spilling over onto the land on either side. A cardboard box lay crushed, bright-colored fabric spilled out, the sleeve of a shirt flung out as if an invisible arm was pointing the way. Cass scanned the scene for Dor, for Sammi, but saw neither, and then she heard the cries above the din of the crowd.

There were five of them, standing together on the other side of the road, past the drainage ditch and the cattle fencing. They must have come across ragged land rather than by the pathway—and worse, they must have been making their way entirely by memory, instinct, smell, because in this light they would be essentially blind, only able to detect the most basic shapes. Judging by how the things clutched at each other and stumbled, they might have been seeing almost nothing at all.

Suddenly there was a deafening explosion behind the citizens on the bridge, followed by a second, smaller blast.

Cass spun around to see the community center in flames, the top of it blown clear off, debris swirling in a red-orange cloud. Behind it, the quarantine house was nothing but a pile of burning rubble. Someone staggered out the front of the community center and collapsed on the porch, hair on fire. The screaming grew even louder, the terrified crowd caught between the ruination of the island and the Beaters ahead.

"What the hell was that?" Cass demanded.

"Holy…who would have done such a thing?" Zihna said. "And how—where would they get the…"

"There were explosives in the storehouse," Red said

grimly. "Someone must have gotten into them, after it was unlocked last night."

"But why? What's the point of—anyone in there was doomed anyway."

Maybe this was a more compassionate death, Cass thought, at least for Phillip. But if Owen had been involved, she somehow didn't think compassion was what drove him.

Yet there wasn't time to worry about it. The Beaters had paused at the first flash of the explosions, but now they were staggering forward again, testing the air with their outstretched hands.

"They must be able to hear our voices, or the rumble of the cars," Red said.

"They've probably been here all night. After they all took off, what do you want to bet some of them came back? Too chicken to come all the way to the water but…"

"Why doesn't someone shoot them?" Cass cried, but it looked like none of the people close to the Beaters were armed.

An escalating roar came from the front of the crowd, and then two vehicles—the old dented Accord and a motorcycle—hurtled straight for the things. The motorcycle gained speed incredibly fast, and when it reached the edge of the ditch the driver leaned forward and lifted off the seat a few inches. Cass's breath caught as she watched the bike shudder and jerk on impact but after a split second the rider miraculously righted the bike—

black hair flashing silver

—and *oh my God it was Dor,* it was Dor on the bike and he was headed straight for the clump of Beaters—

And Cass was running, running through the edge of

the crowd, knocking into people—why was everyone just standing there letting him do this crazy thing?—and then there was an earthshaking crash because the car following seconds behind Dor hit the ditch and couldn't make the jump, its front bumper smashed into the earth, and she saw it crumple, saw the hood accordion against the berm *what the hell had the driver been thinking* and who would have even taken such a crazy chance—

Cass ran past the smoking wreck, a burning smell coming off it, engine whining like no engine should and then going silent, a pop, another, a small defeated dying sound. And the windshield was red. It was splintered and red and what was that oh God, against the glass, inside the car, that thing that was someone's head no matter how many times you saw the many ways a person could die you never got used to it, not ever—

But Cass was not fast enough to catch Dor and he circled once and came back at the Beaters, who were moving at full sprinting speed now, at full speed himself and smashed into them and two went flying and one went down and one, somehow, got latched on to the bike and dragged and the bike tipped and hovered, defying gravity, before it slow-mo wobbled and fell and by then Cass was there.

How had her blade come to be in her hand, it was her nature now, as running had become her nature in the days when she thought everything had been taken from her but she didn't know the half of it, the days when she first found comfort in the tarry punishing blacktop of a summer afternoon. Sweat and ravaged lungs and legs pushed past their limit. And now she was a machine of a different sort, one who could wield a blade that had become like another arm, slash it down on the Beater who was crawling on top of Dor, watch the man who'd held her only days ago as he was sprayed with the blood of the monster and heave the thing off of him and step on its skull as she leaped to the next one.

Behind her there was screaming but where were they, where was help? The closest ones backed away and ran, good God they were running, didn't they know they couldn't outrun this? They had to kill them, kill them all because a Beater would never stop. The cunning hesitation of moments ago, when they shuffled and snorted and bided their time, that was all over now as their instincts kicked in. Kill them or be killed. Kill them or be eaten.

Dor rolled to his knees and swung his arm up and he took his shot before Cass could find the killing cut and its skull exploded, brains chucking on the ground like a spilled snow cone. And then she was being hauled roughly up by the armpit, Dor yelling *to your right* and with their backs against each other they stood in the field of gore waiting for the attack and finally, finally someone else joined in the fight, two more shots from the crowd and Dor took the last one down with the gun barrel pressed to its throat as it reached for him, hands scrabbling, humming-keening, like a lover reaching for him, and it never took its eyes off him even as it slowly dropped to its knees, a hole in its throat, its head finally toppling forward onto its chest as the rest of it sank to the earth.

"Are you hurt?"

His hands on her arms hurt, his grip was iron. Cass shook her head, then did the mental checklist—none of them had been close enough to bite her. The blood alone could not infect; the pathogens were in the saliva. It didn't matter anyway, in her case, because she was an outlier. But Dor...

Already he was stripping out of his coat, his shirt, his body steaming in the morning chill. The sun had inched higher in the sky, and his burnished skin glowed rosy. Cass saw the fine hairs that trailed to his navel, the smooth planes of his chest bisected by two scars; she knew the map of his body like a town she'd lived in forever and she did not look away. She knew they all watched but she did not look away.

She was pushed roughly aside. "I'll check him."

Dana. Of course it was Dana. Though where the hell had he been during the fight, that's what Cass wanted to know, as the crowd pressed forward, stopping at the edge of the rusted and ruined cattle fence. Some stood in the ditch. Many crowded around the busted car and then a gasp went up as a small man opened the door and pulled the body from the dashboard so they could see who had died, who among them had been brave enough to fight.

Dor, grimacing, put up his hands and turned slowly for Dana's inspection. There were no marks on him, no new ones, anyway. Dor was blessed, if you could say that; he'd been in a dozen Beater attacks and survived them all. He nodded curtly at Dana and started getting dressed; Dana took off at a half jog to the car.

"That car's not going anywhere, but Dana'll probably appoint a fucking committee to make sure," Dor muttered.

"What were you thinking?" Cass demanded, trying to keep the hysteria out of her voice. "The odds of you landing that jump—you could have gone on foot—

they weren't going anywhere—one more minute, or you could have, you could have shot them from this side of the fence, you could have—"

"Cass." Dor paused with only one arm through a sleeve, and reached for her. He cupped her face with one strong hand and forced her to look at him. "This isn't the Box. Or haven't you noticed that? Ten of these people aren't the man George was, or Three-High or Joe or Elaine. If I'd waited, the Beaters would have split up and surged into the group and there's no way this crowd could have responded, they'd still be standing there with their mouths hanging open and their pants down as they were tore into and there's no telling how many we would've lost."

He let go of her, but Cass could feel the mark of his fingers on her skin. She felt bruised. But he was right. There had been no training in New Eden like there was in the Box. No drills. No security. They had the bridge and they had weapons and they thought that was enough. It was enough, until the day it wasn't, and no one, including her, had seen it coming.

"Who was in the car?" she asked softly, acknowledging that he had been right.

Dor frowned. "Pulte. Should've been Hank, but he let Pulte drive first."

"Oh, no…"

"Yeah, they were going to take turns. Hank's—there he is. He's got the fuel wagon."

Cass looked where he was pointing; there—on the other side of the crowd—was the three-wheeler Elsa had lovingly maintained and even took the kids for rides in it a few times in the yard, on special occasions. It was pulling a beat-up U-Haul trailer loaded with cans and gallon jugs and soda bottles, all of them filled with gas.

"Fucking Pulte."

Cass said nothing. She'd known the guy, a little. Not much older than Roan, and in fact the rumor was they were together. But not until after he'd tried with Cass. He ran hot and reckless, and Cass had known what attracted him to her and hated it and stayed away. And he'd found his thrills elsewhere.

Like in that car.

"I have to go," Cass whispered.

"I hear Smoke's with you." Dor stopped her with a hand on her arm, his voice hard, his eyes unreadable. "That he's made a remarkable recovery."

Cass only nodded, at a loss for words.

"I want to see him."

It was hardly the time for reunions, but Cass was not about to argue. She led the way through the crowd, her heart pounding with adrenaline and fear and something else, some vague foreboding about Dor and Smoke.

Smoke saw them coming and scrambled off the trailer, dragging his bad leg. He staggered toward them, his face contorted in fear and anger.

"Dor—"

"Smoke, it's great to see you—"

"How could you let her take a chance like that?" Smoke's voice was choked with fury and he did not take Dor's offered hand. "All she had was a blade, she—"

"You've been gone for a while," Dor said tightly, and slowly lowered his hand. "She's tougher than you think. She's done what she had to do."

Done what she had to do. There was no mistaking the implication in his voice, and Cass shot him a furious look. So he wanted their affair out in the open. Well, it was just as well; someone would tell Smoke soon enough. After the scene with Valerie at the water's edge, it was common knowledge.

Smoke looked from one of them to the other, his eyes narrowing. "I know she's tough, MacFall. I *lived* with her, remember?"

"Hey." Red stepped between the two men. "Now is not the time. We can catch up later, my friends. Everyone's fine, that's what matters."

"What the hell, Cass?" Smoke turned to face her, his face twisted in fury and pain. "What were you *thinking?*"

"I had to, they were about to attack—"

"Dor had it handled."

"He couldn't have held them off by himself."

"Then you should have let someone else."

"No one else would!" Tears of frustration stung Cass's eyes. The aftereffects of the adrenaline surge had left her shaking and trembling and she felt dizzy.

"You can't take risks like that, you can't—"

"You don't get it, Smoke, this isn't like the Box! These people, they're soft, they're afraid, they don't—"

"Ruthie needs you." Smoke took her hand and pulled her toward him, turning his back on everyone else. "I need you," he added, more quietly.

Dor made a sound of disgust and strode away, back toward the front of the crowd. Cass did not allow herself to watch him go. She stared into Smoke's eyes, the pallor of his winter-skin reddened by exertion, and knew that he did not mean that he needed her in order to become whole again or to finish healing. It was his spirit he was speaking of, but he couldn't know how far she'd fallen, how little of what was good in her remained.

Maybe he'd forgive what she'd done with Dor, but it wasn't just that. She was weak now, a drinker, a shirker of duties. If she hadn't given herself away to Dor, it would have been someone else, some other path to release. Cass was weak, she was barely able to take care of Ruthie, and there was not enough left even for her to care for her own damaged self. How could she reconstruct enough of her shattered soul to be anywhere close to what he needed?

She shook her head. "Zihna," she said, turning away. "I think I need to sit down. Just for a minute."

And Zihna, who made a specialty of knowing what people needed, pushed aside the blankets to make a place for her, and put Ruthie in her arms and when the crowd started moving again, a few moments later, it was Red who pulled the trailer and Smoke who pushed the empty stroller, using it like a walker, his face set in such grim determination that Cass didn't doubt he'd walk to the end of the earth before he gave up.

25

They'd gone less than a mile before they heard the cries start up again.

More Beaters.

"Goddamn it," Red said. "Who would have thought the fuckers would have it in them? They always go back to their nests at night. *Always*."

Cass jumped off the trailer, carrying Ruthie; there would be no time for resting now. She craned her neck to try to see but they were in the back of the crowd and all she could see was the others, bodies with their burdens, and in the front the remaining vehicles. She searched for Dor, found him through the crowd, walking near the front, having abandoned the downed motorcycle.

"Red," Zihna muttered urgently. "We need to get everyone to the center."

Smoke was already reaching for Ruthie. "I can get this," he said, settling her into the stroller.

"You know I have to go," Cass said.

His jaw tightened, but he said nothing as he fastened Ruthie's buckle.

"They need me. There aren't enough who can fight."

Finally, he looked at her, and she saw the grim determination written on his face. "It should be me, protecting you," he said.

"It will be, soon, I promise."

"Get me a gun, a blade, anything—"

Cass looked away. "Yes. Fine. I'll see what I can do. But meanwhile, please, please take care of Ruthie, okay?"

"Yes, of course." Smoke closed his eyes for half a second, took a breath. "Look, I'm sorry about—with Dor. I know I overreacted, I know I had no right, I just want, I need…"

"Your place is here for now, Smoke," Zihna said firmly, stepping in between them.

Cass turned away from him so he couldn't see her face, caressing Ruthie's cheek, kissing her silky hair.

"Go," Zihna urged her, adamantly. "You too, Red. Cass, we'll be fine."

"Zihna!" Sammi burst through the press of bodies, dragging Sage. "You have to talk to her, she won't stay in the car—oh my God, Smoke, it's really you, I can't believe it—"

Ahead, another of the Beaters' frantic cries, and another. Gunshots and human screams mixed in with the other sounds in the field ahead. The sun breached the horizon, momentarily blinding all with the first rays of the day. People jostled each other in an effort to see or to flee. Several ran backward, dropping their suitcases, headed back toward the island.

"That sounds like more'n a handful of 'em," Red said grimly. "God be with you, Cassie girl."

Cass threw one last look at them—Zihna and Red, the girls, Smoke and Ruthie—and then she ran.

She caught up with Dor and they dodged scattered and abandoned belongings. The cars had pulled bumper to bumper, making a barrier, and the drivers were out of the cars, yelling to each other.

"What now?" she demanded.

"I don't know," Dor shot back, frustration in his voice. "There's no coordination, nothing—"

He stopped abruptly as they came around the side of the cars. There, lying in a thatch of kaysev, were three dead Beaters. A man stood a few paces away, holding his arm and trembling.

"He's bit! He's bit!" a woman was wailing.

A dozen paces away, there was a commotion surrounding more dead Beaters lying on the ground. One of the creatures remained on his feet, lurching toward a wiry man, maybe Nathan, Cass couldn't tell. The man dodged close and jabbed and even from far away Cass could see the spray of blood from its neck. It walked, stiff-legged, in a semicircle before falling to the ground, the blood petering out while it twitched.

That was the last of them that Cass could see; all the Beaters lay dead or dying. There were shouts from the crowd, triumphant cheers. People began pouring around the cars now that it was safe.

The woman who had been wailing latched on to Dor. "He tried, he tried to kill them but that one, it bit him."

"You're sure?" Dor said. He seized her hand and dragged her away from the man.

"I saw, I saw it, on the arm, the arm," the woman babbled, and Cass saw the bleeding puncture down near his wrist bone. He was still staring at his wound, at the blood dripping onto the ground, his expression a mixture of disbelief and horror.

Dor shot him.

He moved so quickly that Cass didn't even see him reach for his gun and certainly didn't see him aim. The man stumbled back and a hole appeared in his forehead so neat and round it looked as though it had been made by a giant paper punch. The woman's screams turned incoherent and she pounded at Dor with her fists, but he pushed her gently away and others came forward, and led her away from the body.

"What are you armed with?" Dor demanded.

"My blade," Cass said. "And I have a spare. There are guns on the trailer, Red didn't think—"

"Red is not in charge," Dor said angrily. "You got that, Cass? You don't follow Red."

"I don't follow *anyone*," Cass snapped, staring into Dor's flashing ebony eyes. But it wasn't exactly what she meant to say—she'd followed Dor into the canoe, hadn't she, with barely a thought; they found their rhythm immediately, the canoe rock-steady as he rowed and she fired, and again at the bridge.

"You'll follow me now," Dor growled. He put a hand behind her neck and pulled her closer, making her falter so she had to grab his arm for balance. "This isn't about you and me right now. We can sort that out later. This is about there being too damn few people who know what they're doing and too many sitting ducks who are going to die if we don't do this right. Now, I've got Nathan and Steve and Brandt covering the other end. You and I will take this end. We'll get Glynnis out in the front and everyone else will drop back. You got that?"

Cass nodded. It made sense, better than anything she could come up with, at least while his hand was heavy on her neck, his face inches away, his eyes reflecting the battleground behind her.

"Now take these," he demanded, releasing her only after he put a gun and extra rounds in her hands.

Up ahead the others were silhouetted against the rising sun, leading the Edenites across the field.

But then she looked again. It was wrong, all wrong. They were coming closer, not moving away. Their gait was ragged, jerking.

At least two dozen of the beasts, and behind them Cass could see more, stumbling toward them in groups that split and re-formed as they heaved against each other and thrashed their arms and howled.

Gasps quickly turned to screams as the rest of the crowd saw them too. Dor stepped out in front, and fired into the sky.

"Everyone! Listen to me. If you are armed and you know how to use your weapon, come to the front. Keep the children, the old folks, to the back. Stay put. No one goes back to the island. It's not safe there anymore."

For a moment there was panic and then, incredibly, the crowd began to follow his orders. Cass spotted Zihna and Red on either side of the trailer, pushing it to the back, and Smoke, standing in front of the stroller, protecting Ruthie with his body. He had a gun in his hand, one of Red's, no doubt.

"Deal with the ones who come to you," Dor shouted to her. "Don't worry about the rest. I've got it."

Cass readied herself, crouching down, weighing the gun in her hands, getting used to the broad grip. The extra magazines, jammed under her belt, were high-capacity—at least a dozen rounds each. That gave her thirty shots, give or take, assuming she survived to re-load, assuming she was steady enough. She wished she hadn't allowed herself to become complacent with the rest of them. All those mornings when Dor went out alone on North Island, doing his target practice and run-ning sprints, working with the set of barbells he kept under a tarp—she should have been there too. She'd heard the way people made fun of him, calling him Rambo, but they talked in whispers about her too, and it meant nothing, less than nothing.

She had allowed their judgment to matter. It was the mistake she seemed doomed to make over and over, and once she let their criticism in it became way too easy to go the rest of the distance, to become the thing they accused her of.

But it wasn't who she really was. It *wasn't*. Here on this field of death, Cass seized on the lesson she'd for-gotten in the past few months: she was who she made of herself, and no other. She breathed deep and forced herself to exhale slowly, feeling the steel warm to her touch, and vowed to survive.

Dor fired and a gangly, thin Beater who'd sprinted ahead of the others suddenly jerked and staggered back-ward, right into the path of another, who fell sideways, screaming.

A trio of them ran straight toward her. The crowd had dropped back, scattering in confusion, and she was alone in the open field, the target of their focus and their desperation. She crouched lower, putting one knee to the ground, waiting. Fire too soon and she'd waste a valuable bullet and risk scattering them. The moment they split up they became ten times more dangerous.

She counted in her mind, mouthing the syllables silently. *One one-thousand, two one-thousand, three…*

Down the line shots were fired, screams and yelps erupting from the Beaters who were hit. But Cass did not dare take her eyes off her targets.

Closer, closer, and Cass could see the bare swinging breast that hung out of the open shirt one of them wore. It had no hair left on its scarred, filthy scalp. Its mouth yawed in a lipless leer and one of its eyes had been ruined, the socket red and pulped, bone protruding from the edges.

Cass shot that one first.

She hit its shoulder and cursed as it fell to the ground screaming and immediately started trying to crawl. A poor shot, nonfatal, but at least one of the others tripped over it, and Cass was able to get a clean shot at its dropping head, which opened like a rose.

The final one crowed, waving its arms wildly, and Cass waited until it was only a few yards away. She pulled the trigger and the gun jerked in her hand but did not shoot.

Oh God oh God it had misfired—who knew where Dor had found this gun, if this had been the Box it would have been cleaned and maintained but no *This was New Eden* land of peace and prosperity and complacency and the Beater was coming closer. Cass fired again and this time the gun responded and the bullet went a little bit wide but it took a good chunk out of the thing's skull.

It wobbled on its feet, close enough that had it still been human Cass could have had a conversation with it. Spinning, grinning, lipless mouth opening in a slow-mo scream; reaching for Cass as if it wanted to make a point, caress her cheek, fix a button. Cass wavered and wondered if the next second would bring its fetid teeth closing on her skin.

No no no

She'd beaten them before, somehow. She had to beat them again. Rage uncoiled inside her and she clenched her teeth and adjusted her position, distributing her weight better. She didn't trust this gun, didn't know how many bullets remained. And at this range she couldn't miss again. She switched the gun to her left hand and grabbed for her blade. That, at least, was as comfortable as it had ever been; Cass kept it sharpened because she used it for all kinds of tasks in the garden. Now she held it tightly and when the Beater was only a few feet away, she dodged around it, reached out for its neck from behind, and cut straight and deep across its throat.

She had killed them this way before, not often. A human throat was surprisingly tough to cut through, cartilage and muscle and arteries knotted densely. And a Beater had been human once. It might chew its skin off, it might lose digits and eyes and chunks of flesh but underneath its gory exterior it was still wrought of the same innards, and she threw herself into the motion and did not hold back, and the Beater's last cry was severed along with its windpipe as it landed face-first on the ground.

The first one that had fallen was crawling toward

her, its useless arm bleeding from the shoulder wound. It was making gasping, panting sounds and these, too, ended abruptly when Cass stepped on its shoulders and repeated the swipe of the blade, this time leaving the side of its neck half-severed. It gurgled and jerked as it died and Cass left it and went looking for Dor.

He'd left his own trail of dead behind him, two of them mounded together as though they were embracing, others splayed awkwardly alone. He was standing in the brilliant glow of the rising sun, arms loose at his side, and for a moment Cass thought he was praying—but when he lifted his gun and jammed a fresh magazine onto it, she knew she was mistaken.

There must be more.

She covered her eyes with her hand and squinted. Something sprinted into view, and Dor took a shot but missed, and the thing ran between them. It was heading into the crowd, yammering as it ran, hands flapping.

Why hadn't it attacked them? Beaters always went for the closest prey. It was gospel that the people in front were most likely to die, so raiding parties always put their weakest members in the back. But this Beater had ignored them to go after the others. Had it figured out that Cass and Dor were its greatest threat? That the weakest, most vulnerable targets were the people in the midst of the crowd?

Where Ruthie was, where Smoke was

"Up ahead! Cass! There's more ahead!"

But Cass plunged through the crowd after the rogue Beater instead. She could not let it reach Ruthie, could not take that risk. People screamed and knocked each other over trying to get out of the way, but by the time she caught up with it, it had seized the pink sleeve of a puffy coat, wasn't that Mrs. Prince—there was her dull gray hair that she'd valiantly tried to pin-curl for so long until she finally gave up one day and had Tildy cut it all off in a pixie that suited her surprisingly well, but the Beater knocked her over as easily as if she'd been a bowling pin and fell upon her and when Cass grabbed its hair, because it still had a greasy topknot of the stuff, studded with chaff and greasy in her hand, she saw that its mouth was sodden with Mrs. Prince's blood and the poor woman was gasping through a hole torn from her throat.

Cass stabbed at the Beater with her blade, slicing through the soft skin under its jaw, bringing her arm down again and again until its head nearly came away in her hand, and only then did she finally stagger away from the scene of carnage.

The Edenites continued to retreat in every direction—the worst thing they could do, inciting the Beaters to ever-greater excitement. She didn't see Red or Zihna, Smoke, any of them, and she couldn't waste time searching. She ran back toward the abandoned cars, the Beaters streaming past the paltry barrier they made. There were so many. Where had they all come from, where had they been hiding? A couple dozen more at least, and more dead on the ground. To the right, she saw Brandt being set on by a clot of the things, saw the gun fall from his hand as they slammed his body to the earth in their favorite technique and then each seizing a limb, an arm or a leg, and then dragging him away, back the way they'd come. Ordinarily they went back to their nests, but there were no buildings here, only open fields dotted with shrubs and clumps of trees. There was a leaning ranch house far in the distance to the east, but the Beaters did not head that way. Maybe they meant only to get their prey out of sight, to hide in the tall grass to feast. No matter what, Brandt was lost, his screams fading as they dragged him away.

Others approached. Too many. It was impossible.

Cass tried to choose among her targets, a pair that were making an end run around the panel van, bypassing her to get at those behind her, and a knot of four or five that jostled each other as they ran.

She could not stop them all. She would die here. Cass wondered if she could shoot herself at the last minute, if she could be disciplined enough to kill as many as she could and save that last bullet for herself. Rage surged through her but rage would not be enough, it could not make her faster or more accurate.

But she had to try. She focused on a squat, limping one, steadied herself, and was about to fire when it suddenly jerked and fell. And then the one next to it spun, its head burst in a cloud of blood.

Who had shot? Not Dor, who was fifty feet ahead, crouched over a fallen Beater, finishing it with his blade.

The ground pounded under her feet and a blurred form approached, moving faster than any human or Beater.

A man on a horse, galloping toward them from the east.

As it grew closer Cass saw that it was a brown horse with a white diamond on its muzzle, its lips bared in furious effort as its rider dug into its flanks, urging it faster, leaning slightly out of the saddle as he fired again. And there were others—three other horsemen riding directly into the battle. The blinding rising sun had obscured their approach, but who were they? Cass had not seen a horse since early in the Siege and the bioagent that killed the cattle and made mass slaughterhouses everywhere. But these were healthy-looking specimens, large and powerful, their hooves pounding the dry, cold earth.

The Beaters seemed confused, catching the scent of the humans on the horses, torn between them and the prey on land. Cass heard the sound of an engine and saw that someone had gotten back into the pickup and was heading straight for the Beaters. The undercarriage and wheel wells were red with gore from running over corpses. It came too close to one of the horses, spooking it, and it reared up on its back legs. For a moment the rider looked as though he would be thrown from the saddle, but then the horse settled and braced stiff-limbed with its ears flattened, until the rider spurred it on again.

The horsemen circled the remaining Beaters, cutting them down efficiently. In moments there were no more of them on their feet. One of the horsemen galloped after the ones who'd dragged Brandt away, and a series of shots proved that he'd found them.

Suddenly, there was quiet on the field. The screams of an injured Beater were abruptly cut off when the pickup drove over it, and seconds later, the driver cut the engine. Dor turned to the scattered crowd.

"Everyone, stay together until we're sure there aren't any more," he yelled. A few yards from Cass, Mrs. Prince lay under the Beater that had killed her, her legs sticking out awkwardly. Behind her, the crowd started to draw back together, the silence punctuated with cries and sobs.

Then a new voice rang through the air.

"People! Anyone with an injury of any sort, stand here to my right! Line up single file! Everyone else, stand with four feet between you and the next person! We will come around to check you out. Please, do not fall out of line until you are told to."

The speaker was the rider of the brown horse, a broad man with red hair and a graying red beard. He wore sunglasses of the sort that were once favored by snowboarders and skiers, his expression inscrutable behind them.

"Who the hell are you?" Dor demanded.

"My name is Damon Mayhew. I'm—we're—here to help." He gestured at the other riders, who had spread out along the front edge of the crowd. Now Cass noticed the gear stowed on the horses' packs, all of it dusty and hard-used. "We saw your flares. We were sheltering a few miles from here, to the northeast, along the river. Took us a little while to break camp but we came as soon as we could."

"We're obliged for the help," Dor said, but there was no mistaking the suspicion in his voice. "But I'll thank you to let us handle this."

Mayhew spoke impatiently. "Look, we can hash this out later. Right now we've got a real problem and we need to deal with it *now*. We need to make sure no one was compromised."

"*We?*" Dor demanded, his lip curled in contempt. "*We?* Correct me if I'm wrong, but didn't you just get here a few minutes ago?"

Mayhew's frown deepened, but otherwise he didn't react to Dor's challenge. Instead he pointed at the ragtag crowd. "Like I said, there'll be time for this later. For now, you get one person infected in a group this size, think about how much damage he can do. Not even knowing it, even. What we have to do, anyone who came anywhere near those bastards, they strip and we check them out. No exceptions."

All eyes were on Dor, who glowered at Mayhew. "None of that's exactly groundbreaking," he said. "We have our own procedures."

Dana stepped forward from the crowd. Only then did Cass realize that she hadn't seen him anywhere in the fighting, again—again he'd stayed behind in safety with the others, despite the fact that he was armed and carried a weapon with him everywhere on the island, an exception to the council's own policies.

"I'm in charge here," Dana said. "Why don't you and I discuss your proposal, Mayhew. Your men can start this safety check or whatever you want to call it."

"No." Dor practically spat the words. "Mayhew's right about one thing, we don't have a lot of time. Here's how we'll do it. Anyone who's armed, who was in the fight, we stay away from the others. Tonight or whenever we find shelter, we'll check then. The fever takes at least that long to turn. But we can do that on our own, Mayhew. These people don't answer to you."

"They answer to *me*." Dana's voice rose, belligerently. "You're a laborer, Dor, and a, a *philanderer*. We're all grateful for your bit in the canoe yesterday, but you're not a council member. And this isn't the time to start pretending you are."

The crowd buzzed, but no one contradicted Dana. Cass knew it was a critical moment, that whoever played the crowd's fears most skillfully would lead, qualified or not.

"You're weak, Dana," Dor said, not bothering to hide his contempt. "You'll get us all killed. And you—*May-*

hew—we don't know you. We don't know what your agenda is. Why should we trust you?"

Mayhew was implacable behind his dark lenses. "You want to know my agenda? Fine, I'll lay it out for you. We come from the East. Like, beyond the Rockies, get it? We're here to *help* you, but unless we get moving, we're all screwed."

He reached for his gun, but Dor was faster, his own out and ready before Mayhew had his out of his holster.

"I'm offering to hand this over to you," Mayhew said tightly. "Mine and the rest of my men. As a symbol of trust."

"Dad. Stop it."

Sammi burst from the edge of the crowd, hugging herself, looking miserable.

"Please, you're just making it worse," she pleaded. Her face was flushed with anger and embarrassment, and Cass realized she was ashamed of her father. "Just do what the guy says, okay?"

Everyone looked from Sammi to Mayhew to Dor. Dana opened his mouth to protest but then shut it after it became clear that no one was going to be following his notions.

The resolve seemed to drain from Dor as he watched Sammi, flanked by her silent friends, fade back into the crowd. Dor, who'd taken the front line without a second thought, who was wearing the blood of the creatures that he'd killed, bowed his head and turned away.

The crowd shifted its attention expectantly at Mayhew.

"I promise that tonight, once we find adequate shelter, we'll share everything we know," Mayhew said as though Sammi hadn't spoken. "We're not here to take over your people. We're trying to carve out a future for everyone and we're all in the same boat now that the fever's gone east. When you hear what we've got to say, you can choose who you want to lead you, but you'll be doing it from a place of knowledge because right now, my friends, I think you're acting from fear, understandably."

This man said his words gently, his face sympathetic. But behind his sunglasses, Cass was certain his expression burned with thoughts and plans that he wouldn't be sharing.

As everyone began to divide into the groups he had asked for, Cass watched Mayhew's frown curve—ever so slightly—into a smile so brief that Cass wondered if she'd conjured it from her imagination, the spoils of Dor's defeat.

26

Mayhew's men dismounted their horses; one of them stayed with the animals as the rest moved into the crowd.

"If you were within eight feet of a Beater, go with Bart here," Mayhew ordered, indicating a tall, broad-built man with ruddy skin and pale hair cut almost to his scalp. "If the person next to you was, see that he goes."

Those who'd stayed with the crowd separated themselves from those who fought, some sheepish, some defiant. Soon eight people had assembled around Bart: Cass and Dor and five other men and Darla Piehl, who had surprised them all by producing a little .22 from her backpack and hitting a target some thirty feet off.

The examination didn't take long. They took off their shirts and coats and examined each other's bare skin, Cass shivering in just her sleeveless undershirt. Fat Mike squinted at an old scratch she'd gotten while pruning, tracing its shape delicately with his finger, then nodded his approval.

"What's that?" Terrence Godin asked, peering closely at Owen Mason's shoulder. Everyone looked to see what he was pointing to—a small gash smudged with drying blood.

"Got it when I fell," Owen said. "I tripped on the first one I put down when I was trying to get close enough to take a shot at the rest."

Terrence was silent for a moment, bringing his face closer to the wound.

"I don't know, I guess—"

"Quarantine," Mayhew said. "It's the only way."

"What do you mean, *quarantine?*" Dana demanded. Cass wondered if he was beginning to bristle from ceding away his position of leadership and was now looking for a fight. "You see any, like, locked rooms we can stick him in around here?"

Mayhew stared at him from behind his dark glasses for a moment before answering. Off his horse, he did not seem quite as imposing, but he was still well over six feet tall and at least two hundred twenty or thirty pounds, his hair held in a loose ponytail secured with a bit of leather cord.

"Way we handle it, the man walks ten paces behind. We post one armed man back there with him. Deal is, if he comes closer than the ten paces he gets a warning. Three warnings and he's shot. Not shot to kill, but in a situation like this, being on the move, I guess you don't need me to tell you that's a death sentence anyway."

There were a few protests from the crowd, a crescendo of voices as the issue was debated. Owen started to object, then appeared to think better of it. He touched his wound, his fingertips coming away bloody, and he stared at them for a moment before wiping them on his pants.

"Come on," Dana protested. "There's no need for that. He'll be glad to stay back, without a guard, won't you—"

"Mayhew's right."

Dor, who had been standing silently off to the side, spoke quietly. He'd regained his composure since Sammi's outburst, but his eyes were deeply troubled.

"We can't take any chances," he continued. "And we've got to be a lot more systematic about these things. You have my vote, Mayhew." His tone implied that his vote did not necessarily carry much respect with it.

Mayhew stared at him for a moment, then nodded. "Look, you—what's your name?"

"Owen Mason." He mumbled, but that was nothing new; Cass couldn't recall a time when Owen met anyone's eyes when he spoke.

"Owen. You need to understand that there's nothing personal about this."

"What the hell, man, I don't even know you. How could it be personal?"

"I'll watch him," Dana said. "Since you've decided to take over my job, Mayhew, I guess I might as well make myself useful somewhere. Don't worry, Owen."

He walked through the crowd, glaring at his fellow council members. After a moment, Owen followed, taking a wide route around the crowd, already the leper, already the outcast.

"We need to get moving," Mayhew said. "We need to find shelter well before nightfall so we can set up sentry, get everyone fed."

"I think we could have figured that out, at least," Cass muttered.

There was something about Mayhew's placid confidence that bothered her. Or maybe it was only her age-old issue with authority, her difficulty with following orders. That, if nothing else, had made the QuikGo a perfect job for her; after her boss showed her how to work the cash register, the locks, the lottery machine, she was pretty much on her own. And she liked it that way. The gardening was the same—no one told her how to move from task to task, when to start, when to end her day.

"I'm sure you could have," Mayhew said easily. "Cass, is it? I don't suppose you want to ride with me."

"No, and if someone's going to ride, we've got some older folks, some others who might be a better candidate."

Mayhew nodded, raising an eyebrow. "Of course, I'm sorry, I should have thought of that. Maybe you could help me figure out who'd be the best to give a breather to."

Cass nodded, but as the crowd gathered closer and she helped Mayhew sort out rides, she felt everyone's eyes on her. But she couldn't help what any of them thought. Not her dad, or Smoke. Or Sammi. Or Valerie. She was like anyone else, trying to make the best of a bad lot of choices.

But as two men watched her from opposite ends of the crowd, she had a feeling her most difficult choice still lay ahead.

Smoke insisted on walking. Cass held his hand, ready to catch him if he stumbled, but he was surprisingly steady.

"Tell me everything," he muttered through clenched teeth.

She didn't know if he meant Dor, but she wasn't willing to go there. And so, instead, she started with the night they'd freed him from the Rebuilder headquarters in Colima.

She told him that she and Dor had killed four people that night, and that other innocent people had died in the fighting. When she described the baby farm, he winced and squeezed his eyes shut for a moment. "God, Cass," he whispered. "Did Sammi..."

"She's fine. We got her out before they—before anything happened. But we brought some of the other girls with us. Pregnant ones. One of them miscarried when she got to New Eden, but the others...one's due in a couple of months. The others not long after."

For a moment neither spoke, considering the damage done to those girls, just another new variety of horror.

Cass told him about coming to the island, about the welcome they received in the waning days of the year. About the Mothers' House, and the House for Wayward Girls; the social committee and the friends Sammi had made. She described Garden Island and the many plants she'd cultivated. She said nothing about Dor, and Smoke didn't ask.

That was not the only subject Cass stayed away from. She didn't tell Smoke she was drinking. Besides, she had quit; even if she wanted to, she couldn't drink now. There was no liquor among the vehicles' paltry supplies, and she'd abandoned her half-empty bottle at the last minute. So far it wasn't too bad, but then again the first few days of sobriety were never the worst.

The other two times she'd quit, she'd had to deal with

headaches, clammy skin, heart palpitations, even a faint tremor in her hands. But she'd been drinking much more then. On New Eden, she almost always limited herself to just enough to dull her edges, which was sometimes harder than being sober. She could do this. She *would* do this, and not just because she didn't have a choice.

The last two times, she'd quit for Ruthie. In the lonely nights on the back step of the Mothers' House, she thought about quitting so she could gain the approval of the others, for Ingrid and Suzanne and Jasmine. Even last night, she had thought she was quitting for Smoke. But now, as she caught him up to the world he had missed, recounting the details of the night when she and Dor had rescued him from the Rebuilders, she realized something unexpected. She'd done a few things right.

She was far from perfect; she'd faltered once they arrived in New Eden. But she had come a very long way with little help. She'd been strong when the chips were down, and brave when courage was called for. Today she'd spilled Beater blood and lived to tell about it, and tomorrow she would get up and do whatever it took to protect her loved ones.

She would do everything for them except this one thing: this time, she was getting sober for *herself.*

When she had told Smoke everything she could think of, he was silent. The crowd's energy was beginning to flag, the scenery changing very little as they traveled north on county roads, but at least they had seen no more Beaters.

"The men I killed," Smoke finally said. "Have they been missed?"

Cass shrugged. "We've already lost more than a dozen people. People seem to have assumed those two were among the ones who ran back with the first wave. I...didn't correct them."

Smoke thought about that for a moment, before speaking softly. "Were they good men?"

"No. Getting rid of Charles...and then you...they took that task on themselves because it excited them, I think. No one on the council ordered it."

"But..."

But they didn't deserve to die. Smoke didn't say it, but the truth hung between them like a palpable thing. His actions were self-defense, she wanted to say, and that was true, but she also knew Smoke, knew how he thought and felt. Honor was everything to him, and valor and retribution. He'd nearly died exacting vengeance, and now she wondered if he would punish himself since there was no one else to do the job for him.

But weren't his weeks of pain, his scars, his severed fingers and broken bones enough?

They resumed walking, holding hands now. The children stopped playing, lulled by the motion of the trailer, and fell asleep like a litter of puppies, sprawled together in a heap. Red took over the trailer duties for Ingrid, and Zihna moved through the crowd talking to the most distraught.

When they came to a prefab ranch house whose windows were all smashed, the leaders in front pulled in and word traveled through the crowd that they were taking a break. Water and crackers were distributed. After Cass checked on Ruthie, still sleeping next to Twyla and Dirk, she took her ration and found Smoke sitting with his back against an old live oak whose gnarled branches had once shaded an above-ground pool, now crushed and seeping brackish water. He made room for her and patted the ground next to him.

"Look," he said. "I just wanted to say…whatever went on, while I was in the hospital…"

"I'm sorry. Oh, Smoke, I'm so sorry, I—"

"No. I want to put it behind us, starting now. I don't—none of it's your fault. We're together now, and that's what matters."

"I came to see you at first," Cass said, unable to cast off her guilt that easily. "I came every day. But you were so…broken."

"Cass." He tipped her chin up with his fingers so that she would have to look at him. "Please, listen to me. I mean, *really* listen. I don't blame you for not coming. I don't…if it had been you, if I thought I'd lost you, if I thought you'd never wake up—"

His voice cracked and he swallowed hard before he could continue. "I wouldn't have been able to come either. I don't think I could bear it."

Cass wanted to let his words heal her, wanted to take hold of the branch he offered her. But instead, her guilt grew. It hadn't been fear of losing him that kept her away, not entirely. Smoke hadn't even been gone from the Box forty-eight hours the first time she fucked Dor, and since then it had been practically every opportunity they got. Yes, their coupling was a comfort, a desperate response to fear, to despair, but it was a comfort she couldn't seem to get enough of.

If Smoke knew how often she'd been lying in Dor's arms while he was struggling for his life, could he still forgive her? If he knew that sometimes, when Dor touched her, she was glad of the forgetting, glad to have Smoke out of her mind, glad to have everything out of her mind, would he still want her back? What if he knew that the only time she didn't want a drink was when Dor was inside her?

How could Smoke ever look upon her with anything but disgust when he understood what she had really become?

He would turn away from her and it would be what she deserved; he would reject her and she would know it was her due. And in one small way it would make everything easier. Because if Smoke didn't want her she would never have to choose between two men. And if he didn't expect her to be good then she could continue to be bad, to fail everyone and everything. As long as she took care of Ruthie, Cass could simply cease to try in any other way.

27

They passed an uneasy night on a dirt track that had once been used for stock-car racing. By the looks of it, several years had passed since the stands had been filled with crowds, but the travelers were exhausted and on edge. Despite their promises to explain what they were doing on this side of the Rockies, Mayhew and his men kept to themselves, taking posts around the perimeter of the track along with a few of the others, and no one had the energy—or temerity—to complain. Dana and Owen slept under the overhang of the sagging snack stand; everyone else clustered close on the center of the track, where grass once grew and kaysev now provided a soft surface.

In the morning, a hasty meal quickly gave over to repacking the vehicles and other preparations for travel. Yesterday's fears seemed both distant and magnified; few had slept well, and there was a general sense of wanting to put distance between them and the bloody battlefield they'd left behind. Surely Cass was not the only one to realize that the Beater threat was undiminished, no matter how much ground they covered today—as numerous as grains of sand on the beach, they would always be out there—but by the time the pink dawn gave way to day, they were on the road again.

The progress of the crowd was frustratingly slow. They stuck to the road, leaving the meandering waterways of the Delta behind for the flat farmland south of Sacramento, passing skeletal orchards only now beginning to come back to life, acres of table grapevines that were nothing but dead, woody spirals clinging to supports. At the end of the rows of vines, the rosebushes planted to give farmers early warning of fungal diseases were beginning to send up new shoots from the hardy rootstock that had waited, dormant, for more hospitable times, and Cass tried to interpret the appearance of the reddish canes as a hopeful omen.

They skirted small towns, taking farm roads to avoid the possibility of Beater nests. They passed shacks, ranches, commercial buildings; fairgrounds and schools and stadiums, and at a distance it all seemed almost normal from time to time, a walk in the country on a long-ago day when one's only concerns were sunburn and getting home in time to catch the game on TV.

At least the day was warm and clear, and the roads were mostly passable. Twice they had to go around obstructions, using the Bronco to drag the little hybrid up a steep grade next to a wreck at one point while the walkers edged past on the narrow shoulder and tried not to look inside the smashed cars at the long-decayed bodies inside. They had spotted no Beaters by the time they paused for lunch in the shade of a billboard advertising the Silver Bear casino, a fact that buoyed flagging spirits and seemed to support the idea that the creatures were avoiding the sparsely populated countryside.

In the afternoon tempers began to fray. Smoke refused to ride until he'd completely exhausted himself, and it was hard to watch his limp get worse as the day wore on. Ruthie and Twyla darted around him playfully when they weren't riding on the trailer.

Only the children were in good spirits. They danced along the road, gathering pebbles, and picking the occasional dandelion or wild orange poppy growing at the side of the road. Occasionally Ruthie would come to Cass to be picked up, snuggled, reassured. She would bury her face in Cass's shirt for a few seconds and then she'd wriggle down again, not wanting to miss any of the fun with the other kids.

Cass marveled at this little cycle. Courage was not that hard to come by for children. No matter the hardships they faced, given a little love and encouragement, their spirits rebounded and thrived. After everything Ruthie had been through, she was a normal, happy little girl again.

Adults were different. Their habits and experiences made them inflexible, welding their routines in place, cementing their hurts and joys to create expectations of life that were not in line with the new realities. All around her Cass saw the dazed expressions and bleak weariness that were the hallmarks of the early days of the Siege. When the president made his final broadcast a few days before the media shut off forever, already secured in the secret location from which his administration intended to "navigate the crisis," a phrase that

was repeated first with reverence and then with deri-
sion—when the infected entered into the new phase of
the disease and began picking at their skin and mum-
bling, when riots destroyed entire neighborhoods—that
was when you began to see people with expressions
like these. That was when they first took to the roads,
driving their cars until obstacles prevented them from
going any farther, then carrying their suitcases and their
children until, in so many cases, they simply sat down
in the street and gave up.

This lot had not given up, though. They were the ones
who survived, who had been tough enough, determined
enough, angry enough to keep going, eventually finding their way to New Eden. But as Cass watched Mrs.
Kristobal shuffling along with tears leaking silently
down her face, as she watched Luddy and Cheddar race
along the edge of the crowd on their longboards, taking
greater and greater risks, as she glimpsed Dor walking
alone, face set in rigid fury, disgraced and powerless—
as she took in all of this she knew it was Siege days all
over again and she feared for their future.

First they faltered. Then they panicked. And then
they began to give up. That was how the cycle went,
and Cass knew in her bones they were going to see it
all happen again.

When the sun was low in the sky, they had gone
a dispiriting ten miles. Mayhew and the other riders
stopped in front of a big house set back along a road
lined with dead saplings, and the cars pulled off the
road and the people followed.

"We'll go in and clear, but we won't say no to a couple of you coming along," Mayhew called out to the
crowd, as he jumped to the ground.

"I can take care of the horses."

Valerie stepped from the crowd. Cass had seen her a few times earlier, walking with Collette's crowd. At lunch she'd helped serve people, gathering up the cloths and bags in which the cold kaysev cakes had been packed, making sure everyone got some water. Cass had hoped this return to her usual generosity signaled that she was doing better, that she was coming to terms with what had happened between her and Dor, but she meant to keep her distance.

Now she went up to the white horse and stroked its muzzle and patted its muscular neck, speaking quietly to it. She and Mayhew exchanged a few words that Cass couldn't hear, and then one of the other men helped her tie them to the split-rail fence that lined the drive.

Smoke started to limp toward the men assembling in front of the crowd and Cass ran after him, stopping him with a hand on his arm.

"What are you doing?"

"Going to check out the place."

"Smoke, don't be crazy, you're not strong enough, you can't—"

Smoke put a hand on her face, forced her to look at him. A couple of days in the sun had restored some of his color, and he looked far better than he had in his sick bed. "I'll do what I need to to protect my own," he said coldly. "I'll thank Dor, later, for taking care of you when I couldn't. But I'm here now and I'm taking the job back."

Cass felt the sting of his words, the unspoken anger. Smoke blamed Dor, not her, and that wasn't right, it wasn't the whole truth.

When they arrived in New Eden, Dor had been willing to stay away from her. He'd kept his part of the bargain, and for weeks they'd avoided each other, until the day when she begged him to…

Cass felt her face burn with shame, remembering the things she'd begged Dor to do to her, with her, anything to make her forget for a little while, anything to make her feel alive when her path had gone so terribly wrong. All the time she'd told herself she would stop, that she *could* stop, anytime she wanted. But just the memory of him, two nights ago or the time before that or any of the times, just the flash of memory was enough to make her breath catch in her throat.

And she knew now that she couldn't have stopped. He was her addiction, her vice, her crutch, and just as she waited for that first burning swallow of kaysev wine each night, so she waited for his touch, thinking about it even while she worked the fields or waited for sleep to come, or endured the judgment of the other women.

Cass realized that Smoke was waiting for her to say something, to respond to his declaration. "I still can't believe you're here," she said, a poor substitute for what he wanted to hear, and pressed her face against his chest so he wouldn't see the turmoil in her eyes.

For a moment they held each other, and then Cass finally pushed him away, not having the right words to make a promise that she wasn't sure she could keep.

"Go," she muttered, and it was a condemnation as much as an entreaty.

28

Tildy Carmichael joked that the house looked a little like her old pool house in Sacramento, but her eyes were red from crying. Her best friends—Collette and Karen and June—were all missing and presumed dead back on the island, blown up in the community-center explosion. Rumors flew about the blast: someone had been careless while packing the explosives for travel; it had been a suicide bombing by Milt or Jack, who had finally been missed enough for people to really begin to speculate upon; it had been a mercy strike meant only for the quarantine house but had somehow jumped to the community center in a secondary explosion. The dead had been counted and then not spoken of again, as though the Edenites feared that the mere mention of their names would bring more bad luck.

The house was enormous, constructed a couple of decades ago when relatively cheap land was enough to entice people to build the houses they could never afford in a city, maybe grow a few grapes or keep some cattle and retire a twenty-first-century DIY gentleman farmer. A for-sale sign still stood, barely, in the yard, rusting. One of hundreds they'd seen so far, sad reminders of the waves of financial crashes that came even before the Siege.

Whoever had built this house had gone in for details that might have looked a little more at home in Tildy's old neighborhood than in the dusty central valley. The arched windows and columns and faux shutters had not stood the test of time well, cheap construction that was easily defeated by the rigors of Aftertime. The stucco walls had been crushed in places; window glass lay in shards on the ground; and most unsettling, someone had dragged a couple of roomfuls of furniture out into what had been a rose garden. The brocade sofas and chairs were overturned and mildewed, a home to rodents. Some were stained a suspicious red-brown that might have been blood baked by the sun.

Still, there was an empty five-car garage that would make perfect shelter for passing the night. People wandered the rest of the house while there was still daylight, the dormant habit of browsing closets and master baths mindlessly awakened. Open houses used to be one of Mim's favorite pastimes; she'd pretend that she and Byrn were "looking for a little more space" and poke around the most extravagant listings in Silva, running her fingers along granite countertops and custom draperies and five-inch moldings with all the other looky-loos. The few times Cass went along as a teenager, she looked for clues to the people who lived there, reading the titles on the spines of books, checking out framed photographs and the grocery lists people left on their fridges. She was desperately trying to figure out how other people managed to live.

She suspected that the others, exhausted from fear and the journey, were doing something similar, looking for stories that reminded them of another time. Looking for echoes of their own lost lives in the remains of the American dream.

The house had already been picked bare by raiders and vandalized, mirrors smashed and the remains of unidentifiable food and cleaning products strewn across the floors. There was an abandoned Beater nest in the formal living room, a pile of rags whose stench drove them to close the French doors. Still, if you didn't look too closely, if you let your imagination fill in the holes, you could imagine the holiday dinners that had taken place in the dining room, the kids who might have lived in the rooms upstairs with their wallpaper borders of ballerinas and airplanes.

Cass took the kids to the backyard with Ingrid and Suzanne. A play structure stood more or less intact, and Cass pushed the little ones by turns in the bucket swing, trying to come up with the right words to talk to the others, who sat at a picnic table chatting quietly.

Dor came around the house and, ignoring Ingrid and Suzanne, joined her at the swing set with a stony expression on his face. "I want you and Ruthie with me. There's a room upstairs we can use, I can secure the door."

"We all shelter together," Cass said, echoing what Mayhew had announced when he and the others emerged from checking the house.

"Fuck that." Dor's eyes flashed angrily. "I'm getting Sammi too. Maybe her friends. I can guard a door as well as any of these guys. No—I can do it better."

Cass could sense the fury of his gaze on her, and she felt her skin flush. Ingrid and Suzanne glanced at each other, and Cass could only imagine what they were thinking. She'd caught people staring—at her, at Dor, at Valerie—and she could only guess where she fit into their assessment.

"They've got a system," she said, avoiding his eyes. "And it's only one night. We can—"

"It's *not* only one night. It's every night we're on the goddamn road, and those dickheads don't know what they're doing."

"They've gotten us this far...we haven't lost anyone since they got here, right?"

"Cass," Dor muttered, voice like grinding metal, abrading her senses. He was angry, yes, but something else, as well.

Not pleading, but—

A man like Dor did not plead. He did not even ask. But in his way, in ordering her around, he was—what? Staking his claim on her? Reminding her that she belonged with him, at any rate. And Cass knew she should rebel, because no one told her what to do anymore, she did what was right for Ruthie and right for her, and now for Smoke, and everyone else would just have to look out for themselves because she couldn't let them matter.

So why was she still standing here, rooted to the spot, the dangerous connection between them unbroken, staring into his flinty ebony eyes, letting her gaze drift down to his mouth, that mouth that was both hard and soft and—

"We'll talk later," she snapped, forcing herself to

look away, and then she took Ruthie out of the swing and walked purposefully past the other women. She gave them a fake smile to cover the fact that she was shaking all over, and went around to the front of the house where they were setting up the evening meal.

At dinner she sat with Red and Zihna and the girls. Sammi was there, and though she said nothing, she moved over to make room for Cass on the soft patch of kaysev where they were sitting.

"Won't Smoke be joining us?" Zihna asked, and Cass followed her gaze and saw that he was sitting with what Cass supposed had emerged as the new leadership. Two of the men from the East were busy with the horses; that left Mayhew and Bart, along with Shannon and Harris and Neal, engrossed in what looked like urgent conversation.

At the fringe of the group sat Dana, his back to the others, facing Owen, who sat alone twenty feet away. By morning, Owen would be cleared to rejoin the group— the fever never took more than a few hours to take hold, and the physical signs quickly followed. For a moment Cass's heart constricted at the thought of Phillip, abandoned in the quarantine house, blown into a thousand pieces, dead and disappeared on a deserted island where nothing human remained.

Still, that was a better fate than the alternative. The slow madness, the feverish twitching. The picking of the skin and pulling of the hair that slowly morphed into an unnatural, unquenchable hunger. The first nip at your own skin, finding it pleasing, the pain was nothing against the need. The hunger, growing and overwhelming, whispering in your ear as the last of your sanity slipped away, stoking the furnace of desire, until you went out into the world, no longer human but a thing of singular purpose: a hunter of flesh.

Cass had known it.

She felt her blood warm in horror and shame. This was a place she never let herself go. This was dangerous. But there was Owen…and in his expression was the faintest doubt, wasn't there? A darkness that weighed on his features, even as he joked with Dana and spit kaysev beans off into the side yard. He was wondering, wasn't he? Wondering what it would be like? And Cass was the only person here who could tell him.

Except she couldn't remember.

Frustration racked her, stinging her eyes with tears and making her dig her fingers into the dry earth, breaking her nails and scraping her knuckles. Pain helped, pain always helped; it was her last and often her only defense against the burgeoning anxiety. Cass was masterful with pain, having learned early; during the bad days with Byrn, after Cass realized that even her mother would not listen and would not help, she learned to use the pain to control the panic. After…he was done, she would go to the bathroom, and once she'd scrubbed herself raw she would get the nail clippers out and use them to snip away bits of her flesh. Places no one would ever see, the tough skin of her heels, the calluses on her fingers and the soles of her feet. And when that wasn't enough, she got the X-Acto knife from the garage, and made tiny, delicate, curved designs on her thighs, her sides. So pretty, the way the blood bloomed in the tiniest droplets, the stinging making her bite her lips.

Why couldn't she remember?

The scars on her arms had disappeared completely, the ones on her back, where the Beaters had torn into her, had faded to burnished whorls. One of the hallmarks of the very tiny percentage of the population to recover from the fever—along with the startling bright irises and the elevated body temperature and the speed at which her hair and nails grew—was the hyperefficient healing, and even scars from childhood had virtually disappeared.

Cass knew with absolute certainty that she'd been attacked, and then recovered. It was everything that happened in between that haunted her. Several weeks were unaccounted for. She'd come to in a field in the foothills, thirty miles down mountain from Silva, in clothes she didn't remember, her wounds still weeping and excruciatingly painful, her hair pulled from her scalp. In a stranger's clothes.

Owen set down the plastic bottle of water from which he'd been drinking, and his gaze landed on her. For a moment he just stared, and then his mouth curved in a slow, calculating, cruel smile. As if he knew what she was thinking, as if he knew what had happened to her.

As if he knew.

Cass looked away, face burning. She had been one of them. A Beater. The thought never failed to bring a wave of nausea; usually she was able to force it back with sheer will, but this time her gut rolled and lurched and she knew she was not going to be able to contain herself.

"Excuse me," she muttered hoarsely to Zihna and Sammi, who'd been talking across her. She got shakily to her feet and hastened around the corner of the house where the remains of a pergola was twined with dead vines. It wasn't a very effective screen, but it would have to do.

Cass knelt on the ground, the thoughts swirling relentlessly along with the pounding of her head and the roiling of her stomach. She'd been a Beater, a devourer of flesh. After she pulled out her own hair and savaged her own skin, she'd hunted. They all did. She would have. She had hunted and if any human quarry had crossed her path she had done what Beaters do, because they were driven by one need. Cass had wished and prayed and offered her soul in the bargain, those nights when she could not avoid facing the thing that had happened to her, if only she had never hurt a person, a man or woman or child, while she was changed.

But that was stupid and she knew it. Her stomach heaved one last time and Cass brought up bitter bile, gasping and coughing and retching onto the cracked earth. Beaters did one thing. It would have taken some miracle to keep *this other her* from following its need, and Cass was not a believer in miracles. She had to face the fact that she had committed abominations, that she'd done unnatural things, evil things.

Cass emptied herself onto the ground while not far away children played and people shared a meal and survivors dared to hope. She was only allowed to be a part of this community because they didn't know. If they knew what she was, they would most likely banish her. They might even kill her.

And she wasn't sure she blamed them.

When she returned, having wiped her face on her sleeve and chewed a few kaysev leaves plucked from a plant that had rooted along the house's foundation to cleanse her mouth, Cass returned to the gathering as nonchalantly as she could. Zihna gave her a concerned look but Red was in the middle of a story so Cass just forced a smile and pantomimed that she was fine, then settled back into the group and watched people finish their meal.

Dor was sitting with a group that included Jasmine and Sun-hi. Jasmine had ridden in the panel van all day, but she looked drained and exhausted, her enormous belly clearly making it difficult to get comfortable on the ground. When Dor dragged over a dusty ottoman for her to lean against, she smiled at him gratefully.

Dor was incapable of sitting still; he was always on the lookout for things that needed doing. She was watching him rig a footrest from a sofa pillow when voices raised in argument caught her attention.

"Aw, man, let him," Luddy said. He was talking to Dana, the sack that had held his dinner dangling from his hand. Luddy and Dana had never gotten along—punk and do-gooder, Cass figured there were probably some sort of father issues going on there—and it looked like Luddy was trying to provoke him, as usual. "Come on, if he had it you'd know by now."

Owen looked on, chewing on hardtack. Luddy was right, he looked fine from a distance, and it did seem cruel, leaving him alone at the edge of the group after their long day. Dana said something quietly and shrugged, but now they had the attention of the rest of the group.

"Come on, are we really gonna sink to this on our first day out?" Luddy demanded.

Owen got uncertainly to his feet, wiping his mouth with the back of his hand, stuffing the plastic bag that had held his dinner into his pocket.

"We need to be consistent enforcing the rules—" Mayhew started to say, but Dor turned on him.

"The only *we* here is *you,* buddy," Dor snapped, his hands in tight fists at his sides. "You've done all right so far, but I wouldn't start thinking you've got a free ride to go around giving orders."

That was apparently all the encouragement Owen needed. He walked toward Dana and was only a couple of steps away when a gunshot blasted and he went down, a hole ripped in his thigh.

She whipped around to see who'd fired—Smoke, his gun now aimed at Owen's heart. "Nobody go near him," he yelled. "Not until we're sure."

"What did you *do?*" a woman screamed.

"Stay where you are!"

"Put that gun away!" Mayhew had drawn too and was aiming at Smoke. It wasn't an easy shot—too far, too many people in the way.

"Smoke—" Cass started, but he cut her off, his voice calm.

"Fine. I'll go myself. I am going to walk over and check him. I'll leave my gun here." He slowly lowered it to the ground, in reach of Cass and away from the children, then stood with his hands in the air. "Shoot me if you want, but I'm telling you, if you don't know if he's infected and he's close enough to touch a citizen, he's the one you need to shoot."

Owen was sitting on the ground whimpering, his hands over his thigh, blood coursing through his fingers. Dana had scuttled back a few steps.

Mayhew said nothing for a moment and then nodded. There was silence as everyone watched Smoke limp painfully toward the downed man. When he got close enough, he knelt down, slowly, using a hand on the ground to brace himself.

For a moment the two men stared at each other. Cass knew what Smoke was looking for—the same constricted pupils citizens checked for at the buddy-ups, and the sheen and flush of the skin. If Smoke was wrong, the man was still as good as dead unless the group was willing to give up a cherished spot in one of the vehicles, as well as precious medication. But if he was right—

Suddenly Owen sprang at Smoke, knocking him over. He pinned Smoke and pounded on his chest with his fist, yelling curses. People screamed as Smoke struggled to hold off the attack. Owen was skinny and now he was also wounded, but Smoke was exhausted from the day on the road, and Cass saw that he was weakening fast.

Cass snatched up the gun from the ground and ran, stumbling over people and abandoned meals. In the seconds it took her to reach them, Smoke had managed to force Owen off him and had rolled to the side. Owen was snarling and desperately trying to grab Smoke's kicking legs.

Cass shot him. She was running when she took the shot and it went wide, hitting his shoulder rather than his head, but he stopped trying to grab Smoke and lay in the dirt, howling and bleeding from both his wounds.

Mayhew came running, followed by Dor. "Get him still," Mayhew ordered to no one particular.

"You think I'm getting close to that?" Dor demanded, and then, contradicting himself, he went within a couple feet of Owen's writhing body.

"Stop flailing around, goddamn it," he yelled.

Cass's gun hand shook. If Owen wasn't infected, then it was the second shot that had doomed him. Hers. There was no way they'd risk transporting a man with two serious wounds, a man who wouldn't be well enough to work for months, if he recovered at all.

He didn't appear to hear them. He was sobbing as he tried to stem the flow of blood from his wounds. Dor toed him in the good leg.

"Look at me, you bastard, or I'll kill you right now."

That finally got Owen's attention. "Bitch shot me…" he said, turning his unblinking eyes up at Dor.

They all saw it—Cass knew by the gasps from the crowd. Owen's irises were tiny black pinpoints, and though he was staring straight into the setting sun, he didn't squint at all.

Cass knew she only had a second. She crouched down as close to Owen as she dared.

"It was you, wasn't it?" she demanded. "You blew up the island, didn't you?"

Owen's expression turned into a smirk and he looked at Cass defiantly. "We're all gonna burn, baby, it's just a matter of when."

He barely got the words out before someone shot his face off.

29

Sammi sat on a little swing that had been hung from a covered arbor that once had plants growing on it, watching the sky go from purple to gray. There were dead spikes on the arbor, probably roses or something. Sammi had seen things like that Before, benches no one sat on, ponds with fountains that no one ever threw pennies in, paths that went nowhere. Just another way for rich people to spend money on nothing.

She'd been sitting here trying to forget what Owen Mason looked like after he'd been shot, how half of his face looked kind of normal and the other half looked like a steak dipped in barbecue sauce and covered with pink cottage cheese. There was no way she was eating anything ever again, and she kind of wished she could just lie down and sleep and not wake up until the world was normal again.

"Wondered where you went." Sammi jumped, but it

was only Colton. He'd sneaked up on her—not really, but he never made a lot of noise. He was quiet, and Sammi liked that. Most of the time she loved hanging out with Kyra and Sage, but sometimes she just wanted to not talk.

That's what they did for a while. Colton put his arm along the back of the swing, and Sammi leaned into it, and that was nice. There wasn't anything going on with them, despite what anyone thought. After Jed, Sammi wasn't…well, it would be a long time before she looked at a boy like that again, if she ever did. And Colton wasn't like that anyway, he never did anything. Maybe he was gay or something. Which Sammi wouldn't care if he was, that was cool. But whatever.

Everything was just so fucked up. Again.

Tears leaked down her face and she didn't try to hide them. Colton said, "Oh," and dug something out of his pocket, a rag or something, and it wasn't all that clean but it was nice when he dabbed at her face with it.

"That thing with Owen. Jesus," he said, shoving the rag back in his pocket.

"Yeah…I know."

"Sammi, listen, I need to tell you about something."

She said okay but a little warning went off inside. People didn't say that unless it was something big, something important. "Well, it can't be someone else dead, right?" she asked, trying for a joke.

"No." He sounded even more serious. "Owen…he was into some really bad stuff."

"No shit. He blew up the *island*. Everybody says so."

"Yeah, but…" Colton's voice trailed off for a minute, and then he took a breath and continued, kind of in a rush. "That wasn't the first time. He, uh. One time?

Shane and me were over at his place. He had, like, a whole drawer full of explosives. Electronic stuff, timers and shit, I don't even know what all. Like, to make bombs? Seriously, Sammi, he scared the crap out of me. I think he was going to…do something. He was talking about taking out the whole island."

"Well, he just about did!"

"No, I mean, before that. He said he was working on something big enough to destroy the whole place. I didn't believe him. I got the fuck out of there. But Shane, he stayed. He told me that Owen said there was all this stuff in the storehouse. He was trying to figure out how to get it. And then when the Beaters attacked and we had to leave so fast, he somehow got it all out of there."

"Owen did? Or Shane?"

"Owen. He didn't have time to rig it up to the thing he was working on, the remote or whatever, but he and Shane…it was them, Sammi. They went back when everyone was on the bridge and they blew up the community center and they blew up the quarantine house. Shane only went along because he felt bad for Phillip, he wanted to put him out of his misery but—but listen, Sammi, you can't tell anyone. Okay? You can't tell *anyone*. Now Owen's dead it doesn't matter, and Shane, no one would get it, what he was trying to do."

Sammi's skin felt cold all of a sudden. "They blew up Phillip?" she whispered.

"Only because—I mean, Sammi, Shane said he was thinking about him going crazy in there, losing his mind. He said he'd want someone to do it to him, if it was him in there."

"But…" Sammi thought of the last time she saw Phillip, of his hand reaching out through the narrow slot. She couldn't do it, no matter how much he was suffering. There was no way she could pull the switch or light the fuse or whatever. "Why are you even telling me this?"

"Because I need a favor."

In the morning Cass woke to the clang of shovels hitting dirt. She went out into the mist-thickened dawn, wrapped in a blanket, and watched from the porch as a small band of people dug a shallow grave. Owen's body lay nearby. They had not wasted so much as a tarp on him, and his corpse, awkwardly arranged and gray-pale in the morning light, stared sightlessly into the sky. Smoke was among their number, and Cass could see the perspiration on his face as he took his turn with the shovel. He should not be exerting himself like that. But who could stop him?

Dor had been as good as his word, watching over Sammi and some of the other kids upstairs. When they came down the stairs he scowled at Cass. She shrugged, but her indifference didn't reach inside. It was easy to believe, as he stepped heavily past her and the other mothers, washing their children from a shared tub of water in the house's mudroom, that he might have stood sentry all night, and she wondered if she were foolish not to take that extra measure of security. His eyes were shrouded and tired, but his body was tense with stored energy. He walked like he was looking for a fight.

But when he assembled with some of the other new council on the porch as the group loaded up for the journey, he stayed near the back and let Mayhew do the talking. He stared straight ahead, detached and almost indifferent as the Easterners addressed the Edenites.

"Many of you have come to me with questions," Mayhew began. He had tied his hair back in its leather string and trimmed his gray beard. Cass had seen him sitting at a window in the kitchen, a small mirror propped on the sill, leaning close with a pair of small scissors, unmindful of the rotted-food stench in the place. "And I promised you answers. I won't take up too much of your time now, because we want to cover a lot of ground today. But I want you to know that you can come to me and my men anytime. Questions, concerns, what have you. Last night I think we all learned something."

Red, tying down their belongings on the small trailer, made a sound in his throat, making no attempt to hide his skepticism. Zihna shot him a warning look.

"I'd like to thank Smoke here for his quick thinking, and Cass, and all of you who shared in the unpleasant... duty. Well, it's always difficult." He pursed his lips and stared at the ground for a respectful moment. He was good, Cass had to give him that. He'd taken little responsibility for the screwup with Owen, and yet here he was directing a moment of silence for him, and people were going along with it. She caught Smoke's eye; he sat on the edge of the porch, his back against a column, resting his hip. He gave little away in the tiny flash of a reassuring smile he gave her.

So neither of her men was going to challenge Mayhew, not over this. And none of the others, who were clustered near the group—Shannon, Neal, certainly not Dana, who was tightly rolling a ground cloth and stuffing it into a small nylon sack, his mouth tight and his eyes lowered—would either.

"Until six weeks ago we were doing fine," Mayhew began. "We—all of us here—were on the border patrol across the Rockies. We'd stop people trying to come east now and then, heard what they had to say about conditions *west* of the Rockies before we sent 'em back. No one got through. No one.

"Then one day the blueleaf showed up in our lands, too. Had to be avian migration, we're figuring, but it doesn't really matter because in one week—*one week*—there were six cases in town. We locked the whole town down, put everyone in a six-block area until we could get a handle on whether it had spread any further, but then a couple cases popped up in town five miles away, and then suddenly there's rumors of people going missing from one place and the infected showing up wandering around somewhere else, feverish. It's terrible over there now."

"Welcome to our world," a woman muttered not far from Cass, but she was quickly shushed. This was the first confirmation any of them had of the stories that occasionally reached New Eden.

They'd heard rumors of the arming of the natural border created by the Rockies a few months ago, when people who'd attempted to travel east returned to tell the story. There had been a couple of guys in the Box who claimed to have tried to cross at the Eisenhower Tunnel. They told of seeing rotting corpses on the west side of I-70, would-be émigrés who didn't take no for an answer and were shot for their efforts and left to serve as a warning. There were only a few other places where a crossing on foot was even possible, and these were all patrolled, or land-mined.

There had been considerable resentment of the East after that. Calls for quarantine—you could hold people for a week, and it would be clear who was feverish from blueleaf kaysev and who was not at that point—were re-buffed by the border patrol, who were rumored to shoot not only those who attempted to force their way across but also those who merely argued too strenuously.

Dana looked up from his task, his face puffy and pale. He evidently hadn't slept well, and his expression was petulant. "So you're just getting a taste of what we've been dealing with," he muttered. Cass couldn't help thinking that what New Eden had been dealing with was, largely, keeping its head in the sand and going soft, that until now they'd been well fed and comfortable.

"Maybe so," Mayhew said coldly. "But we've been sending patrols north, too. That's where we're headed. Beaters can't tolerate the cold and neither can blueleaf. We've got a plan. And a destination. Now, look. We never meant to come barging in on you and take over. But if our two groups pool our resources, our intelligence, we stand a lot better chance of finding a place where we can build a *real* community, somewhere that we can actually thrive, where we're not looking over our shoulders every second of the day."

"How far north are we talking?" Phil Booth demanded.

"Word is if we get up into the Cascade range, both threats drop off significantly."

"Jesus. How far exactly? How many days on the road?"

Mayhew's expression didn't so much falter as harden, but when he spoke his voice was calm and even encouraging. "I won't lie to you. This is going to be a few hard weeks. But think about the alternatives, my friends. We try to shelter anywhere around here, we're into the same problems you've already been up against."

Silence. People stole glances at each other, shuffled their feet, fidgeted with their things. Cass watched Dor, his arms folded across his chest, his jaw set. His gaze bored into hers and he did not look away.

Then a woman near the front of the crowd raised her hand. It was one of Collette's do-gooder friends, Cass didn't remember her name. She was still soft through the middle, fleshy and wan, somehow.

"The Beaters, the way they learned to swim," she said breathlessly. "Everything was fine until a few days ago when they decided to try to get in the water and then it was like they all decided to jump in the water all at once. If they can learn that, what else are they gonna do next?"

"They've got their own language now!" a man called from the back of the crowd.

"That's ridiculous," Dor snapped, raising his head and uncrossing his arms, craning his neck to see who'd spoken. "There's absolutely no indication of that, and spreading rumors isn't going to help. You people need to calm down."

"It's okay, Dor, I've got this," Mayhew said calmly. "Everyone's just a little on edge."

Sure, Cass figured darkly, watching your friends die horribly might put anyone "a little on edge." And yet people seemed to find Mayhew soothing.

He stopped clear of taking any sort of vote, and Cass wondered if it was because he wasn't confident he had the majority convinced yet. As they set out into the morning, she saw the subtle shifts in the company people were keeping.

Dana walked alone, kicking stones and occasionally talking to himself. Shannon tried to talk to him when they stopped for lunch near a murky pond, taking the opportunity to boil water to refill all of their reserves. Cass overheard a little of their conversation as she took Ruthie and Twyla looking for pretty rocks in the field next to the pond.

"...don't know who he thinks he is," Dana was saying angrily.

Cass glanced back at them a few times while she and the girls strolled; she saw Shannon gesturing, pleading maybe, before finally giving up and going to join the others.

Cass had volunteered to watch the girls to give Suzanne a break, but the truth was she needed a little time to herself. No. The truth was that she was fighting an urge for a drink. Not that there was one to be had, but the unsettled feeling left over from Mayhew's little speech had spiraled into a full-on tangle of worries, the sort that usually found her deep in the night.

Days tended to be easier. Last time she quit drinking, Cass filled them with work, with running, with caring for Ruthie. And she could usually stave off a craving by throwing herself into arduous physical work. Digging stones from a field. Weeding between rows. Anything at all to drown out the anxiety.

On the road was different. She had no sense of control. She moved when the group moved, stopped when they stopped. Everyone else seemed to be content knowing only that they were headed "north," but the uncertainty of the future only added to her anxiety.

She walked, head down, with her hands in her pockets, reciting the litany of phrases she'd picked up in her long-ago meetings, inane little sayings that did nothing to boost her confidence in herself but sometimes, occasionally, could pull her back into that feeling of thin hope, that she really might be able to get through this, that she really could survive without a drink.

If God brings me to it, He will bring me through it
I am not failing as long as I am trying

She heard, in her whispered words, dozens of other voices. Since the end of everything she had seen no one from the meetings. Not one of them. They were all probably dead. What would they have chosen, Cass wondered, if they knew how few days they had left—to keep coming back, or to go on a bender the likes of which no one had ever seen? Would they have drunk themselves to death?

She had the start of a headache, a faint breathlessness. Nothing too terrible. And food would help. She could get through this, she could—

Cass looked around. They'd walked to the far edge of the field—strawberries, it looked like, the long-dead plants choked now by kaysev—and there was a worn split-rail fence that might have been pretty if the vines twined around the wood weren't all brittle and brown.

But though Cass turned around, a complete circle, she did not see the girls.

"Ruthie!" she called, her voice hoarse. "Twyla!"

Oh God, she hadn't been watching, hadn't been listening, she'd been lost inside her own head, her own cravings. For a second Cass was frozen in terror and mortification, eyes darting everywhere, gathering her breath to scream—

And then she heard their voices, bright peals of laughter spilling from behind a tractor that had been abandoned in the field. A second later Twyla's head popped up on the bench, followed by Ruthie's.

"Mama!" Ruthie called. "Look, we're farmers!"

Cass forced a smile, her stomach seized with adrenaline and fear. She felt like she would throw up again, but that couldn't happen, not here, not in this moment of the girls' delight.

"Oh, *look* at you two!" she called through a smile she dredged up from her paltry heart. "Show me how you grow your crops!"

And she hastened toward the girls, fixing her gaze on their sweet faces. If she couldn't beat her cravings, then she'd just have to outrun them, keep running toward the next right thing and the next.

That night she had thought to speak to Smoke, to confess how bad she'd gotten. He would be disappointed in her, but he would be compassionate, too. Smoke was like that; he wouldn't let her suffer alone. And she was willing now to trade a little of her dignity for a few moments of his comfort.

But as they set up camp for the night in a feed and supply store, after first clearing out several long-abandoned Beater nests and searching the much-looted supply shelves for anything useful, Cass could not get a moment alone with Smoke.

His limp was far more pronounced in the afternoons, after the day of exertion had taken its toll. His face was slightly ashen and she knew he was in pain. And yet he wouldn't take a break. He helped Davis and Bart— and Valerie, Cass couldn't help noticing with an uneasy feeling—to feed and water the horses, and then he and Mayhew and Terrence and a couple other guys made a tour of the other buildings in the town while there was still daylight, looking for anything useful. They made a decent raiding party, well armed and cautious; they came back with a few tools and several armloads of firewood. Terrence had found someone's rainy-day stash in a canister. He shook it out upside down on the fire once they got the kindling going, and dozens of bills fluttered down and caught flame, the kids laughing at the spectacle.

But throughout the meal and the cleanup, Smoke stayed away. He talked to Mayhew, to Davis and Nadir, even to Dor for a few tense moments. He made his way around to the kids, impressing Colton and the other boys with a brief knife-throwing demonstration. When Cass came back from taking Ruthie outside to wash before bed, he'd set up his bedroll near the front, along with the Easterners and others who were well armed, and was already deeply asleep, his face sheltered in the crook of his arm.

Sleep was slow to come, despite Cass's exhaustion. She knew what Smoke was up to because she had seen it before. He was doing what he did best, building the collective courage of the group, just as he'd once encouraged and developed the security team in the Box. And there was no doubt that it needed to be done; without the cohesiveness he provided, they could easily splinter into factions, start blaming each other for the things that had happened.

So why did she feel so empty every time she spotted him in the crowd?

Yet again, Smoke was not choosing her. He was a good man, a great man, even; these were the qualities that had made him a hero long before his last battle with the Rebuilders. But in his heroism he acted alone. Even when he'd been working with Dor, he was solitary. When he sought vengeance he sought it for himself. He wanted Cass with him, she knew that, but only in the moments left over after he'd vanquished his greater thirst, to fix a world that he could never forgive himself for allowing to go to hell in the first place.

Cass knew there was something at the core of his drive that he'd never shared with her, the key to this crushing sense of responsibility, the blood thirst he carried with him everywhere he went. Smoke had told his secret to only one man, and that was Dor, and that was as good as any vault. She knew she might never know. Whatever Smoke had done, it plagued him, consumed him; the truth was a lover from whose arms Cass could not entice or drag or trick Smoke.

She tossed and turned long after the room was silent, dozens of her fellow survivors deep in their own private dream landscapes, where the luckiest visited memories of Before and others battled horrors real and imagined.

As people began moving from their homes to shelters during the Siege, it was hard to get used to the nights at first. Some people compared it to prison—

overcrowding in California meant that many prisoners shared small spaces lined with back-to-back bunk beds, images of which frequently made the evening news—but Joe, one of the guards in the Box who had actually been in prison, said it was worse. Worse because at least in prison there were clear hierarchies of power, of who got the best bunk, who could tell who else to shut the fuck up or quit snoring or crying or beating off. Joe said it was the *politeness* that got to him on the outside—when the Siege made *everything* part of the outside—everyone forced to lie next to people they might not even like, to quietly endure their sounds and smells and proximity, then get up and pretend to have had a good night's sleep.

Cass forced herself to lie still, trying to will the thoughts from her mind, counting backward from a thousand, anything to quiet her restless thoughts. When someone whispered her name, her eyes flew open to find Red crouching next to her, a ghostly presence in the glow of a lantern turned low and hung from a nail.

"You're not asleep, are you, Cassie? Wanna talk?"

She hesitated only for a moment before getting up carefully so as not to disturb the others, and following him into the house. They felt along the wall in the darkness, to the front door where one of the Easterners was sitting on the ottoman that Dor had brought for Jasmine earlier.

"She had nightmares," Red murmured to the guard. "We're just going to sit out here for a bit, okay?"

"Suit yourself," the man said.

There was enough starlight to find the benches that faced each other across a flower bed. They sat close together and Red unfolded a blanket he'd brought, spreading it carefully over the two of them.

"Aw, Cassie darlin', who would have thought it." He sighed.

Cass couldn't help a cynical laugh. "Who would have thought which part? That the world would be taken over by zombies? That we'd be grazing like cattle on a plant invented in a lab, just to stay alive? Or that by some miracle you'd show up in my life again after abandoning me for twenty-three years?"

After the words were out, Cass wished she hadn't said the last part. She knew exactly how many years it was since her dad left. All those years, she'd kept track. But why give him that satisfaction? After all, she'd long ago quit caring that he was gone.

"It wasn't a miracle," Red said softly.

"Okay, a curse. Is that better? You were cursed with having to run into me again. In all the bars, in all the—"

"No, that's not what I meant. I *found* you, Cassie. It wasn't an accident."

A tickle started along her spine. "Um, well, if you remember, you were already living in New Eden when we got there, so technically, *I* found *you.* And since there aren't all that many places to live left out here, it's not exactly a miracle that we both ended up in the same one, know what I mean?"

"I don't mean in New Eden. I mean before that."

"Before that, when? Before I came here I lived in the Box and I know for a fact you weren't there. Before that I lived in a library and I never saw—"

"The day you were taken, Cass. The day you were attacked. By the Beaters. I was *there.*"

31

He'd still been going by Silver Dollar then. Or Tom Haverford, his real name, to his oldest and closest friend in the world, Carmy Gomez, with whom he'd been traveling the highways and byways of the West Coast, playing in clubs and bars and music festivals, opening for other acts and generally making enough money to cover their costs and salt a little away. Tom had even been paying for rock-bottom health insurance, really a lottery Madoff scheme run by a local charity, but even that was a bit of a trick given his lack of a permanent address, but lately he'd begun thinking about the past, about things he wished he'd done differently. And the last thing he wanted, assuming there was anyone who still cared about him, was to be a burden to them now when he'd managed to be a burden way too many times already in his sorry life.

His mother. Over eighty but still hanging on to the

little bungalow he grew up in, last he called, a few months back.

His half brother, Burt. Burt hated him, sure, but Tom figured he'd given him cause, the way he'd tormented him during their childhood.

His ex-wife. Well, there was no chance she gave a shit about him anymore. Still, he added her to the list of beneficiaries; she'd more than earned it.

And Cassie.

Tom thought more and more about the past as the days ticked by. He thought about telling Carmy about it, but Carmy wasn't that kind of guy, not someone you spilled your guts to, even though Tom knew his old friend would take a bullet for him. Carmy had always had a way with people. He played bass, could pitch in on a set when needed, but mostly he was their manager—finagler of gigs, extractor of payment, riler of crowds and bedder of women. He was good-natured, funny—and fond of anything he could snort, inject or ingest. But they worked around that. It was a scheduling thing more than anything; Carmy could go three, four weekends in a row keeping his shit together and then they'd just hole up somewhere for a while and he'd go nuts and Tom would find a used bookstore or a movie theater or a pretty waitress and while away a week.

The truth was that Tom was content to sit on a beach, or in a park, or on a bench in front of a city hall, or even in a motel room while the rain came down outside, and play his guitar and hum along, throwing in a phrase or two when it struck his fancy. If he'd written down a fraction—a hundredth—of the great lyrics that came to him when he was messing around, he'd have a million dollars, but he was too lazy. He just liked playing.

The things Tom could do with a guitar on his best days rivaled anything Knopfler had ever done, and the crowds would always notice eventually. If he and Carmy had managed to keep a band together for more than a season, they could have written their own ticket, but the truth was that their lifestyle didn't suit that many people. Especially as they'd gotten older. Sometimes they'd pick up a young guy to sing or play horn or whatever, but even they got worn down after a while. So be it—Tom and Carmy were content with their lot.

Then in a cheap motel in a little town an hour north of L.A., two things happened.

First, Carmy met a woman, disappeared for a week and somehow ended up in the hospital with a gash in his chest that he claimed was accidental but which had nicked a lung and threatened to keep him laid up for a while. And second, Tom saw his first case of the fever, a woman who'd been staying in the same motel even longer than he had and, if he wasn't mistaken, with whom he was pretty sure he'd previously spent a drunken night.

Her name was Beverly or Brenda, something with a *B,* and when he bumped into her on the stairs, she reached out to touch his face and for a moment he thought it was an invitation. His room was on the second floor, hers on the first, and he'd been trying to figure out how to politely decline the come-on and edge past her. He was headed for the bar across the street, where he planned to watch the news on the big-screen TV; everything was so fucked up, with the terrorists and now the rioting in the cities, that Tom was starting to get a little alarmed.

"Hey, darlin', in a bit of a hurry here," he'd said

smoothly, giving her his best smile. That's when she pinched the skin of his jowl hard and pulled his face toward her, her mouth opening and her eyes unfocused.

Tom knew now that if he hadn't been so startled that he tripped over his own feet and fell down the stairs, that would have been the end of him, and he and Bev would have been roaming the streets together before long, looking for snacks. Instead, he made it to the bar with only a little bruising, talked to some folks and figured out that if there was ever a time for making amends it probably ought to be now.

His ex-wife wasn't hard to find—ten minutes on the library's computer got him her address, not five miles from the house he'd last called home, and within the hour he was hitching his way back to Silva. The trip was terrifying, as traffic from the cities clogged the inland roads and gas stations started putting up signs that said NO GAS HERE and the cost of a slice of pie quadrupled. He made the last six miles on foot after the driver of the car he'd been riding in crashed into a stalled RV.

All that momentum…and when Tom got back he suddenly lost his nerve. He walked to his ex-wife's new house and stood across the street for an hour, cursing himself for not using the long journey to figure out what to actually say. Finally, he walked another half hour to a bar and got good and soused, drunk enough to bloody the mouth of the guy on the next stool over, who told him not only did he know Cass Haverford, but he'd been a year ahead of her at Silva High and had screwed her once in the locker room and once six years later in the parking lot of the same bar where they just now happened to be sitting. And so had most of his friends, one of whom happened to be at the same bar and who, after some hard persuasion, was happy to share that she'd gotten knocked up and changed her last name to Dollar. And then he threw in her new address for good measure.

On the way to his daughter's house, Tom thought about the fact that his little girl had changed her name. The last time they'd been together, he'd taken her to a baseball game and promised her that he'd be big someday, that the name Silver Dollar would be up in lights in places twice as big as the stadium. He'd said she would always be able to find him just by looking for those bright lights—but that had been a lie, hadn't it?

When he saw the dump his Cassie was living in, Tom suffered an even bigger setback. Because it had never occurred to him that his little girl, despite the benefit of not living under his influence, would grow up to be just like him.

He spent the night in an apartment building across the street from her trailer park. Someone had broken all the windows in the ground-floor apartment, and the occupants had fled, but the bedroom still had some furniture in it and Tom slept on the sagging box spring with a knife under his pillow. The next day, while he waited for courage to find him, he boarded up the windows and took stock of the place. Maybe it would do for a few days while he figured things out. Meanwhile he could keep an eye on his daughter's comings and goings.

Except she never went anywhere.

Tom grew bold, squeezing between her trailer and the thick oleander hedge that separated it from the next one, and peering through the windows. The oleander was dying, its leaves curling and turning that baked-red shade that signaled death by the biological agent drifting in from its rural targets. The government said the stuff didn't pose a threat to livestock or humans, but Tom figured once it got in the groundwater, they were all fucked. Still, he had bigger things to worry about.

Cassie sat on her couch a lot. She also cried a lot. Sometimes, she lay on the floor and cried.

Also—even worse—there were children's things in the trailer. A crib, toys on the floor, one of those things you stick them in to keep them still, with all the bobbly devices attached to it to entertain a baby. But there was no baby.

Tom puzzled over what it all meant. He supposed he could knock on the door and ask her, tell her who he was and why he'd come, but all his instincts told him that she would not receive that news well. And who could blame her?

It tore him up more than he could have ever imagined: his daughter, all grown-up and heartrendingly beautiful even in dirty clothes and no makeup, had clearly arrived at her own rock bottom. As one day turned into two, and then three, Tom began to understand that it was now his life's purpose to help her back up. Maybe—he sometimes thought, during those yearning days—that had been his purpose all along and every set in every nightclub had just been the sound track leading up to this moment.

He was determined not to screw it up.

He considered and abandoned dozens of ideas. All around him, the town was going to the dogs. Before long the apartment house in which he was squatting emptied out, except for a few of the freaky fever people who moved into the other ground-floor apartment. Red talked to people in the streets who urged him to find a shelter. That's what everyone was doing, moving into movie theaters and city hall and grocery stores, big open places where they could pool their resources and keep the scary fuckers out—the rumor was that they were starting to attack people and infect them, too. Rabies, they'd called it. If only. And frankly Tom thought everyone was right, that until someone got a handle on this epidemic, holing up like scared little girls was exactly the right thing to do. The fevered were terrifying as shit.

But he wasn't about to leave until his daughter did. By then he'd evolved a sort of plan—when Cassie moved into a shelter, he'd just follow along and see if he could get into the same one. When they were safe, and maybe fed—Tom was getting damn tired of eating out of cans, and he wasn't keen on eating the K7-whatever-the-hell the government was calling it, like a damn horse—then he'd test the waters and figure out how to tell her who he was.

He almost missed it. One morning she walked out the door carrying a duffel bag, and Tom only saw it because the plumbing had stopped a few days earlier and he'd gone out to take a morning whiz against the side of his building.

He followed her, not even bothering to go back for his few toiletries, afraid to lose her.

When she went to her mother's house, Tom was surprised. He'd sort of thought they were estranged.

When she came out a little later carrying a little girl, he was stunned.

He followed them to the library, but when she went inside, he stayed out.

He wanted to come in. Meant to. Planned to. But this was truly the end of the line. If she said no to him now, if she didn't want to see him here, where else could he go?

Across the street, that was where. From the upper floor of the municipal center, in a big room still decorated with crepe paper from a bat mitzvah—Mazel Tov, Jessica!—he watched the sun go down on the library and wondered if this was to be his lot until the end of time, stalking his daughter, too afraid to come close, too desperate to make amends to ever truly walk away from her.

She came outside the next day looking like his little girl again. The grown-up version, anyway. The smile was back on her face. Her clothes were clean and she'd pulled back her shiny hair. Her necklace glinted gold in the sun. She walked tall, cradling her own little girl in her arms, pointing out the clouds and the mountains to her. When they got to the curved drive, Cassie set the baby down to play, and she toddled around the dried-out lawn. The little girl had the pale fine hair and big round eyes that Cassie had had at that age, and Tom's throat closed up with emotion and for a moment he felt like he was looking through a lens that erased time, almost three decades, and he wanted to run and swing her into the air and make her a promise that he'd never leave her, but just when he was thinking that this time he might actually take the first step someone screamed and Tom had the terrible premonition that he had waited too long, that Fate waited to snatch away the daughter he did not deserve.

"You were there?" Cass asked softly.

"I was there. Cassie...I always wanted to be there. With you. I just—well, I fucked it up. I was a fuckup. I admit it. And I know admitting it's not enough, really, I do. I'd have to live nine lives like a cat to make it all up to you, but all I've got is this one."

Red—her dad—reached for a corner of the blanket that had fallen from Cass's shoulder and tucked it up around her again, and she saw that he was shivering.

"Here, we can share," she said, and shook the fleece out and let it drift down over both of them, scooching closer. As the soft fabric settled she leaned against him, lightly. It was probably wrong. It was definitely stupid to trust him like this, when he'd been in her life for what—a couple of months, if he could even be believed—and out of it for decades.

But Aftertime had a funny way of jiggering the math, of coming up with conclusions that weren't supported by the facts. Because the *facts*—death and infection rates, life expectancies, chemical hazards, the evil hearts of humans—were devastating on their own, unleavened with little miracles like hope and forgiveness and redemption.

"Tell me the rest."

Tom was paralyzed, leaning on the second-story window frame and looking down at the scene across the street, hearing the screams coming from the library's little entrance area where a few people had been smoking and getting some air.

The entrance area would have been a good place to play, because you could get back inside and slam the door shut in mere seconds. But Cassie hadn't stayed there. She had wandered out to the circle drive with her daughter, and they were bent down looking for bugs or something, oblivious to what was going on around them.

When the screaming started Cassie lifted her head and looked for the source of the trouble, already scrambling for her daughter, but the little girl pranced out of the way, focused on whatever caught her eye on the ground.

And then Tom saw the things. Four of them, bursting around the corner, running like a bunch of drunks on wobbly legs, grabbing at the air and making gobbling sounds—headed straight for Cassie.

Then he ran, too. Down the hall, the stairs, stumbling and slamming into the wall of the stairwell but he didn't care. He got to the bottom and unbelievably—the door jammed.

Tom heaved and kicked and when he realized there was no way he was getting through he ran back up to the second floor and down the hall to the front apartment. He yanked up the window roughly and crawled out onto the ledge and dropped, aiming for a hedge, feeling the dead branches scrape his flesh as he landed and rolled, and then he was on his feet and running and just in time to see the things dragging his beautiful girl away, holding on to her legs and arms.

Tom didn't hesitate for a second but he knew he had to be careful, had to be craftier than they were because he'd heard tales of what they could do, and he would be outnumbered and outmuscled if they turned on him. He didn't much care if they ripped him to shreds, but he had to get to Cassie first, had to get her away from them before they bit and infected her.

It wasn't that hard to keep up with them, racing along dusty backyards, catching glimpses of them loping down the street, dragging his poor little girl along the road, swinging her from their crabbed hands. She'd gone limp, and he hoped and prayed she'd got-

ten knocked out somehow, because he couldn't imagine anything more terrifying than to be carried by these
monsters and know there was no one there to help you
and no one around to care about your fate.

But that's what he'd always done, wasn't it? Hadn't
Tom left her behind half a dozen times before, heading
down the driveway when she ran out after him, clutching his hand with her little ones, holding on to the car
door when he started the engine, bursting into tears
as he drove away? He'd always promised to be back
again—*"Soon, you won't even notice I'm gone"*—but
somewhere on the inside, he'd known that the promises
were a lie. There was always a new town, a new gig,
a riff he wanted to try or a song he wanted to cover,
or a woman with long eyelashes and satiny shoulders.
And the road—there was always the road, calling to
him, seducing him, making silvery promises that he
couldn't resist.

Tom ran faster, sickened by his many failures. He'd
trade his own future, his own life, to give Cassie another chance.

The monstrous things turned onto a small alley and
headed for a shed, a nice one someone had built the
right way, timber construction over a poured foundation. One of the barn-style doors had come off its hinges
and was leaning against the building, letting light into
the small building. It was a mess, garden tools and a
ride-on mower and cans of paint strewn everywhere. In
the center was a thick mound of rags, and Tom understood that this was their home, that they had brought
his daughter here to eat her.

Now he didn't worry about staying hidden. He ran
into the open like he was on fire, ignoring the burning

in his lungs, the pain in his knees. He got there as they threw her facedown onto the nest and fell upon her. He saw them pin her down with their knees, watched them rip the clothes from her back. They were screaming nonsense syllables now, something that sounded like "mam-mam-mam-mam" and he thought he might vomit when he saw that one of them was actually *drooling,* a long string of saliva falling from its mouth.

That was the one that Tom tried to pull off first, but it only lashed at him with surprising strength before returning to the exposed flesh of his daughter's back. Red was flung back against the wall of the shed, hitting his head on a bare stud, knocking over a bottle of coolant that hit the floor and burst open, pink liquid seeping everywhere, a sharp note in the nauseating smell of the nest.

Frantically, Red looked for a weapon. He heard his daughter moan and saw the things bite into her, tearing open her skin, rich red blood pouring from the wounds.

Later, he would wonder why it didn't occur to him then that she was lost—that she was doomed to the disease in those seconds, infected like the rest of them. But he was frenzied in his purpose, determined to stop them at the cost of anything: his life, the world, the universe, anything at all.

His hand fell on the handle of an axe.

Tom swung the axe up and over his head before he was even fully aware of it. Its weight as familiar as the boots on his feet. Tom had been raised high in the Sierras where it took two cords of firewood just to get through a single winter, and as the only son of a working man he'd split more than his share of good dry mountain pine, the scent of the sap and the seasoned wood coming back to him now in a rush as he brought the axe blade crashing down onto the neck of the Beater who'd shoved him, cleaving his head off and burying the blade into the floor inches from his daughter's hip.

He took a little more care against the second one, because he was for damn sure not going to hurt so much as a hair of his daughter, and he sank the blade through its shoulders, severing the spine and lodging the axe so that it took some effort to pull it back out.

Only two of the things remained now, and they looked at him curiously. They were covered now with the blood of their companions, Cassie unconscious beneath them. One crawled toward him, right over the body of his daughter, and for that affront earned itself a blow from the side, the axe head hitting with such force that the skull cracked and splintered like an Easter egg.

That left the last one, and it glared at Tom with its mouth wide open, bellowing in rage and excitement. Tom saw with disgust that it had bitten off its own tongue, leaving a ragged lump of meat bobbing in its mouth. It sprang at Red, knocking him down, the axe falling from his hands. The thing was about his size and weight, but as it threw itself on top of him and knocked the breath from his chest, screaming one last time in triumph before lowering its blood-spattered, scabbed and mangled face to feed on him, Tom realized that he was going to die here, in this shed, covered with the blood of the monsters that the earth had spawned, and his daughter would die and would never even know that he died for her.

That realization twisted him savagely, jerking him back. He put everything he had—every synapse, every nerve ending, every muscle and thought—into one last heave and the monster toppled, its face hitting the floor, and even though it recovered immediately and twisted like an eel to grab him again at the ankle, Red had found the handle of the axe and he was just a little bit faster, a little bit wilier and a hell of a fucking lot more determined than some mindless feeder, and it was an awkward blow, that last one, without the benefit of a good windup or gravity on his side, and when the blade crashed down it didn't finish the thing off entirely.

So when Tom used the last of his strength to pick up his daughter and carry her from that hell place, the inhuman mass watched from the floor, its neck broken and bleeding, its eyes blinking and fluttering, and though its cries weakened and its body twitched, it was still scrabbling with its broken-nailed fingers to reach her.

That night, Tom didn't get very far. He found shelter in a house a few blocks away. He dragged a dresser in front of the front door and ran the taps dry, collecting the water in every pot in the kitchen as the sun slipped down and the light bled away into night. He bathed his poor daughter, so gently, laying her out on a rug in the bathroom, letting the water run onto the floor, where it pooled in the tiled corners. He gently squeezed the water from what was left of her hair, and more water seeped into the cracks. Who was going to care if it ruined the walls below? Her wounds were horrible, entire strips of her flesh missing, muscle and sinew and even bone exposed, but somehow the bleeding had slowed and he was able to bandage her roughly with sheet strips torn from one of the beds and supplies he found in the linen closet.

If she died that night, it would not be for lack of effort on his part.

When he'd wrapped her as well as he could, finding some soft knit pants, a sweater, socks in a closet, he placed her tenderly on the bed in the master bedroom and arranged the blankets so that they would not weigh on her wounds. Still she remained unconscious, her eyelids twitching and small mumbled syllables escaping her from time to time. He kissed her forehead, her hair, her fingers, and then he gently closed the door to the bedroom and sat down in the hall outside, a knife from the kitchen in his hands and several more on the carpet at his side, and as he waited for the long night to pass he prayed for God to understand that he had done his best and would do his best again and again, as long as He demanded it.

32

Cass barely remembered to keep breathing while her father told his story. He'd been there. He'd been watching—keeping vigil, really—while she and Ruthie played outside in the sunshine.

How many times had she berated herself for her foolish choice? She knew better than to risk venturing outside the walls of the library. And for such a poor trade: she'd exchanged their safety for dandelions, when surely she could have found Ruthie a dandelion growing in the sheltered courtyard; for the same breeze that blew through the screens in the conference room; for a chance for a few moments of alone time with her baby girl, when she was dooming them both to a solitary death.

Cass had replayed those moments outside a thousand times in her mind. She'd opened the library's heavy metal door, giving the frowning door guard a sunny grin—no one was forbidden from coming and going, at least not back then—and let Ruthie scoot ahead of her out into the bright sunshine of a spring day. She'd promised Ruthie that she would show her the paving brick that had her name on it, the one bought by her mother and stepfather during the library's fundraising campaign the prior year, before anyone realized that the world was about to end.

Ruthie had skipped and sung, clapped her hands in delight at the tiny yellow buttons of dandelions growing among the kaysev. She'd picked a handful, marveling at the stems' bitter milky juice, and Cass had been so busy being grateful for the moment that she never saw the Beaters until it was too late.

But her father had been watching over them. He'd set aside his own safety for them, and the novelty of that knowledge was warm and curious, unfurling slowly inside her mind. He'd cared about her, enough to search for her, enough to fight for her. And as for not being able to gather the courage to come straight to her— well. Cass was certainly not one to judge. Shame had prompted a thousand of her own missteps and mistakes, and if things might have been different if her father had knocked on the door of the library before Cass ventured out that day, well, she had learned that you could never rewrite history, that Fate would always prevail.

She had not winced and she had not looked away when her father described the carnage in the shed: she was trying too hard to remember. But, nothing. She had no memory of the things carrying her to the shed, no memory of their teeth tearing at her flesh, no memory of the axe and the blood and the screaming and her father lifting her, cradling her, rescuing her. The bath…there was something there, a faint shadowy flicker, a notion of floating, of water sluicing away her blood, cool and healing, making her weightless. Maybe it was nothing but a sense memory of unconsciousness, but Cass wanted to believe she could remember something good. She'd seen Red's gentle way with Ruthie and the other kids; surely he'd been just as gentle with her.

Already she was intoxicated with the notion that he cared for her. That her father, disappeared for so long, loved her. She'd despised him for so long, disguising the pain of his abandonment in stubborn fury, but all of that was slipping away as he talked. She knew it was supposed to take a long time; she expected to take a lifetime to forgive him, as so many of the people at the A.A. meetings made clear, early hurts were often permanent.

But Aftertime, a lifetime was a luxury that could not be counted on. If she ever hoped to forgive, she had to start now. If she hoped to absorb the fact that she had been loved, she had to seize it and hold fast.

She wanted her father to keep talking, to keep spinning this tale whose words felt like silken strands weaving themselves into a shield that would protect her, even—especially—from her own self-contempt. Only…there was more to the story. A lot more. Not least of it the fact that when she woke, she was alone.

"So I never woke up?"

"No, not that night, and not for a long time after."

Cass was silent, thinking about her father keeping sentry outside the room. She wanted to know if he had the beard, then, or if he was clean-shaven, the way she remembered him. She knew it didn't matter, and she wondered anyway.

"What did you do in the morning?" she asked instead.

Tom shrugged. "There was a car in the garage, an old Honda Civic, beat to hell. My guess is it was a kid's car or a second car or something. Keys on a rack by the door, believe it or not. It couldn't have been much easier. I got you laid out in the backseat, took everything I could from the house, medicine and food and whatnot, clothes. Pulled up the garage door and off we went. Kind of amazing, now that we've all heard the stories."

Cass knew the stories he meant—by that time, there were roving bands of marauders at the edge of town who waited for cars to come by and then shot out the tires. They were after the gas, the things people carried—the sport. Later, you'd find these cars abandoned at the side of the road, often with corpses with holes in their heads draped over the seats, or on the ground, shot in the back when they tried to run away.

"So no one stopped you?"

"No. But it might have helped that I went all back roads. I knew enough to avoid any of the main roads, but mostly I thought I was avoiding the Beaters." He laughed mirthlessly. "I guess I didn't understand them very well. I'd a made a shitty anthropologist. I figured they'd stick to the main roads because it was easier or something…I was probably giving them too much credit."

"Well, at least you were right about one thing. If you'd gone on the highway you probably wouldn't have made it far."

"Yeah. As it was, I just took farm roads and dirt roads. A lot of 'em I hadn't been on since I was a kid, but it's funny how that stuff stays with you."

"Why did you go down mountain? As opposed to up?"

Red shrugged. "No good reason, I guess. I mean, if I'd had the balls I would have taken you back to the shelter, I guess. But I thought Ruthie was dead, and I figured you didn't have long for the world."

"You mean because I was infected."

"Well, hell yeah. I thought there was no way you'd survive."

"So why…" Cass's breath caught in her throat and she took a minute to steady herself before trying again. "Why didn't you just kill me?"

Red didn't answer for a moment, but his eyes shone wetly in the darkness.

"I couldn't," he finally whispered.

Cass nodded. The strongest men—Smoke and Dor among them—had become killers in order to be merciful. The ones who couldn't kill an infected person ended up bringing more misery for everyone.

But she wasn't in a place to judge. She herself had walked away from a victim nearly senseless with shock and pain after the skin had been chewed from its body, unable to do what needed to be done, leaving the job for someone else.

"It's just that it was *you,*" Red said. "Someone else… in the days that came after that, I did have to kill, twice. People who were infected. One asked me to. One…well, no sense dwelling on that now.

"Anyway, I got almost as far as the foothills but it took me all day. Kept having to go around wrecks and shit, even on the back roads. Saw a couple Beaters too, scared the crap outta me. So when it started to get late in the day I just picked out a farmhouse, one of those ones on cattle acreage, up on a rise. Drove up and moved us in."

"That's right near where I woke up," Cass said haltingly. "The first thing I remember is lying in this field in clothes I didn't remember, with all these half-healed cuts."

But this could be good news. If she had woken close to the place where her father had taken her, then it stood to reason that she hadn't had time to travel very far. And the less time had passed, the less distance she covered, the lower the chances that she'd encountered any humans.

Any *victims*.

If she'd been alert and conscious long enough to escape from the farmhouse, then she had to have been practically recovered. She'd tired, obviously, and lain down to rest, spent a night perhaps, lying under the moon in a field not far from where her father was frantically trying to find her. But the next day she woke for real, and that was when her real memories started.

And there was one other thing, Cass realized with growing excitement. If she'd been recovering, the fever would have been driven from her body. And it only made sense that its effects on the brain had disappeared, as well.

Simply put, she wouldn't have been hunting. Whatever caused her to leave the safety of the room where her father had kept her—hunger, thirst, boredom, restlessness—it wasn't flesh lust.

She hadn't consumed

For the first time since that day, Cass was sure that she hadn't attacked and feasted, hadn't doomed another innocent to the fever. The realization was dizzying, and she felt for a moment that she would faint; she clutched her father's arm and a small exhalation escaped her, sounding almost like a sob.

"Goddamn," Red said, misinterpreting. He wrapped his arm around her, comforting her in a way Cass had not been comforted in a very, very long time—not since she was his little girl. "It's my fault. I didn't have a way to lock the doors to that place from the outside. The day you disappeared, I was only planning to be gone an hour—I just went looking for more food. Hell, we could have survived on kaysev, but I hate that shit. And I wanted to feed you better."

The tears Cass had been holding back spilled over. How to tell him what she was feeling—that she'd given up on being cherished like that. No man—not even Smoke, who'd loved her well and attentively—had made her feel as safe as she remembered feeling in her father's arms.

But she felt suddenly shy. This was all too new, and she had to absorb it, process it before she could trust the feeling to last. She brushed the tears from her face, counting on the darkness to hide the gesture. "Kaysev's the best thing you can eat," she said lightly. "It's good for you."

"I never was good at knowing what was good for me."

"So…you fed me? How'd you do that, weren't you worried about getting infected?"

"Well, you were in and out, kind of. I know you don't remember it, but you'd kind of wake up now and then, look around a little, say nonsense things. It reminded me of this one time when you were little, and you got a really high fever. I sat with you while your mom was at work. You were just a little jabberer, saying all kinds of crazy things."

"You sang to me," Cass said, suddenly remembering.

"Yeah, I guess I probably did."

She had a thought. "Did you sing to me this time? I mean, in the farmhouse?"

Red laughed. "Honey, when I figured out you were getting better, I sang all the damn day long."

"How long did that take?"

"Just a few days. At first—don't get mad, Cassie honey, but I had you tied up. I figured I had to, you know?"

"I don't blame you. I…" Cass hesitated, and then decided to take a chance, share at least some of her fear with him. "There've been a lot of times I wondered, you know, what I did. When I was sick. When I was… one of them."

Red cursed and grabbed her shoulders, turning Cass toward him, hard. "Cassie…you were never one of them. *Never.* You didn't do anything wrong, sweetheart. Not one thing."

All the fear that Cass had stored up threatened to tumble out. She struggled to get herself under control and nearly succeeded, and then a sob escaped her for real this time, and her father pulled her close and hugged her hard, and let her cry.

"It's just that I, I saw what I did to myself, I mean, it had to be me, on my arms, even my knees, and I thought, if I could do that then was I out hunting? Did I attack people, did I hurt them? Oh God, I was so scared…"

"But, Cassie, nothing bad happened. After a few days your fever broke and your eyes got normal again.

I mean, the irises, anyway. They stayed bright, and that green, like they still are. So I wasn't positive, at first, but man, I prayed like hell. Sometimes…aw, shit, I'll go ahead and say it—sometimes maybe I thought I prayed you well. The deals I was putting out there, for God, if you only knew. I must have offered him my soul a dozen times over." Red squeezed Cass even tighter, crushing her against him, but she didn't care. "You let me feed you, almost like when you were a baby, and sometimes I'd catch you chewing on your arms, but you never came after me. Mostly you just slept a lot. Real restless, like you were having nightmares, so I sat in there with you."

"And sang."

"Yeah."

"And when you ran out of food…"

"Yeah, so I left, and like I said I was going to come right back, but it took me a while to find a house that hadn't been raided already, and when I finally got back…you were gone."

"I don't, I don't remember it. The house, or leaving, or anything."

"I went nuts. I looked for you for hours. I finally went up and down the road, used up the last of my gas, before I figured out you must have left the road, covered some serious ground."

"I'm so sorry I put you through that…Dad."

Red went still, hearing her say his name, and then he awkwardly patted her on the back. "It's nothing, baby angel. Look at us, in this whole damn state of California we found each other again. If that ain't the answer to my prayers, well, I don't know what is."

"Why didn't you tell me sooner?"

"Because I'm a damn coward, is why. I just kept biding my time, and biding my time. Zihna tried to get me to say something a dozen times, but I was so scared I'd run you off, that if you knew who I was you wouldn't want anything to do with me. And then when you… aw, honey, I don't know how to say it, but you've got your share of troubles, and I didn't want to make them worse. I've tangled with the bottle myself."

Cass felt her face go hot with mortification. It was on the tip of her tongue to deny it, to say it wasn't a problem, that she'd quit. Well, she was one-day sober, anyway, and she'd been in that scary place twice before and managed to stay for a while. Maybe this time it would be a longer while. Maybe…no. She wouldn't tempt the Fates by asking for forever, not yet.

"You won't make it worse," she said softly. "But you can help me make it better."

33

It was another thirty-four miles to the next big town, where there was a huge shopping mall that was rumored to be sheltering close to a hundred citizens.

At least, that was true a couple of months ago. Jay and Terrence and the other raiders hadn't traveled this far since before the new year. They didn't want to waste the gas, since everything raidable this far north was the domain of the mall shelter, by dint of the common law that had evolved as shelters consolidated. Bigger groups tended to be more successful, since they could post round-the-clock sentries and assign specialized tasks, and send only their strongest and fastest out to harvest and raid.

The last anyone knew, the mall shelter—nicknamed Macy's, after its onetime anchor store—was holding its own. Dor himself had sent a guard there earlier in the fall, to spread the word about the Box and find out

what the Macy's people could tell him about the Rebuilders' progress.

This was the only reason Cass could figure that the
new leadership invited Dor to participate in the early-
morning discussion. She wasn't spying on them, exactly; they were sitting in a loose circle on the front
driveway, using the abandoned furniture, and breakfast
was being served under the house's broad front porch.
Rain threatened, the air heavy with stinging moisture,
thick gray clouds low in the sky. Cass had taken Ruthie
around the back for their turn at the "bathroom" and on
the way back, she stopped to tie Ruthie's shoe.

It was an old ruse. Cass didn't care. The feeling she
got from Mayhew—that he was hiding something, that
he had an unspoken agenda—had only grown stronger.
She'd slept well after her talk with her father the night
before, but when she woke up the Easterners were conferring quietly inside the house. So this was their second
meeting of the day, and Cass couldn't help wondering
if there were things that had been said earlier that were
being left out now that Edenites were listening.

But no one else seemed to care.

Once they got moving, everyone stayed in more or
less the same configurations as before, though Smoke
joined those at the front, keeping up despite his limp.
Cass walked with her father and Zihna, though the
other moms had invited her to join them in the car. It
seemed like their relationship was warming, and Suzanne thanked her for letting Twyla stay with Ruthie,
alternating between walking and the trailer as they had
the day before.

Throughout the morning, the group had a bit of a
festival air. There was food for at least a week, includ-

ing all the cans they'd been hoarding in the pantry, and they'd had a good breakfast. The rain held off, the clouds rolling and gusting. No one spoke of those who'd been lost, though the bitter count lay just below the surface of everyone's minds. A week ago New Eden had been home to seventy citizens; after the battles on the water and on land, the people dragged away and shot and blown up in the community center, they were down to fifty one, plus the four Easterners.

Cass was walking by herself along the abandoned two-lane highway, pushing Ruthie in the stroller, taking a break from the company of the others to think about her father. She had replayed the conversation from the night before a dozen times, and every time she felt the thrill of relief when she realized she'd never harmed anyone while she was feverish. *Relief* was not a big enough word to contain the feeling—it was joy mixed with disbelief, a sense of good fortune so unexpected that she was afraid it was illusory, that it could disappear the same way it came to her.

But it had come to her via her father. Her *dad.* Cass smiled, saying the word in her mind, a word she'd never expected to use again. She knew she needed to be cautious, to prepare herself for the inevitable disappointments that would surely follow. To remind herself that her father had hurt her grievously and that leopards don't change their spots, to use an old saying of Mim's; that the more she trusted him the more she risked.

But she was just so damn tired of protecting herself all the time. Didn't she deserve—just a little, just for now—to see where this went? To maybe enjoy it a little?

A glimpse of orange caught her eye, off on the side of the road where the asphalt was broken and kaysev had taken root. There—growing practically sideways under the gray chunks and clods—was a California poppy. Its wiry stalk and fringy leaves strained to poke through to the air, and it held one tightly rolled bud and one fragile bloom, a tiny spot of brilliant tangerine that wavered and trembled in the breeze.

No one else seemed to take note. Cass pushed the stroller, fast, murmuring, "Oh, Ruthie, Babygirl, you're not going to believe—do you remember—"

But Ruthie was dozing, lulled by the afternoon sun and the rhythm of the big rubber wheels on the pavement, and it was Cass alone who stroked the tender petals, caught a breath to see that there were others, small and stunted seedlings close to this first one. She thought about calling to someone— Zihna, Sammi, her dad—but they were hidden in the depths of the ragtag group making its slow and stolid way along the road, and her moment of ebullience would not withstand their indifference. Better this way, keeping the bloom to herself, remarking on the poppy's return with the joy of one who'd loved them, Before.

The poppy was a challenge to cultivate. Seeds often failed, even under the best of conditions. Transplanted seedlings nearly always died. But wherever the native plant rooted on its own, it was tough and wily. It could grow in the smallest crack, the meanest soil; it was not daunted by weeds or sought by predators. Up close, it was indelicate, even coarsely figured, its leaves stubby and its stem workmanlike. But from a distance there was nothing like that glorious shot of pure color.

Cass smiled, wondering what it was about this particular spot, this homely stretch of road in the midst of dead fields, that inspired the poppy to grow here. It was not for her to know—but perhaps it was no mistake that she was the one who noticed it.

She didn't pick the flower. Let it go to seed; let the seed scatter and find its way across the healing land. For now it would remain her secret.

By late afternoon, the rain began. People were tired from walking, tempers were thin and fears had resurfaced, and they spent a cold and uncomfortable night at a stable, sleeping on the malodorous straw in the stalls. The next day dawned clear and brilliant, water sparkling on the kaysev leaves, and spirits were restored. Near evening they disturbed a clump of Beaters sun bathing on the turf of a mini golf course in front of an RV campground. The things rushed out, hollering, but John and Glynnis, riding sentry with Nathan in the hybrid at the front of the crowd, picked them off easily.

The campground would have made decent shelter, with its large bathhouse, but everyone was too skittish from the Beaters—and who knew if there weren't more Beaters that belonged to this particular nest— so they went a couple more miles and sheltered in a trucker rest stop.

Smoke continued to keep his distance. He was polite to Cass, solicitous of Ruthie, but he was dividing his energy between pushing his body to catch up from its forced inactivity, and conferring with the new council.

Each night he slept elsewhere, bunking down with those closest to the doors, the guards and the raiders.

"Zihna, is he crazy?" Cass asked, as they walked along in a steady drizzle on the fourth day. Everyone was miserable, their clothes soaked. People were beginning to sniffle and cough, and it seemed like a spring cold was starting to spread through the group. Sun-hi was riding with Jasmine, who had started her labor that morning. It looked like her baby was going to be born in a moving car.

Zihna narrowed her eyes thoughtfully. She was taking her turn, at her insistence, pulling the trailer. Ruthie and Twyla were playing with a bowl full of pebbles that they had collected from a landscaping bed at the rest stop, protected from the rain by a pop-up play tent that Ingrid had brought, chattering and laughing.

"I don't think he's crazy," she said. "I think he hasn't been entirely truthful."

"What do you mean?"

"Well, you know I'm not a doctor, but these last few weeks I couldn't figure out why he was gaining his strength back so quickly, and now it makes sense, he was awake. He was pretending during the day. It makes me want to kick myself, 'course, since I could have saved him a lot of trouble by just talking to him. And you know I've talked to plenty of patients that didn't talk back. Only with Smoke, it had been so long, and it was like…well, nobody was coming around to see him anymore."

"I know. It's my fault."

"It's no one's fault. I'm just saying he started to seem like, I don't know. We were always so busy, and we had Omar's burns, Crystal with the staph infection, Charles…we all just started treating him like an object. A…houseplant. And the whole time he was, you know, coming back to life. Well, look at the man, I've never seen that kind of determination."

Smoke walked a dozen yards ahead. He'd set his cane aside today; it was resting on the trailer, a long tree branch trimmed and sanded for him by Steve the first day of the journey.

"That's Smoke—determined," Cass said softly. She could give a thousand examples of her own: how he'd scavenged lumber in the Box until he could build her a bed frame, how he'd stayed up with Ruthie two nights straight when she had strep throat, how he'd killed a man who'd just saved his life but been bitten in a Beater attack.

How he'd gone hunting the Rebuilders, alone, out-numbered, outmatched, hungry for justice and willing to sacrifice everything he cared about to get it.

"How quickly do you think he could get back—I mean, I know he'll never be exactly like he was before, but, you know, back to himself?"

"Hard to say. When he really was unconscious, his body was focused entirely on mending. First order of business was to fight off the infection he had when he got here. Rebreaking his arm set him back, but Sun-hi was right, it was the right thing to do. The limp, he's gonna have that for a while. Maybe forever. Everything else—well, he's doing exactly what we'd tell him to do. Work on those muscles, rebuild. Kaysev's probably per-fect fuel for him. He's doing everything right, darlin'."

"He just seems so…spent, at the end of the day."

"Well, you would be too, with a regimen like that. Bet every muscle in his body is screaming." She smiled slyly. "Or are you really asking me something else? Like…how soon he can expect to be sexually active?"

"Zihna!" Cass reddened. In fact, that hadn't been what she was asking—and then she wondered why not, why she hadn't been stirred by him the way she used to be, in the Box.

"Because let me tell you I've seen every inch of that man, and I didn't see any evidence of injuries that would prevent a full recovery. Heck, probably be good for him."

"Stop it, I didn't—"

"Oh, come on, it's just us. And it's perfectly natural. Where do you think me and your dad get our robust good health?"

"Oh, Zihna, you do not need to be telling me that. I'm barely used to the idea that he's my dad—I don't think I want to know anything about his...about his...eww."

Zihna turned serious. "Honey, I know what you're saying, it's different when someone's your parent. But you might want to keep that in mind when you're dealing with Sammi."

"Sammi—what does she—"

"Just, your relationship with her is important—she needs other adult women in her life, not just me. And the quality of that relationship is going to be dependent on how you and her dad are getting along. Or, to be more specific, the state of things between you two... romantically."

"Zihna..." Cass said softly. "Do you, um, I would hate it if you thought, I mean, things have been so weird with everything and I've done things I shouldn't, I know—"

"I don't think badly of you," Zihna said cheerfully, squeezing Cass's hand. "If that's one of your worries. You make your own choices and as your friend my only hope is that you learn from the wrong ones and enjoy the right ones. And while we're talking like this, I am very glad you're going to quit drinking. I hope you don't mind that your dad and I talked about it."

Cass blanched, and for a moment she did mind, she minded a lot. And then the anger subsided and Cass saw it for what it was—the desperation of the addiction trying to maintain its hold on her.

She'd been here before. And she knew what she had to do. *Fake it till you make it.* That was the program's answer, and—annoyingly, frustratingly—it worked. So she would pretend she didn't mind, and pretend some more, until one day it was a little bit true, and the next day it was a little more true.

"I'm glad you and he talk," she said as evenly as she could.

"I wouldn't be here without him. I would have given up."

They walked in companionable silence for a while.

"Where did he get the name Red?" Cass asked. She could see him up ahead walking with Earl and Old Mike, talking. She recognized his gestures, now that she knew it was him; perhaps she'd noticed them all along, somewhere deep down. There it was—the way he rubbed the back of his neck when he was considering something, the way he stabbed the air with a finger when he was making a point.

"*I* was the one who gave him that name," Zihna said. "Actually, we named each other. Once we decided to make a go of it, and we were on the road, on the way to New Eden though we didn't know it at the time, we had plenty of time to talk. And it turns out neither one of us much liked the names we'd been saddled with."

"What was yours?"

Zihna grimaced. "Mary Chastity."

"Oh, no." Cass laughed and then Zihna was laughing too.

"Your dad said that didn't fit me at all. And then he told me that Zihna means 'spinning' in Hopi. And, well, I thought it was pretty."

"And what about Dad? Was he still going by Silver Dollar?"

"Yeah, he was. Showed me this old band flyer he used to carry around—'Hammerdown, featuring Silver Dollar Haverford.'"

"You know...I took his name when I turned eighteen. Cass Dollar, it's legal and everything. Mostly I think I just did it to piss off my mom."

"Well, how about that." Zihna grinned. "Save that up, maybe tell your dad the story one day when he needs a lift. I think he'd get a kick out of it."

"So...how did you come up with Red?"

"Well, I asked him if I should just call him Tom, but your dad said it brought back memories he'd rather forget, that he wasn't proud of being that man and he'd just as soon start over with something brand-new. And I said, anything I want? and he said, yes, anything, and I was going to tease him and maybe call him Skeeter or something but he was so...serious."

Her voice went soft and dreamy and Cass felt like she was intruding on a private moment.

"Your dad can be a very serious man, for someone who makes me laugh every damn day," Zihna said, smiling, but Cass didn't miss the way she wiped her eyes with the back of her hand. "Anyway, when I was a little girl, my grandfather used to listen to this old co-median named Red Skelton. We kids thought that was such a funny name. It made me think of a red skeleton, you know, the bones...anyway, your dad has this amazing thick hair for a guy his age, and when the sun hits it just right, I swear there's these glints of red."

Cass laughed. "I think you're just a little dazzled. He's pretty much gray all over."

But secretly she was having a hard time keeping her emotions reined in. It shouldn't matter to her, what her father did, who he was, after all this time.

But then again, why not let it matter?

"But that's just it. Everyone has their own reality, right? I mean, we see the same things, but the thoughts in our head and the experiences we've had, all of that changes things, so the pictures we carry around with us are all different. Like, look up there…lot of folks would say that's a ruin, a junk heap."

Cass had been walking and thinking, not focusing on the horizon, but up ahead the torn flags and hulking wings of the mall stood out against the steely, damp clouds.

"But for a lot of folks, that's home now. I imagine it's got a certain kind of beauty when you think about how it couldn't be much more secure, how it's probably got a pretty good stockpile of necessaries, plenty of room to spread out."

Cass tried to see what Zihna saw, but instead she got a deep foreboding, a tightening in her gut that could not be entirely explained by the bad architecture and gloomy weather.

"We shouldn't go to the mall," she breathed.

"What's that, honey?"

"I have a bad feeling about the mall."

"Well, let's just send these East Coast yokels in, then." Zihna laughed. "I don't much care for them, they're kind of uppity."

Cass forced herself to brush the feeling off. It was true that they all needed a rest and a chance to dry out, as well as to restock their supplies, if possible. There was the unspoken but very real hope there might be room for at least some of them to live in the mall too, at least for a while. But the idea of all that concrete, so few windows... She wished she'd appreciated the freedom of the island more, the ability to step outside her home without worrying about Beaters, to walk in her garden without looking over her shoulder every second.

So many days and nights on the island, she worked so hard to forget that she failed to take notice of the good things—the beauty of the moon reflected in the river, the wind riffling the reeds that grew along the bank, the laughter of the children playing in the yard. The only time she let go of the tension lodged inside her was when she was with Dor. It was no wonder they came together with a passion that was almost violent: they both had so much loss to obliterate. And that's what it had been, wasn't it—tearing holes in their dreary and painful reality and letting in sensation, longing, even joy, if only until the tears skimmed over and their lives were shut tight again.

And now even that was lost to her. But she shouldn't need him anymore—Cass berated herself; she had Smoke now, her heart, her love. Dor was in the past, just a phase she'd gone through, a crutch she'd relied on. As soon as Smoke was well, as soon as they were settled, it would be as before, the two of them together, being everything to each other.

Only...Smoke had been spending all his time with the new council. Reunited only days, he was already strategizing and planning, eager—maybe too eager—to work with the Easterners. It wasn't glory he was after, Cass was sure of that. But something else…something familiar, something she had thought, had hoped, he had left behind on the battleground where he killed the Rebuilders.

He was still avenging. Even after the Rebuilders were no longer a threat, he was seeking…something. Maybe not vengeance, exactly, but atonement.

And still she didn't know what he was atoning for. The thing that had always been between them was still there. He cherished his self-punishment more than anything else in the world, and nothing could banish it, nothing could ever be enough. He'd almost given his life as trade, but even that was not enough—as his strength came back he was already seeking ways to matter, ways to give, give of himself. And there would never be enough left over for her.

Knowing that had chilled Cass's feelings. No longer did her heart race at the sight of him. No longer did the brush of his hand against hers excite her. He kept his distance and she, if she was truly honest with herself, kept hers.

Maybe the mall would be a fresh start. Maybe she needed time to be alone, without any man at all. She had a lot more in her life than she had a few weeks ago. There was Red, for starters, a father she'd given up for dead, for lost. There were the moms, the fragile peace between them. There was Zihna and Sammi and the other kids. And always, always, there was Ruthie.

It would be work, all the complicated messy relationships she'd damaged and scorned, learning to trust and to earn trust, to take risks and take deep breaths, try again and again, until she got it right. But God willing there would be time for that too.

"You're right," she said to Zihna, as cheerfully as she could. *Fake it till you make it.* "It's going to be fine."

Someone had been working on the mall parking lot. The cars had been dragged away from the innermost spaces around the central entrance, and an area had been walled off with chain-link that looked like it had been scavenged piecemeal and then welded together. Inside the fencing were mismatched outdoor chairs and tables that looked like they had been taken from several different restaurants. A fire pit in the center made from stacked brick pavers was blackened and piled deep with ash.

They left the vehicles and horses at the far edge of the parking lot. There had been an undercurrent of excitement buzzing through the crowd all morning, a yearning to be indoors again, to see other citizens, but the council insisted on a break before they went inside, a chance to eat something and drink water. No one argued. Experience had taught them to take dehydration and hunger seriously enough that they broke their progress for a meal of kaysev, chewing methodically and with little satisfaction. The mothers coaxed the little ones to eat. Colton and Kalyan practiced tossing hard little dried kaysev chips into the air and catching them in their mouths, people good-naturedly cheering them when they managed a direct hit.

Still, the excitement and anticipation were palpable. When the meal was finished, the group hurriedly assembled and made its way through the parking lot, threading through the maze of cars. A few were parked neatly, as though their owners had come for a final trip to buy a sweater or a tube of lipstick, but many more were abandoned haphazardly, crashed into others or blocking lanes.

Nobody looked inside the cars. The smells had abated, but you never got used to seeing the decomposed corpses, the hair that was still styled the way it was on the morning they died, the leer of exposed jaws and teeth always making cadavers look cheerful and jaunty, in stark contrast to the horror of the eyes, which were often eaten away by parasites or dried to thin, flaking tissue.

But there were always remains outside of cars in places like this, people who waited until hunger or thirst drove them out of their cars, who made it a few yards or even a few hundred yards until they were set upon and devoured. These bodies—little more than skeletons, their clothing ripped from them and abandoned nearby—were the worst, and Cass and the other mothers held their children close and shielded their eyes from the sight of them.

Dor had somehow managed to get Sammi talking to

him in the past couple of days, and though she didn't look happy about it, she and the other kids stayed close to him. The girls who'd escaped the Rebuilders had remained silently loyal to him after they reached New Eden—Cass wouldn't be surprised if Dor planned to protect them all. Other little cliques—Valerie and her friends, Luddy and his, Corryn and Rachael and the other kitchen staff—merged into one tight group as they neared the doors.

A hand on her shoulder, and there was Smoke, his cautious smile. "I'd like you to remain near me."

Before she could respond, Mayhew leaped nimbly to the hood of a blue sedan at the edge of the cleared area. The rain had abated and weak sunlight forced its way through the clouds, and Cass had to squint to look at him.

"Everybody." His voice carried easily through the stillness of the parking lot, rebounding faintly, a trick of echoes. "Davis and Nadir went ahead to check things out. They found a couple of old kills around the corner, so we need to be careful. I think we're better off all sticking together and going in. Once we get the lay of the place we can send some folks back out to deal with the cars and the horses."

All of this was already in place, of course, so he wasn't so much asking permission as building consensus. Not so different, it occurred to Cass, from the way New Eden had been run. And Mayhew was good at it, too, playing on people's fears; at the mention of the Beater kills the crowd seemed to press in on itself.

"Did they see the Beaters?" a woman called…maybe Cindy, Cass thought. "The ones who did it? Or the nest—did they see the nest?"

"I think they may be using a mechanicals shed for a nest," Mayhew answered easily, keeping his voice in a reassuring, even timbre. "Makes sense they're around, trying to get into the mall, since there's folks sheltering there."

"Did you talk to anyone inside?" Dor, stepping out from the crowd.

"Not exactly. We got a visual. There's a, what do you want to call it, like a sunken lobby in the middle, bunch of coffee shops and restaurants, seating. There were about eight or ten people there, but Davis couldn't get their attention from up here through the windows. That's good glass, by the way. Solid as all heck, just needs some Windex." He smiled at this joke, a gesture reminiscent of television.

"So maybe we should send in one or two people first," Dor said, ignoring the few titters Mayhew's joke earned, his tone making it clear he thought Mayhew was an idiot. "Before we risk our entire population. What do you think?"

Mayhew stared at Dor without blinking, and the people in the crowd looked back and forth from one to the other. Cass knew the popular opinion had swayed to Mayhew, but there was enough uncertainty that she knew the outcome hung in the balance between them.

"The way to risk lives is to keep standing out here, where there's a known Beater threat," he said impatiently. "Davis saw citizens, they were sitting together talking, eating, whatever. Just like you guys were doing a few days ago, just like I was, with my own loved ones, a few weeks back. Look, at least two of you have been here recently and confirmed that it's a friendly group—"

"If you call two months recent," Dor cut in, his voice rising angrily. "Things change fast. As I guess you might know, Mayhew."

"And so I suggest we break into this door here and if nothing else, we'll have a warm and dry place to let the kids run around a little," Mayhew continued, as though Dor hadn't spoken.

"You won't have to break in. This group doesn't lock their doors from the outside," Dor said, disgusted. "The mechanical ones don't work at all, but there's a safety latch on the emergency doors, under the push bar. The Beaters haven't had the dexterity to work them so they leave them unlocked so citizens can come in quickly. They only lock them on the inside."

"So much the better." Mayhew smiled, his expression chilly. He walked over to the door and ran his hand along the bar. There was a click and the door opened. "Okay, look, MacFall, if it makes you feel any better, I'll go first. We can keep the women and kids in the back. Let's just get in there, everyone can take off their packs, rest a little while we look around, talk to the folks."

"Only a damn fool would go in alone," Dor said, and strode to the door.

"Guess we're two damn fools, then," Mayhew said sarcastically. "But I appreciate the company. Anyone else?"

The Easterners stepped up, as well as a few others. The rest of the crowd murmured approvingly. Clearly the popular vote was for Mayhew. Again.

They entered single file, Nadir holding the door open. Inside, there was a faint hint of the smell that permeated every mall, Before, industrial cleaners and plastic and perfume. But there was also the shelter smell—notes of burned food, urine and bodies living in close contact with little opportunity to bathe.

Oddly, Cass found it comforting.

"I think you should carry Ruthie." Smoke had appeared quietly at her side. "And stay in the back of the crowd, with me."

So he felt the same as Dor and as Cass herself, that there was something off here. But she wasn't about to stay outside without protection from the Beaters, no matter how long it had been since they'd swarmed in the area. She picked Ruthie up without a word.

"Hello!" Mayhew called, as the crowd walked along the broad hallway into the mall's upper floor. The entire ceiling was made of glass and plenty of natural light filled the open areas. Many of the storefront windows had been shattered, the contents looted, but the debris had all been swept away and the mannequins and displays stacked against the walls, leaving most of the stores clear in the center. As they passed, Cass could see that many of the clearings had been made into homes; shelves held personal possessions, stacks of clothes, stores of food. Curtains had been hung to lend some privacy to the living quarters; posters and lamps and other merchandise had been moved into the spaces to personalize them. Other than the fact that everything was new, the atmosphere was not so different from the middle of the Box, where the employees made their permanent homes.

But where was everyone?

The group reached the rail overlooking the atrium. Just as Mayhew had described, there were restaurants with tables arranged in the center area, even evidence of a recent meal, dishes and cutlery on the tables—but no one was around.

"So where are all these citizens you were talking about?" Dor demanded.

"They were right down there," one of the Easterners said, puzzled. "We looked in from that window up there, there's stairs up there from the parking lot. There were at least eight of them before. Mostly women. Maybe they're cleaning up, they must have a separate area for the kitchen "

A hollow sound stopped him, footsteps echoing from around a curve in the hall that led to another wing. A man stepped into sight. He was good-looking, exceptionally so, with curly brown hair and wide blue eyes. He wore an expensive-looking red sweater that fit him well. His mouth curved in a hint of a smile, and he moved slowly, confidently, a hint of swagger in his stride. There were weapons on his belt, but he made no move to reach for them.

"Hi," he said.

From behind him, three more people followed, two women and another man. All of them looked healthy and well fed, if slightly disheveled. "Hi," one of the women said, touching her hand to her face. None of these others held weapons.

"Good to see you," Mayhew said, stepping forward with his hand extended. "We're up from the south, a shelter about fifty miles from here. New Eden, you know it?"

"Eden…" said the man. "Eden."

The uneasiness in Cass's gut unraveled into full-scale alarm. Something was wrong, very wrong. "Those people," she said to Smoke. "They're not right."

Mayhew reached the little group and stood awkwardly for a moment with his hand extended. After a pause, the man in front reached for his hand and they shook.

"I'm Damon Mayhew."

The man stared at him with his mouth suddenly slack. "Havoc."

"Havoc...I'm sorry?"

"Sorry," the man repeated, with an odd little grin. Then he lifted Mayhew's hand to his face, as though he meant to kiss it with a courtly flourish.

And Cass screamed.

And kept on screaming, joined by other voices, other terrified Edenites, because instead of kissing Mayhew the curly-haired man licked his wrist delicately, and Mayhew, who hailed from the East and had never seen a Beater in the early, airy stages of the disease, who had time to run but didn't, didn't, didn't, stood there doing nothing while the man smiled wider and then nipped into his skin with perfect white teeth.

Mayhew yelped and jumped back, grabbing his wrist with his other hand but not before Cass saw the little jagged rip dotted with blood. The man who'd bitten him had been recently turned, still had the initial shine of the fever, and he would not attack. This little group would not tackle Mayhew and drag him away to feast upon, even though Cass now noticed the cuts and scabs on their hands and wrists, a gash on one woman's face, the rosy sheen and bright eyes that were the hallmarks of the sickness. In this phase, they merely nibbled idly, on themselves and each other, their bites more exploratory than savage, nothing like the ravenous hunger that would soon follow. In their fever, they practically glowed.

Mayhew still didn't understand what was happening, rubbing at his arm and scowling, but the Edenites did.

They ran. Most ran back toward the doors they'd entered through, though a few raced in the other direction toward a T in the rows of shops. Cass had Ruthie in her arms and Smoke at her side and they were not as fast; others—including the Easterners who finally figured out what was going on—passed them by, hurtling with a speed born of terror.

"Go on!" Smoke yelled at Cass. "Take Ruthie, just go!"

He was fumbling at his belt, he had his gun—they had Red to thank for that, Cass's father had outfitted Smoke with his second-favorite piece in a gesture that seemed oddly old-fashioned, a courtly tradition of another era. Now she was grateful. Now she understood what Smoke meant to do and prayed for the bullet to find its target.

The curly-haired man went down first, his head canting to the side in a burst of blood, his body thrown against the half wall overlooking the atrium, his hands clutching air.

Smoke shot Mayhew second, taking off the top third of his skull, dropping him to his knees with a surprised expression on his face, and as Smoke fired twice more and Cass's ears rang with the echoing report, the thought that came to mind was that Mayhew would never know why he'd been killed, he'd never know why the people of New Eden turned on him.

But he should have. On this side of the Rockies, at least, everyone knew. Everyone had seen a new Beater and knew they were every bit as deadly as the oldest ones that shambled, flayed and broken, toward their inevitable end.

The female Beaters lay on the floor, one of them silent and still, the other gut-shot and trying to move, shrieking in pain and rage, crawling over her own entrails toward them. Smoke fired again and she crumpled like a moth hit with a garden hose.

But the screaming continued, and Smoke grabbed Cass's arm and pulled her toward the walkway bridge that led across the atrium, to a Victoria's Secret store that still bore a pink-and-red banner decorated with sequins and stuffed felt hearts.

"That's not the—"

That was all she got out before one of the Easterners, the barrel-chested, lisping one named Davis, ran past her, knocking into her with his shoulder, spinning her against the wall.

Then she saw what he was running from. Three of them, much further along in the disease, old Beaters whose flesh hung in ribbons from their chewed and wasted arms and whose faces were a ravaged tarmac of wounds and self-inflicted assaults, lips chewed away and broken teeth, eyebrows and eyelashes long ago ripped out with the nervous savage fury of infection. These creatures were not handsome, like the ones who'd greeted Mayhew, damned spirits with one foot in this life and one foot in hell, gorgeous with the first flush of the poison, their skin radiant and their eyes bright and depthless. No. These were the befouled foot soldiers of the curse, their humanity drained from them as they mortified themselves, obscene stinking mad lustful organisms of hunger and need.

These were the ones who must've breached the mall somehow, compromised a barrier or overwhelmed a guard, forced their way in and found their prey captive and defenseless, trapped in a prison of their own making. Who knows how many they'd devoured until, momentarily sated, they'd let some of their prey live. And those, the newly turned, were the ones who doomed the rest. Just as Owen's curse would have spread like wildfire throughout the Edenites had he lived, the barely feverish had doomed the other mall-dwellers until the entire place was one giant festering nest of Beaters, all of them longing for uninfected flesh.

It was nothing she hadn't seen before, nothing any of them hadn't seen before, except, perhaps, for the Easterners, so perhaps Davis could be forgiven his terror, his desperate attempt at self-preservation that left Cass reeling and struggling to hold on to Ruthie.

"Come on," Smoke yelled again, waiting until she took his hand. Ruthie was heavy and restless in her other arm, wakened from her peaceful afternoon slumber yet again by tragedy and disaster.

Cass could tell that Smoke's strength was ebbing, his body racked with pain and his muscles weak, but he kept up the pace past a cosmetics store, a kitchenware shop, to a clothing store that still, all these many months after the final shopper overpaid for the last logo-embroidered shirt, still reeked of a signature cologne.

Cass had hated malls, the chemical smells and lack of natural light, the forced cheer of the window displays featuring impossibly thin mannequins and spotless suburban tableaus, all of the tableware and underpinnings and electronic toys and scented candles, the thousand varieties of *crap* that didn't even add up to a single decent meal Aftertime. All of this, the entire compendium of suburban marketing fraud, coursed through Cass's mind as she allowed Smoke to shove her and Ruthie inside the somewhat fortified store.

"I'm going back for your dad and Zihna," he said, and then, in the dim mote-speckled light of a postconsumer skylight, in what had been a shopping mecca Before, he seemed to be about to kiss her.

He stared into her eyes and ran his fingers through her hair and pulled her closer, but in the last minute, one of them hesitated, one of them flinched, and Cass would always wonder which of them it had been, because all she remembered of the moment was the cornflower-blue of his eyes and the regret that he couldn't love her enough, couldn't love her as much as his cherished ideal of justice.

In the next instant he was gone.

35

Smoke had seen carnage and Smoke had killed men, but the blood-slicked panorama before him caused him to suck in his breath. For a moment he thought he'd vomit, and he leaned over the stuccoed wall, heaving and gulping air, ready to unloose himself onto the vinyl sofa directly below.

The moment passed, in a second, a fraction of a second. Disgust was not an emotion he could afford to indulge. Smoke swallowed down his bile and plunged forward.

At the entrance, half a dozen citizens were throwing themselves against the doors, using their bodies as battering rams. Locking the exits from within—the shelterers had mistakenly believed they were making their small world safer, protecting their number from the temptation of outside, never anticipating the horror they'd accidentally spawned. Smoke could not help them now: at this point his focus needed to be on the threat of the moment.

The Beaters had dragged off their first victim, a slender middle-aged woman with long, graying hair they wrapped through their decrepit fingers for leverage. Smoke recognized her—she'd asked him if she could help him when his bum leg gave him trouble, offered him half of her lunch, but now she was being shoved facedown on the floor in the entrance of a Hallmark card shop. Behind the broken glass windows were canting displays holding Mother's Day and graduation cards and gifts—because it had been that season, hadn't it, a year ago when things fell apart? The woman screamed and gargled in terror as the creatures yanked her limbs straight out and knelt on them. He could hear the ripping of her clothes as they were torn away. Her back was smooth and pale, and then it disappeared under the four monstrous heads as they assaulted with their wide greedy mouths, their sharp and tearing teeth.

"Anyone who's armed, help me," he bellowed, shooting into the writhing mass. One of the Beaters squawked and fell away, its face slimed with blood and its mouth wide and grimacing, but immediately squirmed back into the feeding frenzy, dragging one bloodied arm uselessly at its side.

No one seemed to have heard him, so Smoke shot at the doors, hitting the reinforced metal above their heads. The sound echoed all around them, and several people screamed or fell and the crowd tried to run in both directions. "If no one helps me we're all going to die here," he yelled before turning back to the Beaters.

He edged closer to the mass, trying to find his opportunity. He managed to get a clear shot at the woman when one of the Beaters threw his head back to tear a long strip of flesh from her back down near her buttock. Smoke aimed for the back of her head and tried not to see it burst, focusing instead on the Beaters, now sprayed with her blood and brains and enraged to find their quarry unresponsive.

Their angry cries ricocheted and echoed down the mall, and he glanced down the corridor to the farthest end where people poured out of a JCPenney, a dozen, two dozen, more of them. From this distance they looked normal, orderly, a congregation emptying out after church, fans leaving a stadium, patrons leaving a bar at closing time—only they walked with a certain shuffling, unsteady gait and they bumped into each other and occasionally lifted their fingers to their lips and chewed.

The new ones. The ones who, if they'd come a week earlier, would have still been living here as survivors, not so different from the people of New Eden or the people of any shelter, making the best of things, trying to scrape together enough optimism to see them through another day, when somehow—a door forced open? an HVAC duct? a tear in the cheap stucco wall, the things' hunger driving them to tear and chew through insulation, plaster, whatever it took until they reached the inside of the mall?—the Beaters got in.

And all it would have taken was a few bites. A population like this, trapped, no light at night, all those halls and empty shops and dark corners for hiding like this— it would have spread geometrically, madly, instantly. With nowhere to go, the mall sealed shut tight save the one breach, the uninfected didn't stand a chance.

Hordes of the things outside, inside would still seem more survivable…

All of this flashed through Smoke's mind while he was shooting, then reloading from the stash in his pocket. There was more ammo on the trailer—but the trailer was out there, in the parking lot. The bullets were slippery in his hands, maybe twenty of them, and he jammed them into the cylinder with shaking hands while the Beaters grew frustrated with their immobile, unresponsive meal and howled their disappointment.

They liked it alive. They'd eat a dead body if they had to, but with far less zeal. They'd wander away from it and circle back, grazing on the corpse for a few days as children might pick at a fruit bowl if denied their Halloween candy. But for now, with the air pungent with the scent of living citizens, they would lose interest in the dead woman and come after the fresh uninfected.

In fact it was already happening. Two of them had turned away from the woman's blood-soaked, naked body and were crawling, slipping on her blood, toward the crowd of terrified people. One tried to rise, slipped, and fell down again, its elbow cracking on the hard floor. Smoke's damp and trembling fingers had not managed to load the entire cylinder but there was no time, and he jammed it shut and fired the way he'd practiced so many mornings in the Box, on the fly, his body turning already to the next target.

But before he could aim, the thing lurched sideways, taking a shot in the upper chest. Not a fatal injury, but enough to slow it down. Smoke looked for the shooter and saw three of the others, no—four, all armed, one man with only a blade—coming tentatively closer.

Smoke shot the last two uninjured Beaters in quick

succession, and they collapsed on top of the poor dead woman. One of the Edenites, a short wiry woman, ran to the Beater that was crawling along the blood-slicked floor, jammed the muzzle of a gun against its forehead and fired, getting splattered with gore.

Smoke approached her, wary that she might fire again. "Hey," he said gently, putting a hand on her shoulder. "Don't get so close if you don't have to. That's taking a hell of a chance."

The woman looked at him, wild-eyed, her mouth trembling. "It's just I never shot a gun before," she said. "I wanted to make sure I didn't miss."

Damn. The last thing they needed was weapons in the hands of people who had no idea how to use them. "Whose gun is that?"

"It's some…somebody dropped it. Over there."

"You did good," Smoke said, taking it carefully from her hand, pushing the barrel down. "You didn't miss, not one bit."

"What do we do now?" One of the slacker guys, the ones who had been skateboarding along the edge of the crowd, was tugging on Smoke's sleeve like he was five years old. Smoke didn't bother asking him if he was armed. "There's more of them down there, did you see? Did you? Oh, Jesus, what're we going to do?"

"I saw. Look, maybe you can help out here, okay?" Smoke pointed to the entrance lobby, where several people had been knocked down in the panic to reach the doors. One woman had a gash on her forehead and was leaning against the locked door, crying. "How about you see what they need, okay?"

The boy turned dubiously toward the fallen. "Yeah, I want to help and all but—"

"Then *do* it." Smoke had run out of patience. He scanned the mall in both directions, saw a couple of the Easterners conferring at the junction with the other wing, past half a dozen storefronts. They, at least, were armed. And there. There was Dor, working at the heavy door. Someone had hacked away at the hinge and the thick metal had split, exposing wires from the security system and the mechanical closing mechanism.

Next to him was Sammi, holding something, a narrow tool of some sort. Her face was pale but as her father worked she remained steady, handing him what he needed from a small leather bag. Smoke recognized that bag—back when he'd been second-in-command in the Box, he remembered Dor carrying his tools with him on his belt. Back then they'd been useful for repairing sections of the chain-link fence that surrounded the Box—or for opening the occasional bottle of beer after a good raid.

How many mornings had the two men trained together? How many overcast days and chilly dawns had they raided together, watching each other's backs at each unfamiliar house, each closed door? They'd been as close as two men so stubborn could be Aftertime, sharing confidences and, eventually, trust as the weeks turned into months and they soldiered on together.

And all that time, Smoke thought Dor didn't like Cass. She'd told him so herself, described the way he avoided her, never looked her in the eye, found an excuse to leave whenever she arrived at the fire or one of the food-merchant stalls where he'd been passing the time.

But Smoke had never bothered to wonder why Dor avoided her so studiously. If he had, if he'd paid even a little more attention, it would have been so clear. Dor had loved her. Even then. And though he'd respected Smoke's claim enough never to allow himself to be tempted, once Smoke left, all bets were off. No: after Smoke had nearly gotten himself killed, after he'd chosen a battle he could not win over a future with Cass. It was what she had been trying to tell him, that last day, when he left without saying goodbye because saying goodbye would have hurt too much, would have stolen his focus—he *had* chosen.

And she'd come for him anyway, saved him anyway. But what was left, after that battle, was a broken man, an un-whole man—and who could blame Cass and his old friend for letting down their guard, for giving up resisting, for seeking a little comfort?

He could. He could blame them, or at least Dor, and if it was wrong he didn't care, and if it was pointless he didn't care. He looked on his old friend and felt the burn of betrayal and the stirrings of hatred, and he knew he had to master these emotions or they would all certainly die. Dor, with his dexterity and determination and focus, was their best and possibly only hope for finding a way back out. Smoke would have to fight the Beaters without him. He turned away, forcing the bile of his hatred down, down and thinking only of the challenge of the next moments.

He had learned the Easterners' names during the past few days of cavesdropping on their conversations. Mayhew—now dead. Davis was with the group that had pressed to the front and Smoke saw him now, crouched next to Mayhew's body, rifling through his blood-soaked shirt. What was he looking for, his weapon? Blade? But all the Easterners were well armed—in fact, he'd admired Nadir's ebony-handled tactical knife.

The other two were working at the entrance—Nadir, the most outgoing of the four, the one who chatted with the older folks and made wisecracks with the kids, and the Mack-truck-built Bart. They were kicking at the emergency exit door a few yards from Dor, grim-faced and silent, Bart putting his shoulder into it and making the frame shiver with each assault. It was possible that he'd dent the thing, but nearly inconceivable that he'd break through. And definitely not in time. The mall architects and then its dwellers had made sure of that, locking everyone in with great care.

The issue came up every time someone wandered out of the Box, drunk or bored or simply looking for a little solitude, and managed to get themselves killed instead. Then there would be calls for securing the exits, for preventing people from leaving. These demands had been put down firmly by Dor: personal liberties were not taken for granted in the Box. But here—in this temple of suburban consumerism, it was not hard to imagine a different outcome.

Smoke made his choice. He didn't know any of the group, other than Dor, well enough to be certain who would be best in a fight, but the Easterners were disciplined, at least, and armed. "Nadir. Bart. Come on, we need to deal with these fuckers."

The men joined him, the crowd closing in around the doors behind them, and considered the shambling crowd of newly turned, still at the far end of the mall. They moved slowly at this phase of the disease, their languorous quality one of the things that made the early stages deceptively appealing, the thing that caused people to call it "the beautiful death," like tuberculosis a hundred years earlier.

They stopped using that term when the suffering advanced to the cannibalistic stages of the disease.

"They're all infected, aren't they?" Bart said, and Smoke saw that he was afraid. Which shouldn't have been a surprise—who wouldn't be terrified?—but the Easterners had accumulated, in very short order, a mystique around themselves, one that all the Edenites had bought into. It was so easy to grasp on to anything when you had nothing. Smoke should have known— *would have known,* if he had been paying attention— that they'd given away their allegiance too fast, that they'd bought into the flimsy illusion the strangers held up, giving too little thought to the dark side they were hiding.

Because every man had a dark side. Smoke knew this more than anyone, didn't he?

"Nadir, you take the front line with me," Smoke said, motioning them to hurry. "Bart, you next." He scanned the people nearby for anyone who could help. "Terrence, Shel—you too. Do you have extra ammo?"

Shel held up her handgun and nodded; her face was pale but her hands were steady. Terrence stepped up without a word. The street-sweeper auto he carried had seemed like a ridiculous affectation to Smoke earlier, but now its bulk and power seemed like a good idea. So what if Terrence was a boy with a man's weapon? If there was ever a day to become a man, today was it.

"Okay. Let's go."

Smoke was conscious of his limp, of the trembling that started in his chest and radiated out his arms. He gripped his gun harder and made a fist with his other hand. He knew it was more important to appear strong than to *be* strong right now. The others would follow his example, a lesson he'd learned over and over in the Box when he trained with the other guards. He'd never been the strongest, the fastest, the most accurate—but he'd been the most determined.

He had the most to atone for.

And that was the thing he held in his mind as he led them down the mall walkway. It was another day of atonement and that was all right, and if his body screamed with pain and his thoughts fell away until all that was left was this blood-rimmed shadow of the man he'd been, that was all right too. The coward's way, the easy way, would have been to die back in the stinking concrete basement room where the Rebuilders had taken their vengeance upon him, where they left him to lie on a floor streaked with the blood of others, but Smoke did not die.

Because he wasn't done atoning.

And because of Cass.

He sought her out in the huddled crowd of Edenites. There—there, she had retreated to the center, with Ruthie in her arms and her father close by. Red would keep her safe, for now—another man who'd give his life for Cass, and that was all right with Smoke.

Nadir knew what he was doing. He kept pace with Smoke, though Smoke knew he itched to go faster, and focused on the group ahead.

"Get 'em in the chute, boss, what do you say?" Nadir said quietly.

Smoke saw what he meant—if they could get the infected to come across one of the narrow pedestrian bridges that crisscrossed the atrium, they'd be tightly clustered, a better target than they were now. Not yet close enough to catch the Edenites' scent, they stumbled and wandered in a loose formation along the side of the mall, momentarily distracted by the brilliant flashes of light being spun by some sort of crystal hanging in the display window of a Hot Topic.

"Good idea." He turned to the others. "Everyone… we need to get them to come across. I'll stay on this side with…how about you, Shel? You and me. Then when they're in the middle, Terrence, Nadir, Bart, you guys get to the other side and we'll box them in. But you'll have to be fast because you're going to have to take the long way, see?"

He sketched the plan with his finger, pointing out the circuit made by the two pedestrian bridges and the walkways on either side of the mall.

"Got it," Shel said. The others nodded their assent.

"Okay, we're ready?"

He was more aware than ever that he was the one slowing them down, and Smoke threw himself into the short journey, holding on to the brass rail overlooking the atrium, and favoring his good leg, letting the other drag a little. The Edenites had stopped screaming, at least, though he could hear the moaning and whimpering from those who'd been trampled and injured. In the relative quiet, the voices of the infected echoed, a trick of the acoustics of the place. The mumbled syllables and nonsense words blended together when there were so many of them, almost losing their oddness; they could have been a polite crowd at an art gallery, a group of suburban parents at a middle-school open house.

When they reached the far side of the bridge, Smoke

took one side of the opening and motioned them to spread out. "Now we make some noise."

They started whooping and hollering, and the infected paused and turned their heads. The expressions on their faces were disturbingly, stirringly innocent, a combination of curiosity and good-natured interest, like children at a matinee when the curtains part. Their babble went up a few decibels and they turned gracelessly, bumping into each other and squawking with irritation, shoving at one another.

A couple of them lumbered toward the bridge, but most of the others, their attention fixed on the Hot Topic display—sunglasses and belt buckles and sequined tops all hung just out of their reach—stayed where they were.

Without warning Shel ran forward onto the bridge. She whooped and shot at the ceiling, hitting the skylight with a tinkling of glass that rained down not far from them, sparkling as it fell.

"Come and get me, cocksuckers," she screamed. "Come on, I know you want me. I'm good, I'm good, I'm sooooo good, you know you want to sink your teeth in me."

She danced along, shimmying and waving her arms, dangerously close to the other end. If any of them decided to run for it, she was doomed.

"Shel, you're too close!" Smoke yelled, and then Nadir burst past him, sprinting to her, grabbing her free hand and dragging her back.

Shel fought him, screaming. "No! Let go of me! Come on, I had them!"

It was their struggle that seemed to make the difference. There was a swell of excited chatter, a few garbled cries of excitement, and the group of infected turned toward the bridge. Several pressed forward onto the ones closest to them, knocking one of them over, a middle-aged woman with a fussy short haircut that was sticking straight up on one side and a necklace of purple beads that bounced against the ground when she fell. An overweight man with his shirt unbuttoned, exposing a hairy, pale stomach, stepped right on her outstretched leg and reached in front of him with grasping hands.

"Shit," Terrence breathed at Smoke's elbow.

"Keep it together, boy," he snapped. He was trying to get a shot at the heavy infected, but Shel and Nadir were in the way.

"Get back here!" Bart screamed. "Nadir, come *on!*"

Smoke saw what had scared him: a skinny Beater in a velour tracksuit was pushing her way through the clump, moving more quickly than the rest of them, her mouth open and her tongue waggling.

Nadir tugged Shel, dragging her backward, and with his free hand he fired. He hit the big man in the chest, slowing him, but not stopping him. Others pressed around him as he wobbled.

Nadir's second shot took out the wiry woman seconds before she reached him.

"Go, *go,*" Smoke ordered. "Bart, Terrence—you'll have to take the other side by yourselves."

They ran for it. Smoke could hear their footsteps ringing through the great empty cavern of the mall, echoing through all the wasted space that had once cost untold sums of money to heat and cool, Before. All that money, all the shit in these stores, mountains of crap that no one really needed.

The crowd of Edenites was yelling, a terrified sort of cheering. Smoke hoped they'd have the sense to stay where they were. He heard banging, and prayed Dor was getting closer with the door.

Two-thirds of the infected were on the bridge now, stepping on and around the bodies of the big guy and the wiry woman.

"Hold back," Smoke yelled to Nadir. The worst thing he could do would be to create a blockage on the far side of the bridge; then the things would split off into two groups, get distracted, wander in different directions.

Nadir seemed to understand. He quit firing and dragged Shel back with him. In seconds they were back on Smoke's side of the bridge, out of breath, Shel's eyes red and watery.

Terrence had made the circuit down the hall and across the bridge and back up the other hallway, Bart right behind him, but they were going too fast. They needed to let all the infected follow the first ones onto the bridge, where they would be sitting ducks.

"Wait up!" Smoke yelled. Terrence looked over at him and nodded, then stopped, pressing his back against the entrance of a candle shop.

There was a noise from below.

A scream and a great clanging from the first floor. Smoke looked over the rail. A coffee shack in the center of the lounge area shuddered, and four figures burst out of the door, knocking over a café table.

Beaters. Mature ones.

They must have been nesting inside the little shack. And they were headed for the escalator. The one that would take them straight up to the end of the mall where the Edenites were huddled.

"Oh, Jesus God," Shel breathed, and then without

pause she shot, over the edge, down into the mall. It was an impossible shot and Smoke grabbed her arm.

"No," he yelled into her ear. "Save your ammo. Focus on the ones here. The others will deal with those."

It was the only thing they could do. But once the Beaters got up the stairs, there would be nothing to stop them from attacking. Even if Smoke and his companions laid every one of the things on the bridge to waste, it could well be at the cost of losing everyone else.

But there was nothing else he could do. The roving mass had nearly made its way entirely onto the bridge. Terrence was slinking down the hall toward them, waiting for the stragglers to catch up. Bart was a few paces behind him, looking like he was about to throw up.

He still had a couple more clips—how many rounds, he wasn't sure. He'd just stand here and pick off the things that staggered toward him until he ran out, counting on the others to herd them onto the bridge or blast them from the other side.

A scream rose above the din, singular among all the others because he knew that voice.

Cass

Smoke forced himself to stay focused on the scene ahead of him, knowing that if he abandoned his post to go to her now he'd doom them both. And yet every fiber of his being rebelled as he lined up his shot.

36

Cass ran to the side and looked down, just in time to see them reach the escalators. Three of them had no hair at all, and one had a few greasy hanks at the back of its head. At least one of them was missing fingers. These Beaters had been infected for a long time, and their bodies were starting to disintegrate. In a month, maybe two, they'd finally die from the sheer punishment they routinely suffered and inflicted on each other—even their hyper immune system couldn't save them after they lost enough blood and took enough blows to their savaged bodies.

But until then, they were more dangerous than ever. Hungrier. Faster. Unstoppable.

She ran back to her father, who was cradling Ruthie, rocking her and singing. "Dad, I'm going to help Dor. Just—just keep her safe."

She pushed through the crowd, knowing how ridiculous her words were. There was no way to help. There was no such thing as safe.

"Where are we at?" she demanded, after forcing her way to Dor's side. Sammi made room for her, her face white with fear.

"Last one," Dor muttered, sparing her a quick glance with his flint-spark eyes. "Got the other two hinges out. Shot off the caps and pried out the pins, but this one's corroded or something, can't get it free."

His hands were bloody, and the screwdriver he was using to chip away at the blockage slipped from his hands. *"Fuck!"*

"Let me." Cass seized it from him and wiped it on her shirt, leaving his blood streaked on the fabric. "Tell me, show me—"

And he did, his quiet voice in her ear, speaking slowly, steadily, the way he'd done so many times before when it was just the two of them, when he'd cajoled and urged her to the dark heights where they both sought release. She let everything else fall away until it was just her and him and the thing that must be done, his voice, his lips brushing her ear, her hands and the glinting metal and the greasy mechanism and every bit of her energy focused on the task until suddenly the pin fell to the floor with a clang and then everything, the sounds and the people and the fear came rushing back and she was pushed away from the door as the crowd surged forward.

"Back, *back!*" Dor yelled from three feet away that felt like a thousand, and he and others jammed their blades into the space between the wall and the door and heaved and pulled until it gave a little, just a little and down the mall there was screaming and shooting and Cass could not bear to look so she turned away and found Red and took her daughter back, burrowed her baby's sweet face into the crook of her neck and kissed her hair and swore it was going to be all right.

Sunlight and screaming. An earsplitting metal-on-metal groan as the door was pulled away from the frame. Four, five men grunting and sweating with effort, and the metal door bent but did not break. The opening grew until it was a foot, eighteen inches wide, and the crowd roared and pressed forward and they would not be stopped now, but the space was not wide enough for them all to pass through, they would kill each other trying, there was Craig Switzer shoving Mrs. Nguyen out of the way, his hand on her face, mad with fear—

And then his throat exploded, blood everywhere, his mouth open with surprise, and his hand slipping slowly off poor Mrs. Nguyen.

"Stand back or I'll shoot again," Dor yelled, and the crowd hesitated and backed up just a fraction of an inch, enough to spare the ones suffocating at the front, and the door budged a little more and a little more, until there was room for a person to slip through sideways and Phil Booth forced his way out to the other side before Dor could do a thing about it.

He cursed and shot at the floor, chipping up a chunk of concrete at the base of the door. "You go when I say you go or you're dead. Harris. Benny. Go through and man the other side. One of you help the people through and the other keep everyone together. Women first. Kids. Old people. Line up and so help me God you fuck this up I'll shoot you so fast you won't know what hit you."

It was working. The crowd had retreated—just a little farther, but enough—and the women were being helped along, sliding through, crying. Ingrid went with all the children and then Suzanne, and Dor seized Cass's arm and tried to push her through but she fought him.

"They're going to be here in a second," she shouted, but Dor had been so focused on forcing his way out that he didn't know, he didn't know about the four struggling up the stairs, and he'd sent two of the only armed men through the door, and Cass knew he had to stay here to make sure the others got out.

"Who—"

"It doesn't matter," she said, and then she told a lie, the only way she could make him let her go. "I'm just going to get my dad, I'll be back in a minute."

Red was at the end of the line of older people, him and Zihna, and Cass handed him Ruthie and kissed his cheek, and he gave her his gun and whispered that he loved her, her father understood what she was going to do, his eyes were terrified but he took Ruthie and followed Zihna through the crack to the outside—and Cass ran.

Far ahead, on the bridge, there was fighting and screaming and dying, but that was not Cass's fight. Behind her the terrified crowd continued its exodus. She was alone, she was the only one left to face the ones coming up the escalator. They were terrible at stairs, they stumbled and lost their balance and that was all that had saved her so far; one had stumbled and was splayed upside down halfway down the metal staircase, but the other three clutched each other in a grunting scrum that had nearly reached the top.

They spotted her, and the closest one—God, it was

impossible to believe it had ever been human, with its gaping mouth-hole and sunken eye sockets and torn-off ears and pulped flesh—it saw her and it screamed, and Cass couldn't help screaming back as she shot it, the gun jerking in her hands. She did not know this gun, it was her father's gun, it was unwieldy and old and it was too heavy for her, the report traveling up her arm through her elbow into her shoulder, and her palm slipped as she tried to rack the slide.

And the thing kept coming. She'd shot it in the chest and it had gone clear through, but too high, too high. A shard of bone protruded and one arm lay limp as it seized at her with the other. No, no, no, it was too late to run, they were too close, she'd fucked it up, it was an easy shot and she'd failed, and then it was on her, its bone-fingers clutching the fabric of her shirt, yanking her toward it, its mouth open and drooling and its rotting brown teeth shiny with saliva. She put her hands on its head and shoved, anything to keep the snapping teeth away, but she was not strong enough. The mouth closed on her forearm even as she fought it, pushing and writhing with all her might, but there was nothing in the world stronger than a Beater's lust and this one was mad with its hunger for her and she felt the sharp pain as it bit down, saw the blood spurt from her arm as it ripped her flesh.

Explosions, so close, and the thing fell away from her, rolling back onto the stairs, falling on its companions who shoved it out of their way and kept coming. Then more shots, a staccato burst of them, and their bodies jerked and seized and went limp, and there was Terrence, leaning over the edge with that insane gun of his and one more burst took out the last one and it died upside down on the stairs, staring up at the skylights with empty eyes.

Cass, sinking to the floor, her hand closing over her wound—she looked up and found that she was staring into the barrel of Bart's gun.

"No, no, don't do it! Don't shoot her!"

It was Sammi, racing toward them, her hair flying behind her.

"Sammi, stay back," she screamed. Bart's gun hand was shaking from adrenaline; there was no telling what he'd do in the heat of the moment. "Go to your dad!"

"No, Bart, don't, you don't understand." Sammi ignored her, her sneakers slapping on the smooth floor of the mall, echoing around the giant space. Behind her was pandemonium, the crowd pushing through the narrow opening, Dor yelling, people screaming. "Cass can't get the fever, she's immune."

"What the fuck are you talking about?" Bart waved the gun back and forth between Cass and Sammi.

"Sammi, go, please," Cass said, her heart caught in her throat as she prayed that Bart would stay calm. "Please just back away. Go outside and we'll, I'll—it's going to be fine, I promise."

"No!" Sammi's voice turned into a wail, and tears glistened in her eyes. "Cass, he doesn't understand, make him understand. Bart, she got attacked a long time ago and she got better and she can't get the fever again. She's, like, *immune*."

Bart stared at her for a long, breathless moment, his eyes narrowed, and for a second—a quivering, hopeful second—she thought he might lower his gun.

But then, instead, he raised it and pointed it squarely between Cass's eyes.

"Look away, little girl," he muttered.

Cass heard the click and squeezed her eyes shut and when the shot came she was thinking that she would have done the same.

Down on all fours, pain searing her forehead, the echo of the sound filled Cass's ears. Blood poured into her eyes, but she was alive.

In front of her, Bart was clutching his hand and screaming, and his gun lay on the floor.

Smoke. Smoke staggered toward them and then his leg gave out and he sank to the floor. His strength had finally run out. He'd used every bit of adrenaline for the fight, and then somehow he'd made it close enough to shoot Bart in the hand to keep him from killing her. Cass put her hand to her scalp, found that the bullet had only grazed her, felt torn flesh but no bone. It was nothing.

"Sammi," she said weakly, and the girl knelt down and leaned into her, sobbing, and Cass hugged her hard, feeling her strong heartbeat against her neck.

"We've got to move," someone yelled, his hand on her shoulder. Cass looked up, blinking. Terrence. He offered her his hand, then withdrew it. "That's true?" he demanded. "You're really immune?"

"She is, damn it," Smoke said, and with a huge effort forced himself to his feet. "We need to get them out of here."

"We *all* need to get out of here," Terrence said. He helped Sammi up, supporting her with an arm around her waist, and Sammi leaned against him, still snuffling, wiping at her tearstained cheek.

Despite the gravity of the situation, Cass felt a stirring of gratitude and hope. The dam between her and Sammi had broken; the girl had let Cass comfort her, embrace her. Sammi could have left Cass for doomed, could have been rid of her forever, but instead she'd tried to save her.

"Let them go first," Smoke ordered Terrence, but he looked like he was going to fall again so Cass hooked an arm around him and half dragged him to his feet. Terrence hastened Sammi along toward the exit and Bart followed after him, bleeding a trail of droplets.

Cass took one last look at the mall. Bodies lay everywhere, blood pooling on the floor and dripping down the escalator. There were undoubtedly more of them, the shelterers who'd made innocent mistakes as they tried to save each other, who'd paid with their souls. Even now they were probably rousing themselves from their delirious fevered slumber, staggering out from their dark corners, from the remains of the shops where they once bought their designer shoes and their thirty-dollar lipsticks and their coffee grinders and cell-phone accessories.

She and Smoke were the last ones to leave. Dor pushed Bart and Terrence through and then he looked at her, taking in his blood on her shirt, the bite mark on her arm, Smoke nearly unconscious.

With surprising gentleness he lifted Smoke, dragging him to the opening and handing him off to the men waiting on the other side, who pulled him through. Sunlight hit Cass's face and she blinked and ducked back into the gloom, just for one minute more, one second more.

"He saved you," Dor said quietly. Outside, Cass could

hear the shouting and cheers of the Edenites who'd made it, but inside the mall it was stunningly, eerily still.

Dor put a hand to her cheek, tenderly tracing a path from the superficial bullet wound down to her mouth, brushing her lips with his thumb. "Are you back with him, then? Are you together?"

His voice was a whisper, his mouth so close. Cass's body was so numb from terror and exertion she knew that she could collapse right here and sleep for a dozen hours, a thousand years. And even in that state she could feel the electricity between them, the memory of the taste of him seared in her mind. She wanted to kiss him. Wanted to consume him and be consumed by him, to ignite and burn down to ash.

Instead she had to go on. They both had to go on.

"I don't know," she whispered, and then she slipped out the door into the blinding sun.

37

That night, there was a memorial service for everyone who died in the mall. They made a forced march north, five or six miles, along pretty country roads greening with budding kaysev, and the clouds vanished and sun streamed down to earth.

They stopped at a chicken ranch. The fowl had been among the first casualties of the Siege, laid waste by a bioterror agent believed to have come from North Korea, though it was never proved and remained anybody's guess. Even after all these months, the place still reeked. Red, who was walking with Cass, asked her if she remembered helping him in the garden, unloading the chicken manure he got for free from a friend who kept a few dozen hens.

"Chicken shit's the worst-smelling shit in the world," Red said. "Oh, sweetheart, you should have seen the look on your little face. What were you, eight? And your mom was so pissed at me..."

"But everything grew that year," Cass remembered, smiling. It was becoming a little more okay, talking about things like this with her dad. Everything—every story—was tinged with a little sadness, a little anger over the fact that it had all come to an end when he left. But it still felt right to talk.

"Yeah, you remember the carnations?"

Carnations, for her birthday. Every month had a birth flower. January was hers. They'd planted larkspur for her mother and narcissus for her dad. When Ruthie was born, Cass looked it up—the September flower was aster. Nobody really cared about things like birth flowers anymore, but Cass decided that—maybe, if they ever found a place to settle again, if she ever had a garden again, if Red and Zihna wanted to—they could grow a little patch of asters for Ruthie.

The laying sheds were unusable, layered with desiccated shit and straw, a few chicken carcasses they'd somehow missed collecting and burning. But the ranch house was pretty, an old rambling square wood-sided edifice with a wraparound porch. Whoever had built it had situated it well; the back porch looked out over fields to the mountains miles beyond.

It was in the field that they had the service. The sun was sinking behind the house when they gathered in its long shadow.

Shannon had assembled a list of the lost. There were thirty-two names on it, including the two Easterners who'd died—nineteen from the Beaters' attack in the river and the day of their departure, thirteen more at the mall.

Sh'rae Bellamy had done the services on New Eden since the Methodist minister died, and she did so now. She opened her Bible to a page that she had marked, and began to read, but she made it through only a few words before she stopped and went very still. She raised her eyes to the mountains in the distance and the evening wind whipped her long cape around her, and the silence was deeper than Cass could remember in a very long time. There was only the wind and the mewling of the baby, the soft sounds of crying from somewhere deep in the gathering.

After a while Sh'rae found her place and began again. "From the Book of Isaiah," she repeated.

"'Do you not know? Have you not heard?'

"'The Lord is the everlasting God, the Creator of the ends of the earth.'

"'He will not grow tired or weary, and his understanding no one can fathom.'"

38

The evening meal was a somber affair. There was little conversation as the bedding was laid out in the various rooms of the house. Sentries were chosen, four to a shift—it was not a particularly secure house with its front and back doors, ground-floor windows, screened crawl space below—but no one seemed especially concerned about what might come in the night. After the horrors of the day, perhaps they were numb to fear.

She found Smoke sitting on the steps of the porch as the sky deepened to indigo, talking to Nadir. There were others on the porch; Red and Zihna sat in rockers with blankets over their laps, and a few people sat alone or in pairs, staring off at the mountains disappearing into the night. Sammi and Colton sat at the far end of the porch, their legs dangling, eating tender young kaysev pods and tossing the beans out into the darkness. It was an evening for reflection. Tomorrow would be another day of travel, and while they would not forget the losses and tragedies of today, they would have to store them carefully and well so that they could go on.

Cass had hoped to find Smoke alone. She asked awkwardly if she could join them, and sat on the top step, so that they made a triangle. Nadir had set up a small tripod flashlight that illuminated the papers that were spread out between them with a soft yellow glow.

"You need to hear this," Smoke said without preamble. "Mayhew lied to us."

Nadir winced and shook his head. "We all did."

"What do you mean?"

"The shelters they've built up north? They're not meant for us. Definitely not meant for anyone from the West."

"But what—then who—"

"There are four new settlements, that much is true," Nadir said. "Two months ago, the first wave went north. They had the resources to build communities that could sustain three hundred people each for a year or more. Only thirty were in each party, though, enough to build, and stock, and secure the settlements. Men and women, all of them strong and healthy, so that if for some reason the others never made it, they would have the seeds of a new civilization to build on."

"It was all decided very democratically," Smoke said, a trace of contempt in his voice. "They practice *concordance* in the East."

Cass was surprised at his bitterness. "But you've always believed in cooperative government. That's what we did in the library."

Smoke stared into the space between them, his eyes

unfocused. "And what happened to the library? Burned, and everyone dead or worse."

"Concordance was not the problem in our community," Nadir interrupted. "If I may be so bold as to share my opinion. We had a good government, a well-meaning government. The plan was a good one. But when all of these good people went north, who is left behind— the ones who are not so good, yes? The ones who are not so idealistic. Who are thinking maybe about themselves, not about abstract values."

"They had a lottery to figure out who would come in the second wave," Dor explained. "Twelve hundred people, that's all that would be allowed. Four groups of three hundred, minus the hundred and twenty who went first. That was less than half of the people living in their town."

"Mayhew was not chosen," Nadir said heavily. "Nor was I. Nor Bart, nor Davis."

Cass was beginning to understand. "And those who were left behind…"

"There was an agreement, one we all voted on. The unlucky ones would stay, and deal with what was to come. We had reinforced our shelters, much as you have here. After today I can appreciate how small our efforts were against the threat of the fever. We would have been caught unawares. We would have made mistakes."

"It would be just like here," Smoke said. "Just like the West, all over again. They just knew what they were in for, that was the only difference. They knew what was coming."

"The stories we heard, from the border—they did not prepare us, not for what I have seen. I could not imagine…"

His words hung in the air. Cass understood. Until you'd seen a Beater, they way they moved, their child-like hungers and rages, their sheer determination, you could not imagine the terror.

"And Mayhew?" Cass asked, though she had a feeling she knew the rest.

"He sought us out. He went to Davis first because of the horses. Davis owned many horses and he had given many away, for people to ride, but he had kept his finest for himself. Me and Bart, he chose us because we had weapons, and we are strong and young. Mayhew said to us, there is no reason we cannot go to this settlement. Let the others build it. Four more people, that is not a lot—once we arrive, they will not turn us away. These are good people, compassionate people.

"Davis taught us to ride. We stayed out on his ranch, and no one knew what we were doing. We gathered the things we would need. I taught Davis to shoot. The rest of us practiced. We were biding our time, to give the first group time to reach the destination and make everything ready. We thought our chances were best if we arrived around the time of the second wave, when everything was still confusing.

"That was a mistake. Because you see, we were not the only ones to have this thought. We found out about the others. People like us who were not content to be left behind, who were also gathering weapons, and among this group were bad people, killers and criminals. Mayhew tried to meet with them, to reason with them. He said we should split the settlements among us, each group should go to a different one, but there was no agreement. The more Mayhew tried to lead this discussion the more it disintegrated. It almost came to violence. Threats were made.

"We left that night. But Mayhew had an idea. He thought that we should make our numbers stronger, that we should find others—fighters. Survivors. People who already knew how to deal with Beaters. We would take the settlement by force, if we needed to.

"He thought we should come West, for two reasons. First of all, anyone here would have the advantage of experience with the Beaters and the fever. He was convinced we would need that knowledge to survive, even once we made it north. And second, the Western settlement is the harshest, the most difficult conditions. It was taking a chance, because there was some doubt about whether the first party could make it work, that it might not be able to build the infrastructure. But it was for that reason that Mayhew thought the other groups would avoid it.

"The first few days of the trip were difficult, and we made mistakes, but we learned. We lost Jarvis to the Beaters during our first day on this side of the mountains. He…" Nadir paused, his voice roughening. He swallowed before continuing.

"We grew closer. Bart and Davis and I did, anyway. Mayhew…he held himself apart. We did not begrudge him leadership, but we began to see that he could be cruel. The night we saw your flares, we did not come to help you, not the way we said, anyway. But when we found that you were well supplied, and already on the road, he saw a way he could turn this to our favor."

"But we're not all strong," Cass said. "Not warriors. Not what he wanted."

Nadir frowned and stared at the ground. "No, not all

of you," he agreed softly. "Mayhew planned to take the women and the strongest men only. He was willing to wait a few days, because he thought the difficulty of the travel would soften people up to the idea of leaving the weaker ones behind. But he was ready to kill them if that didn't happen."

"He thought—?" Cass was incredulous. "Mayhew thought that of us? Even after he got to know us?"

Nadir looked miserable. "We tried—Bart and Davis and I, we tried to tell him…but he didn't care to listen. In every society, some people get left behind. Not all your people made it off the island, so I guess he was thinking it might work. Anyway, he had other concerns. He wanted, um, more women. More women of child-bearing age. He thought—well, that's why he was so determined to get into the mall. His plan was to take their women too."

"How the hell did he think he'd accomplish that?" Smoke demanded. "Just walk in and issue an invitation? Hey, girls, wanna come with us?"

"He thought once we'd spent some time with them, maybe there could be a big meeting of the leadership. A bargain could be made. He thought they might be willing to come, a few leaders and some of their women, once he explained about the settlement. And we would leave the weak members of our party there. He said it was humane, you see, because they would be protected, they would have resources."

The chill of this knowledge traveled through Cass. "And you went along with this?"

Nadir's expression darkened further. "I am ashamed to say that I did, at first. I was very afraid. Seeing the Beater, what it did to Jarvis…I believed we did not have a chance unless we did what Mayhew suggested. But now…I cannot continue as he wanted to. My heart is not in it."

"Either that, or you've figured out the truth is your only option," Cass said bitterly. She herself knew how powerful self-preservation could be, but she'd also learned to part with her trust very reluctantly.

"Cass, he's giving us everything," Smoke said. "The plans for the settlement, the coordinates, the notes on the conditions. He doesn't even want to lead. He says he'll accept whatever role we give him."

"Oh no," Cass said angrily. "If we do this, you're not getting off easy. You know the most about this plan, you're going to be one of the people making it happen."

"I have seen what this man can do," Nadir said, indicating Smoke with a palm placed flat on the step between him. "It would be my honor to follow him."

"All right—but it can't just be me," Smoke said.

Cass was stunned. Since the first day Smoke and she had met, he had been adamant that he did not want to lead. Even in his role overseeing security in the Box, he avoided anything resembling a hierarchy, and rarely told anyone else what to do.

"I'll do this," Smoke said, knowing what she was thinking. His blue eyes bored into hers, and when he spoke again, it was only to her. "But you have to convince Dor to do it with me."

"What?"

It was the last thing Cass expected. Since the first day on the road, the two men had barely spoken. Cass knew she was the reason. Before, in the Box, they had been each other's closest confidant, each other's best friend. Now, they were rivals. They both wanted her—and she did not know what she wanted.

The months in the Box—the time on the island—these were illusory, brief expanses of peace when it sometimes seemed like life returned to the way it had been Before. Except…in the Box Cass had something she'd never had: someone to love, who loved her back. Who loved Ruthie. Who wanted to make a family with her. Wanted to be with her forever…until the day came when he wanted vengeance more, when he left her and Ruthie and their home and their dreams, left everything behind to fight an impossible battle.

With Dor it had been different. They'd never talked about love. The thing between them was dark, needful, sometimes almost violent. It was an affair twisted from the threads of their hungers, their losses, their sorrows. At times it seemed like it inhabited only the fringes of their lives, especially because they always met in secret; but when they were together it expanded to encompass everything. When Dor touched her, everything else fell away, and it was like the world had never broken. No: it was like the world had never existed, like only they existed, in a free fall from time and space and everything they'd known. And yet, when it was over, they parted without promises, without words of love, without even a tender kiss, and they pretended there was nothing there.

Thinking about Dor was an endless loop, a puzzle with no answer. She had to stop.

"What is it that you're proposing?" Cass asked Nadir.

"We have the location." Nadir stabbed the paper with his finger. "We have the exact coordinates. We have routes, here. Weather conditions, population density from Before, everything. The first wave should have gotten there a week ago. They'll be putting up the frames for shelter, figuring out the water source, building cooking facilities and latrines, and fortifying all points of egress. If we stick to the schedule on here, we can be up there in eighteen days."

Cass examined the stack of printouts, the topographical map on top. "Where is that, anyway?"

"Mount Karuk. Fourth-largest peak in the Cascades. It's national forest land, so it hasn't been densely populated, but the site of the settlement—" Nadir pointed to the star inked on the map "—has been used by humans for, well, forever, because it's got hot springs, waterfalls, great volcanic soil for farming. It's perfect—except for one thing."

"Yeah?"

Nadir shuffled the papers, selected one. "Here's a detail map. The settlement is on this land, here. You can see the river, here—well, technically it's a stream but these cliffs are hundreds of feet high. The falls, here, carved out this gorge, and you can see where the river breaks off here, so that's impassable most of the year. Bottom line, it's very hard to get to. But there's some good news, too."

"What's that?"

"This bridge." Nadir showed them an aerial shot, fuzzy in black-and-white. "Wait, I can do better. I'm trying to conserve battery, but…"

He took a cell phone out of his pocket and thumbed it on.

"Are you going to call up there?" Cass asked, looking at the little machine a bit incredulously. She was aware that high emotion was making her sarcastic, and she regretted it, especially because this was the first good news they'd had in a long time. "Tell them to order pizza?"

Nadir grimaced but didn't respond. They waited for the phone to power up, and he clicked a few buttons. "Here."

He turned the screen face toward them, and Cass looked close: a crystal clear photo of emerald-green treetops, the winding break of the river, and there—a straight gray line.

"A bridge," Smoke said. "Four lanes. Put in by some multinational group that wanted to build a resort."

"So, assuming the bridge is intact—"

"That's a big assumption," Cass said. "Don't you think?"

Nadir shrugged. "Those photos were taken last March. Not even a year ago. Since then there's been no air traffic, hardly anyone on the roads. Sure, it's possible to get there on foot, but I'd say most people spent most of last year trying to go toward civilization and not away from it."

"The Cascades are hundreds of miles long," Smoke said. "And there's higher elevations. Why did they pick this one?"

"Because it's relatively easy to get to, especially coming from the southeast. They spaced the settlements out east to west, and this was supposed to be the westernmost camp. But if they'd gone up to Washington or Oregon, that'd take weeks longer. And they wanted the settlements to be forbidding enough that Beaters couldn't survive, but not so hostile that everyone else couldn't either. I mean, I wouldn't want to be in Minneapolis right now, know what I mean? At least in the settlements, a day on foot gets you down mountain, above freezing almost all year round. Put in a few satellite farms and you got four growing seasons, too. Couldn't really ask for much better."

Cass considered Nadir's argument, trying to find the holes in it. She had to admit that, other than the uncertain welcome they were likely to receive, it was better than anything they'd come up with. "So you really think this will work for all of us? What about the slow ones—the weak ones?"

"Everyone goes," Smoke said adamantly. "Everyone."

Nadir nodded. "I understand. We have the advantage of the vehicles. That should make up for any…problems we could experience. I mean, anyone who's slower, the kids, the older folks. If you don't mind me asking…are you concerned about loyalty? Why do you wish to involve this other man?"

Smoke addressed Nadir but his eyes were on Cass. "I am not well-known here. I've been sick. People might question my strength."

"Dor's only been here as long as I have," Cass protested. "Two months."

And no one liked him, she wanted to add. But things had changed so much. Of the council leadership, only Shannon and Harris remained; Dana was dead and Neal was among the missing.

Dor had been a hero today. In times of great upheaval, people were judged by their last trial, their last triumph. Without Dor they'd all be dead; she had a feeling that Smoke was right, that people would be expecting him to play a role in what came next.

"Is there anyone else?" Nadir asked. "Anyone who will challenge you?"

Smoke and Cass looked at each other. "No," she said slowly. "Dana would have, but he's dead."

Nadir nodded. "And what role do you see for me?"

"What do you mean?" Smoke asked.

"Am I to…assist you in some way?"

"You're the one with the maps, my friend," Smoke said. "You've put a lot on the table. You'll forgive me for assuming that you want something in return."

Nadir raised his hands. "A new life," he said. "A chance at something. To matter. To…know people."

"What did you do Before?" Cass asked.

Nadir shrugged. "I worked at a Best Buy. Went to community college. I was engaged…but I was thinking of breaking it off. I wasn't anything, really. Just an average guy."

"And now?" Smoke asked. "What do you want from life?"

"I'm twenty-six years old," Nadir said. "I've lost everyone I knew before a year ago. I'd like to live to see twenty-seven, and have a couple of friends when I get there."

Smoke nodded. He looked at Cass, slipped his hand around hers. "That's not the worst goal I ever heard."

People adapted to the new order with surprising complacency. Or maybe it wasn't all that surprising—and on second thought it wasn't complacency, but more like stunned acceptance. No one was unaffected by the terrible losses suffered at the mall. People were silent much of the day, prone to crying jags, more likely than ever to wander off in search of solitude when they did stop for rest.

Cindy, who had treated Rosita like a second mother, had taken to wearing the scarf she took from the dead woman's body outside the mall after she died from her head injury. It was still stained with blood, but Cindy didn't seem to care.

Sharon, whose partner, Elsa, had been among those crushed to death when people swarmed the door of the mall, stopped speaking to anyone. When people approached, she turned away; she seemed to blame them all. She walked several paces behind the crowd and slept outside at night and Cass worried that one morning they would find her gone, having slipped away in the night to be alone with her grief.

No one seemed to miss Craig Switzer much. Or Mayhew, for that matter, after a somewhat condensed version of his plan had been communicated at a meeting Smoke led with Nadir and Bart, Dor doing his customary silent-and-glowering thing a few paces away. A vote was taken, and, not surprisingly, it was a unanimous decision to continue northward toward Salt Point.

People were given a quick glimpse at the images on Nadir's phone before he shut it down to conserve the battery. Jay said it reminded him of skiing in Whistler, up in Canada. Kyra, who had begun talking about the baby from time to time, said she thought it would be nice to have a log-cabin school for the kids.

The days took on a rhythm, early mornings around fires made from whatever lumber they could scavenge, the last of the canned and preserved food doled out parsimoniously along with whatever form of kaysev was on offer that day. A new kitchen crew had formed from a few volunteers, including—surprisingly—Kalyan, who was a sort of apprentice to Fat Mike. Fat Mike wasn't the least bit fat anymore, but the name stuck, and he and Kalyan spent the evenings experimenting with kaysev and whatever other ingredients could be scrounged. Several times there was rabbit and even squirrel that Nadir or Dor or Bart shot. Cass found wild shallots and ginger, serviceberries, squawroot and nutsedge tubers. In her pack was the seed collection she had brought with her from New Eden, and she daydreamed about the garden she would grow if they reached Salt Point safely.

When, she corrected herself every time. *When* they reached Salt Point. But optimism was in short supply, despite everyone's efforts to practice it.

One reason Kalyan was spending more time with Fat Mike, Cass figured, was that Colton was spending most of his time with Sammi. Only Shane, among the young men, seemed to have failed to find a new diversion. Sometimes Cass saw him with his slingshot, shooting stones at billboards, wrecked cars, rabbits—though he never managed to hit those—always with the same vacant expression. If he missed his friends' company he didn't let on.

Twice they encountered Beaters: once, they pulled off the road at an orchard, the dead trees eerie with their clinging brown leaves and withered fruit. A pair of long sheds seemed like a reasonable shelter for the night, especially after Dor and some of the others went in to clear them and found nothing more vexing than a corpse lying next to an open refrigerator surrounded by empty beer cans. But as the group was settling in, a pack of four Beaters came sprinting from the tiny farmhouse that had been nearly hidden by the trees. Since the travelers had taken to posting sentries the moment they arrived at a new shelter, two of them were killed before they could enter through the open metal doors, and the others after they tripped, screaming with frustration, over their comrades. They were all old Beaters except for one, who had been a young man in his twenties recently enough that he still had all his hair and tattoos, elaborate colorful skulls and roses on both arms. He was the last to die, exhaling for a final time with what Cass imagined was a flicker of regret in his bright eyes.

The other Beater encounter was more disturbing still.

Late on a warm day, when they were looking for some-where to shelter, they passed by a tiny town, really noth-ing more than half a dozen small bungalows and a brick general store. All were abandoned, windows cracked and debris spilling from doorways. A stench rose from several cars parked in the middle of the intersection, and the group gave it a wide berth, walking through the field on the other side of the road.

They passed this site by because it would be too risky to try to check the buildings. Anytime there were more than two or three buildings clustered together, they gen-erally stayed clear. The paucity of Beater sightings on the journey confirmed what they'd heard from the hand-ful of settlers and freewalkers they'd encountered: the Beaters were generally concentrated in the larger towns and cities still, though with their quarry more and more elusive, as survivors dwindled and reinforced their shel-ters, it wasn't unheard of to find a nest in a tiny town or ranch, especially near the roads.

Still, nothing stirred in the dusty streets as the group rolled silently by, the horses' hooves clopping hollowly alongside the cars and trailers and wagons. They'd gone perhaps twenty-five yards past the edge of the town, far enough for a collective sigh of relief, when a fright-ened yell pierced the air and a figure came sprinting toward them.

As he gained ground, Cass saw that it was Shane, his long hair flopping on his forehead, his baggy pants sag-ging below his stomach. A second later a pair of Beat-ers came loping after him. One of them had something wrong with its leg, which dragged along behind it, and Shane quickly outpaced it. But the other one had man-aged to get a hold of Shane's flapping jacket before it tripped and let go as it staggered, trying not to fall. A bullet from Smoke's gun dropped it instantly, but Shane kept running, gibbering with terror, until he was in the midst of the group.

Cass didn't like the boy, but he was still a child, as much as any sixteen-year-old can still be called a child. She wasn't the only one to feel that way, it was clear, because several of the women surrounded him, checking for injuries, exclaiming over him, as Smoke walked to the injured Beater and shot it in the neck.

"Let's keep going, let's just keep going," Shane repeated, his voice thin and terrified.

"What the hell happened, son?" Dor demanded. Shane was not a big kid, and he had to look up to meet Dor's eyes. "What were you doing back there?"

"I was, I was, I just saw, I thought I saw, uh, cans, like food cans."

"Where, through a window? On a porch?"

Bart and Nadir had their weapons out and had flanked Smoke on either side. Neither of the downed Beaters stirred, and there were no further sounds from the camp.

But there was smoke and, as everyone turned to stare, a small popping sound.

Shane turned away, muttering, as Dor exclaimed softly under his breath.

"Stay here, everyone," he ordered as he joined the other armed men.

It didn't take them long to find the fire. The shabbiest of the bungalows was in flames all along the back, where the paint had long ago flaked off the siding and a porch railing made excellent tinder.

They were back in moments.

"I smelled kerosene or something," Dor said, cuffing Shane on the shoulder. The boy kept his head down, his face burning.

"I said something to you, boy."

"It was there. It was sitting out. And it wasn't kerosene, it was deck stain."

Dor cursed and spun Shane around in the street. Cass was torn—like the others who kept walking, she trusted Dor to handle it. But her father, who had been walking next to her, had backtracked to join the pair, and Cass followed.

"So you found deck stain sitting on the street? I don't—"

"Didn't say it was in the street. In the garage."

Two of the houses had detached garages behind them. Both were missing doors and windows.

"Boy," Red said softly. "You like watching shit burn?"

Shane flicked a glance at him but didn't answer.

"Check his pack," Red said, as he hooked a large hand under Shane's chin and forced him to look at him.

A quick search turned up a Ziploc bag full of small boxes of matches, a motley collection of knives and a cheap imitation throwing star.

"That's a lot of matches, son," Red said softly. "Anything else you might want to be getting off your conscience?"

Shane shook his head as Red squeezed his jaw, finally wrestling free and stumbling off at a jog.

"I think you just found your firebug," Red said.

Everyone was talking about Shane, and Sammi wanted to talk to him, ask him if it was true, if he'd really done the things they were saying. They'd taken everything sharp or flammable or conceivably dangerous away from him, and spread the word among the entire group. Bart suggested leaving him behind at the next shelter they passed, but he was quickly voted down. Watching the boy trudge along behind the group, face flaming and an expression of utter dejection on his face, seemed like punishment enough.

Besides, they had another problem to worry about. Jasmine had gone into labor that morning, and it wasn't going well. She'd been riding in the panel van with Sun-hi all day, and when they came to a long, low-slung cinder-block building set at an angle on a giant gravel lot, broken neon signs spelling out TRIPLE-X GIRLS LIQUOR COORS LIVE NUDE, it was decided that she and Sun-hi would stay in the van while everyone else made camp inside.

Twenty yards behind the building was a surprisingly pretty creek. The water was shallow and murky, but grasses grew along its banks, and butterflies and water bugs flitted among them, the first anyone had seen Aftertime.

A fire was built along the bank and dinner served there as the sun set. People waded into the water, the first chance for a bath or laundry in many days. There was laughter as people emerged shivering and stripped behind blankets, hanging their clothes from the branches of a sycamore tree.

Sammi was helping to dry the little boys after a dip in the creek, toweling Dane off and smoothing his damp hair, which had grown long enough to hang into his eyes.

"Sammi, oh my God, Sammi." Kyra came running up, holding her side, wincing.

"Kyra, what are you doing, you're not supposed—"

"It's Jasmine. Sun-hi sent me. It's bad. The baby won't come and—"

Sammi exchanged a look with Sage, who was trying to get a struggling Dirk back into his clothes.

"Go ahead, we'll watch them," Sage said, her face pale.

"Who does she want?" Sammi asked. "Does she want you to get Zihna?"

Kyra nodded, gulping air.

"Yeah, I just, I can't catch my breath—"

"I'll go."

She ran over to a clump of people sitting on the ground on the stream bank. Zihna was sitting and talking with Cass, slightly apart from the others. Sammi skidded to a stop with her arms wrapped awkwardly around herself.

"Jasmine's baby won't come," she said, out of breath. "Kyra says it's bad. Sun-hi needs you."

"Take me there." Zihna transformed instantly from earth mother to all business, though she held Sammi's hand as they ran, and Sammi squeezed back. They raced back up the incline to the ugly building, around through the parking lot to the front. One of the side doors of the panel van was open and next to it, on the ground in the shade of the car, was a pallet made of blankets unpacked from someone's luggage. Jasmine lay on it, naked from the waist down, her legs impossibly pale and still, with blood-soaked towels covering her belly and between her legs.

Sun-hi was holding a baby.

It was the ugliest thing Sammi had ever seen. There had to be something wrong with it—it was purple and wrinkled and dented and covered with slime, a disgusting kinked cord hanging from its belly, its mouth wide with fury and its eyes squinched shut, and it was wailing, the most terrifying hiccupping cries Sammi had ever heard. It didn't sound like a regular baby, even—it just sucked air and wailed over and over again.

"Dear God," Zihna said, so it must be bad. When Zihna put a strong hand on Sammi's shoulder, she stayed put. "Wait here a minute," she said, and jogged the rest of the way.

She and Sun-hi conferred quietly and Zihna examined the freak baby. They looked down at Jasmine, who was apparently dead, and back at Sammi, who was suddenly cold. Freezing, even, shivering as the wind blew trash up off the asphalt and skittered it along under cars.

"Sammi." Zihna's voice was gentler, but still urgent. "This is important. You need to get your dad and Cass. Hurry, okay?"

"Cass? Are you sure?"

"Sammi, it's obvious she's an outlier, I've known it since I met her. She has all the characteristics."

"But some people think "

"They're just scared. By morning they'll realize she's not a threat. But for now, we need her here."

So Sammi made the trip back, jogging more slowly this time. Her dad and Cass—well, that was just great. Figured that they'd have to work together on whatever came along. In there, in the mall, it had been the two of them that finally got the door unstuck. It was like no matter what happened in their lives, they were thrown together. It had to be the two of them. What did they know about babies? Other than they'd both had one— but then again a lot of the people in New Eden had had kids, once.

Besides, Smoke was here, Smoke was doing fine, he'd made his miraculous recovery, shouldn't Cass be with him now? He was a hero again after the mall, so why wasn't she back with him? Why couldn't she just leave her dad alone?

For a minute Sammi considered disobeying Sun-hi and Zihna and bringing back Smoke instead of her dad. She was pretty sure he could do whatever her dad could. Only, Smoke looked like he was going to pass out, and besides…

Jasmine

Sammi squeezed her eyes shut hard for a moment,

nearly tripping on a clod of dirt. She'd seen about a million dead people, some of them way more disgusting than Jasmine, people who were eaten or rotted or burned. Compared to that, Jasmine just looked like she was sleeping, and it wasn't like Sammi was a little girl or anything, she didn't need her dad to tell her it was going to be all right, because she'd figured out a long time ago it wouldn't, so it wasn't that, but only yesterday she'd seen Jasmine in the morning with her hands on her huge belly, stretching with her eyes closed and this little smile on her face and Sammi had wondered what there was to be so happy about. Jasmine wanted that baby so bad, she'd told Kyra that after she turned forty she figured she'd never get to be a mom, and she had about thirty names picked out, for boys and girls, and she said she'd just know, she'd take one look at her baby and she'd know what its name was meant to be.

So maybe it was a good thing she'd died, maybe it was a good thing she hadn't seen the disgusting thing she'd given birth to. Sammi reached the others and practically collided with her dad, and to her surprise she was crying so hard she could barely get the words out.

Sun-hi shook her head when they ran up, and Cass knew that Jasmine had died. But then Zihna lifted the soft blanket and showed them the baby in her arms, and she was beautiful, face bunched and lips puckered, suckling air, her tiny hands in fists and faint pink lines at the bridge of her nose. Angel kisses, they called them, harmless little birthmarks; Ruthie had them too, but they'd faded away over time.

The baby's head was a little misshapen from the labor. "Unproductive" labor, they called it, when the baby wouldn't come—just one of many horrible euphemisms for the pain of becoming a mother. Cass had delivered Ruthie in a stark hospital room in the wee hours of the morning, and it had been an unremarkable labor, according to the doctors, but to Cass it had been one miracle after another. She'd suffered plenty—they wouldn't give her painkillers because she was an addict—but thinking about what Jasmine had suffered before she died, before Sun-hi had taken the baby from her lifeless body, made Cass want to weep.

But this was not the time for weeping.

"We can bury her by the creek," Dor said. "The soil will be soft there."

"All right," Sun-hi said. She sounded exhausted. Cass could only imagine that the disastrous labor had crushed Sun-hi, mentally and physically, as she tried to hold on to Jasmine's life while the others battled for their own lives inside.

Dor was already wrapping the body. Cass saw his tenderness, his reverence; such a sharp contrast to the man most people thought they knew.

"I think there's a little bit of evaporated milk in one of the cars," Zihna said, her brow furrowed with worry. "But not enough. Oh, Cass, what are we going to do, this poor little thing—"

"I have an, an idea," Cass said, the audacity of it making her stammer.

She told the others. They were all silent for a moment. It was far from ideal.

But nothing was ideal anymore, and after a moment they nodded and she took the baby in her arms—so tiny and precious, memories of holding Ruthie coming back like it had been yesterday—and she and Zihna set out to try.

It was too dark to dig another grave tonight. So while the others carried Jasmine's body carefully to the shed attached to the building, Cass found an unlocked extended-cab Ford a few rows over and waited there with the baby.

Zihna was back soon with Ingrid, whose flustered, bewildered expression told Cass that she didn't know. When she saw Cass, her face went stony.

"To what do I owe the pleasure?" she asked sarcastically.

For a moment Cass feared she'd made a terrible mistake. Ingrid with her judgments, Ingrid with her certainty that only she knew what was right, with her righteous condemnation—how could she be the one?

"Please," Cass whispered. "Just—just let me talk for a minute."

It took less than a minute. There was very little to say. A death, a birth, another Aftertime tragedy marked with blood and loss. Cass did not embellish. She did not entreat. She did not even say the thing that had made her seek out the woman who probably despised her most, of anyone in New Eden—that only Ingrid could save this child. She opened her jacket and showed Ingrid the baby, who, miraculously, was sleeping.

"Oh my God," Ingrid whispered. "Oh God, oh."

She reached for the baby and Cass knew she did it without thinking and was only a little bereft to hand her over.

"You have to feed her," she pleaded, but Ingrid was already unbuttoning her shirt.

In the morning, Dor and Steve and Earl and Smoke dug the grave. They had brought a shovel in one of the cars, but the barns revealed a vast assortment of tools, enough for all of them. It did not take long.

Jasmine's body was brought from the shed and lowered, in its wrapping of blankets, into the ground. Everyone scooped a fistful of dirt and tossed it in.

Sh'rae was ready with her Bible. She had a gift for gentleness, and she chose her texts with care. Today she read from Revelation; when she got to the end, many people were crying as her words drifted away on the morning breeze. For a moment nobody spoke. Then Sun-hi crouched down and dug a fistful of dirt and tossed it into the grave. She brushed off her hands and started toward the building, not looking back.

The others followed. Cass held back until the end, and when their turn came, she set Ruthie down. Ruthie had been quiet since the mall, thoughtful almost, staying close to her mother. Now she bent to the earth with her mouth pursed in concentration and dug into the ground with her small hand. She dropped her fistful of dirt into the hole with a reverence far beyond her years.

The news of Jasmine's baby had spread quickly through the group. During Jasmine's funeral, Ingrid stood in the back, and when the baby began to fuss, she slipped away, out of earshot. But when the service was over, Cass saw Kyra sitting in an old glider chair, on the building's back porch, cradling the baby gingerly, Ingrid showing her the proper way to hold her head.

Back on New Eden, there had been lots of teasing— not all of it good-natured—as Dirk approached his second birthday; the public opinion was that he was too old to still be nursing. But no one said anything now.

Days passed, a lengthening string of them, until it had been nearly three weeks since they left New Eden behind.

In two days' time, they would arrive in Salt Point. Nadir said they called it that because of potassium deposits in the soil, but considering he'd never actually been there Sammi was skeptical. The people who were trying to get the place set up would be in for quite a surprise. The Edenites were down to thirty-three now, including baby Rosie, who turned out to be healthy and not nearly as bad-looking once she was cleaned up and fed for a few days.

They'd lost five more since the mall. Old Mike and Terrence had died when they stumbled on a Beater nest in the warehouse they were clearing one night a couple of weeks ago. Richy Gomez and Paolo had to be shot the next day after being bitten doing the good deed of trying to save Old Mike. Cheddar had hit his head on a stone outcropping while longboarding, been unconscious for several hours and suffered noisy seizures for a few days after that until someone—no one had come forward—had strangled him during the night.

Sammi was ready to move into the next empty building they saw, as long as it meant they could stay put for a while. Her blisters had blisters from all the walking, and her body ached from the moment she woke up in the morning until the moment she went to bed—if you could call it "bed," since most nights she was sleeping on the floor in some shed or barn or church.

Worse, she couldn't get warm unless she was walking. When they stopped for the night, she volunteered for every task she could think of because the alternative, which was to sit still, meant she'd be freezing before she went to bed. Once she was lying down she'd never get warm, even though she and Sage and Kyra had taken to sleeping huddled together.

According to the plan that the new council had drawn up, she was entitled to ride for forty-five minutes twice a day. That was the shortest amount of time since she was in the youngest age bracket with no health issues, and she wasn't pregnant. But the reason she skipped her allotted time most days was that she was only allowed on the trailers, not in any of the three cars that still worked. And that meant getting colder and colder until she could get off and walk again.

Kyra took her trailer time most days. She said the baby was starting to press down on her bladder and her back hurt. They all felt the baby kick—every time it moved, it was good for a little entertainment, which was way hard to come by—but when Kyra rode, she liked to nap. How she managed it, Sammi couldn't figure, though Kyra said she got something like hot flashes now, with all the hormones zinging through her body.

Part of the problem was undoubtedly that Sammi was so skinny. She wasn't the only one—they hadn't had much besides kaysev since the food ran out. There wasn't time to hunt, and though they raided every promising building they passed, nearly everything had already been ransacked by others.

It was March now, almost a year into the Siege. A year of desperation, a year of people making do with whatever they could find. Lots of times they'd come to a house and there would be a pot in front of the door. That meant it had already been raided of all the food and medicine, anything worth taking, but that didn't keep people from wishing, hoping, for a miracle.

Sometimes when she and Kyra and Sage walked with the boys, they played a game to see who could imagine the best meal. The boys always won, probably because they declared themselves the winners. Colton always started out with his mom's Caesar salad. No one ever gave him a hard time about his lack of originality, because his mom was one of the first to die; she was the manager of a high-end grocery store and was shot when she tried to stop looters from taking all the bottled water.

Kalyan was the most creative. He described elaborate feasts featuring all his favorite take-out menus in the Oakland neighborhood where his parents once developed online content from home.

Sammi would never admit to it but the meal she most longed for was the one her dad used to make her on her birthday—giant rib-eye steaks grilled black on the outside and practically raw in the middle, with an iceberg-lettuce salad with tomatoes and a few slices of red onion on the side. Her mother had declared it inedible back when they were still together, and Sammi had called it disgusting the last time he'd ever fixed it for her and only eaten the narrow band of meat that was cooked medium.

But her dad used to wear an old red apron that Sammi gave him in first grade, her handprints in acrylic paint on the front. He paraded the plate of raw meat around the house acting like it was so heavy it hurt his arm. He'd bring a bone home from the butcher for Chester, too, saying that since he was a mutt and no one knew when his birthday was, he might as well share Sammi's.

Her dad had kind of sucked as a dad, spending way too much time at work and missing a lot of her soccer games and forgetting her friends' names, but at least he'd cracked jokes and tried to spoil her on the weekends.

Ever since the mall, he'd somehow gotten himself on the new council along with Nadir, the Easterner who Rachael and the de Ceccos didn't trust because he was a Muslim, and Shannon and Harris and Smoke. At first Sammi worried her dad would be upset because of Smoke, who was almost back to normal now and so everyone figured he and Cass would just take up right where they left off. Only that hadn't exactly happened. Cass spent most of her time with Ingrid, helping with the boys since Ingrid had to nurse Rosie, like, fifty times a day. But Sammi thought the real problem might be that Cass was avoiding both of them.

And to be fair, there was a lot to keep the new council busy. They'd given everybody jobs, made up all these procedures for how to check and clear a shelter when they stopped, who would cook and clean and all of that. Smoke was kind of like how he used to be back when they lived in the school, he let other people make the big decisions, but now he would have his own opinion a lot of the time instead of insisting everyone keep talking until they came up with a decision together.

They'd been off the main roads for a week now, the terrain getting more and more uneven. Nadir had explained about how Mayhew was planning to crash the shelter, and in a lot of ways it seemed like that was still the plan, but somehow it was okay now since they were just trying to survive.

Sammi and her friends constantly discussed what would happen if the settlers weren't happy to see them. What if they told them to turn around, find their own damn camp? Sammi couldn't imagine that her dad and the rest of the new council would fight people over what was, to be fair, theirs.

They'd probably have one of their stupid secret meetings where they went walking after dinner, talking it all through. Then they'd come back and tell everyone they would just have to keep going and make the best of it. They'd act like it was no big deal, at least to Sammi and her friends, because they still thought of them as immature, even though Kalyan was going to be eighteen in July and the rest of them were all over fifteen. If her dad could see what Colton had given her, well, then he might change his mind…but she still hadn't figured out how to give it to her dad without getting Colton into trouble. The adults wouldn't understand how none of it had been his idea, that he'd thought they were just messing around, that he'd never realized it would go so far.

Nadir's lists said that Salt Point would get below freezing at night through April. That was almost two more months like this. There was no way that they would be able to build adequate shelter for that, not right away, anyway. And if they went down to lower elevations, they would need Beater walls, just in case, and they were right back to the same problem.

Sammi wondered if they should have just picked someplace on the way and made the best of it, like so many other people had done. Only…she'd seen what happened on the islands. At the mall. Before that, at the school and the library and almost every other place she could think of since the Siege. If the Easterners thought the only place to make a new life was up north, at least until someone figured out a way to get rid of the Beaters once and for all, then Sammi had to admit they were probably right.

They crested a ridge and there, on the other side, was a scattering of farms with a few buildings at the center making a tiny town. And in the center of that was a sweet little white church with a spire on top, looking like a postcard against the blue blue sky.

"It's so pretty," Sammi couldn't resist saying.

"You think? I've been in a hundred of those," Sage said sourly. "That's a Methodist church, bet you anything. They go in for the wooden pews. No cushions."

"Huh," Sammi said, as they trudged on.

Sleeping in a wooden pew didn't seem like the worst thing in the world. Nadir might say one of his pretty Muslim prayers—that would be kind of nice.

She knew it was all the same God, just different ways of talking to Him. But in a way, it would be better if there was a whole team of gods they could pray to. Sammi had a feeling they were going to need all the help they could get.

In the vestibule of the old church Cass found a bride's dressing room. It looked like it had once had some other function; perhaps it was a supply closet before a steady stream of city brides discovered this perfect little setting that practically guaranteed enviable photos, with the drifts of wildflowers and the mountain backdrop. All those brides…they'd adjusted their veils in the mirror, checked their makeup, quelled their nerves and stepped out with breathless anticipation in their satin high heels and French manicures and updos constructed with a hundred tiny hairpins. All of this to launch marriages that, more often than not, would end in tears and bitterness and regrets.

Nevertheless, here she was, alone in the twilight of an early March day in the year 2022, wiping a year's worth of dust from the mirror, regarding her reflection and thinking about love. When Ruthie was born,

Cass had sworn off all love but that which she had for her daughter. Back then it had seemed that her damaged heart would have to struggle the rest of her life to be worthy of her daughter, that it would have to work overtime learning the lessons of devotion and faith and support. But all of that had come instantly, hard, crushingly, the moment she held Ruthie in her arms.

Then there had been Smoke. They'd come together in the threat of the unknown, first loved each other while on the run and then—when she'd rescued Ruthie and they were safe at last—clung to each other and built something real from the tender shoots. They'd had three months together in the closest thing to bliss that Cass had ever known. She'd been shocked to discover that she had learned to trust him; at the end of each day he came back to her and that was a sweet miracle, that alone was enough.

But then he'd left her. It had to be: he could never have been at peace knowing he hadn't tried, that he hadn't avenged the loss of those he cherished. Smoke could not have continued to love her if he hadn't made the quest. And now, finally, after this journey, Cass accepted it. She'd forgiven him for leaving, he'd forgiven her for Dor, and she trusted that he was ready to love her again.

Why, then, was she hesitating?

Cass leaned closer to the mirror, dust motes swirling prettily in the last beams of fading light, and looked at herself critically. She was different—different than she was a year ago, different than she'd been after the attack, even different from the start of this journey. There were the obvious things: they were all thinner, their bodies pushed to the limit each day, with little to eat other than kaysev. But the changes that eluded her, things she noted as one sees shadows from the corner of one's eye, were as compelling as they were subtle.

Her eyes were still the startling clear green of those few who survived the fever, her pigment altered forever. But there were depths to them, a weariness accumulated from all the stories of hurt and loss that she'd not only witnessed but lived through. Phillip, Jasmine, Terrence...all the lives she'd moved through had changed her, both hollowed and intensified her.

Her hair was startling, too. It had grown long and thick and fine, silvery-white strands supplanting her old honey blond. At times she thought it looked like a botched dye job, but in this mirror it looked startling and lovely, like an ice queen from a book of European fairy tales, flowing around her shoulders and tumbling over her forehead no matter how many times she pushed it back.

But even these were not what she was looking for. Cass was convinced there were answers to be found in the set of her lips, the cant of her cheekbones, the fine lines that had appeared on her brow. Somewhere inside her was the knowledge of whether she could truly ever be with a man, and if so, who she was *meant* to be with, and it was hard to resist the notion that if she just looked long and hard enough, she might find it here, in the glass.

But the harder she looked, the more it eluded her.

There was a soft knock at the door, and it creaked open.

Smoke.

"Okay if I come in?" he asked. "I've got room service."

"Oh, are they serving dinner?"

"Yeah, if you can call it that. Kaysev again. But I have something special…" He rattled something in his pocket, and took out a small can of smoked almonds. "Not even opened."

"Oh wow, where on earth—"

"Nadir gave it to me. He'd been saving a few things for tonight. He and Dor and Bart are drinking twelve-year-old scotch right now, if I'm not mistaken. I asked him if it was okay if I took mine to go."

"Oh." Cass's mouth watered at the thought of real food, but she hesitated. "I guess someone probably told you by now. That I was drinking again."

"And that you stopped."

"It's been hard." That was an understatement; a dozen times each day she yearned for the sharp taste of the first swallow, the oblivion that followed.

"Which is why I'm here and the bottle's not."

Cass smiled. "Thank you," she said softly.

Smoke sat down on the upholstered bench, and Cass sat next to him. He popped open the can, but for a moment neither of them moved to eat.

"It's not going to work out between us, is it?" Smoke finally said quietly.

Tears sprang instantly to Cass's eyes. "Oh, Smoke…"

He closed his hand over hers and squeezed gently. "There's something I need to tell you. Something I did, Before."

Cass blinked and looked at him carefully. His face was lined and scarred, and the past months had left a permanent wistfulness that lifted when he smiled, but always settled back into place afterward.

As long as Cass had known him, he had been a man

of secrets. He'd told her only that he'd done something that he could never make right, but it was clear that guilt and self-recrimination were never far from his mind. She often found him staring into space, or soaked with sweat from a workout that was never hard enough to drive the memories away. She'd asked him to tell her what was wrong a hundred times, a thousand, but he'd always brushed off the question, saying it was nothing, or not saying anything at all.

And only now, when she'd finally let go of her need to know, was he ready to tell her.

"You don't have to do this," she said softly.

"I'm not telling you for your sake. I'm— I need to. For me."

Cass swallowed. Now that they were on the brink of it, she wasn't sure she was ready to know. But she owed him this, the freedom he might earn from the telling. It was one gift she could still give him. "All right."

"I told you what I did Before, right?"

"You were a corporate coach." The phrase he'd used, on the day they met, as they walked through the streets of Silva, was "career consultant of last resort."

"Yeah. And I was damn good. You want to know my specialty? Weak guys. Guys who lacked resolve. Guys who were…" Smoke's expression was pained as he made air quotes around his words: "'Weak on fol-low-through.' 'Soft leadership.' 'Unable to build con-sensus.' But those are all just euphemisms, Cass—you want to know what for?"

His self-contempt was as clear as if it was painted on him.

"No balls. Those are all MBA-bullshit ways of say-ing a guy's got no stones. And when that happened, they'd bring in the fix-it guy. Me. I charged heaven and earth for my services, but I gave a guarantee—you give me your hopeless case, I give you back a man who can whip it out when he needs to. Six hundred twenty-five bucks an hour, that was my top rate, and there were half a dozen clients in San Francisco who couldn't get enough of me. Hell, I had a waiting list—seemed like there was no shortage of guys who tended to freeze in the clutch or hide behind the other guys' skirts.

"What I'd do, I'd get a guy on his own turf. His office, sometimes his house. His club, for the ones who'd made it a little ways up the corporate ladder. See, Cass, they weren't stupid. They were never stupid. They knew I was there because they were failing, and they wanted to *impress* me. It was fear, that was what drove most of them, fear that they didn't measure up, as if my opinion of them mattered at all. But a lot of these guys, their daddies told 'em they weren't worth shit and they got into the office and all of a sudden the guy in charge can seem damn intimidating. Bring in Ed Schaffer, the guy who listens, and they'd tell me their golf handicap, the women they'd bedded, hell, the car they drove. Take me out and buy me drinks even though their companies were paying me a goddamn fortune. I ate a hell of a lot of rare filet and drank my share of single malt in those days."

Smoke laughed, a hollow sound that chilled Cass to the core. "I'd listen and drink their booze, and all the time I'm reading them, figuring out where their fear came from. Once I knew that, I had all I needed. I broke them down and built them back up, tore down the fear, taught them to go in for the kill, to man up on the job. 'There's a leader inside us all'—that's what I had printed up on my business cards, Cass, but you know what it really should have said was 'There's a scared-shitless fuck inside us all' and all you get for your six-fifty an hour is learning how to turn *that* guy into the bully. Go from the stepped-on to the guy who kicks sand into everyone else's face.

"And the amazing thing was that no one ever figured it out. They loved me. 'Ed, you've changed my life.' 'Ed, I feel like I can do anything now.' I just smiled and bought them a final round and cashed my checks and never told them what they were really feeling was *power.* I didn't teach anyone to lead, Cass, I taught 'em to *take.* To look at the world as their candy store and start turning over the shelves. Hell, I got Christmas cards from guys saying they'd dumped their mousy little girlfriends and finally told their families to fuck off and wasn't it great, and deep down I knew what I was doing was not something I could be proud of—but I didn't care. Because I think my biggest client was me. I was never a hopeless case, I wasn't the class loser or the guy who couldn't get a date or the one who got stuck in an entry-level job. I was just…unexceptional. But when I hung out my coach sign, it was like telling the world I knew things they didn't. I liked the mystique. Hell, I *used* the mystique."

Cass remembered how Smoke had described his old life: the sports cars, the mountain getaways, the skiing and boating and women. It was hard to imagine the man she knew—so carefully unassuming, so determined to maintain his low profile—in the picture he was painting. But she let him talk.

"So around the holidays a couple years back, I get this call from Travis Air Force Base. You might remember, I told you I used to work in that area, in Fairfield, and drink with some of the guys from the base after work. That wasn't exactly true. They hired me, on a consulting basis, to come in and work with one of their guys who was losing his shit. Big project, top secret, very hush, I had to sign all these papers and I wasn't allowed to talk about the project itself when I met with him, only about his job in general terms. The brass was in a tough situation because their leadership on the base had been stretched thin—I mean, it's not hard to figure out why, now."

In the summer of that year, bioterrorists attacked livestock in the U.S. and Asia; by fall there were reports of dead livestock on every continent. Overseas travel was halted and remote nations began to go dark, and skirmishes escalated and nuclear tensions were on the rise. Banks began to fail and currency was devalued worldwide.

"My guy Charlie—Lieutenant Colonel Charlie Benson, right out of central casting, looked like he'd been painted in his uniform by Norman Rockwell—he had somehow risen to be the number-two guy on the base. Only, the top guy, he got called to Wright-Patterson after the Christmas strike. Charlie was losing his shit because he had personnel problems, discipline problems, protesters every day right outside the gates. They send me in and for a while things are going okay. At first he's just repeating everything I tell him to say. We take a tough stance, zero tolerance, a civilian guy misses a shift because his wife's injured in a protest at a bank, we can him. We go out into the protesters one day with tear gas—next day it's rubber bullets. The shit was hard-core, Cass, and it didn't even matter because the media had bigger stories than a few tree huggers getting their feelings hurt.

"Only Charlie—he surprised me. He may have been the only guy I ever worked with who wasn't a coward. He just wanted to think everything to death. How he got that far in the military I'll never understand, because old Charlie's response to everything was to commission studies and conduct interviews and draft plans. And he didn't really have a taste for power, either. His heart wasn't in it. At first he went along with what I told him to do because he was worried about his job. But as the country fell apart and we started hearing from the top brass less and less, he began to push back. He didn't want to act, he wanted to wait. 'Let's see what the outlook is in six weeks,' he'd say. 'Let's not respond out of panic,' that was one of his favorites. Made me fucking nuts.

"I guess by then I figured this was the last big job I'd have until things sorted themselves out. It might sound funny but I wasn't too worried about my own future. I had my place in the mountains, it was well stocked because we were always having power outages up there anyway. Nobody really believed this was the end of the world back then, more like a hell of an inconvenience that might wipe out the underclass and decimate a few island nations no one had ever heard of.

"So one day we get this order. The K734IV order, the one that went to all the bases around the country. By then I was reading Charlie's mail before he did, confidential and otherwise. There's about three hundred pages of scientific crap about the plant, but all we were concerned about was the flight schedule and maps. It's a direct order, there's no decision to be made.

"Except that the order has an attachment for bases in California only. Says how down in UC-Colima, they've developed this second strain that appears to boost immunity. They're making it available on an optional basis, recommending a seed mix that includes two percent of this strain, which has some long name with initials and numbers, just like kaysev did back then. There wasn't time to get approval in any other state. And on the back page there's a test schedule and you can see they haven't done even a quarter of the tests, and the results of the ones they have are either blacked out or marked 'inconclusive.'

"So Charlie, he gets on the phone with the other guys, in Beale and Edwards and so forth. He wants to know what they're thinking of doing. Now this is *ex-*

actly the sort of behavior we've been working on for a month now, how he's going to be accountable, immediate and decisive. *A-I-D,* that was his acronym, and I made him repeat it every morning when we started the workday. So when I hear him dicking around, should we do this, should we do that, I pretty much lose my shit. 'This is where you *take charge*,' I tell him. 'This is where you come out strong, make a name for yourself.' I ask him if he wants to go back to driving a desk in a cubicle when this is all over, or if he wants to be remembered as the guy who saved California's ass— at least, a few more asses in his region than elsewhere.

"And *still* he fights me. There wasn't enough testing, the results are inconclusive, the blacked-out data is troubling, blah blah blah. I'm ready to deck the guy myself. We've got a 4:00 p.m. deadline to make the decision, and by three o'clock all the other bases have checked in as no. They all lack the balls—at least, that's the way I see it, that's what I tell Charlie. I lock the door to his office and I start screaming at him. I can feel this vein in my forehead standing out, I'm giving it everything I've got, everything in the Edward Schaffer bag o' tricks, calling him names, questioning his manhood, and he just sits there staring at me, shaking his head. Finally, when I have to stop for breath, he says to me in this calm, tired voice, 'Ed, the only way that call's getting made is if you do it yourself.'

"He didn't mean it, of course, he never believed I'd do it. And, Cass, I've thought about it a thousand times and I didn't ever think I'd do it either. I was giving him one last chance—that's what I really believe—and I just wanted him to *act,* he could have punched me in the face and that would have been better than him sitting there with his dick in his hands waiting for the apocalypse and letting the inmates run the prison.

"So I pick up his phone and all the time I'm thinking he'll stop me, and then I'm dialing and we're staring at each other, neither one of us blinking, and the guy comes on the line and I say, 'Benson here,' and he says, 'Yes, sir,' and still I'm waiting, I give it an extra-long pause and the guy on the other line is like, 'Sir, sir, are you there?' and Charlie, he does something that— He gets out of his chair and he goes to the window and he turns his back on me. He turns his fucking *back* on me, and I tell you, Cass, every cell in my body turned into the bully I'd failed to make him into and I remember thinking I'd show him, I'd *show him what it means to lead,* and I gave the order."

Smoke was perspiring as he came to the end of the story. "After that I went home. It was the last time I ever saw Charlie, actually. After—later—I tried to find him. But you know what happened to the base and...well, I didn't try all that hard. After a week or so it didn't matter anyway. And by the time I realized what I'd done..."

Cass listened, horrified, as Smoke's voice trailed away.

This was it. The thing Smoke had done for which he could never forgive himself, the sin that he would spend his whole life atoning for, putting ahead of everything and everyone else—including Cass.

And she knew how he saw it: Smoke believed he had single-handedly unleashed the Beaters. If he hadn't made the call...if the mixed seed had never been loaded into the planes alongside the otherwise fine kaysev seed...if the first blueleaf had never sprouted...

"But you can't believe it's all your fault." The words

burst from her before she had a chance to think. "There were a thousand parts to play in what happened. The people who developed it, who were supposed to test it, Charlie's commander…"

But she realized that Smoke wasn't really listening. He was looking off into space, reviewing the story that would never leave him.

She wanted to make him see, to shake him, scream at him, until he finally gave up his steadfast determination to suffer. But Smoke wouldn't even listen.

Anger bubbled below the surface of Cass's sorrow. It was a terrible waste, throwing his life away like this, over something he could not change, a mistake he never intended.

But what was worse—he'd thrown away more than his life. He'd discarded their love the day he left the Box, abandoned it as though it was worthless. It was no wonder, Cass realized, that she'd felt so hurt. Because even though his error had terrible consequences, even though it had changed him irrevocably, it still was not enough. Not enough to trade her for. Not enough to have made her feel so small, so hurt—to have driven her into the arms of another man.

But no. That was wrong. She would not blame Smoke for that. When she went to Dor, she went willingly, and when she loved him, she loved him fiercely.

Cass held Smoke's hand for a while longer, considering and eventually abandoning her anger, forgiving a man who did not seek her forgiveness. Finally it was time to leave the darkening little room. By then Cass finally understood why Smoke had to leave her back in the Box, why he would always have to leave her for one justice quest after another. He could never fully give himself to her, because he'd already given himself over to the job of punishing himself, forever, one agonizing day at a time.

45

Two mornings later, she was the last to linger at the foot
of the trail, watching the small party ride up the incline
through the binoculars she'd borrowed from Bart. Bart
had stayed back to tend to one of the horses who had
picked up something in his hoof and been favoring it
all day; he was worried that a trip to the settlement and
back would be too much for the horse. Besides, three
men were more than enough to do the reconnaissance.

There were only two possible outcomes. The first
was that the settlement party had reached Salt Point,
and were now in some state of construction. The first
wave would probably not be thrilled to see them, but
the new council had put a lot of effort into how to pres-
ent their case, and even Cass had to admit that it was
a compelling one, focusing more on the skills and resources they brought, and less on the challenges they
presented. Though no one voiced the thought out loud,

they'd lost their weakest members; they would not have to beg passage for their elderly or injured.

The other possibility nagged at her no matter how she tried to force it from her mind—that no one waited for them at Salt Point, that there was nothing there besides beautiful scenery and spring snows, a plot of land perfect for a well-supplied, well-rested party with the luxury of a plan and the means to implement it. But the Edenites had come with only what they could carry, enough food for another week. They had children and old people; they were demoralized by loss and lacking clear leadership. Cass was certain that, if nothing waited for them but bare land, they would lose more people before the summer came.

Still, the little advance team seemed to lift everyone's spirits as they took off at a brisk pace up the mountain. Dor and Smoke had become competent riders. Bart had been training them for the past week, after they determined that Smoke and Dor and Nadir would ride ahead. Smoke had lingering stiffness in his hip and leg, and getting in the saddle presented a challenge, but by the third day he had mastered the move. Dor tended to impatience with the animals, but once he started riding Rocket, who had been Mayhew's mount, it went more easily; Rocket was as stubborn and headstrong as Dor himself.

Nadir was the key to the group's cohesiveness. Smoke and Dor spoke mostly to—and through—him; Cass didn't miss the way the men avoided each other. If one walked by, the other would step out of the way, or pretend to be engaged in some small task. The few words they exchanged were brief and barbed.

It made Cass melancholy to remember their old

friendship in the Box. True, Dor had been Smoke's employer, but they'd worked as partners from the start. They talked for hours, trained together most mornings, fought and worked side by side. Now, after so much had passed, she finally knew the secret Smoke had confided in Dor, and forgiven him for choosing to share it with him instead of her. Dor had never told anyone about the thing Smoke had done, and she understood that the secret would stay with the three of them and someday die with them.

At first she'd thought that the secret should be enough to bind them all, its terrible weight a burden they could only bear together. But now she understood that loving her had driven the two men apart. They were both proud men, both passionate, loath to compromise. Now that she'd separated herself from them both, she saw the way they drove themselves harder than ever. Smoke's regimen of healing left him spent and exhausted each night, but he didn't rest until he'd done a full share of work. Dor often seemed to be everywhere at once, consulting with the new council, helping anyone who asked, and throwing himself into the manual labor of breaking camp, splitting wood, hauling water, anything to burn off his endless supply of glowering humorless energy.

Paradoxically he seemed more and more at home, the farther they traveled from civilization. This was an inhospitable part of the country, far from any mountain pass or even an improved road. Dor was undaunted by the lack of commerce, power lines, any evidence of community. They'd been following the map the Easterners had laid out and found this final camp exactly where it had been marked, eight miles down mountain from Salt Point on what had been an old stagecoach road many years ago and in recent decades had served only the most intrepid sportsmen: cross-country skiers, backpackers and fishermen.

On the map the camp was not named, but a note scrawled in the margin read, "5 cabins, well water, no elec." There was no sign of a well anywhere and only three cabins remained standing, one reinforced sometime in the last decade with repairs to the board siding and a new handrail, the other two in sorry shape. Elsewhere the remains of other cabins were stacked haphazardly. On the positive side, there was no evidence of Beaters anywhere in the camp. Cass, who had been on the lookout for the whole journey, had not seen a single blue leaf in at least a week. Perhaps it was true, that it could not tolerate the harsh winters of the north.

Best of all, neatly parked in a row at one end of the camp were three empty flatbed trucks, and the trail leading up the mountain was deeply rutted. The logical conclusion was that the first wave had arrived and used a compact tractor to take load after load of supplies up the trail.

Last night they'd built a celebratory bonfire from discarded lumber and kept it going all night, and since there was no threat of precipitation, almost everyone slept on the ground near the fire. Volunteers took turns feeding boards into the flames, an extravagance they'd think twice about if anyone expected to be here more than a single night.

In the morning there was an atmosphere of subdued cheer—of hope. People stirred from their fireside pallets, pushed themselves up on elbows, sat up in tangles of blankets. The wood was damp, the fire smoky, but people leaned in close nonetheless, warming their hands. They pushed back their hoods and combed disheveled hair with their fingers and looked at the sky, gasping at the beauty of the mountain face illuminated with the rising sun. There were murmured good-mornings, gentle inquiries as to how the night had passed.

For breakfast there was fresh-caught fish, as much as anyone cared to eat, grilled over the fire. The teens took over the serving and cleanup duties, unasked; a couple of the boys tossed a tennis ball with the little kids.

Not everyone was holding up well. A handful of Edenites sat apart, morose and uncommunicative. The circles under some of the older folks' eyes had deepened, and they weren't eating. Post-traumatic stress, Cass figured, but there was little she could do for it now. She brought food to Ingrid, took her turn holding Rosie. Across the clearing, Valerie glared at her while she helped with the horse; Cass turned away.

Dor, Smoke and Nadir were surrounded by well-wishers when they took their leave, a spirit of cautious optimism pervading the group. Cass stood near the back and watched Dor hug Sammi, and then search her out in the group. For a tense moment she felt both Dor and Smoke watching her, and she looked away, turning toward the path they'd climbed the day before, and focused on a hawk that soared lazily above the valley below.

She waited until they were off, the ground reverberating with the horses' hoofbeats, before she busied herself with cleaning up from the morning meal.

Now, with Ruthie asleep on a cabin porch with Twyla after a long and unseasonably warm day of playing at the edges of the stream, and everyone else either fishing or napping or strolling, taking advantage of their first day of rest in weeks, Cass slipped away from the camp, following the trail where the men had ridden this morning. She wanted to be the first to see them return. She was still looking for clues and, having failed to find any in the mirror the night before, thought she might find them now. Two men had ridden away with Nadir this morning; both had loved her, but she wasn't sure if her future lay with either of them. For several days she'd felt that the answer was tantalizingly close. Perhaps the feeling was nothing but the imminence of the journey's end, but Cass thought it had to be something more.

The horses had navigated the steep incline and thick forest growth well, but Cass had difficulty walking the rutted path. As she ascended the mountain, the air grew colder and thinner. Here and there, in the hollows of rotting stumps, in the loamy soil layered with leaves from seasons before, there were pockets of grimy snow, flecked with debris and slick from melting. Once or twice, Cass saw shoots poking through the snow, pale green fronds tipped with tight-rolled leaves, plants whose delicacy belied their hardiness. Cass wasn't sure exactly what the plants were—checkerbloom, perhaps, that would soon grow tiny pink blossoms—but whatever they were, she counted their presence a hopeful omen.

The notes said that after a couple of miles the path evened out, and crossed a broad plateau before arriving at the river gorge. Salt Point was on the other side, a heel-shaped promontory that had been carved by a bend in the river, when prehistoric waters rushing westward down the mountains met the volcanic rock face

and turned south. Beyond, Mount Karuk rose sharply
to the highest peak for many miles.

There were two ways to the point, the longer of which
took switchbacks up the eastern incline and featured
steep drop-offs and a waterfall that made the path impassable later in the spring when the snowmelt was at its
highest. The other was the bridge, built in the late eighties by the developer whose planned resort never mate-
rialized after cost overruns on the early development
killed enthusiasm for the project among its backers.

It took Cass an hour to ascend to the plateau, but it
was worth the effort for the spectacular view alone.
The path hugged a drop-off down to the roaring river,
a few pines clinging valiantly to the earth at the edge
above the sheer rock face. Hundreds of feet below, the
water coursed over boulders rising from the bed of the
river and formed deceptively placid pools here and there
along the banks.

But the falls that fed the river were even more as-
tonishing. Droplets misted Cass's face from all the way
across the gorge; its roar was thunderous. Rainbows
arced above, glittering against the blue of the sky, darkening the rocks with water. Birds dipped and soared,
suspended far above the water, between the walls of the
chasm, and it was dizzying to watch their aerial play.

The bridge lay far ahead on the twisting trail. It
looked out of place here, its man-made symmetry in
sharp contrast to the natural beauty carved by the vi-
cissitudes of wind and water and time. On the other
side of the bridge, the road disappeared into the forest
that grew, as on this side, practically to the edge of the
cliff. The developers must have planned to cut down the
trees to give access to the views that would have been

the star attraction of the resort, but for now they would make a perfect windbreak for the settlement that was located on the cleared land beyond. In the grainy aerial photos, Cass had been able to see the stumps left from when they began work on the resort; it was like a giant had gouged a huge square into the forest, lifting away the trees and leaving the rich land exposed.

It really was a perfect location: remote, and easy to protect. Would-be attackers could be repelled in so many ways, most of them ending with their bodies crushed and broken on the rocks far below.

She found a spot to wait, a loamy patch of earth below a tall tree, and leaned back against it, enjoying the sun on her face. She'd worn an extra fleece tied around her waist, and she pulled it on and reveled in its cozy warmth, breathing in the good clean scents of sap and kaysev. A bug crawled over her hand and she lifted it closer to her face: an iridescent-winged beetle of some sort, searching for tender leaves, itself food for birds, evidence that the earth's insistent journey back toward life continued apace here in the north.

Cass let her eyes drift shut and daydreamed about the settlement, the home she might make there. She and Suzanne and Ingrid would be the first mothers, but there would be others before long. New babies to join Rosie, new friends for Sammi and the other young people. And the garden she'd have up here! So many things she hadn't been able to grow farther south. She'd have beds of lettuces and kale and beans and squash, an entire patch of pumpkins, every kind of herb. In one summer she could lay up enough to can, produce a cutting garden, a cold frame to see them through the winter. In two summers she could have fruit on the trees, apples and pears.

Real pies, she thought with a smile, not the bitter ones made from hawthorn berries. And she wanted to try growing grains, give everyone a break from the kaysev flour. Wheat should be possible in this climate, maybe barley. As soon as things were straightened out with the settlement, she and Dor—

Dor. She was thinking of him again; he had become the place her mind went whenever she let it roam, the note to which her heart gave voice when she let her guard down. But that couldn't be right…could it? Her life was barely back on track again, far from ready to share with anyone else besides Ruthie. She was eighteen days sober, and she needed to get to 180, and then 1,800. She needed to stay sober forever. She had to learn to live with the hurt and damage she'd suffered and the rocky path she walked before and still walked now. She would take one day at a time and be worthy of Ruthie, and this would be enough.

But Dor. Dor, with his ebony eyes and his voice like sandstone, his breath on her neck and his hands tracing that place on her back—

She could not shake him. She couldn't even pretend to try anymore. Smoke's return had not eradicated him. Danger and battle and bloodshed and loss had not eradicated him.

And even more shocking: she had lost her shame. She was tired of feeling bad about Valerie. She was tired of second-guessing herself about Sammi. She was even tired of thinking of everyone else's needs before her own, when what she needed was more of him, more of Dor, without a plan or a pledge.

Cass drank in the sun and dug her fingers into the earth and breathed the good air and allowed herself to wonder if maybe she was more than the sum of her addiction and her sobriety, more than just Ruthie's mother, if maybe she'd done her penance and suffered enough and deserved something only for herself. Even with the scars and the regrets, some of her spirit remained, and some of it was good, and some of it was worthy, and at least some tiny part of her bid to live came from these depths, from this place that had been there when she was born and hung in there during all the terrible years and survived the addictions and the bad decisions and the self-punishment.

And this part of her, this part that was not mother and that was not pilgrim or penitent or servant, this part wanted Dor. Wanted him savagely.

Smoke had been her lover, her salve, as she had been his.

Dor was her fire. And as long as she lived, she would burn for him.

"Dor…" She spoke his name softly, testing it, tasting it, as though for the first time, erasing for a moment all the history they'd shared, the chaos in which they'd first come together. Her heart raced with the thrill of recognition, and suddenly it was all so clear.

It seemed as though the earth itself trembled in response to Cass's new knowledge, but then she realized it was the approaching horses pounding the earth with their hooves.

They crashed around the bend in a cloud of dust, Dor in the lead. When he saw Cass he reined in his horse, and Rocket reared and snorted to a stop. The others circled around, Nadir in the rear, and it took a second for Cass to realize that the bundle he had slung over the saddle in front of him was a body.

"Cass, what are you doing?"

"I just came to—"

"There's no time, get up here with me." Smoke made room for her in front of him. "We've got to get back to the others *now.*"

Cass stood frozen to the spot, searching their faces. "What? What happened?"

Dor guided his horse forward, in between the others. He leaned down and seized her hand, pulling her up as if she was weightless, and she scrambled onto the horse's heaving, warm back, sliding into the saddle, pressed close against Dor's body. She caught Smoke's expression, his hand slowly falling to his side. He saw. He knew.

"They're coming," he said numbly. "Renegades, from the East. Like Nadir was telling us. They picked the same settlement Mayhew did."

"We have to get there first," Nadir said grimly.

"We're going to help defend them?"

Dor wrapped his arms around her and spurred his horse into motion.

"There's no one to help," he said into her ear, his breath hot on her neck. "The renegades sent a team ahead. They burned the settlement and killed everyone inside."

46

The renegades' advance team had actually killed all the settlers but one. As the Edenites scrambled to gather their belongings, Dor summoned Sun-hi to examine the woman Nadir carried on his horse. Sun-hi declared that she would probably live. The blow to the head that had knocked her unconscious had saved her; she'd been dragged to the center of the settlement and piled with the other bodies as the four men who attacked them soon after dawn lined up the people eight at a time and shot them, execution-style.

The woman moaned when Sun-hi probed the wound on her scalp, and winced when she wrapped it in bandages made from a torn shirt. "Janet almost got away," she said listlessly. "She made it to the trees before they got her."

Smoke and Nadir stood on the porch of the sturdiest cabin and Smoke whistled for attention. He described the horror that lay up the trail, the mismatched battle they faced.

"I know who these men are," Nadir said, barely controlling the anger in his voice. "They were trouble back home. There are stories of things they have done, bad things. I do not know who they have convinced to come with them here, if they recruited others like themselves, but we must plan for the worst. They have already killed dozens of innocent people. They will not hesitate to kill more of them."

"We could turn around," Smoke said. "We could retreat down the mountain, reach our cars and be safely out of the area by the time these people arrive. We could keep looking for shelter elsewhere...."

"But we will not do that."

He waited a moment for his words to sink in, for everyone to grasp the scenario he painted. Cass knew she was seeing evidence of the talent that had made him such a good coach, his conviction and charisma.

"We will not retreat," he repeated, and there was silence among the gathering. Everyone was riveted. "If we do not take this settlement for our home, odds are we won't survive the spring. We've lost half our number so far, and conditions here are nearly intolerable for those who aren't prepared. Yes, we will be living off the hard work of the slaughtered—at first. But I am not afraid to tell you that it is better for us to seize the spoils than for them to fall to murderers.

"Might does not make right, my friends." Smoke paused again and searched the crowd, making eye contact with each of them. When he got to Cass he lingered for a moment, and the look they exchanged was tinged with a wistful sort of pain that she knew would only be cured by the passage of time.

And then he moved on. "But sometimes, the right can be mighty. We are in the right here. I have not known you long, but I think I have known you well. I've fought beside you, grieved with you, and now I have the audacity to hope with you."

The applause started with a single pair of hands, echoing across the camp. Cass was surprised to see that it was Valerie. She had not returned to her headbands and her tentative smiles. She stood apart in her black clothes and her dark glasses and slick-backed hair, and a scowl so fierce Cass didn't doubt she was looking forward to a fight.

When the applause died down, Smoke outlined the plan, such as it was. Get there first. Dig in deep. Shoot like hell and hold nothing back.

If the Edenites were disappointed with this bare-bones strategy, they didn't let on. The procession set out, grim-faced and silent. The Easterners led the horses at the front. Steve and Fat Mike carried Dane and Dirk, and Twyla squeezed into the jogger stroller with Ruthie, Red and Zihna pushing it up the incline. Ingrid strapped Rosie to her chest in a papoose Valerie had rigged from a blanket.

Cass waited to take her place in the procession. People filed past until finally it was just her and Dor. She fell in step next to him, but they'd only gone a few feet when Sammi came racing back down the trail.

She was out of breath, unslinging her backpack and digging around inside it.

"Don't say anything, Dad, because I don't want to hear it. Only I thought you should have this."

Cass knew the taped-together package of plastic bricks and wires was the real thing because of the way Dor's face went utterly white.

"Where in the name of everything holy did you get this, Sammi?"

Sammi's face looked like it was going to crumple. "I said don't—"

"You don't want to talk about it? That would be fine if you were late coming home from the movies, but this—shit, Sammi, this could have killed us all. There's enough here to blow up this entire camp."

"This was Owen's," Cass said. "Wasn't it, Sammi?"

For a second Sammi looked confused, and then her eyes met Cass's and cleared. Cass had no doubt Sammi had gotten the explosives from Colton, but whatever poor decisions the boy had made in the past, Cass felt that the time for punishing him for them was over.

"Yes," the girl said shyly.

"But how—" Cass knew it was fear that raised Dor's voice—not for the dangers ahead, but fear for his daughter, for the fact that she'd been ferrying this terrible load in her backpack. But Sammi would only hear the anger, and the fragile peace between them was not strong enough yet to withstand such a test.

"It's not the time," she said, taking Dor's arm. "Look at me. Please."

He did. She saw the indigo sparks in his narrowed eyes, the scars that started at his hairline and bisected an eyebrow. The fine lines that had appeared at his eyes and the corners of his mouth.

"Sammi did the right thing," she said softly. "She was brave, and strong, and you are so lucky to have her."

"All of that is true, and I wasn't saying—"

"So thank her."

Dor frowned at her for a moment, then turned back to his daughter.

"You're—" He stopped, his voice cracking. "You're my world, Sammi, I couldn't stand if anything happened to you. Thank you for bringing this to me."

"Oh—Dad." Now she did cry, fat tears rolling down her cheeks and splashing to the ground.

"Go, go. Find your friends, and stay with them. Stay with them, no matter what, Sammi, you promise me?"

"I promise," she mumbled, and kissed him on the cheek before dashing back up the trail after the others.

"For God's sake, put that thing away," Cass said, and she held his pack for him while he settled it into the outermost compartment. Then set it down and grabbed her hand, pulling her close. He circled his arms around her waist, but his touch was not gentle.

"Cass." His voice was low and rough and he made her name sound like a threat. "You're…"

He shook his head, and Cass understood that words eluded him, because her own thoughts were in disarray. Declarations of love were not for them. Gentle endearments would never pass between them. There would be no private names, no anniversaries. He would not sing her love songs or write her letters, and she would not be his helpmate, she would never wear his ring.

But they would continue to find each other as long as the fire burned within them, and Cass knew the fire was at the very heart of her, that it would not dim until her life was at its end.

"You're mine," he said, and then he kissed her, hard. His hands slid down to pull her against him and she felt her body respond, the heat inside her unfurling as she returned his kiss.

It was over in seconds. It was not the time—and yet it was always the time, and as they headed up the trail, late-afternoon sun filtering through the trees to dapple everything with enchantment, Cass wondered how she could have ever not known.

47

They rested at the same clearing where Cass had stopped earlier. Ingrid nursed Rosie, while the children played tag and Bart watered the horses.

When they started out again, the broad plain was a welcome change from the steep climb. The sound of the waterfall grew louder as they drew closer, and the air was chilly with mist. The cold seeped into their clothes, and by the time they reached the bridge they were thoroughly damp and miserable.

But the bridge itself was nothing short of miraculous. It had never endured automobile traffic, since the roads from the highway to the resort had never been built. The asphalt here was smooth and pristine, the yellow striping fresh. Other than bird guano and the litter of workmen's lunches from long ago, nothing sullied the surface.

Kalyan gave a whoop when he set foot on the bridge,

and the mood brightened perceptibly. There, on the other side, was their future. They were so close now that it was tempting to forget the battle they would have to fight to keep it.

Smoke and Dor and Nadir had decided their best bet was to travel past the cleared space through the thick forest to the steep face of the mountain, and make camp there for the night. Only those who were armed—a dozen of them—would spend the night in the settlement, hiding behind the framed structures, ready to defend their claim to it when the renegades came back in the morning. Depending on how many were in the renegades' party, they would either capture them, kill them or fight them. In the event that there were enough of the enemy to prevail, even after being ambushed, then at least the other Edenites would have a chance to escape down the mountain, circling back along the path that bisected the falls. There was no guarantee the falls were passable, though the snowmelt had barely begun; that was a chance they would have to take.

The bridge was almost a quarter-mile long, according to Mayhew's notes, and as they walked Cass alternated between staring over the edge at the breathtaking drop to the boulder-strewn river rushing below, and the falls. As they drew closer the falls' force and volume seemed to grow and Cass became increasingly doubtful about whether anyone could find solid enough footing behind the wall of water to cross to the other side—especially a person carrying a child.

She did not share these fears. The crowd had fallen silent except for the gentle snorting of the horses and the sound of their hooves; the children rested in the arms of those carrying them. Sammi and her friends held hands near the front, all of them except for Shane, who walked by himself off to the side. The girls tossed the occasional pebble into the chasm beneath them, but otherwise they were silent and serious.

When they had nearly reached the other side, a sharp crack sounded all around them, bouncing off the canyon walls and echoing back. Then there was another, and another—a bullet flying a few feet from the crowd, and people screamed and ran for shelter along the bridge's sides, where a small overhang on the waist-high concrete walls offered almost no protection.

"Where are they shooting from?" Nadir demanded, frantically sighting along the forest in front of them, which was dense and dark in the late afternoon. There was nobody there, but another shot was followed by screaming, and Tanner Mobley fell to the ground with a bloody hole ripped in his side.

"Cass, look," Dor muttered, and she turned to look back the way they'd come.

There, emerging from the clearing on the other side, were men. A dozen of them, eighteen, twenty, wearing camouflage and hunting jackets, all of them armed. They were racing toward the bridge, and a couple of them with long-distance scopes were shooting as they ran. Tanner moaned and spasmed as more bullets struck the walls of the bridge.

Cass felt her entire body go cold with terror. If the Edenites continued ahead onto the point, they would draw the battle into the settlement. Running might delay the inevitable, but the fact was that they were mostly unarmed, weighed down with children and pregnant women.

If those who were armed took up positions at the

edge of the forest, sheltered by trees, they could pick off their attackers as they approached. Cass had no doubt that between her and Smoke and Dor and the others, they would manage to kill a few of them. But what then? They had only the ammunition that they carried, and most of them were barely adequate shots. Even if they took out half their attackers, that left ten more who would make it into the clearing where the rest of the Edenites would be waiting like sitting ducks. The inescapable truth was the Edenites were insufficiently armed, unskilled and mostly untrained—mothers with children, teenagers, ordinary citizens with the perplexing luck to have survived more than most.

By contrast, the men racing toward them looked as though they had been training for survival, as though they were handpicked to kill: deadly, fit, lean and determined. Their shouts carried across the expanse of bridge, guttural cries, terrifyingly close.

Dor was unshouldering his backpack. He lowered it gently to the ground, then knelt and started unzipping it. "Smoke. Cass. Nadir. Take everyone with you— now. *Go.*"

"What are you going to do?"

He pulled out the brick of plastic explosive and set it on the ground with great care. He looked up at Cass and for a second he went still, his eyes wide with emotion.

Then he looked away. "Go, damn it, Cass, get the fuck out of here."

"You heard him," Smoke said. "It's the only way, Cass. Go."

Nadir was already gone, shouting ahead to the others, who were running as fast as they could, some of them already off the bridge, scrambling up onto the grassy bank of the point. He ran behind them, shouting encouragement, urging them to go faster. More bullets flew around them, and ahead, a bright bloom of red appeared on a woman's back and she went stiff, falling slowly to the ground on her face. The terrified screaming crescendoed.

"Come *on,*" Smoke yelled. It was only the three of them on the bridge now, Dor working frantically at the mass of wires and the pale doughy bricks. Cass looked beyond him, searched out Red and Zihna, Ruthie in her father's arms. There were the kids, Sammi and the rest of them, and the young mothers.

The seeds of a new community.

"No," she said, the decision made before she even considered the alternative. She would not leave him. She would not leave Dor. "You go. Go on ahead. I'll be right behind you."

"Go, Cass, I don't need you," Dor muttered, but the wires slipped from his fingers and he cursed. Frantically he picked them up again, pressing the ends between his finger and thumb.

"Cass—" Smoke's voice broke. "Goddamn it. I'll stay here with him. We've got it taken care of. Please, for the love of God, just get the hell off this bridge."

The men's eyes met and Cass knew they had come to an unspoken agreement, that they were both willing to sacrifice themselves for her, for the others, for the future.

"Leads came out of the igniter," Dor said tightly, and Smoke nodded and took hold of the loose piece. Dor twisted something and pulled, the two of them anticipating each other's moves. "Hold that—here. Steady…"

"No!" she shouted, because without them…without Dor…there was no future for her. "No, look, I can—"

More shots, and Cass looked up to see that the men were terrifyingly close, close enough to make out the red logos on their jackets, the muzzles of their guns. She dropped to the concrete, saw that the wires were back in place, but the minute Smoke took his hand away they slipped out again. Someone had to hold them in place.

Smoke made a sound next to her, a soft exhalation, and when she looked into his face it had gone completely pale. "Cass," he whispered. "Please."

Something warm dripped onto her hand, and she looked down and saw the blood, an enormous round splotch on the back of her hand, slowly dripping down through her fingers. *No.* She looked back up at his face and saw how his eyelids fluttered, how his mouth was twisted in pain.

Smoke, whose face she'd first seen on the broken pavement of a school parking lot in Silva. She'd been broken, stinking, terrified, a thing of need, driven only to find her daughter. But Smoke had loved her. He had helped her save Ruthie, but he had also loved her back to life, his great gift to her, and if in the end it had not been enough, it was not his fault, he had given her more than he gave anyone in this world, more than he could ever give himself, and she would never forget.

Tears filled her eyes even as Dor cursed and wrapped the wires tightly around Smoke's fingers and then gently pushed the ends back into place. He knew. He *knew.* "Hang on, buddy," he said softly, and Smoke nodded, and then his eyes closed and Cass knew he was beyond speech, but still his grip held. He held on.

"Oh God, oh no," Cass sobbed, and she kissed his

face, his eyelids, his lips, and then Dor pushed her and she got to her feet, already running, her legs moving like they'd never moved before, Dor right behind her, pushing her still, his hand at her back, making her faster, getting her there, saving her, and all the while she whispered Smoke's name and remembered that she had loved him once and would always love him for what he'd given her, for the gift of loving her first.

Cass's muscles burned and her lungs screamed and then it came, *then* it came—

The explosion was all sound and blast and then a great shuddering quake below her feet, heat at her back and grit pounded against her neck, her wrists, her face. But the end of the bridge was still too far away. They were not going to make it, Cass saw the truth reflected in the horrified faces of the people waiting, she heard the ripping steel and crumpling asphalt behind her, the screams of their pursuers, the blast of debris hurled against the rock walls of the canyon.

And then the ground shifted beneath her as the bridge split and canted toward earth. The sound was deafening, the sound of hell itself, the air swallowed by the echoing blast, and she fell, her knees cracking against the concrete.

So it was here she would die, broken on the rocks next to the bodies of her enemies, only the very last of the many deadly threats since the Siege, but at least it would be instant and she would be washed clean in the freezing water of the river before her body was deposited, lifeless and pale, on a gravel spit far downstream. It would be consumed by animals, picked to the bones, dried to nothing while far above, the new community took hold, Ruthie and Dor and Sammi and her father

and all the others she'd known, the imperfect people
she'd loved, sometimes badly but always with all of
her heart.

And then she felt herself being dragged again, her
arm nearly pulled from its socket. Dor bellowed her
name and she scrabbled on the crumbling asphalt as
a huge chunk of the bridge split off a few yards away
from her and fell toward the water.

She slipped back a foot, another, and then miraculously her boots found purchase and she propelled herself forward, holding tightly to the hands reaching for
her, climbing with bloodied fingers up the sloping, tearing edifice. Above them, the bridge's concrete footings
began to separate from the earth into which they'd been
poured, like tree roots after a storm, tearing off chunks
of dirt and saplings with them.

She realized Dor was trying to help her, even though
he was about to lose his own grip, somehow he'd managed to climb ahead and had one arm wrapped around
an exposed root, his feet kicking against the gaping
earth, and still he was reaching for her. Above him
people screamed and reached for him, but he did not
take his eyes off her. She slid another few inches, nails
scraping and breaking on the crumbling surface, before she found her footing again and pushed herself
upward toward the rough poured concrete. It provided
a handhold but too late, too late, as the footings separated from the earth and seemed to hang in the air for
a moment before the entire bridge half slammed down
into the gorge.

Cass screamed and flailed wildly, her hand brushing the feathery leaves of a wild honeysuckle vine. She

seized it and held on with all her strength, getting her other hand around the branch as the bridge fell away beneath her feet and she was suspended in the air.

She looked down, and knew it was a mistake when she saw the bridge span split into pieces on the rocks, the water frothing and geysering around the detritus. She thought a body bobbed on the surface of the water for a second before disappearing beneath. Smoke—oh God, *Smoke was down there Smoke was dead he had died saving them.* Her hands slipped on the vine and she realized the shrill screaming was coming from her. Desperately she tried to pull herself up, her arms quivering with the effort, but the vine tore away from the earth, flinging clots of dirt into her face.

A thin network of roots was all that held, the woody vine beginning to splinter at the base. And then strong hands closed over hers and she let herself be lifted, dragged across the muddy outcropping to safety. She lay facedown, heaving for air, exhausted and aching, using the last of her strength to lift her chin and search for Dor and there he was, on his knees in the dirt, he'd made it, they'd lifted him to safety too, and she was weak with gratitude as he crawled to her and took her in his arms and she lay there, cradled in his safety while he kissed her hair and whispered her name.

When she got her breath she twisted to look behind her where the bridge used to be. The earth was torn and jagged on either side of the gorge. Down below, the rushing water had swept most of the bridge away, a few broken edges jutting from the surface where pieces lodged among the rocks. There was no sign of the attackers' bodies. The river had swallowed them whole, and at its leisure would spit them out again, indifferent as the rest of the earth to human struggles, to right and wrong, intent only on coming back to life itself.

48

It was nearly nightfall in the camp. They'd put out the smoldering fires around the settlement and built a new one in the center, feeding it with the lumber from a ruined structure that Nadir identified as the ornamental gate with the symbol of the new community designed by the people of his old town, a clover with four leaves to represent the four settlements.

The attackers had actually left most of the place intact, burning largely superficial structures. Or maybe they had intended to pile the bodies on a pyre to burn, and run out of time. For now, the Edenites carried the bodies outside the edge of the settlement to a grassy clearing. Tomorrow, they would dig graves.

Smoke would have no grave, but Cass did not need one to visit. For her, the river itself would be his memorial. She would visit it in every season, she would look down at the rushing waters, crusted with ice in winter, running with fish in summer, and she would remember and honor him.

One building in the clearing was nearly complete, a long wide dormitory with windows set high in the walls and a roof framed out and nearly finished. The first-wave settlers had outfitted the building with bedding and a few personal items: photos tacked to walls, rolled-up socks and clothing stacked on the floor. They gathered these and stored them at one end, before getting the children settled for the night. Pink insulation lined the walls and roof of the structure; already, the heat of their bodies was warming the interior.

Everyone was silent. The latest losses had stunned them, the terrible memories of the attackers falling into the gorge, the bodies of the four who'd been shot while trying to cross. The daunting tasks that lay ahead of them. All of this was too much to bear at the end of this long and cursed day. Tomorrow they would take up the yoke of their futures yet again, but for now they were spent, and before long everyone went to bed.

Cass waited until Dor's breathing became deep and even beside her, and then she got up as carefully as she could. Her body ached from her scrapes and bruises, and she limped painfully out into the night.

The moon lit her path back to the gorge, glinting off bits of mica in the earth, souvenirs from a volcanic eruption aeons ago. She shivered in the cold, but she would not be out here long.

At the edge she looked out over the river and the land beyond, the sloping trail that led back down to the camp and finally the road back to civilization. Here on this side, they were safe—for a night, a month, a season—

no one could say. The future was unknowable, but she knew some other things.

She knew the sound of her daughter's voice.

The touch of a strong man.

The friendship of people who were no longer strangers.

The love of her father.

She did not yet know the limits of her strength, but she was ready to be tested, and tested again. She would be tempted and discouraged and broken, but she would come back each time, into this world that had been bequeathed to them, into the dangers that threatened them and the joys that waited, buried but not impossible, for them to unearth and cherish.

"Thank You," she whispered into the wind, praying to a God she was not sure existed, whose purpose she did not yet know.

Her words were plucked from her lips and carried into the night, no one to hear them but the spirits of the dead. After a moment she turned and started back to the settlement. Tomorrow she would work alongside the other survivors. Her family. Her lover. Her friends. She would do the next right thing and the next. In small and humble ways, she would begin to live again.

* * * * *

ACKNOWLEDGMENTS

The Aftertime series marks a turning point in my life as a writer. Because of the efforts of my agent and editor—Barbara Poelle and Adam Wilson—I was able to take on a challenge that was far more rewarding than it ever was daunting—and it was plenty daunting.

Thank you, thank you, Harlequin team! I keep wanting to pinch myself. Every writer should be so lucky.

Sophie Littlefield

The world's gone.
Worse, so is her daughter.

Awakening in a bleak landscape, Cass Dollar vaguely recalls enduring something terrible. Having no idea how many days—or weeks—have passed, she slowly realizes the horrifying truth: her daughter, Ruthie, has vanished. And with her, nearly all of civilization. Instead of winding through the once-lush hills, the roads today see only cannibalistic Beaters—people turned hungry for human flesh by a government experiment gone wrong.

In a broken, barren California, Cass will undergo a harrowing quest to get Ruthie back. Few people trust an outsider—much less one who bears the telltale scars of a Beater attack—but she finds safety with an enigmatic outlaw, Smoke. And she'll need him more than ever when his ragged band of survivors learn that she and Ruthie have become the most feared, and desired, weapons in a brave new world....

Available wherever books are sold!

Be sure to connect with us at:

Sophie Littlefield

The end of the world was just the beginning...

Civilization has fallen, leaving California an unforgiving, decimated place. But Cass Dollar beat terrible odds to get her missing daughter back. Yet with the first winter, Ruthie retreats into silence. Flesh-eating Beaters still dominate the land. And Smoke, Cass's lover and strength, departs on a quest for vengeance that can end only in disaster.

Now the leader of the survivalist community where Cass has planted roots needs Cass's help. Dor wants to recover his own lost daughter, taken by the Rebuilders. Soon Cass finds herself thrust into the dark heart of an organization promising humanity's rebirth—at all costs.

Bound to two men blazing divergent paths across a savage land, Cass must overcome the darkness in her wounded heart, or lose those she loves forever.

Available wherever books are sold!

Be sure to connect with us at:

Harlequin.com/Newsletters

Facebook.com/HarlequinBooks

Twitter.com/HarlequinBooks

HARLEQUIN® LUNA™

www.Harlequin.com

LSL353

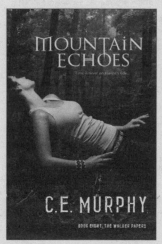

REQUEST YOUR FREE BOOKS!

2 FREE NOVELS FROM THE PARANORMAL ROMANCE COLLECTION PLUS 2 FREE GIFTS!

YES! Please send me 2 FREE novels from the Paranormal Romance Collection and my 2 FREE gifts (gifts are worth about $10). After receiving them, if I don't wish to receive any more books, I can return the shipping statement marked "cancel." If I don't cancel, I will receive 4 brand-new novels every month and be billed just $22.76 in the U.S. or $23.06 in Canada. That's a savings of at least 17% off the cover price of all 4 books. It's quite a bargain! Shipping and handling is just 50¢ per book in the U.S. and 75¢ per book in Canada.* I understand that accepting the 2 free books and gifts places me under no obligation to buy anything. I can always return a shipment and cancel at any time. Even if I never buy another book, the two free books and gifts are mine to keep forever.

237/337 HDN F4YC

Name	(PLEASE PRINT)	
Address		Apt. #
City	State/Prov.	Zip/Postal Code

Signature (if under 18, a parent or guardian must sign)

Mail to the Harlequin® Reader Service:
IN U.S.A.: P.O. Box 1867, Buffalo, NY 14240-1867
IN CANADA: P.O. Box 609, Fort Erie, Ontario L2A 5X3

Want to try two free books from another line?
Call 1-800-873-8635 or visit www.ReaderService.com.

* Terms and prices subject to change without notice. Prices do not include applicable taxes. Sales tax applicable in N.Y. Canadian residents will be charged applicable taxes. Offer not valid in Quebec. This offer is limited to one order per household. Not valid for current subscribers to Paranormal Romance Collection or Harlequin® Nocturne™ books. All orders subject to credit approval. Credit or debit balances in a customer's account(s) may be offset by any other outstanding balance owed by or to the customer. Please allow 4 to 6 weeks for delivery. Offer available while quantities last.

Your Privacy—The Harlequin® Reader Service is committed to protecting your privacy. Our Privacy Policy is available online at www.ReaderService.com or upon request from the Harlequin Reader Service.

We make a portion of our mailing list available to reputable third parties that offer products we believe may interest you. If you prefer that we not exchange your name with third parties, or if you wish to clarify or modify your communication preferences, please visit us at www.ReaderService.com/consumerschoice or write to us at Harlequin Reader Service Preference Service, P.O. Box 9062, Buffalo, NY 14269. Include your complete name and address.

PARA13R